Dragaa

G000150331

Protecy Unbound

Matthew Bunn

About the Author

Matthew first came into the world of fantasy by none other than JRR Tolkien. The Lord of The Rings and other Middle Earth Tales inspired him to one day create a world of his own, in hope to create such wonderful stories as his. Since those days he continued his inspiration into fantasy and fiction by reading the Harry Potter's, The Moontide Quartet, and other fantasy stories.

Growing up aspiring to be an actor, he found comfort in realising his enjoyment in creating and imagination. He landed the role of *Flavio* in The London Coliseum's production of Handel's Rodelinda, which was later commissioned to be performed at The Bolshoi in Moscow. It was here where the luxury of time was presented for him to fully form his trilogy of novels in the Dragadelf series. Combining it with over fifteen years worth of jotting down idea's on paper and the notes on his phone, he found the excitement of his creation.

Father to a growing and wonderful boy, Teddy, and professional tennis coach, he finds himself with more time of late to continue his other interests in chess, piano, football and the occasional trip to the gym (although very occasional it must be said these days!)

Special mention of thanks to my sister, Rae, for the swift editing, my illustrator Charlotte Strong for the fabulous design and Eleanor Prescott for helping piece the bones of imagination together.

And also to Danielle. For life's greatest gift.

For Mum.
May the pages of this book give you your wings to fly.

Rèo

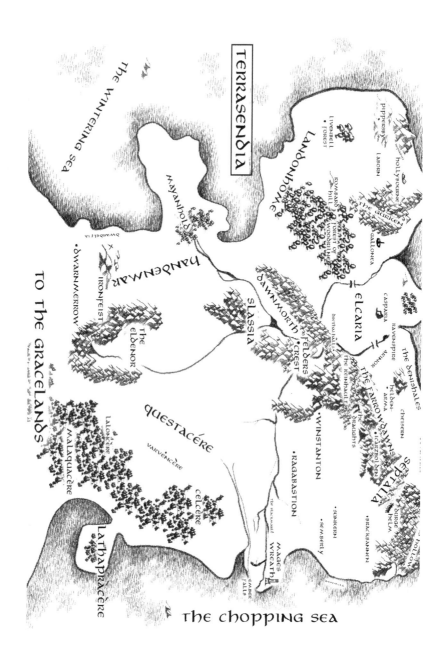

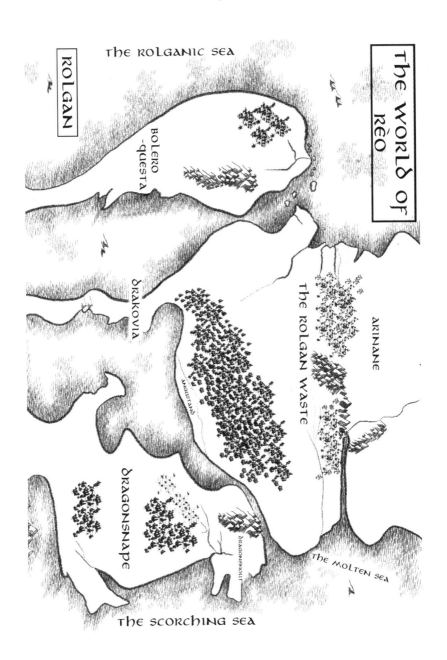

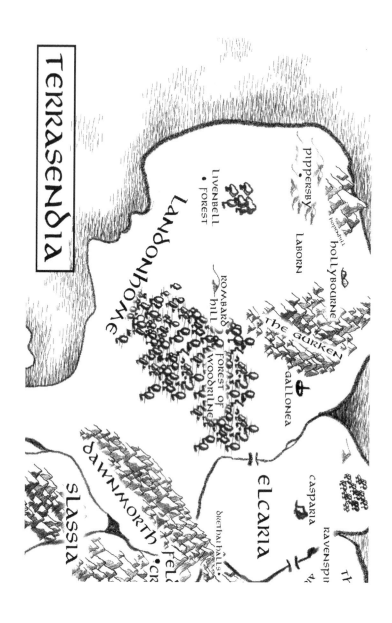

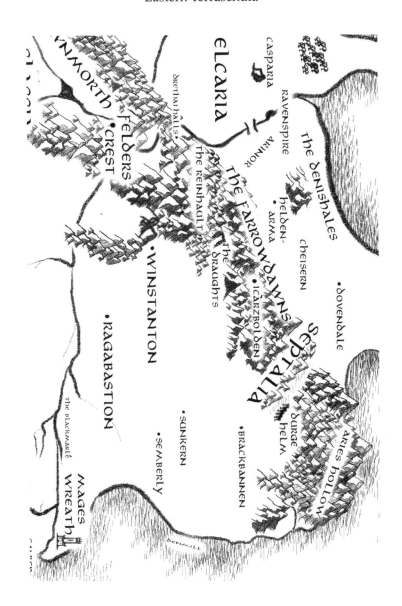

The Prologue

Standing strong above the clouds and beyond, the peaks of Terrasendia pillared the world on Rèo. The great mountain scape of The Farrowdawns ranged from the foot of Felders Crest, the capital and heart of Terrasendia built into the very mountain itself, carving its way through a divided Septalia to the nose of Durge Helm. Wealthy would be an understatement as the foundations of the land contained riches so great, poverty was seldom found.

Woven into these themes of Mother Nature were gold, diamonds, emeralds, but the value that took the eyes of all were protecy stones. Born from the land millions of years ago, great stones of purity and outstanding beauty. Terrasendia looked to these for thousands of years to platform magic called The Protecy, which increased the importance of these stones. The practice of protecy was invented by a small band of enchanters who could never foresee how successful the method would become.

Any Màgjeur could conjure an affinity given that they knew how, but the usage of protecy only enhanced one chosen path of magic. The Màgjeur would enchant their choice of energy: fire, water, air, etc. onto a stone, which would then allow the energy to be conjured through the protecy stone, releasing energy and power for the Màgjeur to use and expel to their desired needs. The clearer and purer the stone, the more energy that could be harnessed through it to cast. The Màgjeur would typically conjure the energy with either one of their hands or even feet if they wished, which then travelled through the stone for the enhancement of energy to then be cast out by the other side to use.

The stone could be kept anywhere in the world provided it was in a safe place. If the stone was somehow destroyed, the use of The Protecy would be lost to that Màgjeur forever. For a cost, protecy stones could be purified by merchants, which many choose to do in order to improve the flow and connection to their stone, enhancing their power.

Days on Rèo were measured by the number of hours into the day and night there were. For instance, miners would spend from the second hour of the day to the third hour of the night, mining for riches that would flow like colourful rivers out of the mountains and caves and into the cities, towns and villages.

The very skill of mining depended on the race. The noblemen would typically carve into rock and stone with their pickaxes, brows drenched in sweat. The dwarves of Handenmar would weave complex networks of explosives into walls, finding cracks and fissures to maximise the effect, whereas the Questacèrean elves would use chemicals and fluids filled with corrosive properties to soften the rocks to sand and dust. Stones were even mined at the bottom of deep lakes by highly skilled air Màgjeurs, cutting and weaving into burrows with intricate magic, capturing the stones inside conjured bubbles then floating very slowly and elegantly to the surface. For the nobleman, if you were to look at these lakes at night, sheer beauty and undeniable awe implanted their memories. A rainbow of colours so beautiful that the starlit sky had competition. But they were all one day outshone by the devastation that consumed Terrasendia.

King Felder, the High King of Terrasendia and his Màgjeurs witnessed a particular stone, not from the origins of Rèo but from the night sky itself, scorch its way ever closer to them. Judging by the stones' speed and velocity, it was futile to attempt to stop it. He ordered the capital to evacuate. The King and his people watched on from a safe distance as the stone pierced through the atmosphere and crashed into the mountain, landing in the heart of Felders Crest itself.

The King and his bands ventured back into the city to determine the level of devastation and carnage. As they rode through, they realised their city was mainly unscathed and remained intact. They ascended the peak of the city towards the throne room of Monarchy Hall, and the real wreckage started to unveil. Part of the roof was smashed on the stones entry, while the heat of the event burned any trees or agriculture nearby to embers. The Hall itself remained mostly intact too, thanks to the reinforced structure given by earth Màgjeurs into the fabric of the building. Rubble and broken windows glittered the floor of the Hall.

As Felder approached the cause of the devastation, his eyes lit up with amazement and genuine humbleness to what was in front of him. A stone of outstanding purity, flowing with colours of lime green, blue, orange and bright white radiated from where his throne once sat, which now was in a thousand pieces.

He held his hand out to take the stone, wisps of white energy circulating. He could feel the warmth and energy which shot spikes of adrenaline through his body. There was no denying the energy and power of this stone, which to some degree, disappointed the King as he could not enchant his own protecy onto the stone, as his affinity was already with fire. Declaring the capital safe, Felder allowed his people to return to the city.

But something felt very strange to all in the capital. The cold and ghostly mist of the Farrowdawns slowly breathed through the city uncharacteristically. From the heights of his Hall, Felder could barely see the bottom of his growingly anxious city, often hearing cries of panic through the eerie stillness. Bone shuddering cold swept through lungs as clothing began to soak. Felder knew something wasn't right.

Meanwhile, he consulted his Màgjeur of clairvoyance who informed the King of the peculiarity that he could not see past the haze. His anxiety increasing, the King asked to project the Màgjeurs sight onto the water of Wemberlè falls, a waterfall that half covered a clearing looking onto the city from the Crest.

As a precaution, The Blessèd Order were summoned - twelve Màgjeurs of undeniable mastership of their chosen crafts. However only eleven of the order were present as Felder's wife, Queen Eveleve, was about to give birth.

They looked together to see what was causing the anomaly. The Màgjeur tried something which might help, placing the glowing stone, still warm to the touch, onto a plinth before the waterfall, channelling his thoughts connecting the clairvoyance to the stone. After failing in the attempt, everyone left the clearing, putting the reason down to a changing of the seasons, Felder pondered alone.

Giving up hope he walked away from the plinth. Upon doing so, he suddenly heard a deep and distant thunder. Returning to the waterfall, he saw black shapes in the mist. The shapes gradually got bigger and bigger before getting too close to the waterfall. All of a sudden, a white-hot flash of fire lit up Felders eyes, splashing through the waterfall and propelling him backwards – his world went black. When Felder came to, the vision was broken, and the waterfall flowed as normal. The King grabbed the stone as he now knew precisely why the mist of the Farrowdawns was upon his city. The Dragadelf were coming.

In this vision, King Felder saw the seven tyrannosaurial, inferno breathing lizards swarm towards Felder's Crest. Their bodies, each as big as several carriages were armoured by thick scales. From spiked backs their strong wings flexed, spanning twenty metres, and in similar proportion from tip to tongue. With teeth as sharp as newly forged sword, and the sound of crackling flames burning as they roar, the ferocious beasts were a sight to behold. King Felder determined that the pure power of the stone was so great, it had attracted the most fearsome and powerful creatures known to exist.

Felder rushed to alert The Blesséd of what was coming, but he knew the city could not evacuate in time. He had no time to dwell on the devastating consequences and ordered The Magjeurs to deploy a spell of containment around Felders Crest once The Dragadelf had passed into the city. The Blessèd challenged his decision, but as the King of Terrasendia, he had a duty to protect and preserve the existence of everyone on the land.

The Blessèd reluctantly agreed being the only way to preserve the safety of Terrasendia and so Felder made his way to the opening of Monarchy Hall where he hoped to hold the beasts off for as long as he could to allow as many people to escape. The Blesséd were on route to be in place several miles dotting around the city to deploy the colossal spell, but they had to time it right. Deploy it too early they would not pass the spell to be trapped, deploy it too late, and The Dragadelf would escape into Terrasendia destroying anything in their paths. Felder was ready to hold them off but was once again distracted by yet another event.

Unable to see the city below through the mist, the people begin to wail and scream as if they were being slaughtered. Sounds of swords clashing and spells being cast hollowed Felders' body in fear, but he had to hold his position for the oncoming Dragadelf. After several minutes of sheer panic in the city below, the mist slowly started to tint a faint red and the gleam of many floating white lights became apparent through the fog below. Felder felt defeated, and despite his legendary power, it was no match for the seven oncoming Dragadelf. The mist from the Farrowdawns started to clear and descend further down the city, the sounds of ear-splitting screaming slowly began to diminish, and Felder looked upon the mountains to see the ancient creatures soar towards him.

The Blessèd initiated what was to be called The Dragasphere, which took time to deploy. Beams of unparalleled magic from each Màgjeur started to ascend above the city, forming a magical dome that spanned for several miles. The sheer scale of The Dragasphere created uncertainty around whether it would be complete in time, accelerating the Orders' determination.

Felder readied his protecy as a wave of heat hit his face merely just from The Dragadelf preparing their inferno. The seven formed a sporadic formation, but in sync, they breathed their belly filled, molten fires onto the Monarch.

The King launched a spell of fire himself which was overpowered but enough to deflect away. The beasts swarmed the capital, often disappearing into the descent, dispelling the fog with their fires and destroying the capital. Felder hurled powerful spells of wrapping fire constricting one of the beasts, but often being released upon having to defend against another attack. The beasts occasionally dipped in and out of The Blessèd's spell, often coming between the lines of their magic which decelerated the process which Felder could not control.

He made a move to lure the beasts away and to give The Blessèd a chance. He rushed to the very heart of Monarchy Hall where his throne once sat, drawing The Dragadelf's attention as they swarmed in. The King was cornered, and with one last roll of the dice, he cast his protecy of fire - creating a flaming wall in front of The Dragadelfs incoming embers. It proved effective as The Dragasphere was nearly complete with all beasts contained, but knew his fate was sealed. Unable to sustain his ward much longer, he used his last moments to plant a rune of ownership onto the stone, branding it with his blood which would own the stone forever.

A flash of white light sparked across the cold morning sky. The Dragasphere was completed. Feeling accomplished with his plan, Felder took a deep breath in, flashes of his loved ones, his reign and his people came to mind as he calmly relaxed his protecy. The embers tombed his body, before his mind floated away into darkness.

The Blessèd stood in amazement and sadness to the sacrifice. Not only their King but the hundreds of thousands of people who did not make it out in time. Only their darkest of imaginations were able to see what would happen to them inside what was seen as the greatest spell ever created, capturing one of the most feared horrors that would ever shadow the land of Terrasendia.

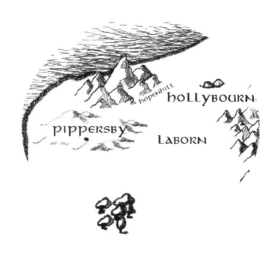

In the Search of Answers

"He has Malerma," was the diagnosis of Mirabella, the district Medimage on Landonhome, "and it has spread far quicker than we anticipated. Jàqueson has responded well to the initial treatment, but the disease has spread to his shoulders and should it spread to his heart; it will have fatal consequences."

She explained to the parents of the ten-year-old boy, who lay resting on his bed inside the home of Alexandao and Amba.

"We need your honesty Mirabella, what are his chances? Of survival?" Amba asked with the tight rope feeling of anxiety in her stomach. The salt in her tears stained her freckled round face, streaming from sky blue eyes. Red hair curtained her face down to below her shoulders. "I know you have said that if it is Malerma, then there is very little we can do but if there is the slightest route of hope we can pursue we will do anything for our boy."

"The rate of survival is very slim. My job is to brace you with the reality of what we are facing and prepare you for the worst. Several cases of Malerma have been cured before however, so there is cause for optimism. I appreciate the anxiety of not knowing what the problem was has caused tremendous stress, but we will need to see how well he responds from now. I was only able to diagnose his issue by a treatment I only hoped could work."

Malerma was a near terminal disease which is non-contagious. It was exceptionally hard to spot which involved some gentle guesswork from Mirabella to find out what triggered the response of the disease. It starts by attacking the nervous and immune system, adding an age-accelerating agent onto the nerves which make the system grow older and frail more quickly. Eventually, the nervous system will become that old that the immune system will fail and leave the hosts' body vulnerable and eventually die, despite the natural age of the infected.

"Curing diseases which are essentially born from time is difficult to understand, even for The Blessèd Mage of Time. The process I am performing involves slowing down the time in Jàque's body, concentrating entirely on the disease, but it is too strong for me to stop entirely, let alone reverse."

"With the greatest respect Màgjeur," Amba said, "is there any other on Terrasendia that is more learned than yourself in this matter?"

"There are Màgjeurs who do indeed delve into the teachings of time, but I would not recommend it," she replied with caution. "It is highly complex and too exposing."

Alexandao looked at her straight away and back to Amba. Thick black hair topped his head while long stubble lined his strong jaw line. He was athletic, quick and robust. Fair in nature but always fought with his heart, inspired by the love he has for his family. He intensified his stare at the Medimage.

"Why have you not mentioned this before!?" he pressed.

"Because it is exceptionally dangerous. If the understandings were to fall into the wrong hands, the existence of everything we know would be in danger. And besides, I needed to confirm the problem first before issuing blind optimism."

"Mirabella, please!" he pleaded as he stood. "He is our boy. Our only boy. I will do anything to make sure our son has every chance to make it through. Who is this Màgjeur? And where is he?"

The news of hope brought new life to Amba's river strewn eyes too.

"This was my fear. Giving too much hope while the odds are stacked against us."

"You just told us your job was to make us aware of the reality of what we are facing. The reality you have just presented to us involves hope, hope for our child!" his increasingly shaky voice turning into misdirected aggression. "Whatever the danger, whatever the cost, whatever the sacrifice, I will do it!"

They both could see Mirabella knew something she was reluctant to tell.

"Please, Mirabella." Amba breathed.

"I am not a mother. But I understand the risk between parents love and dangers presented in finding answers. You understand the code of Màgjeur's is binding, I could lose my wreath for this."

"We swear to you. Your information and where we can find this person will remain sacred to our deaths. We swear to you!" Alex repeated.

Mirabella took a deep breath, the weight of oxygen inhaled felt like a waterfall inside her chest. The partnership of the parents seemed to be winning her over.

"I give you this knowledge in the hope you would bring good to your findings and help your son. But any findings you must bring to me. Is that clear?"

"Yes, perfectly clear. Where can we find him?" asked Amba.

"That I really cannot tell you," causing slight agitation amongst the parents after the hype of hope.

"... Okay. Where was he last seen?"

"This is the problem. I'm not exactly certain whether it's him you need to find as I believe it to be impossible."

"And why is that!?" he asked, impatiently.

"Because The Blessèd Mage of Time died thirty years ago. You remember King Felder?"

Alex's eyes slumped shut like led weighting down a balloon, feeling heavy with resignation.

"I served him many years ago, Alex. I still serve him now... However, I fear the level of understanding we need is of his quality, and he of course died. But there is something that will help and may just be the answer. Something which luckily aligns with your job, Alex."

He perked back up.

"What is it? Tell me where I can find it."

"Time in the Water."

* * *

Smash, jangle and the roaring of flames. The sounds of the blacksmiths hut of Smithwins could be heard from anywhere in the quaint town of Pippersby, a pure country town located in the realm of Landonhome, northwest corner of Terrasendia. Not loud enough to distract everyday life mind, but just enough to remind the people of their heritage. Plumes of smoke and hot ash flickered from the chimneys which rose high enough to be seen from several miles away. The noblemen of Landonhome took great pride in the forgery of weapons, armour, construction and even jewels. Smithing was an art, and it was their passion. The concept of existing and walking around with something they created with their own bare hands had a sense of pride and sentimentality about it, knowing nowhere in the land would there be a copy of their creations.

Enclosed by the rocky mountains and the slope of Hopenhill, Pippersby was a fair town. The farming of livestock, the growing of flowers, the public houses were all part of the fabric which decorated the town. Butchers, fishmongers and bakeries also peppered the place, perfuming intense aromas of meats and sweetbreads. The town hall was at the top of the hill with Smithwins just behind, overlooking the town. With a population of just over three hundred, it was safe to say everybody knew each other. So recluse was it that in fact, news of the outside world seldom reached the town, save a few messengers and adventurers returning from local visits to families in nearby villages, and even then the news was brief. In a sense, they actually preferred it this way.

Garrison Vardy, an old but surprisingly strong blacksmith, often covered in soot, charcoal and dusty aprons, was found drinking ale at the Spuddy Nugget.

"Rolan, one more for the road?" Garrison asked.

"You said that three ales ago," returned the charming orange haired teenager with a smile.

"Didn't your mother tell you it was good for the soul?"

"Oh dear not this again."

"The soul, dear boy, the soul! I'm telling you, a man with no soul is a bit like a… a sword with no pommel."

"You're always on about the bloody soul! I don't know how mother lets you drink this much."

"It doesn't get any better sober, believe me."

Three men appear in the public house. Branmir, Brodian and Alexandao, all early thirties and noblemen who work at Smithwins. Covered in charcoaled tunics and overalls, they pulled up the wooden stools and sat next to Garrison.

"Your shift ends in five minutes. What am I paying you for gents?"

"This round of beers old man," jeered Brodian, the more bolshy of the three with dirty and ruffled black hair and piercing blue eyes modelling a chiselled face.

Branmir, the larger and far more superior in build to the other two was keeping a close eye on the women behind the bar, otherly known as the gentle giant of Pippersby he had a softer heart for the more sentimental things in life. As the four noblemen cheered their beers away, they notice a rather anxious looking Alexandao.

"How're you holding up?" asked Brodian, directing his question to Alex.

His humble grace was often his mask. Everyone knew the severity of his sons' condition but often tried to avoid the conversation in fear of treating him differently. He would smile, but only to cover up his ultimate pain. Usually avoiding being the centre of attention, but confident in his stature as a blacksmith and swordsman.

"Old cloth ears here not paid you this month?" joked Brodian.

"I think I'm going to ask her…"

The guys dropped their mugs and looked at him.

"… Ask her what?" asked a very quizzical looking Branmir with furrowed eyebrows.

"… How to open up a coconut - what do you think it means when a guy says that Bran!?"

"I dunno do I? I'm not the bloody Blessèd Mage of Mind am I?"

"You look like him!" Brody laughed, causing Bran to punch him in the arm.

"I'm going to ask her to marry me," his whispered words were met with surprise but a sense of jubilation.

"About bloody time an' all!"

"Have you spoken with my brother?" asked Garrison.

"Not yet. To be honest, Joric is the last person I want to ask. I mean asking The Durgeon of Pippersby for his daughter's hand in marriage is more frightening than sparing with him."

"He'll respect you for asking him."

"Will he approve, do you think?"

"No man will ever be good enough for Joric's daughter."

"Right. Thanks for that."

"But you come pretty close," Garrison said with a wry smile as he finished his ale.

"I'm even more scared she'll will say no. I mean with everything going on I think that's a more likely answer."

"Do you have to ask her yet?" asked Brodian. "You guys share a wonderful boy, you've got your thatched roof cottage which you built with your own two hands, and you're a good favourite to win The Bucksman this year. You're a desirable man. If I were a woman I wouldn't think twice."

The Bucksman tournament ran once a year, open to all ages who wished to improve their stature as a swordsman. Fighting with sparring swords provided by The Durge but allowed the use of their own armour. Alexandao was an accomplished blacksmith, creating his with a thin layer of steel to improve lightness and agility in movement, leather-bound under-layers with thick and compressed rope running along the seams underneath the arms. Agility was Alexandao's primary weapon in a fight. He could easily out-match Branmir in a spar due solely to his speed and lightness against the sturdy heavy feet of his friend. He was respected as one of the best swordsmen never to win the event. The next tournament was in two months. Alex had his sights on claiming his maiden title.

"When will you ask her?" asked Garrison.

"When I come back from The Gurken. I haven't even made the ring. I'm hoping to find something nice to make it with. When are you sending us out?"

"Next week. We're all going. Ourselves along with The Durge."

Every year Garrison sends himself and his blacksmiths out to The Gurken, an old mountain of gems plethoric in diversity and value: gold, diamonds, rubies, emeralds etc, for the season.

"Why do you need to ask her now?" repeated Branmir. "Surely you've got the time."

As soon as he spoke the words, everyone, Bran included, felt a little hollowed in the gut as he knew the response.

"Because I want my son at the altar…"

As ever the talk of what seemed like the inevitability of his son's fate brought a cooler temperature to the conversation which Alex was used to dispelling quickly.

By now The Spuddy Nugget had filled its emptier seats, sounds of live music from accordions, harmonicas and ukuleles joyfully singing as the smell of puff pastry from rising pies and fried salty fish clouding its way into the public house. Just as the food arrived for the table which included freshly rose bread accompanied by a beef stew that Branmir sunk his sausage fingers into immediately, sumply tucking into his food, Alex prepared to leave as he had training at The Durge.

"A word of advice," Garrison cautioned, "If you're going to tell my brother you need to be sure. He would probably kill you if you were to break her heart."

"I'd like to think I'm the first person to know that."

As Alex left with doubts and anxiety raining in his mind, he found himself at The Durge sparring yard, gravel and dirt laid the surface, fenced in with wooden surroundings and archery targets. Despite being the eleventh hour of day, it was still light.

The Durge was the name given to a band of soldiers responsible for the defence of the relevant location. Durges of villages and towns were more popular in the hierarchy, followed by Durges of the state which was made up mainly of the villages and towns and the odd city/forts depending on the location, narrowing down to The Durge of the realm. Each of these bands was naturally led by The Durgeon.

Alex equips his light leather under armour, leaving out the steel which he keeps at The Durge next to the yard.

The entry for The Bucksman tournament is up with Alex already submitting his entry, along with many others, including a very surprising addition.

"I couldn't let you walk this tournament without a challenge now could I, Alex?" said Joric in a deep and satisfying voice.

His short white beard sanded his face. His hair was also short, which made his somewhat wrinkled head seem bolder than it was.

"Great. There goes my proposal," Alex thought. "I was wondering when you would come out of retirement old man," he joked.

Joric's rare smile turned into something more characteristically serious.

"Old man!?"

"Yep. There definitely goes my proposal. It's only a figure of speech."

"I see. Let's go."

Alex and Joric made their way out onto the yard where several other fighters were already warming up. Joric stood to one side, observing the warm-ups. The sparing soldiers varied in size, heights and build. Some were very impressive with a sword, others not so much. No man had to sign up to The Durge, but by doing so, they got training free of charge by The Durgeon in return for their services to protect the land. Not military grade but mainly basic combat. Higher level training required one to venture to The Durge of either the state or beyond. Joric lined up his soldiers of roughly twenty men.

"As many of you know, The Bucksman is two months away. For those of you entering for your first time, it's a gentlemen's' competition based on your ability to strike your opponent with a sparing sword. More points are awarded for harder targets to hit, head strikes, for example, give you maximum points of ten. Other body parts including the chest, stomach and back are five points while arms and legs gain you two points a hit. Sword jabs to the head, punches and kicks are illegal, resulting in instant disqualification. Shoulder barges, trips and arm traps are allowed but advised to use sparingly. All participants must wear their helmet at all times. Depending on the number of entrants we will run two halves of the tournament. The final being the two soldiers from each half. Rounds will last ten minutes unless knockouts to the remaining participants end the fight. Every fight will have panellists of three members of The Durgeons choosing. Simple gents. For those of you who are new to the tournament make no mistake, when you are placed in an environment where your human instinct of defence and attack take over, you will find very different people than the ones you thought you knew. A word of advice, fight your opponent, not yourselves. Many challenges face men who fight, don't over complicate it by trying to control yourself. That's Septalian words for you. Let's get to it."

Alex was paired with Jacklatoro, shorter than Alex but just as athletic and very good at turning defence into attack. But Alex's lightness and quick feet were usually able to allow him to take more risks. He ended up taking a swipe with the wooden sword which Jacklatoro caught with the side of the sword, spinning round and giving Alex a pommel to the back of the helmet which sent Alex crashing to the floor.

"You alright, your highness?" Jack said with a sarcastic sense of care. A maverick in his own right, cocky, arrogant and snide.

"The Mrs not giving you any attention, Jack?" Alex retorted.

Jack took a swipe at Alex while still on the ground which he evaded, giving Jack a kick to the back of the knee, which allowed him time to get to his feet. The yard came to a stop to witness the heated spar. Joric watched on with intent. Jack uncharacteristically made the first move with an overhead strike which Alex blocked with an upward guard. Jack followed up with a nasty knee to Alex's midsection then spinning around with a two-seventy degree swipe which Alex luckily just managed to evade. Alex was annoyed as a knee to the stomach technically was illegal, but he had no time to contest. Before he knew it, Jack was going for the jugular. Several overhead swipes which were blocked as Alex retreated back. Getting closer to the edge, Jack pinned

Alex into the corner and their swords met at head height grappling with each-others strength.

"You think you're going to win this year, do you? You're not even going to make it to the tournament this year after I'm done sparing with you!"

Jack finds his balance, and stuck his right foot behind Alex's left, stepping through and launching Alex into the fence, splintering it as he is propelled. The impact and sound of wood cracking for a split second made Alex think it was his own back making the sound.

Alex by this point was furious the sparing session had turned into something so malicious and he had no idea why. Jack went for another swipe of the head which Alex rolled under. Why isn't Joric stopping this? Jack turned and went for a thrust to his midsection which luckily Alex pre-empted, getting his feet organised early to spin round the attack and land his resulting swipe heavily into the side of Jacks helmet who crumpled into the floor.

"Enough!" Joric ordered.

He rushed over to Jack, who didn't move. Alex removed his helmet, and a black hole filled his stomach of fear.

"Is he dead!?" he thought.

A general concern amongst the others grew. He felt like his heart was trying to escape his rib cage as it was thudding that hard. He held his breath, silently praying he was okay.

Joric looked at Alex with eyes that he felt pierced through his soul. Luckily, however, Jack slowly came to and sat regaining his consciousness. Slowly removing his helmet, Jack breathed heavily. No blood or bruising, just a narrow-eyed and zombie faced Jacklatoro staring at the ground.

"Are you alright, lad?" asked Joric.

"Alright? If that's all he's got, I'd say he's a coward for not finishing the job!"

Jack got to his feet and struggled his way toward Alex, but is stopped by other fighters on the yard.

"Just watch yourself, Alexandao! Good luck at The Gurken! I hope those Rawblers don't kill you because when you get back, I'm going to do it my - "

" - GET BACK NOW! Or I'll have you thrown into the bard! Go see the Medimage now! Your head is quite clearly broken. Go!"

Accompanied by several other soldiers Jack left with fury and intent filled behind his eyes. Medimages such as Mirabella use restoration magic to heal. Jack's wound was not severe but was more of an excuse to diffuse the situation.

"What was that about?" Alex asked.

"I told him to start fighting with his heart. Didn't realise his heart was filled with blind and stupid hatred towards you."

"You could have warned me."

"He's just trying to make his mark and put his stamp on being the favourite this year. And besides, I wanted to see how you would react. Fighting for life and death is completely different from sparing in the yard, Alex. And you're a smarter fighter than last year. You didn't rise to the emotion, you kept your head and your cool, the sign of a good warrior. Plus it gives me additional research on how to beat you when it comes to it. Not that I need it," he said with a smile.

"Why are you comparing this to being a warrior?"

"Have you not heard? There's been another attack off Hopenhill. Just keeping you alive is all I'm trying to do."

"What kind of attack?"

"Rumours of Rawblers, but nothing too much out of the ordinary. King Romany is fully aware and investigating thoroughly."

Rawblers were creatures said to be born from the dirt of the earth. Characterised by their curved backs and overly bent knee's they would often travel by scurrying like spiders, dark green complexion armed with jagged weaponry. Often seeking refuge in the dark corners of the world. The news troubled Alex as his venture out to The Gurken not only passed Hopenhill, but the mountain itself was a comfortable home for such foul beings.

"What about him?" Alex referred to Jack.

"You'll just have to keep reminding him I'm not the only one that can teach him a lesson." That brought a small smile to Alex's face. "I sense there is something new that's troubling you."

Alex really wanted to speak with him about his proposal to his daughter, but having just bludgeoned someone's head off he felt it was probably the wrong time.

"No, just hoping we don't run into Rawblers is all."

Alex left the yard under a clear moonlit sky, taking a back route to avoid a potential angry Jacklatoro or his cronies. Coming round a corner, he could see his cottage built under a thatched roof, strong pillars and white decor. The sight of the living room window glowing orange by the fire inside filled his heart with warmth. He was home. He opened the door to the warm smell of roasted potatoes, which hit his nostrils and instantly made his belly rumble in hunger. As he closed the door and turned, he's met with a thud to his chest and arms wrapping around him.

"Father!" Jàqueson said with a booming smile.

"How's my boy!? How was school?" he said with his eyes closed as they embraced.

His son was the spitting image of himself, ten years of age, and the only difference being was his hair which curled slightly, adding to his youthful charm. His round cheeks and booming smile only added to the besotting powers he possessed. The red vines of the Malerma tattooed his neck on the left side, spreading down and underneath his top.

"Jàque come sit please, dinners ready," Amba said as she appeared around the corner of the kitchen, apron on and smiling to see her man home. Athletic and agile in build, she knew how to take care of herself with a sword. As they embraced Amba joked, "So who did you kill today?"

"Everyone, you know, nothing unusual," said Alex.

She kissed him smiling as she pulled away. But as they looked into each other's eyes they saw that familiar sight behind the eyes. The weight and burden they both shared for Jàqueson, who inconveniently was peeking around the corner.

"Get to the table ya tyke!" Amba said.

He scurried off, smiling and laughing. Any slight moment of resignation or defeat in their demeanour was quickly disbanded with positivity or light humour to keep his naivety alive. They kept the details of the severity of his condition away from him as he was too young to understand. Too young to be afraid of death. Too young to be this unlucky. Should Jàqueson really find out how serious his condition was, understandably no child would be expected to keep their spirits alive.

Amba had prepared homemade chicken soup with crusty bread still warm from the stove, followed by a plethora of roast potatoes to go with her minted lamb dish. The smell hit Alex's nostrils like nectar to a bee as he was drawn to the table not eager to carry on waiting any longer. The family tucked into their scrumptious dinner.

Alex listened to his son and Amba all evening, occasionally dropping out of focus to think, *'Time in the Water.' 'Time in the Water.' If Mirabella didn't even know what exactly it was, how the hell am I meant to find out where to look for something I don't have the faintest of ideas about what it actually is. Basing her hope on a rumour which -*

" - Father!! How long will you be gone?" asked Jàqueson.

"Depends how much we find. A week or two maybe. Don't worry, will be back in plenty of time for your birthday son."

"Are you going to bring me back a big emerald? Or even one of those protecy stones? Or what about The Dragastone!?"

The stories of the event of The Dragastone echoed throughout the land. Many had known what had happened thirty years ago, and the terror that lay within The Dragasphere. However, to kids, it was an appealing story of power, force and fantasy which they imagined to one day possess. For thirty years, Terrasendia has existed in fear from the events. The Dragasphere was the only thing keeping The Dragadelf contained and saving Terrasendia from certain ruin.

"And what exactly would you do with a protecy stone, son?" asked his mother.

"I'd enchant it with the same powers as Aristuto and use it to make me fly! Then I could go wherever I wanted in no time! He's my favourite."

"I'll bring you back something nice. Now off to bed, I'll come read you a story once you've brushed your teeth and finished helping your mother," Alex said.

"Ah, dad, can you read me *A Rivalry in Perpetuity* again!? I love that story, how Felder and Melcelore always saw each other's plans but went one step ahead of each other!"

"You'll never get to sleep if I read you that."

"But mum promised me you would."

"I certainly did not, ya bugger!" claimed Amba, met with an over the top groan from her son. "Get and brush your teeth, or I'll get the Blessèd Mage of Fire to come here and burn ya bum off! Go!"

As Jàqueson scurried upstairs, Alex and Amba started clearing up the dishes. As Amba began the washing up, Alex wrapped his arms around her waist, talking on her shoulder.

"He seems lively today," Alex said.

"He's getting more energy ever since he started riding. The horsemaster said he's coming on really well. He's becoming more like you every day."

"He's like you. Getting smarter, more excited every day just to go to school. Makes me very proud."

"And me," she said as she turned her head to kiss him. "Go on, I'll finish up here."

As Alex wandered upstairs to send his son off to sleep, he opened the door to see his room still lit by several candles, Jàque's eyes were already closed, mouth slightly ajar and wrapped himself in his fur duvet covers. He was exhausted. One of the side effects of his condition was that when he rested, it was a deep rest which was needed to replace the extra energy he needed for daily activities. Alex came in and sat on his bed in admiration for his son. No amount of words or magic could ever quantify his love for his family. He placed his hand gently on the side of his sons resting head as Amba quietly came into the room.

"He's just you," she whispered, smiling. "He really is. Such a handsome boy."

A small tear filled Alex's eyes. Humbled, purely from the power of love for his boy and devastated by the weight of his condition. He kissed his forehead while Amba did the same. They doused the remaining candles as they sent their son off to sleep.

"I will find a way, son," Alex said. "I promise."

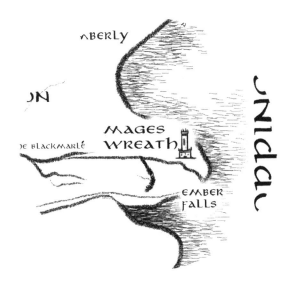

Protecy Unbound

The obliteration of rocks and earth fractured the battleground. Proteìc spells cast by two Magjeurs as they duel in the first round of The Màgjeurs Open.

Crowds gathered to witness the spectacle from heights in the stadium. The stands spanned high and wide, protruding so far away from the large playing field that many spectators in the back rows needed to cast magical orbs of water in front of them to magnify their view. Thousands of balls of water glittered over the arena as they all watched in suspense and exhilaration.

Pierro, a very experienced air Màgjeur in his fifties, was dominating the duel with his counterpart. His elegance with his use of The Protecy looked highly impressive, swishing his wrist cleanly and casting spells of air, narrowly missing their target. One could say he was inspiring to the younger generations for how calm and in control he looked in battle.

His struggling opponent Ramalon, a Màgjeur in his thirties, was clearly struggling with the gulf of experience between the two. His youthful complexion and medium length dark brown hair was un-kept as the waves and curls dangled from the crown of his head.

Being constantly on the back foot, he felt the build of lead in his muscles as he was always on the move. As a result, the connection with his protecy was not as strong and the energy he could conjure was weaker. His affinity was that of fire which was not exactly burning within him at that point.

As he managed to hide behind a large stone to regain any energy he could muster, he felt an embarrassing amount of regret that he could well be going out in the first round. His dream of winning The Màgjeurs Open would have to wait another agonising five years. And that's if he was lucky enough even to be picked to participate in the twenty-four Màgjeur event again.

Pierro took centre stage on the playing field. His confidence grew as Ramalon's waned. He had one more chance. One more real chance to muster enough energy to put up a fight. With each growing breath he drew, the connection with his protecy grew stronger, to the point where he revealed himself from his hiding stone. He prepared his almighty fireball, turned the corner to the open battlefield before rapidly stopping in his tracks. Pierro was not there.

He looked around the playing field and stadium to see where he could be and yet nowhere was he to be found. Ramalon did not relax for one second; he knew to expect a crushing blow any second. The weight of his anxiety was killing him by the second.

"Show yourself!" Ramalon thought as he continued to scan for his opponent.

He tried to hatch the only plan he could think of. He makes his way naively into the middle of the arena. Suddenly his eardrums burst with the screeching high pitched sound of air razoring its way around the stadium, slicing every orb of the spectators to their annoyance. Ramalon's face was that of bitter defeat as the bursting of aqua spheres started to rain onto the arena which not only soaked everything inside but also made Ramalon's fire very much ineffective if it wasn't already.

His sodden, quirky face looked up once more squinting as the rain fell. Before he knew it, his opponent came crashing with an air bomb from a great height onto him, sending him flying sideways and onto the floor. Ramalon felt completely resigned, outsmarted and outplayed. Pierro waded to his opponent for the final blow. The end of the battle was not that of death, but that of submission in this tournament. Pierro let out a huge battle cry which resulted in him wrapping a blanket of air around a helpless Ramalon, suffocating him which he desperately tried to resist. The crowd were shouting as they knew Ramalon would submit and the round would be over...

Ramalon, however, had other ideas. He charged his energy as much as he physically and mentally could while in the suffocating blanket, taking every portion of the air from him. Very subtly he released his embers onto the whirling cloak around him which gently caught alight and started to turn the circulation of air steadily to fire. Pierro's eyes turned from victorious greed to horror at the realisation of what was happening. He tried to relax his protecy and break the cast, but Ramalon returned the favour and turned his gaze full of intent and victory towards Pierro, trapping his protecy. The fires grew around Ramalon much to his deceitful plan, consuming as much as he possibly could. Pierro's battle cry turned to a wail as the trap was clearly hurting him. Ramalon saw the inevitability in Pierro's eyes.

He could not contain the pressure of the fires any longer and expelled the surrounding fireball with epic devastation onto his opponent which blasted Pierro backwards, smashing him onto a rock and crumpling to the ground.

Gasps from the crowd were that of shock and awe as to what they just witnessed. Many of them had not seen with their own eyes devastation of that magnitude before. Ramalon fell to his knees breathing very heavily.

Beyond the clearing smoke and haze, he saw his opponent on the floor, unconscious and burned. Ramalon thought that the might of the blast must have killed him, but all Màgjeurs who participate in the games are given additional protection from Medimages before battle, giving them greater immunity from harmful spells.

With Pierro very much down and out a female voice echoed from the judges' box in the stadium. Anelene stepped forward from a plinth covered by a yellow gazebo. Her regal stance and finely detailed robe were not as noticeable as the thin red feathered wreath draped on her shoulders. An important recognition that she was a member of The Magikai, the order responsible for the protection of magical purposes on Mages Wreath.

"It is the verdict of the panel, that I can announce the winner. Màgjeur Ramalon!"

Huge cheers erupted from the spectators. Ramalon's elation set in. He circled himself on the spot taking in the recognition from the fans, which presented him with the best feeling. The feeling of invincibility. He couldn't quite believe it himself. For most of the contest, he was very much under the cosh and grew weaker throughout. Were it not for his quick and cunning plan he would have been beaten. Planning and trickery were never his strong point, but he managed to recognise that if he could use Pierro's air to his advantage, his protecy of fire would receive a bigger impact, despite the damp that had surrounded him.

He felt overwhelmingly proud of himself; making Pierro believe he only needed to do one more thing to finish him off. He may just have found a new weapon to help him in his future rounds.

He trudged back to his chambers after receiving an official invitation to the second round of the event the next day at noon. His whole body felt broken by the duel. Not one muscle in his body went unnoticed. The deep aches and stabbing pains he received with simple movements made his victory taste bittersweet.

On his journey home, he could not pretend that if he wanted to go all the way and win this event that he needed to be stronger and more efficient. He couldn't wait to get back to his luxurious duck feathered bed as soft as clouds and to drape his toasty pyrovined duvet up to his shoulders, and sleep until his body told him to wake.

He was greeted by many spectators in the street to give him further congratulations, which he took in his stride. Despite his growing popularity, his response was very muted and underplayed.

The city streets all over were lit up by magical fires, lightning and Aquarius swirls to celebrate the opening round of The Màgjeurs Open. Any Màgjeur of any affinity were allowed to enter, but the most popular was that of air, earth, fire, water, ice and volts, the six destructive affinities. Three rounds of magical fighting in the format and location of the organisers choosing at the time. The winner is said to be given not only prize winnings that were enough for retirement, but also honorary status into The Magikai. Winnings did not draw Ramalon but the prestige of being one of the most powerful Màgjeurs on Mages Wreath did. It was his lifelong dream.

The white city itself had many tall buildings amongst the peppered houses. It resided right on the east coast on Terrasendia, overlooking the Chopping Sea to the east. Its high location on the cliff-top had an unwelcoming mile deep drop. Several plinths on its way down - large enough to host several villages and houses for those who loved the sea view.

Its position on the land was subject to controversy as it was declared the most northern part on Questacère. So north was it, that it intruded into the realm of Septalia; the home of Men. But the Questacèrean's claimed it as their own as it was founded by them many years ago and won the right to claim it as part of their land.

King Thorian Mijkàl, the King on Questacère, and the Blessèd Mage of Ice, resides in the capital of Lathapràcère, a city stretching so far south that it bordered The Gracelands. Questacère was not known for its conflicts, but its potential power on Terrasendia did not go unnoticed.

The proudest moment in Ramalon's life was being played out on the streets before he stumbled into his chamber. His small bungalow was decorated by the creations of his students at The Opey Deary - a small school in which he taught basic protecy and other magical forms to students aged eighteen. He loved the school as he loved his job as a teacher. The students he had taught in the past ten years since he started were special to him, and they always stayed close to his heart.

His younger students would knit wool and cotton into the shapes of animals and magical creatures which would move on his shelves by their own accord. He loved how each of the animals interacted with one another, existing peacefully and happily in his home. Considering how it was his students who made these for him, using the magic they had learned, filled Ramalon with happiness. A reminder of his care and responsibility for the youths. The touch of sentimentality. He had a strong passion for passing on knowledge and inspiring the younger generations. Magical paper in the shape of birds, dragons and other flying creatures would also flitter around his home. Near his stove was a plethora of roses of all different colours mainly oranges, purples and scarlet reds for his rose teas which he adored.

He didn't have many friends, not that it bothered him in the slightest. His quiet and reclusive nature prevented his awareness of how uncommon that was. He rarely spoke when not spoken to, unless he was teaching. A sign that he was indeed in his element. He would spend many nights over the years watching the fires burn logs after school. Alone; just staring into the fire. His inspiration. He would never do anything else apart from setting the fire alight with his protecy. Only when the orange embers wisped away into thin smoke would he start the process again, until the weight pulled his tired eyes shut. He would never manipulate or douse the fire in those moments, instead, he would admire the simple process and existence that fire has. The creation and destruction it caused.

His tired eyes started to wane as the fatigue took over. The last of the logs fires diminished, and it was at that point that he suddenly noticed the creatures on his shelves had all stopped and were looking towards the door.

A sudden sound of knocking startled Ramalon and perked him up. It was not a ghastly hour to have visitors, but he seldom received guests at any time, let alone the third hour of night. He went and opened the door before immediately recognising the prestige that was before him.

"My lord, Davinor!" he said, shocked at the visit.

The Blessèd Mage of Protecy, the Head of The Magikai, the most important person on Mages Wreath, accompanied by several members of The Magikai stood before him. Davinor's chiselled face and high jawline gave him a gaunt look. He looked strong and intense despite his older complexion. His well-fitted robes did not flop at the arms nor dangle at the ankles like many Màgjeurs. Instead, it bore a slim fit. He looked upon Ramalon with a subtle smile as he took in Ramalon's nightwear. His chequered red and white bottoms with knitted slippers fluffing at the toes did not present Ramalon in the most prestigious of lights.

"Caught you at a bad time, Màgjeur?" Davinor asked with a hint of irony.

Ramalon took a moment to regather himself, closing his open mouth and scurried his arms to draw his gown across his night clothes.

"I did not expect company," his light and gentle voice said. He took pride in his well-spoken speech too, pronouncing his t's and h's in the proper manner.

"No. And I did not expect to be out at such hour. May I?" he asked, still standing at the door.

"… May you what?" A perplexed Ramalon replied.

The Blessèd Mage looked at his entourage before indicating to Ramalon that he would like to enter his home.

"Would you like to come in?" his question sounding more matter-of-factly than a question.

"I think that would be appropriate."

Davinor recognised the bluntness in Ramalon's voice and cottoned on to the fact that he may struggle in social situations. As Davinor entered his home, Ramalon attempted to close the door after him before a member of The Magikai hurriedly stopped the closing door with his arm.

"My apologies!" Ramalon said.

He did not gather that the others would be expected to follow and thought it would be just Davinor.

"No no, it's quite alright, Màgjeur," Davinor reassured. "Wait outside, Dorovir."

He nodded his head as he backed away from the door before Ramalon closed it shut not entirely recognising the awkwardness.

Davinor wandered around his home taking it all in, not inspecting but merely just noticing the strange house in which he was experiencing. Ramalon felt a very peculiar feeling as though he should say something.

"Would you like some rose tea?" he asked as Davinor noticed the paper dragons and creatures on the mantelpiece.

"These are extraordinary. Did you make these?"

"My students did. I taught them how and they gave them to me, as a token."

"Your students? Do you enjoy your job?"

"I did. Very much so. But I retired since being picked to fight in the games." Davinor was listening, albeit not looking at him.

"A touch of home."

Davinor attempted to touch one of the paper dragons offering his fingers gingerly before the dragon started to freeze, as if it was on edge, waiting to pounce. Davinor recognised the startle in the dragon and slowly withdrew his hand.

"Fascinating. A mind of their own too."

The dragon flittered away to another part of the room.

"How may I help you?"

"I would like to ask you the same question. May I sit?" Davinor felt consciously aware to ask to sit to avoid any further confusion.

"Of course."

"Thank you." Ramalon hardly moved from the door since the Blessèd Mages arrival. "There is no need to feel alarmed."

"Alarmed?"

"You seem on edge with me being here."

"Not at all. I feel explicitly normal right now."

Davinor conjured a small laugh in response.

"I suppose you're wondering why I'm here."

"That would seem natural in this situation."

"Indeed. Have you ever extensively delved into the art of protecy?" Davinor asked inquisitively.

"I taught the basics to my students."

"The basics yes, but have you ever really studied how it works?"

"I guess so. I stare into the fire every night. I observe how it moves. What its purpose is."

"Those are observations of the affinity. I'm talking about the connection with your protecy stone. Where is it?"

"I keep it safe."

"As you are very much advised to do. But fear not, I will neither take it from you nor destroy it."

"Why? Why do you need to see it?"

"I saw you today. No one thought you stood a chance. But something happened in that arena. You found something which fascinates me, and I want to know how it happened."

"What is it that fascinates you?"

"I'm going to take a wild guess and say you've had your protecy stone purified at least five times. Am I correct?"

"Purified?"

He indeed had heard of ways to improve the connection between stone and Màgjeur but never delved into that route as for him it was never necessary.

"Yes. How many times have you brought it to a merchant to improve the purity?"

"My lord, I have never done such a thing."

Davinor cocked his head, truly perplexed. "Never?" he asked slowly.

"No."

"Not even once?"

"No."

Davinor just observed Ramalon from the chair. A silence existed between them, but yet again, Ramalon felt no awkwardness or agitation at the silence. Instead, it was Davinor who buckled.

"That's nearly impossible if I may say so - "

" - I am telling the truth, my lord. My stone is untouched. Ever since the day I bought it from the Rolgan markets many a year past."

"Would you be comfortable showing it to me?"

After a slight pause, Ramalon conceded that Davinor's intrigue might be in his better interest.

"Of course."

Ramalon nodded to his paper dragons to which hundreds more appeared from any paper in the room, transforming themselves into the same mini dragons. They flittered around the room before they all congregated around the burnt out fireplace. They breathed their small fires into the very middle of the hearth. Hundreds of small fires started to produce a shape in mid-air just above the charcoaled logs. Davinor was increasingly excited at the spectacle.

All of a sudden, the dragons dispersed quickly all around the room before returning to their subtle activities. Davinor looked back towards the hearth to see the protecy stone suspended in mid-air. Ramalon went over and took it. Every Màgjeur was encouraged to conceal their protecy stone in a manner of their choosing. Were their stone to be destroyed, their protecy would be lost forever according to the law of protecy. This concealment was Ramalon's way.

"Another touch of home," Davinor said before Ramalon approached him.

He placed the stone in Davinor's hands, looking confused as to how in awe he was. It seemed a murky dark green colour with spots of transparency, which were the parts the affinity flowed through. Judging by Davinor's confusion, it looked like a very inefficient stone, adding to his awe at how Ramalon expelled such energy.

"Good Gracelands," The Blessèd Mage whispered.

"Is there something wrong?"

"Something wrong? This is impossible. This cannot be your stone."

"I assure you it is."

Davinor pondered as he continued to scrutinise the stone.

"Could you prove it?"

"At once."

Ramalon picked up a chopped log and put it on the ashes of the fireplace. Some of the soot and debris floated in the air as he placed it carefully onto the fireplace. He looked over to Davinor in the chair, stone still in hand before placing his left hand by his side and his right hand towards the logs. Immediately small fires were conjured in through his left hand by his side and expelling through his other, pointing towards the fire which lit very efficiently. This would all be the normal process of The Protecy were it not for a gentle gasp of pain from Davinor. He immediately dropped the stone looking very surprised. Ramalon saw that Davinor's hands were shaking slightly as the stone had slightly burned them.

"That has never happened before!" Davinor gasped.

"What just happened!? Are you okay?"

"Yes, I'm fine. But this is irregular. I have never seen a stone itself carry a similar property to its affinity."

"I do not know what to say. Is this a bad thing?"

He went to pick up the stone which he felt was indeed hot, but not too hot that he couldn't handle.

"Your stone and the power you produced does not match up. I have seen many basic stones before, and it is simply impossible for you to have conjured the magnitude of magic in comparison to the impurities of this stone. Simply because it has too many impurities for that amount of energy to travel through, it simply cannot be."

Ramalon too was now confused at the apparent revelation. He never for a second thought that his stone was capable of producing a higher power. Even though his front did not seem startled, behind the eyes, he felt intrigued. Davinor would not be lying. This was his subject.

"How would you explain today's event?"

"If I knew that, I would not have come. I believe your connection was too true to be considered normal."

"So, I'm extraordinary," he rhetorically and matter-of-factly stated once more.

"That remains to be seen."

He pondered for a second, gently tapping his fingers on the side of the chair before announcing his proposition.

"What would you say about meeting me tomorrow? I want to take you under my wing."

Ramalon's expression seldom changed. But on that occasion, his eyes did indeed slowly light up.

"You mean to learn from yourself?"

"With the idea of studying how to improve the connection you have with your stone. Also for me to examine just how you managed this. There is something about you, Màgjeur Ramalon. I fear you may have only scratched the surface of your potential. Something which I don't know thrills me, or scares me... I hope it's the former. What do you say?"

Ramalon stared at Davinor before looking at the stone. He initially thought that should he do it, he may stand a chance of becoming stronger and winning The Màgjeurs Open. He might one day become the greatest Màgjeur ever to live. Out of nothing, the stone suddenly produced a small fire inside the parts of transparency within the stone, as if fate was telling him the answer.

Ramalon smiled back toward The Blessèd Mage.

•BRACKBƏ•

Seeing is Unbelieving

"I saw one. I saw one with my own eyes... It came for us. I don't know why. I don't know how. Wings as wide as galleons. Scales as hard as granite. White as snow! But the one thing I will never forget... Gracelands, it took my soul... Were its eyes. Snaring at me! Relentless. True... I think I died in that moment!"

Rya Al Asharad shook as he replayed the event in front of the council on Durge Helm, the capital of Septalia. His dark brown complexion twinned with his loose black hair struck a terrified figure as he knelt before the Jury. As part of his imprisonment, his hands were bound.

"Just to be abundantly clear. You are describing that of a Dragadelf?" said the stern and masculine voice of Luanmanu, the Head of the council. His square shoulders defined his broad and robust frame. His short grey hair brought out the finesse in his older face. He sat alongside other members on the council who also bore influential roles.

"Yes." Rya nodded.

"Madness!"

"I am not lying."

"And what did it do when you saw it?"

"I told you. It spared me. I don't know why."

"Words of madmen are exactly that. Especially the words of our enemy."

"It's true!"

"The only reason we have entertained the idea of bringing you before us is for one reason. We might have believed it if you told us you saw the constitution of another dragon. A Charzeryx, a Dralen or even a Drogadera, for example, which we would take seriously as to why they are on Terrasendia. But the specifics you have told us are without question a Dragadelf. In conclusion, this conversation is pointless as that is impossible for you to have seen."

"I promise you it's what I saw! The Banamie does not know I have come to you."

"Why?" said the voice of Nedian. A mid-forties knight from Brackbannen; a stronghold close to Durge Helm. "Seems strange, you would tell us and not *your* people."

Rya continued to shake as he looked at other members sat before him.

"I saw what I saw. A Dragadelf has escaped!"

"Yes, we've established your theory."

"It's not a theory - "

" - I want to know why you came to us? Also, you are from Rolgan, correct? A foreign land to us. Why pledge your allegiance to a cause that was born from Terrasendia?"

"You think the enemy are just domestic?"

"So it's *the* enemy now?"

"You have many enemies on Rèo! There were many people of Rolgan in Felders Crest when you cast that spell, killing hundreds of thousands in dragon-breath!" Rya shook more intensely the more passionate he got.

"We will not be insulted by your emotions, Barkler!"

"I feel a little education is needed." Luan calmly said. "Quite right. Hundreds upon thousands of innocent lives were tragically lost when The Blessèd constructed The Dragasphere."

"They were murdered," Rya confidently stated.

"I have no interest in your opinion. But I ask you this. Something your leader cannot answer. How many more would have died had the spell not have been created?"

Luan allowed an air of silence to mist the atmosphere letting the question sink in. Rya looked down, almost in the full knowledge that he knew deep down many more would have indeed died if the spell was not created.

"It doesn't matter. It was still genocide. You cannot choose who lives and who dies."

"Unfortunately, in this case, we can. And we had to."

Rya genuinely started to laugh at how ridiculous that sounded. "And you call them the enemy?"

"Them? Shouldn't you be referring the term us?"

"Would you like me to!?" Rya replied with a hint of venom.

"Forgive me, your honour," another mighty voice was heard. Farooq Manwa's sleek black medium length hair sat on top of his bulged shoulders. His brown tunic tightly fitted as they hugged his giant muscles. "But I would like to get back to the original question here. Educating minds that cannot think for themselves and hide behind an extreme ideology is not only exhausting but time-consuming."

"I have to disagree," Alexa Greyman opposed.

An excellent markswoman, her skill with a bow was unquestioned. Regarded as one of the greatest archers on Terrasendia, she commanded respect among the many speaking voices. So skilled with a bow she was, that she invented the bow-throw. A technique used to capture incoming arrows by throwing their own bow in a spinning motion toward an incoming arrow, trapping it mid-air and allowing its velocity to return to the defender for them to use for their own use. Her stern voice was certainly not overwhelmed, albeit outnumbered heavily by the council predominantly being made up of males.

"But I feel that educating turned minds sends a clear message to others who fell into the trap of extremism."

"Enough," Luan said, "we have lost focus. Barkler, answer plain and simple. Why bring this to our attention first?"

Rya started to weaken when he thought about the answer.

"I was scared." he murmured.

"Speak up!"

"I said I was scared! That's the real reason I come to you now. And trust me when I tell you, when a Dragadelf stares straight into your soul, you'll start realising who the winning side is when it comes again."

"Do I sense confusion in your allegiance?"

"I do not regret my beliefs. But I do regret the decision I made."

"You knew the consequences of your choices," Luan's voice turned more foreboding. A hint of regret in his voice as he knew what would have to happen now. "If made, there is no action on this land that could forgive."

Rya's eyes started to turn softer and less defiant.

"You're saying you will not believe me?"

"Did you honestly think by bringing us such nonsense will soften our hearts? Open our arms with a warm welcome? Draul truly has washed your minds of any sense."

"I made a mistake! A big mistake. Please. Don't kill me!" Rya pleaded.

"You knew the law before you left. And since the information you have brought to us in my conclusion is insufficient, I have no choice but to adhere to the law."

"Please. Please! It's true, I swear!" Rya's honest eyes turned shiny as the fearful tears started to glimmer.

"Rya Al Asharad. I hereby sentence you to - "

Suddenly the sounds of bolts and crucks were heard as the thick wooden doors of the marble courtroom swung open. Everyone's attention was drawn to the oncoming Knight as he marched in with purpose. The sides of his head were finely shaved while the top of his dark hair was also relatively short. The cheekbones on his defined face were straight and regimented. His dark brown leather brigandine was well strapped above his iron-clad skirt which hid his fitted trousers. Every step had additional gravitas from his heavy steel-toed boots, echoing on his march. Only one man in all of Durge Helm had the power to storm into this situation and not be immediately thrown out. The Durgeon of Septalia himself.

"What is the meaning of this!?" his deep heroic voice boomed and echoed throughout the hall.

"Alicèn," Luan said.

Alicèndil had the respect of all in Durge Helm. His genius in military nouse has defended not only the capital itself but many attacks that have existed on Septalia. Mainly from their direct enemy, The Banamie, but he has also been primarily responsible for the scouting of Rawbler nests, destroying them at the source before any damage could be done.

"And what do we owe the pleasure?"

"Is this the Barkler I have been informed about?"

"Indeed."

"May I ask why his presence was not brought to me at once?"

"Careful Durgeon."

"The capture and imprisonment of our enemy should have been brought to my attention the moment he came through our walls. Is it not the responsibility of The Durge to ascertain such matters?"

"It is."

"Then, please enlighten me."

"This man tells us that he spotted the form of a dragon. And in particular, a Dragadelf. Such information warrants our immediate attention."

"And you do not trust my judgement?"

"It is not a question of trust, Durgeon."

"And what is your opinion of what he has told you?"

"A Dragadelf?" Luan laughed. "Insanity."

"It is not a lie!" Rya burst out. "I have proof!"

The atmosphere in the room sharpened. They all perked up as to what proof could be shown to warrant their attention.

"Proof?" Luan asked carefully. "What proof can you provide?"

"Is there a man or woman in this city who studies the constitution of dragons?"

"One is right next to you."

Rya looked at Alicèn who looked back with immediate interest. Rya got to his feet and produced very delicately from inside his baggy garments something which stunned the room, captivating everyone watching. He produced what looked like a large beige coloured boulder with a reddish spike elongating from the main body of the rock which took two hands to hold. Alicèns mouth immediately dropped open as he knew exactly what it was.

"Good Gracelands!" he whispered. "May I?"

Rya handed the boulder to Alicèn who was completely compelled at the rock.

"Durgeon?" Luan asked. "What is it?"

Alicèn examined with growing amazement.

"Your honour... I do believe he could be telling the truth."

The general concern rose immediately at The Durgeons analysis.

"What is it?"

"This... This is dragon-bone! In particular, a smaller vertebrae from one of the beasts itself."

Every single member on the council shuffled and murmured towards each other in complete astonishment.

"This unique fusion of calcium is called Delfenclaw. This is irrefutably such bone from a Dragadelf."

"That simply cannot be!"

"With respect, your honour, it is without question a part of a Dragadelf's spine. Nedian?"

He walked over and placed it to his hands as he also studied with great interest in the constitution and makeup of dragons. After several moments of examination, he lowered the bone and looked fiercely towards Rya.

"Where on this land did you find this!?" Nedian needled.

"It came apart when it thrashed its way in Icarzbolden. I hid when it came. And when I thought he'd gone, I made a move to grab it. And it was then when it appeared behind me. Maybe it was because I had this in my hands at the time, which is why I'm alive now, I don't know!"

"This is impossible! Dragon-bone does not just fall off."

"In this case, it did!" Rya fought back. "I am telling you. A Dragadelf! It escaped! And I do not know how."

"Why did you not mention this immediately to us?"

"I don't know. I - I'm scared."

The wry smiles and moronic laughter on the council saddened Rya. However, there was an air of nervousness and great concern about what had just been revealed.

"What do you make of this, Durgeon?" Luan continued, ignoring Rya's ridiculous comment.

"Is it really so hard to believe?"

"You say you believe him then?"

"I'm saying we should not rule it out as a possibility."

Alicèn noticed several murmurs and shakes of the heads in the courtroom at how ridiculous that sounded to them.

"Let us be clear. This does not prove exactly that a Dragadelf has escaped."

"No, but it does indicate a cause for concern to me. How else could this be anywhere than inside The Dragasphere?"

"Everyone on this council appreciates your dedication to the realm, Alicèn, truly. And we have never doubted your competence. But trusting the word of our enemy?"

"Was this man captured by any of our men? Or was his imprisonment voluntary on his part?" Some of the council members looked sideways at each other. "It is clear to us that he did not need to come with this information. But yet he has done so anyway. We are duty bound to investigate."

"Alicèn," Luan informally warned. "We cannot. Trust. A Barkler!"

"A Barkler he may be. But ask yourself. What if this is the truth? What would that mean for the safety of not just Septalia, but all on Terrasendia? Is it really impossible!?"

"Yes!" The voice of Meryx Meigar quickly stated. The brother of The Blessèd Mage of Earth, Max Meigar, who was one of the Màgjeurs who constructed The Dragasphere. "The Dragasphere is the most powerful containment spell to have ever existed on Rèo. It is simply impregnable. Nothing goes in, and nothing comes out."

"You are fully aware that for all the power The Blessèd hold, there are evils on this land that are just as powerful."

"You question the powers of divine right?"

"Not at all Meryx, I am simply stating that there are still ways this could have potentially happened."

"Such as?" Alicèn paused as he contemplated his answer. The rest of the room watched on feeling slightly nervous; he might reveal something they do not want to hear.

"There is something at work here. Something that is meant to be beyond our understanding. But I vow to you all I will find out what is happening."

"Nothing is happening! It is all false! A ruse. Just stories made up by fanatics to frighten us. The same fanatics as the one before us here!"

"Alicèn?" Luan said "Do you have information you wish to provide?"

"I do. In fact, I believe everything Meryx has pointed out is also relevant."

"How so?"

"How many attacks have happened in the last ten years?"

"Precisely," Meryx said. "Very few! Congratulations."

"I appreciate the sentiment, but it is not because of my efforts that these attacks have halted. I do fear it is deliberate on The Banamies part."

"How so?"

"The possible sighting of a Dragadelf could be related somehow to our enemy. I believe Draul is withdrawing his attacks for one purpose. He plans to attack all who oppose him."

The men on the council murmur towards each other.

"Order," Luan carefully said once more. "Are you saying it is in your opinion, that we are facing an impending threat?"

"Yes."

"How big are we talking?"

"… Full scale, your Honour."

"All on Septalia?"

"Not just Septalia. But all on Rèo. Starting with the realms of men and Màgjeurs." The murmurs grew even louder as the disbelief echoed throughout.

"Silence in the court!" Luan banged his gavel on the wooden plaque. "Are you saying that The Banamie have somehow managed to tame a live Dragadelf?"

"I'm not sure."

The looks of several members significantly grew more shocked at the theory. Some even looked at him as if he had said the most stupid thing they ever heard, which to some of them was a strong possibility.

"The Dragadelf answer to no one. You know this."

"I may have a theory that I do not wish to discuss here."

"I want to hear it."

"Not now your Honour. I need time. But unusual things are happening. Scout reports in Landonhome too have significantly reduced, and that is not normal. Which is why I request the council to release this prisoner to be left in the care of The Durge."

"And what will you do with him? Question him? Torture him? He is a Barkler. He will not break."

"I do not wish to do either of those things. I wish for him to take us to the place where he claims he saw the Dragadelf. To see for myself what is happening."

More outrageous cries came from the council. Words of *preposterous* and *madness* came into fruition.

"RAZING GELLOWS!!!" Rya's voice pierced through the air. The noise died down as they turned their heads toward the Barkler.

"What about Razing Gellows?" Luan sternly asked.

"The Durgeon is right. Draul plans to wipe out the realms of men. He is gathering his legions at Razing Gellows."

Due to the sheer mass and terrain of The Farrowdawns, there were plenty of places to not only gather on masse but also to potentially hide too.

"Your Honour that would make sense," Alicèn confirmed.

"And you believe him?"

"I am concerned enough to investigate both locations."

"Unfortunately, I do not condone this. I cannot accept the words of a madman to set dooming precedence should we act upon it. Soon we will have thousands of people claiming fallacies that we cannot entertain."

"They would not provide key evidence as Rya here."

"Even still, should you wish to proceed with your investigation you will not have the support of the helm."

"I'm sorry?" Alicèn couldn't quite believe it.

"It will be a rogue operation which you will concentrate on your own time should you wish. We need you to focus your efforts on protecting the land from this and any threat. Not expeditions on the word of a madman."

"Your Honour the protection of the land includes investigations as such."

"It is the source of information which forces my hand, Durgeon."

"Explain to me how Delfenclaw has ended up outside of The Dragasphere."

"That is your job! And I expect you to fulfil your obligation."

"May I then ask you to extend any notion of punishment until my investigation has concluded?"

Luan certainly did not want to bend on this. Releasing Rya would indeed be problematic as in effect it would be bending the law, which was clear. Any persons joining The Banamie in any form were immediately declared enemies of the state and punishable by death. However, he could not ignore that Septalia was facing increasing difficulties with their war with The Banamie. Draul was a Master of War. So much so, that he had attracted thousands to his cause which was of great concern to the realms of men. More each day. He knew he needed to be bold if this information were true.

"Very well," Luan said after a long pause of thought. "But this must remain within these walls. Were word to get out, it would set an example for potential followers. Knowing there is a way back into society would not be a useful deterrent."

"Thank you, your Honour. We shall leave early hours to avoid being seen."

"Good. That's concluded." Luan stood, followed quickly by everyone on the council. "The prisoner is now in the hands of The Durge. But I advise with great caution, Durgeon. Trust yourself."

"I will. Stand with honour."

"Stand with honour."

As the council filed out of the room, Rya was ushered out by guards to a nearby cell as Alicèn tried to process what he had to do next. He truly believed there was something brewing that did not sit right with him. His immediate concern was to go straight to Razing Gellows to see if it was true, that Draul was gathering his armies there. But also he had the strangest of feelings that Rya was telling the truth about seeing a Dragadelf.

A theory festered within him for many months. A theory born entirely as to why The Dragadelf came in the first place. And after convincing himself that Rya's sighting was genuine, it made him prioritise seeing the location he claims to have seen it. All in all, despite remaining reservations with trusting the Barkler himself, it made no sense to him why he would present this information were it not to be true. He was the last one to leave the room as he took the bone from Nedian, staring at it for several moments, alone, before marching out with determination.

Alicèn made his way back to his quarters at The Durge. He loved the capital. He would defend it with every fibre and being of his life. And the people knew that too, which filled him with the satisfaction he needed. Durge Helm itself was right in the northeast corner of Terrasendia. Its curved stone walls blended into the mountain of Aries Hollow, the home of Zathos, The Blessèd Mage of Electricity. Seldom does he appear in the city itself but it would take some nerve to attack the city knowing such power watched over them.

The DNA of Septalia and especially Durge Helm was that of strength and regiment. Considered to be the protectors on Terrasendia, Septalia holds itself in the highest honour to protect the land from those who intend to harm it. The history of their direct enemy all derived from Draul who was once one of Felders most trusted friends. He strongly disagreed with the High King's suggestion to create The Dragasphere to the point where after it happened, he could never forgive. Even in his sacrifice he vowed to avenge the tragic deaths of those who did not make it out in time and blamed The Blessèd Order for merely following the opinion of Felder and not acting with reason. As a result, Draul disavowed from all that was good and green to secretly build an army to avenge the fallen. Over the years his persuasion to those who also agreed with his philosophy had developed such a force that it is of great concern to Terrasendia. Not just the men, but to all who believe in the decision of creating the spell of containment.

Septalians strongly believed in the power of the military. Their concept of using The Protecy and magic was primarily shrugged off despite knowing its potential. That was how it was for men who so highly regarding strength of arms as a sign of honour and sovereignty. However, when opposed to such harmful magic, they do agree that the use of magic to defend one's self was acceptable.

Alicèn mustered a small band of his most valued knights to aid him on his quest. He prepared the horses ready to leave in the early hours of the night. The council would have had to tell the city that Rya would be privately executed for his desertion to adhere to the law and keep the peace. But secretly sneaking Rya out of the city to ascertain what was truly happening was top of Alicèn's agenda.

He approached him in his cold cell. Rya struck an apologetic figure as he grovelled against the steel bars.

"Are you lying to me?" Alicèn asked, still trying to find any nuances in Rya's behaviour, which seemed suspicious or could lead to deception. So far, he sensed nothing. Rya shook his head in disbelief.

"Please. You must believe me."

"Did you really see one?"

"Yes! I know what a Dragadelf looks like. This one, white as snow! I studied them in my learning years. All seven beasts mark a different colour. Are you saying you believe me?"

Alicèn sighed in uncertainty. He didn't want to believe him, but his experience has proved never to rule anything out.

"Razing Gellows. How many gather there?"

"Some fifty thousand. Maybe more by now."

"Is he there?"

"Draul? Yes."

"And he plans his assault on Septalia?"

"That's just the start. You were right what you said earlier. He is withdrawing his armies to launch a complete wipe-out. After he conquers Septalia, his retribution on the whole of Rèo will soon follow."

"Do you know where they will strike first?"

"Yes."

"Where?"

"Right here. On Durge Helm. An eye for an eye as he declares."

"How so?"

"He is a very philosophical man, as you know. It's The Banamies signature. Harm them, and they'll harm you with the same manner."

"Killing thousands of innocents on Terrasendia is hardly the same manner."

"He would disagree. He claims that The Dragasphere was a pure stake to the heart of all humanity. The murdering of innocents on Felders Crest. He feels taking out Durge Helm would prove some justice. He is gathering legions not only from the realms of men. But also creatures from the pits of Slassia! Rawblers, Sharwings, Grozlers. Not to mention the more heads he turns every day of not just men, some dwarves and Questacèreans too."

Alicèn listened and believed every word. He tried not to show that Rya's information was of great value to him as he didn't want to give him any leverage. But the truth was that Rya's words were invaluable to him even more so that the bone was undeniably that of a Dragadelf's.

"You seem very easy to give me this knowledge without anything in return."

"Please do not let that concern you. I fully expected to have my life taken from me. If I do show you everything I know, all I ask is that you do reconsider my death. Please."

"Should we get to Razing Gellows and everything you say is true, and that there is proof that a Dragadelf has escaped, I not only assure you your life, I assure you your freedom!"

Rya started to break down at the thought of freedom. The twinkle in his eyes once again began to glisten.

"Thank you. I realise I have made a big mistake. I hope that my actions prove my redemption, not my words. Actions that could help you save the lives of many more."

Alicèn again believed his words. His reservations were still at the forefront of his mind as that was part of his DNA, but he genuinely believed him. Suddenly he produced a set of keys and opened the gate. Rya's expression lightened up as he looked into the space the open gate presented. He slowly got to his feet and crept towards Alicèn.

"Show me."

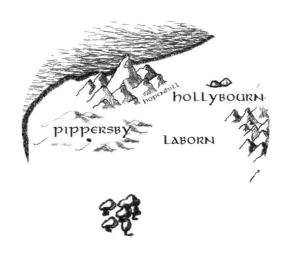

HOPENHILL
HOLLYBOURN

PIPPERSBY
LABORN

The Blessèd Wheel

The next morning Jàqueson packed his bag ready for school at the town hall. Alex would walk him every day on his way to work. Usually, Jàque would be enthusiastic and bouncing to go and learn, but he was unusually quiet on the way to school.

"You okay, son?" Alex asked.

"I'm going to miss you, father," Jàqueson quietly responded.

"And I will miss you too. Tell you what, when I'm back, how do you fancy a trip to Gallonea?"

Jàque's eyes lit up at the prospect. It was his dream to use air magic, like his idol, The Blessèd Mage of Air.

"You want to be like Aristuto? I promise I'll take you, how does that sound?"

"We're going to see him father!?" he excitedly asked.

"Not quite to see him, I think he'll be a little too busy, but we'll walk in his footsteps and learn exactly as he did for sure."

"Father, you're the best!" he said while wrapping his arms around his father's waist as they embraced. "Can we go now, please? Thank you, I'm so ready!" His energy levels soared and all of a sudden it felt to Alex as if Jàque's worries just disappeared. "I'm going to Gallonea!!!!! Woooooah!!"

"Okay son, calm down," he said, half laughing. "Don't want the other kids getting jealous now. Maybe your teacher can tell you a few things about Gallonea. Am I right in saying you're learning about all The Blessèd Order today? And not just your favourite?"

"Yeah, I can't wait. All twelve of them! Oh, father, does that mean I can use a protecy stone when I know how?"

"Maybe not quite yet, son. Using one of those would be far too powerful for such a boy as light as you, you'd fly yourself to Rolgan and back in no time!"

"Please!"

"Off you trot, you monkey!"

They arrived at the village hall, steps leading to thick heavy wooden doors decorated with fine iron and a well-insulated roof. They embraced, and Jàque bumbled off to school welcomed by his teacher professor Gregrick, mid-fifties, grey hair wearing a grey robe. Before he got to the top of the steps, he turned to Alex.

"I love you, father."

The warmth and happiness in Alex's face were not in his smile but in his eyes. He sensed his son didn't want him to go, but he knew he was old enough to understand that he had to work.

"I love you too, son. Have a nice day."

Jàque trotted off into the hall and out of sight. As the doors closed, he heard a familiar voice behind him.

"You both seemed a little troubled today," noted the frail voice of his aunt, Gràcene. Her fading red hair turning to silver streaks, older in stature and her sight was completely gone. Her clouded murky eyes were transfixed looking upwards. Dark navy green cloak bore her attire with fine brown boots. Her weight was almost entirely on her brown walking stick.

"Everything alright?" she said tentatively.

"All fine. Just a little tired," replied Alex.

He dreaded more attention being brought to the thought of leaving his family.

"Come on, boy, I've raised you since you were a nipper and your lies are as convincing as King Romany's beard!" she snapped. "They're worried about your expedition you're going on," she confidently stated.

Knowing she guessed wrong and that finding this so-called 'Time in the Water' was ultimately the primary motivation for him going. Were it not for that, he would ask to stay, not to go and stay with his son. But any excuse to deflect he would take it.

"Well if you knew that why did you ask?"

"Don't get savvy with me you sod! You're not the only one going through the task of convincing your family of the dangers of this job. I've tried to talk to Garrison, but he's having none of it. Even his brother can't reach out to him. He's a tough man, your boss but in a way, it's people like him you want around when things get tough."

"Everyone seems a lot more worried about this than myself. Is there something I should know that everyone else does?"

"Son," she drew closer and placed one of her hands by the side of his arms. "You must understand for the women and children of this village; it's a frightening thing to see the man of the family leave the village. Even for a day, we're not used to it. You'll be fine dear boy but try to sympathise with Amba. She loves you dearly and when you hear Rawblers starting to scout about, it's naturally a cause for concern."

Alex treated Gràcene as if she were his mother that he never had. He looked up to her as the influential parental figure she was and always took to her words with good value.

"You'll be fine boy. When you're away, I'll take care of her. And when you're back, I'll give your blessing when she yes…"

That brought a smile to both their faces.

"What are you talking about?"

"Oh my dear, it's not the biggest secret of this year. People have talked it up for years, you've kept most of us waiting for far too long now it's only a matter of time."

"You can't tell her," he said trying to hide his smirk.

"Don't be ridiculous. She's probably the first to know you will someday. But hurry up! She'll turn to stone by the time you pluck up the courage to ask!"

"Yes, mother," Alex retorted sarcastically, causing Gràcene to whack her stick into the side of Alex's legs.

"Blast you boy! Get to work before I show you up ahead of The Bucksman!" Her regal nature always brought out a smile to Alex.

He made his way back home where he found Amba scrolling through pages of books. At least twenty books were on the table as she sat scrolling through them all. He looked around the house, which was gradually becoming more and more messy the more the days rolled on. A job that Amba entrusted herself to do, until recently since Jàqueson's diagnoses. Instead, her resources were devoted entirely to the teachings of time and what could lie within The Gurken. After page upon page, they both scrolled through learning nothing they didn't already know, and nothing that could help them, to the point where Amba wiped every book from the table onto the floor, sobbing into her shaking hands.

Alex rushed over to her.

"It's alright, it's alright," he consoled, hugging her tightly in the process. She flumped into his embrace as she continued to sob.

"Why us, Alex? Why us?" she cried.

"I don't know. But I promise you I will get to the bottom of this. We will not let our son go."

"How can you be so sure? All Mirabella has done is given us an alibi to give us false hope!"

"She would not do that. Whatever she speaks of must be true, otherwise she wouldn't say."

"But this makes no sense. She told us that somewhere in The Gurken would be something that will help involving this 'Time in the Water?'" her voice was turning a little angry with the force of her emotions.

"I know," Alex tried to calm her.

"She says she has no idea what it is or where exactly it is, which gives us nothing to go on."

This indeed did concern Alex too. What was Mirabella's motivation and intentions of telling them about this *'Time in the Water?'* And who told her about it?

"I don't know what any of this means, and how our son came to this in the first place - "

" - I read that Malerma is very unnatural. A bi-product of impurities on this land."

She pulled away from his embrace and scrolled through the several books which crumpled to the floor until picking out one. She scrolled through pages and laid it onto the table for them both to see.

"See here:

'Malerma is a disease which involves the essences of time. This rare and complicated affliction causes the acceleration of growth within the body, causing a faster death if not cured. Since medicine cannot cure, and no treatment has been definitively recognised to treat effectively, the chances of survival are slim. However, several studies of this rarity have learned that expertise into the delving of time has triggered responses to slow down the complex disease and in one case, even reverse. Furthermore this affliction is not caused by natural elements…'

And that's it! Nothing more."

Her eyes were scrolling for more answers. She couldn't help herself but get angry and upset very quickly, which Alex was very competent at controlling by now.

"We must try to be calm and work this out."

Again she sobbed heavily into his chest which by now was noticeably wet. The warm droplet of tears splashing onto his arm.

"I'm sorry Alex. I am, I am sorry," she sobbed.

"Don't you be sorry! This is no one's fault. When we get to The Gurken, I will not be coming back without whatever is it."

"Good." Her tears did start to dry up. The skin on her reddened cheeks eroded from the salt. "We need to be strong. I need to be strong, just like you!"

"You are strong. I wouldn't be with someone who wasn't," he said while kneeling.

He realised he just put himself into a position where he could potentially propose to her right in that very moment accidentally. He always had a perfect way to propose, and this was not it. Luckily Amba did not recognise what kneeling to her could have potentially meant and Alex continued to console.

He went to work and prepped for the voyage ahead with the other smithies. Provisions, clothing, armour and weaponry were the main components of the trip. The horses needed to be fed well with starchy foods to help last the three-day ride. Garrison gathered the men round to discuss the journey.

"We'll be going with most of The Durge this year, including The Durgeon himself. This is purely a precautionary action and not based on any intelligence we have received from Rombard Hill. Do not feel the additional numbers is because an attack is imminent. We feel that it would calm the town of any fears they may have. I promise you all, we'll be home quicker than you know it. Some of us will be left behind to ensure the policing of our streets until our return. Branmir you'll be…"

Alex's mind wandered away again as Garrison's speech did nothing to alleviate any worries.

" - What if it's true?" interrupted Taryn. Mousy brown and untidy hair topped his stern face. Quite aggressive but can be reasoned with given the conditions were right. A heavy drinker at The Spuddy Nugget after work but also a competent swordsman.

The room focused in on Garrison, who by the impression of the room almost seemed like a relief that someone asked that question. Most of the men felt too proud, perhaps even a little heroic to ask the question, but the fears always had it in the back of their minds.

"What if we get attacked?"

"You afraid of a little fight, son?" Garrison answered rhetorically.

"So the rumours are true?"

"No, they're not. But we're well guarded, and we are doing this whether you like it or not. We can't survive for another year without the materials."

"But why The Gurken? Why not the hills of Handenmar or the sands of Rolgan? We might be able to double or even triple our intake as it's all-new, in demand, people will want to see new product."

"The hills of Handenmar belong to the dwarves, I don't think to start a potential confrontation with them is wise, and Rolgan is far too hot for even the strongest of our horses."

"We don't need horses when we pass into Rolgan, if we took the western plain of Bolero-Questa, we would be back in a few weeks still, beneath the sands are hundreds of thousands of years' worth of compressed minerals inside cavities. We're bound to find something there also."

The mood of the room turned seemingly optimistic.

"And you think you're the first one to think about the alternatives? Rolgan is a volatile and dangerous place. Full of mystery, wonder and secrets. The heat has turned the people who reside there mad. Why do you think north of the Rolgan Waste is called the Land of the Neverseen?" Garrison asked again.

"Because no one has ever seen it..." Branmir slowly answered, completely deadpan. The room tried to ignore the naivety as best as they could.

"All I'm saying is that there must be another option."

"No. There is not. I will not risk the safety of new ventures when the only information we have received is a rumour. Probably from a madman at best. If you want to stay Taryn be my guest. But don't expect to be wearing those overalls when we return. The more men we have, the quicker we'll be back."

Taryn's palms began to sweat at the exchange and the opportunity to not go. But he knew he had to. Secretly Alex was willing Garrison on not to deviate and stick to the original plan.

"So what's it going to be?" Garrison asked. Reluctantly Taryn nodded. "Good lad. Now the road over Hopenhill will be easy for the horses but on the way back may prove challenging with all the..."

Alex's mind faded away once more with the weight of anxiety bearing into his chest. Sparring in a yard was sport for Alex, but the risk of not finding what he is looking for filled his head into bone harrowing fear which spurred every action for the rest of the day.

At the end of the shift, Brody approached Alex.

"How's my little champ doing?" Brody asked. "Little Jàque hasn't seen his uncle Brody for a week! I miss him."

Brody had a soft spot for Jàqueson not only because of his disease but long before that. He always joked around, and Jàqueson adored him. To the point that he called him uncle Brody, which Alex and Amba loved. Brody and indeed Bran were dear friends to the family.

"Come round tomorrow. He will be glad to see you." Alex said.

He embraced his best friend with a man hug, a gentle thud on the back before entering his home.

The usual flump of arms greeted Alex from Jàqueson before sitting him down and educating his father on what he had learned today.

"Today Professor Gregrick told us to draw a picture that would make us relate to The Blessèd Order! I loved it today, father, I really did." His enthusiasm cruelly warmed Alex's heart again. "We learned that there are twelve Blessèd Mages, and as there are twelve hours on the clock, I placed each one of them onto each hour.'

Jàque showed his father and mother who brought in some food for them his highly impressive drawings of each Màgjeur on each hour of the clock.

Aristuto, The Blessèd Mage of Air, at twelve o'clock. Who else to begin with other than his favourite Màgjeur. His protecy stone was believed to have been born in a devastating hurricane, capturing the energy in the stone for his unrivalled use. The concept of air Màgjeurs having the capability to fly by their own accord was commonly misleading. They could often use air to move objects, or propel themselves up to glide for many miles depending on how high up they are, using their powers of air to help sustain their flight. Though very few had enough power to make them ascend from the ground for such a period of time and in affect give the impression that they can fly. However, it was common knowledge that Aristuto went missing many years ago, and has not been seen since the creation of The Dragasphere.

Max Meigar, The Blessèd Mage of Earth, at one o'clock. Muscular in build and charisma, residing somewhere in Septalia. His fascination with preserving life into matters of the earth was what made him so interesting. Not only could he manipulate earth (like other Màgjeurs who study earth magic,) but he was a master of Soul Preservation. His protecy stone believed to have been carved out of the mountain of Aries Hollow.

Ethelba, The Blessèd Mage of Fire, at two o'clock. Very small in terms of height and characterised by a cute tail. But perhaps the most destructive in terms of her overall power. Fire was indeed an obvious choice of offensive nature, but the fascination with her was that she could manipulate fire so destructively to her needs. She was the head of the Rolga-Knights, a famous band of soldiers, all with pyrovines noticeably running through their bodies. Her protecy stone born from the volcanic fires of Dragonsnout.

Wemberlè, The Blessèd Mage of Water, at three o'clock. Elegant and slim in physique, her arms reminiscent of fins. The pale and deep blue colours of her skin gave that aqua feel. A Tsunami tried to hit the east coast of Mages Wreath several years ago. Wemberlè countered the onrushing water with a typhoon in the middle of the easterly oceans which drew the devastation away. Her protecy stone born from the deepest part of the darkest ocean was said to have such power she could control tides and waves of the oceans.

King Thorian Mijkal, The Blessèd Mage of Ice, at four o'clock. The King of Questacère, resided in the capital of Lathapràcère. Building his palace of ice with his powers was a pillar of beauty said to be so great that upon death, their souls will see the magnificent spectacle when they pass into the Gracelands. His protecy stone was said to be extracted from the heart of the glaciers of The Gracelands. A land so cold and peaceful not much has ever come to common knowledge.

Zathos, The Blessèd Mage of electricity at five o'clock. Bald and dark in complexion, married to Wemberlè. Purple and dark blue colours were the makeup of his typical robes. His demeanour was very calm and only spoke when necessary. His stone crafted by a strike of lightning, captured his unrivalled used of volts. He may also be considered The Blessèd Mage of Volts which essentially is the same thing.

Eveleve, The Blessèd Mage of Life, at the bottom at 6 o'clock. Her powers were said to be the preservation and longevity of life. Her skills could not revive those from the dead but could cast the use of life to counter any spells or dangers that would endanger life itself. Her existence became unknown after The Dragasphere while the details of her protecy stone were also unknown.

Mavokai, The Blessèd Mage of Death, at seven o'clock. If life was considered one of the essential elements on Terrasendia, then so should death. Mavokai was a master of death. His heart did not beat but was loyal to the living cause. His protecy stone, buried somewhere in the land of The Understunde. The most evil of places the soul could go after death.

Davinor, The Blessèd Mage of Protecy, at eight o'clock. The Blessèd Order did not consider any one Magjeur to be at the head of the table, however, Davinor's counsel was said to be most appropriate and demanding. His voice would be considered the highest of them all since the death of Felder. His comprehensive study of The Protecy allowed him to have a connection with any chosen affinity. He was the only one in living memory that could excel in any and every element of his choosing, albeit not as powerful as the other Blessèd Mages but, to flow purer than any other connection known to exist. His protecy stone was said to be enchanted by himself to manipulate elements so that he could use more than one. He refused to ever let on how he discovered how to do it, as it directly conflicted the fundamental laws of protecy.

Lestas Magraw, The Blessèd Mage of the Mind, at nine o'clock. The oldest and wisest on the council. He was said to have taken studies from both Zathos and Davinor to manipulate electricity like no other. This helped him work out the patterns of the mind, needing the electrical pulses to make it naturally work. His protecy stone was said to be very weirdly planted inside the head of a genius.

King Thakendrax, The Blessèd Mage of Gravitas, at ten o'clock. The dwarven king of Handenmar, blessed his dwarves with additional gravity on the land of Handenmar which made them strong and resistant. He threw his protecy stone and sent it to the middle of the earth via a volcano to maximise his gravitational powers.

And lastly, King Felder, The Blessèd Mage of Time, at eleven o'clock, on Jàqueson's perfect wheel. The High King of Terrasendia himself. He died during the creation of The Dragasphere which he ordered. A sacrifice he chose to lure The Dragadelf into the trap to ensure its completion. One of the things that made Felder so powerful was that he was the only mage who could wield two forces of protecy to its utmost purity which no one knew how. Even though Davinor was extremely powerful and could learn any element in more depth, he could not excel in the same fashion as Felder when it came to time and fire. His fascination with time was so absorbing he studied the notions himself using his own studies, thus being only one of two known Màgjeurs to possess the art of true clairvoyance, the ability to see not only past and present but also future. Legend has it that he locked away all his knowledge on the subject of time into a stone of glass which later became known as The Time Stone. However, it was said to have been lost or stolen much before the escape of The Dragasphere.

It was the efforts of all Màgjeurs which created The Dragasphere which is widely known as the greatest spell ever created. Not even the fires of The Dragadelf could pierce its magical walls. Nothing goes in, and nothing goes out. For all the legendary powers and good that The Blessèd hold, there are forces of evil on Terrasendia that hold powers that could rival them, and have done for many years.

"This is really impressive stuff son," Alex proudly said. "What did professor Gregrick say?"

"He told me he was delighted I came up with something so simple. It's been my favourite topic so far."

"Even more than *The Tales of Felder and Melcelore!?*" Amba pointed out.

"Ah yeah! I can't pick, I love them both!" Jàquesons smile really did beam. He was happy, and they both wanted to keep it that way for as long as they could. "He loved how I gave brief descriptions to the protecy stones too. He said that it was really important to understand how it can help enhance energy…"

Suddenly Alex's brain hit a windsail. As Jàque continued to talk about his wonderful day, Alex rushed off and out of the house.

"Alex!?" Amba called out.

"Father, where are you going?"

Alex ran as fast as he could scudding round the corners of the pebble streets under the dusk sunlight, heading straight to the library. He flicked through sections of bookcases and looked for the book Protecy Stones and their Origins. He managed to locate the book which was relatively used due to its popularity, and luckily few copies were available.

He laid the book onto the table in the library and started scanning. He was looking at different types of stone from fire stones to ice stones which the information regarding these was plentiful. Until it came to him at last. Right at the very end. One page on what he had hoped… The Time Stone.

After hearing his son's learnings that King Felder created a stone to conceal all his learnings of time, he gathered that this must be what Mirabella is asking him to find. It gave him a sense of direction to go in, not just for him, but for the survival of his son. It did, however, dawn on him at that moment that Mirabella knew Felder, and it was entirely possible that it was Felder who told her such information. But why she could not tell him it was a stone was again unclear. Maybe she didn't know it herself? Questions rained inside his head again. Questions that he wished Mirabella was right there. He raced back to his loving home to tell Amba what he has learned.

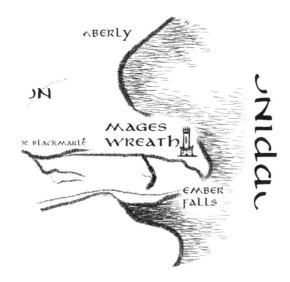

The Next

Much of Ramalon's day was looking forward to starting his training with Davinor. He could not quite believe that a man of his calibre was so interested in someone like him, a Màgjeur from the lower levels, satisfied with his quiet life of teaching his students. Seldom did he get excited, but this was an occasion he couldn't wait to start.

The autumn air chilled Ramalon's face as he made his way to The Skyurch. The highest tower on Mages Wreath where Davinor lived. The purpose was twofold in that he was there to meet with him in the afternoon but also to receive an official invitation to the second round with the eleven other Màgjeurs.

Because of its location in Terrasendia, Mages Wreath enjoyed the typical four seasons with autumn being his favourite. Despite his loose fitted dark cloak being enchanted with pyrovines, he chose on most occasions not to use them. Despite his affinity with fire, he loved the cold. The chill that nature had to offer. He always slept with the windows open, even in the harshest of winters.

He arrived at The Skyurch where he entered the humungous hall which was so tall he could barely make out the ceiling. Once he stepped inside the building, he noticed other Màgjeurs from the first round once again already there. He had his ideas as to who would make it to the next round. He suspected that not one of them would ever have imagined he would make it to the next stage. His suspicions were confirmed when several Màgjeurs looked sideways at him before quickly making sharp comments to their mini bands who collectively reacted. He noticed that he was the only one who was alone. Not that it bothered him, he was used to it.

The remaining Màgjeurs gathered at the foot of the steps which led up to a stone pedestal where several members of The Magikai were stood. He felt very much outclassed by some of the others. Their confidence came across overwhelmingly cocky and arrogant.

A member that Ramalon recognised approached the pedestal to announce the details of the next round. Ronovin was an exceptional earth Màgjeur, relatively young for a member of The Magikai but his talents were not in question.

"Warm congratulations to you all!" his voice was crisp and well spoken. "A fine first round indeed. The games this year have brought in a record number of spectators. As many of you will have seen, a higher influx of Handen's, Cèreans and even Elcarians have flocked into the city to watch this year. A fine show you put on, all worthy of your place in the second round. Many of you…"

Ramalon drifted away from the conversation and observed the competitors around him once more. Some were looking at him, smiling with intent. He knew that they were all hoping to get drawn with him in the next round. He looked over and noticed Pyros, another fire Màgjeur who he wanted to avoid as he believed him to be stronger in the same affinity. His skin was dark while the black beads of his eyes and sneering smile attempted to intimidate Ramalon. He also didn't want any water Màgjeurs as that would prove difficult for him in a fight. All in all, he didn't like his chances whoever he got.

Ronovin produced twelve sheets of paper which floated in the air before him, all with the names of the remaining participants.

"As you are all aware, to preserve the integrity of the games, you shall not know which format the next and indeed third round shall take shape until the day of the event."

He flicked his hand upwards, and the pieces of paper flew high into the air.

"Depending on the order in which name falls into my hand will be your opponents. All I can tell you is that this round you will competing in three's. Good luck to all."

Ramalon's anxiety went through the roof, along with the papers. He liked to think it was the same for every other Màgjeur, but their confident thick exteriors gave him more reason to feel the shuddering of his teeth as the nerves kicked in.

The pieces of paper floated down on their own accord into the direction of Ronovin's outstretched hand. It took a while before they could see even one float down as they were cast up that high, adding more sweat in his undercarriages. The first name finally floated into his hands.

"Lauru!" a water Màgjeur - fair natured and elegant.

The second name floated down into his hands. Ramalon was hoping his name would not come as he would immediately be up against a water Màgjeur.

"Rybon!" a fire Màgjeur from the city.

Even more reason to not want his name next as he would be drawn into a three with two tricky opponents.

The next paper floated down into his hand. The waiting clamped Ramalon's diaphragm…

"Lazabeth!" a Màgjeur with the affinity of volts.

Her young and beautiful charm dazzled some of the males. The clasp released, allowing his breathing to continue, his anxiety subdued temporarily.

"Our first trio of Màgjeurs. Water, fire and volts. Very interesting! Now for the next trio."

Ramalon and Pyros were the only two fire Màgjeurs left. He knew of the others by name and affinity only. Ildreàn, another water Màgjeur, Allaremsah and Enzo as volts, Peter Palgan as the remaining earth, Chloen and Allenade air and Xjaques Croller as ice.

The one he really wanted to be in a trio with was Xjaques as he stood a chance with his fire against ice. His attention drifted off again as his mind ran and ran into endless possibilities of *what ifs?* and what his plan against each one of them would be. His mind in total overdrive with overwhelming possibilities. So much so that he completely missed the next trio.

"Allenade, Chloen and Ildreàn! Our next trio. Two air and one water!"

Ramalon's chances of being drawn with Xjaques grew more likely. The next papers floated down.

"Enzo!"

Ramalon only knew of his erratic and unpredictable nature but could immediately feel he was dangerous.

"Xjaques Croller!"

This was it, the one Magjeur Ramalon needed to draw to stand any chance. It all stemmed down to that moment. Ronovin pinched his fingers around the next falling paper. Ramalon's lungs once again tightened – his anxiety constricting.

"Ramalon. Ramalon. Ramalon!" he thought…

"Peter Palgan!"

And with that Ramalon's shoulders slowly lowered and his hopes began to fade dramatically. He tried not to change the look on his face but it was unconvincing, even to him. Luck, it seemed, was not on his side that day. Ramalon was hit with the realisation that he was in a trio with another fire Màgjeur in the smirking, cocky and full-of-himself Pyros. Not to mention Allaremsah who he felt was the stronger of the three-volt Màgjeurs. His heart told him that this was perhaps the worst group to be drawn in. The remaining three papers flew down with Ramalon's name being the last.

"Two fire and one volt! Very interesting, indeed."

The air grew tighter, despite the enormity of the hall. The suspense among the final twelve grew sharper and spiked more intensity among the competitors. Ramalon knew how much they all wanted to win. No more than him.

"There we have it! The second round shall begin next week where you shall know of the format in which your battle and task will take place. Good luck to you all!"

And with that, Ronovin and the other members of The Magikai bowed their heads and left. As they disappeared from the hall, the silence pierced through every competitor. Nobody moved, even when Ronovin left. Only awkward shuffles and sideways glances toward each other. Ramalon did not feel uncomfortable in the silent awkwardness, only nervous of his competition. He could sense something was about to happen. Would somebody's nerves crack and use their protecy on another? It would certainly be a justifiable release of tension it was that high.

It was Ramalon being in the middle of the crowd, who was the first to eventually move. He left the congregation in the hope it would stir up and disperse the crowd. It didn't. He made his way down the hallway to his right, looked back to see the tense eleven looking at him. He had no idea why, but he conjured a small smile as he turned from them, as if he found the situation amusing. Taking in particular note of

Pyros who returned the smile with a smugness that stank out the hall.

Ramalon continued his walk and just like that his nerves and anxiety subsided. He couldn't quite put his finger on why and put it down to his lack of empathy helping his temporary struggles. But as he made his way to the peak of The Skyurch and thought about his meet with Davinor, he realised the real reason for his surge in confidence.

He recovered very quickly from the jangled nerves and noose-like feeling he had when experiencing the draw for the next round. Ascending so many wide steps in The Skyurch he felt his legs would fall off by the time he got to the top. His mind regularly raced with excitement, wondering what Davinor would be doing with him. The apprentice he presumed. To learn from the best. Maybe it was those thoughts that produced his smile to the other competitors. A sense of bragging rights that he had. None of the others had that singular attention and he couldn't wait to get inside the high chambers of The Magikai.

The steps were soon surrounded by uninterrupted glass instead of the granite and white marble decor. He looked out to admire the view of the white city and beyond. The sun was at its highest point on the fresh and crisp day. As the stairs spiralled around, he saw the cliffs The Skyurch were perched upon, which overlooked The Chopping Sea. The higher he climbed, the more invincible he began to feel. The more confident he grew. He got to the final step and saw the famous doors of The Magikai. Thick stoned doors, detailed with the most intricate and exuberant of illustrations of all the recognised affinities. Beautiful bright colours clashed with affinities which Ramalon had seen in pictures, but they did not do it justice. The detail was impeccable and took Ramalon by surprise by just how in awe he was.

Suddenly the doors opened to reveal The Blessèd Mage of Protecy himself on an impressive chair. Davinor welcomed him as he entered the circular room taking it all in. Other chairs in the style of different affinities laid out around the room. The stained-glass windows lit up a vast array of different colours, making the cold stone floor seem alive.

"I'm glad you found your way," Davinor said.

"It's hard to miss."

"Indeed. Are you pleased with your draw?" he asked quickly.

"No."

"No?"

"It was quite frankly the worst draw I could have asked for."

"I see. Do I get the impression you fear the competition?"

"You have an astute and correct mind, my lord."

"I do, do you have the stone with you?" he asked as he approached Ramalon.

Davinor's gait almost looked as if he did not need to move his arms, merely gliding toward him. Elegant but purposeful. Ramalon produced the stone which was tucked safely in his robes. He placed it into the hands of The Blessèd Mage.

"I will try not to burn you this time," Davinor scoffed audibly at the thought that someone as low as Ramalon could hurt him.

"Curiously enough that is something I want to find out. As you are aware when you use The Protecy, the affinity will indeed travel through the stone. But because of the protective lining that cases a protecy stone, we are assured it stays within the stone itself. Which is the first part of my intrigue as to how it managed to burn my hands last night."

"It does not burn my hands."

"Is there pain?"

"No. I feel the warmth, but no pain."

"I see. And the trap you cast for Pierro, did you feel any different at all?"

"I always feel different," Ramalon bluntly replied.

"I mean your protecy. Did you feel anything more? More of a connection?"

"Nothing out of the ordinary."

Davinor furrowed and began to cut an inquisitive figure rather quickly.

"But you must have felt more powerful when you released your fire onto him, yes?"

"Indeed, I did. But you ask if I felt anything different to which I did not. I felt the most power I have ever felt. But purely in the hype of the moment, I guess."

"I need to study this. Would you consent to me looking at your stone for several weeks? I have never experienced anything like this."

Ramalon was a little concerned about giving his stone away from his protection. He also felt that the situation was becoming more about Davinor's interest and not his.

"You mean, whilst I am here?"

"No, I do not. I need time alone to study how so much energy could filter through such impurity. In exchange for my studies onto your stone, I will purify it for you. That is my offer."

The thought of purifying the stone never really seemed like an option for Ramalon and was not instinctively drawn to it. He stared at the feet of Davinor, considering his proposal.

"I assure you, you will have it back before your next round intact."

"Forgive me but am I not here to learn more about The Protecy from you?"

Davinor paused before contemplating his answer.

"As I said, in exchange for the findings of your stone I will purify it for you. Is that not fair to you?"

Ramalon didn't feel he could say no. He was The Blessèd Mage of Protecy after all. Ramalon was annoyed that his excitement and eagerness to learn from Davinor was misplaced.

"With respect, I feel a more appropriate trade would be to learn how you can conjure every affinity so powerfully. Something no other Màgjeur can do."

"That is not on the table. I do not want this to turn into a bargaining race. I have offered you a chance. A chance to win The Màgjeurs Open! Which we will keep to ourselves."

Ramalon could not hide his disappointment but at the same time was conflicted by his powers potentially growing stronger as the result of a better protecy stone.

"So I give you the stone, you do what you need to do, and then you purify it for me?"

"Can it get any simpler?"

"… On one condition."

Davinor did look a little annoyed that his trade was not enough. Nevertheless, Ramalon weighed up that he would not go to such a length to reject a proposal now.

"Which is?"

"In addition to purifying my stone, you share every part of what you find with me."

"Ramalon - "

" - Every. Part. I feel I have the right to know."

Ramalon was surprised at how angry this made Davinor. His top lip stiffened and his jaw started to pulse.

"This is how you show your appreciation, Màgjeur Ramalon? The studies I will partake in are not for the minds of yourself!"

"Regardless, it is my stone. And should you find something that should benefit me, is that not fair trade?"

"It is fair that I excel your power and help you accomplish your dream. That is my offer. You can choose to take it, or indeed leave it and I wish you well."

Ramalon's choice seemed like it had already been made up. Despite the hesitation, it was not to contemplate the decision, but merely to plan what would happen next.

"I wish you well. My lord."

He bowed his head but not too far before he took his stone back without permission. It was not an aggressive retrieval, but Davinor took it that way before Ramalon rummaged his stone back into his robes.

As he turned and walked away from The Blessèd Mage of Protecy he saw Davinor's stunned face. Almost as if it turned to stone with his judging eyes bearing down onto him. He felt it was a massive shame to turn the opportunity down, but he felt an uncharacteristic ownership over the stone. Much more so than he ever had before. Previously he never thought of the stone as something he cherished more than anything. But the intrigue of Davinor made him realise he has something unique, which he treasured for his own. He even thought to himself if Davinor could learn about this stone, he could learn about it too.

"Màgjeur, stop!" Davinor implored as he reached the doors. He waded over to Ramalon with haste. "I agree to your terms," he said, trying to conceal his frustration with a calmer tone. "I will share the knowledge that is fitting and relevant to you - "

" - No! You will share all knowledge you find, regardless of whether it is fitting to me or not."

Davinor's face was even more irked. But Ramalon felt a slight enjoyment at calling his bluff. He knew Davinor wanted this.

"Every. Part. And the purifying of my stone. Do we have a deal?"

Ramalon offered his hand, not for a handshake, but instead to offer back the stone. Davinor took a brief moment of admiration of the stone, before quickly staring at Ramalon while contemplating the deal. He took the stone from Ramalon and did not shake his hand.

"Tomorrow. Noon. Be here."

Strange Arrivals

The blue of the moon lit up Durge Helm as if it was the seventh hour of day. The moonlight bounced off the cool steel and slate which made up the many elaborate structures and buildings of the capital.

Alicèn mustered his most trusted band members from The Durge, to aid his expedition onto Icarzbolden, the place where Rya claimed to have seen a Dragadelf. After which they would turn their attention to Razing Gellows to confirm what Rya said was true. If so, it would give him and the rest of Septalia a considerable advantage in their defence, allowing more time and preparation to fend off the impending invasion from Draul.

Alicèn kept a very close eye on his prisoner. Despite the proof of the Delfenclaw, his reservations were still at large. The prisoner still struck a very nervous figure as he mounted his horse. He could see in Rya's eyes, he felt lucky to be given a chance. A chance to redeem himself from the wrongs he admitted to having done.

Deonrick was Alicèns second in command and perhaps his closest friend. A mid-thirties aged man whose medium length black hair was tied behind his head while his sides were smooth and short. His finely shaven beard gave him a somewhat dazzling and heroic look, often being labelled as *Helms Hunk*, a member of the renowned Helda-Knights, originating from Helden-Arma, the band specialising in their signature use of boomerangs. However, despite his muscular strength and humbleness, he bore more qualities in his wisdom and courage. Alicèn would often consult his best friend when confronted with challenges he alone could not overcome.

Then came Athrempitritus and Falcone. Mighty men of brute strength. The former wielded a giant broadsword while the latter chose the Warhammer. Both men, members of The Itranir that resided in Brackbannen. Their specialty being to take centre ground in a fight, using their sheer size to make opponents move around them and improve efficiency in a fight. Their chosen mildens, huge and muscular shire horses, a suitable match for their horse-masters. A milden was another term for horses.

Also included in Alicèns band were the only two females of the group, Snira and Nutat; elves from the realms of Questacère. Athletic and lean in their physique. Great admirers of Alexa Greyman, they are naturally accomplished in archery. Their focus and stillness reflect their silent nature. Their bows were immensely beautiful, crafted from the woods in The Gracelands in the south. With the exception of Alexa Greyman, Alicèn considered them to be the most competent marksmen on Septalia.

Next, two men descended from the lands of Rolgan to the north. Dark in complexion with satisfying smiles. They knew very few could match their skills with a spear. The impressive Seyfi Alamori and Radja Gahani had many followers throughout Durge Helm.

Perhaps the quickest of them all was Ryuchi, by far the smallest member of the band. His low centre of gravity and light feet aided his nippy speeds. Exceptionally dangerous with two small-swords – his weapons of choice, needling sharply at the tips. One small slip from a larger foe could easily be their downfall with his impeccable timing. His source of training originated from Ravenspire, a place on the very edge of Septalia to the west, almost invading the crossing leading into Elcaria.

And lastly, a younger man of average build but intelligent mind, Xjazen from the stronghold of Ragabastion. Very few there fully study the specification of fighting which is very shrewd. Wielding the use of a typical sword, it was within the movements of the warrior which they believed in. Varying syncopation with one's feet, making rhythms in fights harder to read and therefore improving the Ragabastion follower to dictate fights. Common foes fall into the trap of naivety, often striking when believing the moments are right, only for them to realise their fate when falling into a syncopated trap. A hard skill to master but once accomplished, an advantageous way of defeating opponents.

All the knights of the band were hand-picked by Alicèn himself for their expertise and the fact that they would not only die in a heartbeat for their Durgeon, but they would do anything for the preservation of all that is good and green. The variation of DNA's appealed greatly to Alicèn. Should they be attacked on route, he felt comfortable that they would out-skill larger bands.

Alicèn himself was brought up in Durge Helm. He never knew his parents, instead being raised by The Durge itself. His specialty was the balance of all varieties of fighting which he studied for many years, often wielding a large shield and typical long sword to aid the all-round fighter. *One of the greatest commanders the helm has ever seen*, it was commonly said. Loved amongst all Septalians, not that he enjoyed the accolade. If anything, it was perhaps the only thing that embarrassed him. *Far too humble for your own good*, others would say. Honour compelled him to get on with the job. A true man of military. He would not hesitate to give his life for the realm. A realm that he took much pride in defending.

Draul kept his ever-growing militants hidden not only within The Farrowdawns but also forests and cities within Septalia and Landonhome. But such a gathering in one place at Razing Gellows would be very concerning. Its strategic position within the mountainous terrain would make it impossible to predict an attack given there were many paths it could lead out of the mountains.

Alicèns band filtered out of the city through passages carved into the mountain of Aries Hollow to avoid unwanted attention. Despite the pitch black surroundings of rock and stone, The Durgeon knew these paths well. The passages themselves were heavily watched as it was a way out of the capital as much as it was a way in. However, The Durge had traps and blockades in place should any unwanted attention arrive. The only realistic way in from their enemies was through the heavily protected front gates.

An occasional ascend on their journey brought them to a clearing out of Aries Hollow which overlooked the illuminated lands, lit by the moon above. They could see the eastern plain of Dragonsnape leading into Rolgan, one of the three main ways the lands connected. It's name given because its area looked like the nape of a dragon. Often considered the most fearful and dangerous of ways to cross lands as it is home to many species of dragons. Seldom do they leave their provincial home except for the terror that gripped the world thirty years before. It was the birthplace of The Dragadelf who descended onto Felders Crest.

The moon glimmered off of one of the great lakes which divided the plains. The band were clear of any potential sightings from the helm as they turned their journey southwards to Icarzbolden on the outskirts of The Farrowdawns. At a canter and occasional gallop, the journey would last more than a day.

They stopped off at Dovendale in northern Septalia, a historic but quiet village. Their hospitality was greatly welcomed, and their discretion appreciated profoundly by Alicèn. The mildens refuelled and band members sumply tucked into their hearty meals. Loaves of bread and meats were consumed greedily, while the fruit and veg over spilled a little in their baskets.

Generally, the men would banter amongst themselves while Snira and Nutat listened, often rolling their eyes to the ceiling. Occasionally they could not hide their reserved smiles behind their demeanour. Rya ate alone at the end of the long table within the public house. He was too scared to interact as he felt largely unwelcome. The rest of The Durge were fully aware they were ignoring him. Despite their instructions, they still had reservations and hate for Rya in joining The Banamie in the first place. Even though he was trying to do right, they could not overcome the treasonous perception just yet.

"Do you have family?" Alicèn asked Rya, feeling a little sorry for him as he sat opposite.

"I did." Rya sheepishly replied, keeping his gaze away from him. "Two boys. And my wife."

"What happened?"

"They're no longer with me."

"I am sorry to hear. How did they die?"

"They didn't die."

"No?"

"They didn't want to leave. No matter how hard I tried. No matter how hard I told them they were not going to be safe there, they wouldn't listen. They grew up not knowing anything different."

"And who's to blame for that...?" Athrempitritus retorted.

"Alright, Arthur," Alicèn calmly said.

"No, he's right! It was my fault. I should never have gone all those years ago. But just like many of us, my mind was turned. I was...

vulnerable. Suggestible."

"Weak?" Athrempitritus' suggestion sounded more like a statement. "Because that's what you are."

"*Were*, Arthur." Alicèn once again tried to defuse tensions. "I think there is value in redemption. It takes bravery to keep the balance of right in order. But it takes true courage to admit you were wrong." He took another glug of his ale.

"Still doesn't make up for the thousands who have died because of his contribution."

"It might. If what he says is true."

"You're putting a lot of faith in this man, Alicèn. You really believe him?"

Alicèn once again looked at Rya whose confidence seems to shatter at confirming the hatred towards him.

"I do. Not only because of the proof he has brought forward. But because he is here." Athrempitritus hummed with disapproval.

"I tell you, boy. If you're lying to us, I'll kill you my - "

" - Arthur that's enough!" Rya tried to conceal the shaking and fright at the threat. "You must excuse him. His honour occasionally gets the best of him."

"I understand," Rya's response was so quiet it was almost a whisper before sipping his own ale. Athrempitritus concluded the conflict by taking a substantial bite from his fluffy cob of bread.

The next morning Alicèns band gulped down their thick syrupy coffees and sticky sweetbreads before saddling up the mildens, and bade farewell to their host. As dusk approached and Alicèns band neared The Farrowdawns, the temperature dropped dramatically. A crisp freshness to the air was upon them, breathing in the moisture from the thickening density of the clouds. Several of the band members started to cough amid the additional moisture in their lungs which took a short while to get used to.

"Hold!" Alicèn commanded as the band stopped just short of the ascending rocks before them.

The Farrowdawns naturally had many entrances and exits weaving into the mountains before the main paths. He couldn't quite put his finger on it, but something seemed very strange to Alicèn.

"Alicèn?" Deonrick asked, approaching level with him. "What is it?"

"I'm not quite sure. It's just a feeling, that's all."

"A feeling like we shouldn't be here?"

"No. A feeling that we should."

Deonrick furrowed his eyebrows.

"How so?"

"It's just a feeling, my friend," Alicèn quickly smiled before staring straight into the misty abyss ahead. "Knights. Stand with honour."

"Stand with honour!" they all replied perfectly timed together.

Alicèn turned into the opening and walked his horse forward into nothingness.

The mountains became more and more mysterious the further in they went. Covered entirely in mist which rarely dissipated, it was easy to get lost in the stoney surroundings. If lost, survival was very slim. Not only nests of Rawblers festered there but also bandit camps and creatures so dangerous it was suicidal to enter unprepared. Venturing in was indeed a perilous task, but Alicèn was too noble and honourable not to have gone himself and seen with his own eyes. By keeping his band small, he hoped his expedition would go unseen.

However, there was one place that Alicèn feared above all on Terrasendia. And that place resided in the very heart of the terrain. The Draughts. A man-made underground chasm built by one of the most feared Màgjeurs ever to exist - Melcelore. Although his capture by King Felder was very well known, he still vowed unless absolutely necessary, never to venture in. Alicèn could never forget the amount of evil said to have existed there, which surpassed all level of horror. One day he promised himself to learn precisely why Melcelore created The Draughts in the first place, a question he was not ready to answer just yet. He knew himself it was perhaps the only place he truly feared.

Before too long, the road presented itself with several forks of different passages to go down. Alicèn knew the way and took the right-hand fork heading west. They had journeyed for several hours into what felt like miles of pure cloud. That particular route he assumed was a much quieter route to avoid being seen. What unnerved some of the knights was how quiet everything became. An eerie chill ghosted around them. Suddenly the mist started to thin out, and they noticed more and more of their rocky surroundings.

"Most peculiar," Deonrick furrowed as he noticed the orange haze above them, which was not visible before.

"It means we are here," Rya said. "The dragon-breath pushes the mist away."

"Just like thirty years ago," Alicèn said, relating to the tragedy of The Dragasphere.

"Exactly."

They came to a huge opening within the rocks to reveal a small town, the town of Icarzbolden... Everything in their sight was blanketed in charcoaled soot.

"It can't be!" Deonrick gasped, along with many other members of the band. "Dragonstorm?" he asked Rya.

His head nodded as his eyes closed, almost as if he was replaying the horror in that moment.

"Alicèn!?" he noticed his Durgeons eyes in some confusion before him.

Alicèn dismounted his milden and carefully approached some of the rubble and wreckage before him. Others also followed to examine some of the carnage.

"Any bodies?" Radja asked.

"Not that I can see," Seyfi said. "If there were there would probably be a horrible smell by now. And it wouldn't be Falcone for a change."

"Real funny, Seyfi!" Falcone's deep voice replied.

Brackbannens notoriously did not have much of a sense of humour which the knights from Rolgan knew all too well.

"So you believe me now?" Rya asked of Alicèn who continued his examination of some of the woods with great detail. "A Dragadelf! I swear to you."

The tension in Rya's body language started to increase. His pupils dilated a little more as the sense of edginess crept in. Alicèn was not listening all too much. He was more concerned with picking up a plaque of wood before him. His horror evident on his face as the realisation dawned on him. He quickly snapped his head towards the Barkler.

"What is it!?" Rya nervously asked.

"Graceland save us!" Alicèn whispered.

"Alicèn!?" Snira worryingly asked.

"The breath and incineration of a Dragadelf would not have left even a bark behind!"

The band immediately grabbed their weapons to stand fast. Athrempitritus looked straight at Rya as a wicked smile spread across the Barkler's face. He took his giant porky hands and grabbed the Rya by the neck, but it did not stop his sinister sneer. The gargled sound of air trapped in his windpipe sourced his hysterical laughter.

"Fools!" Rya spat, shaking as his face bulged from the strangulation. Athrempitritus gritted his teeth and tightened his grip so much, Rya's head threatened to burst open like a grape.

With no time to contemplate what was going on, the sound of a single whistling arrow appeared from the clouds behind them, landing right into the back of Xjazen's neck. He took one last look into the eyes of his Durgeon before sliding off the saddle of his horse and crumpled head first onto a stone slab before him. The rest of Alicèns band together took a circular defensive approach before more whistling of arrows appeared from the mist on the other side of where Icarzbolden once stood. One arrow aimed straight for Nutat who launched her own bow in a spinning motion directly ahead of her which caught the incoming arrow to perfection before returning to her hands. She tried to aim the same arrow to her attacker but could not make out a target. The same eerie silence chilled to the bone.

"Alicèn! What do we do?" Ryuchi asked.

Alicèn could not believe it. He could not believe how Rya managed to convince him to betray his better judgement. Maybe it was too late, but he realised that perhaps he was so preoccupied proving his own theory that it blinded him of logic. He looked over at Rya's face whose eyes had turned bloodshot, still radiating with satisfaction. Clearly, it was a trap set up by The Banamie to capture him and as many of Septalia's warriors as possible. But Alicèn was still terrified at the thought that they could have found the bone of a Dragadelf.

"The Delfenclaw! Where did you get it!?" he demanded.

"You have - no idea - what is happening!" he strained. "You will now!"

Sure enough, the band turned their attention to the clouds behind them. The glow of approaching fires made the shadows bounce higher and higher the closer they came. Before long the band saw the torches held by their attackers begin to come into view. By the sheer mass of oncoming flames from both sides of the valley, Alicèn estimated they were outnumbered at least forty to one. Were they to initiate the attack they would surely be defeated.

"HOLD! STANDFAST!" Alicèn instructed as the Barklers came into full view.

Their clad rags and tatty armours matched their rugged ugly faces, full of scars topped with matted hair. They enclosed in a circular formation around the band, they were trapped.

Rather than attack, however, the Barklers held off. As Alicèn and his band began to realise their daunting prospects, three men appeared on horseback and slithered through the parting crowd. Alicèn knew exactly who the leader of the band was.

"Well. Well. Well," said the slithery voice of the white-blonde leader. His slick-backed hair revealed his pale face and blue eyes. His armour was more impressive than his band members but far less than Alicèn's band.

"Slair!" Alicèn quietly said, his eyes narrowed as he watched his approach - Draul's second in command and on Terrasendia's most wanted list for being an influential voice in rallying forces to their cause. It was no wonder he was a vital crux in Draul's organisation. His slithery nature matched his annoying tone. The other two were Mulrek and Standl. Both equal in build and strength, looking much angrier than their smug band leader.

"And how came to pass that Alicèn, greatest commander Septalia has ever known, was fooled by a Rolgani?" Slair said with a wry smile. By this point, Rya's eyes threatened to burst from his skull, bulging unnaturally. "Release our friend. Now."

Alicèn nodded his head and instructed Athrempitritus to release his grip which he did so thrusting his force into his neck, sending him crumpling away from them in a heap. His desperate wheezing coughs and spluttering of mucus inflated Rya's lungs.

"Well done Rya, well done."

Slair's genuine gratification comforted Rya as he instructed men to help him to his feet. Even the men who lifted him up, slinging his arms around their shoulders patted him on the chest with massive triumph.

"Now, drop your weapons." The band did not heed, instead turning to their Durgeon.

"Alicèn?" Deonrick asked. A brief moment passed before Slair calmly reinforced.

"Drop your weapons and no one will get hurt."

"Listening to cowards isn't really our thing." Falcone said.

"Falcone…" Alicèn interjected before gently nodding his head to the band to lower their arms. They reluctantly did so as the sounds of thuds and chinks hit the ground.

"Excellent!" Slair smiled. "No need to explain what happens now."

"The Delfenclaw! Where did you get it, Slair?"

"Oh, I'm afraid you'll have to ask him yourself. But keep the questions to a minimum, our King is rather a busy man. Bind them."

The Barklers approached and bound the hands of Alicèns band, much to their reluctance. They knew they would be taken to Draul, most probably for interrogation and torture.

"Septalia's finest!" Slair laughed. "All in a hamper."

They found themselves with their hands bound behind their back with thick rope. Alicèn noticed the appreciation for Rya in the crowds and how it maddened him. Their little project, how easy it must have been perceived for them. A masterful stroke, presenting the bone of a Dragadelf, without which none of it would have happened. As the sounds drowned out amid his plethora of thoughts and feelings, he noticed something very unusual on the ground.

A slight wind brushed the soot and ash on the floor which had been clearly torched by The Banamie and not a Dragadelf. But it did not blanket sweep along the ground as a gust of wind would usually do. Instead, it weaved the dust, snaking its way from underneath his knees toward the crowd. His concern grew as he saw more ash about five metres to his right and five metres to his left all snaking soot to the same place. His fears became more alarming when he noticed just how dampened the sound became. A typical trait of one of the most feared prospects to haunt Terrasendia.

His heart started to race faster and harder, adrenaline burned through his veins. Deonrick noticed his Durgeons growing panic and physical growing energy.

"Alicèn! What is it!?" he worryingly asked.

Alicèns eyes widened as he knew that what was about to happen was far worse than their impending imprisonment. Instead of blurting out and alarming the Barklers, he nodded his head to his band members at the travelling debris, making its way to the same point and shared the same rising concern. They too knew what was coming.

Suddenly the sound ultimately dampened to a point where all they could hear was a faint high pitched scream which gradually grew louder and louder. The light from their surroundings dimmed and was absorbed by the same point the ash was drawn too. Slair, Mulrek and Standl all turned around to view what the growing orb of energy was. They had a three-soldier deep wall in between them and the growing mass of debris, which was collecting the whole atmosphere around them. The light, the sounds and even the air, building a figure in front of them. During the spectacle, the Barklers merely stood and watched as it grew. Alicèn knew for sure they had no idea what this was. If they did, they would be running for their lives.

By this point the high pitch scream grew so intense that it started to pierce the ear-drums of all in Icarzbolden. The air stretched thin as the mass developed enough to take the shape of a grey and black figure the size of three men. The wails of Barklers covering their ears and gasping for air were faintly heard. Alicèn preserved his own breath in preparation for what was about to happen.

"IT'S DREANOR!!!" he yelled.

The build-up of pressure and life into the shape exploded, sending the force outwards in every direction, obliterating much of the remains of Icarzbolden and sending everyone flying back off their feet. It took a short moment before consciousness was regained. Alicèn and his band huddled together before the explosion to minimise the impact, but as his sight resumed through his blurred vision, Alicèns horror was confirmed through the rising dust.

Dreanor, one of The Ancient Drethai. One of the thirteen royal men and women promised ultimate power by Melcelore. But unknowingly to them all they were betrayed by him and attempted to steal their souls for himself. Luckily for them, they were powerful enough to defy Melcelore of any right over their souls, but it came at a price. Their souls would live on, but their bodies would be sacrificed. In the process, they managed a spell which would allow one to preside the constitution of their bodies to live one at a time, while all souls live on in Drethai Halls. When one body dies, another takes its place on Terrasendia, spawning wherever they choose.

Despite their situation of being captured and interrogated by Draul, Dreanor was far worse. The Ancient Drethai have haunted Terrasendia for many years, killing all with no motive, no inspiration and no mercy, just vengeful hate for the world they were no longer accepted in.

Alicèns blurred vision became clearer as he noticed the growing gloom in the cloud. Dreanor slowly got to his feet to reveal the ten-foot tall Shadow Knight. He slowly turned with closed eyes, to come into view of everyone in sight, who also slowly got to their feet, petrified at the sight of the inherent evil before them. The black and dark silver armour perfectly fit for a King. His black cape wisped off his shoulders with a black gas around his plated calves. His sword thick and wide, cruelly indented in several places on the blade which resembled a black flame, held by black plated gloves. His pale face had a glowing darkness underneath as his cold eyes flickered open. He bore a crown made of thirteen small blades, each resembling a member of the Drethai which spiked up around his head. He was indeed, King of The Ancient Drethai.

Some of the Barklers fled as soon as Dreanor's eyes opened. The wall of soldiers in front of their three commanders nervously pointed their spears in the direction of The Drethai. In two minds whether to attack or defend, Mulrek issued the order.

"ATTACK!!!" he bellowed.

Only two Barklers were brave and inherently stupid enough to follow them. They charged and thrust their weapons into the direction of Dreanor's torso together. And just like a ghost he calmly waded in between the two spears, turning his back on everyone, sheathing his sword behind his back in the process and raised both his giant hands above the sorry Barklers heads as they were sucked upwards like magnets sticking onto Dreanor's palms. The gravity and force squeezed their heads into his hands as their bodies left the ground. Their weapons instantly dropped, the white of their eyes exposed as they rolled into the back of their heads, while their faces pruned and dishevelled as the life was sucked out of them. As Dreanor slowly turned around, carrying his outstretched prey in both hands, the horror on The Banamie's faces was utterly terrible. Dreanor's face calmly and satisfyingly stared down the remaining Barklers.

"RETREAT!!! RETREAT!!!" Standl barked, issuing a fracas and melee of evacuation, upon which Dreanor drew his mighty sword once more, stepped in and swiped with such velocity and venom each strike took out more than five retreating men at once, slicing and carving them to shreds.

Honour and duty compelled Alicèn to fight. And with that so did his band members. With their captors fleeing for their lives they were free to find their weapons which were left in a heap and began to untie themselves ready to fend off the terror. Dreanor made his way through roughly fifty Barklers before turning his attention to Alicèn and his band. He was still bound before he felt the cool steel of his eyes fix on him.

As The Drethai approached with an overhead swipe, Athrempitritus heroically stepped in trying to parry the attack with an upward guard. However, the horror in Alicèns eyes rang true when the defending blade was sliced in two, much to everyone's surprise. Before the reality sank in, blood-spattered onto Alicèns face as he saw the tip of Dreanor's black sword appear out of Athrempitritus' back in an additional thrust.

"ARTHUR!!!" Falcone shrieked.

Snira and Nutat recovered their bows and fired straight at the Shadow Knight, but before any such blow landed, black fire flared from one of Dreanor's hands, disintegrating the arrows and quickly torching the only two females in the band to their burning deaths.

Falcone impulsively jumped and duelled with Dreanor for several blows. Even his mighty size and brute strength was no match for his counterpart who was far quicker, and more efficient and elegant in his moves. So predictable were Falcone's movements that he did indeed slip a particular swinging motion, only to realise the same fate as his Brackbannen brother.

Deonrick released Alicèns binds before arming him with his sword and shield. No amount of training could prepare for a warrior as great as a Drethai. Their best and only hope was to work together.

"PORCUPINE!" Alicèn instructed.

The remaining band members including himself, Deonrick, Ryuchi, Seyfi and Radja circled their foe. Alicèn knew one whirl of black fire would instantly kill, which made him valiantly step first into Dreanor's attention, resulting in the fires being unleashed onto him.

His shield was coated in a warding magic to protect him from such magical attacks. But it would not last, the flames were too hot to withstand. Luckily it proved a useful distraction as Seyfi's spear landed in Dreanor's shoulder, disbanding the fires. The deathly screech of The Drethai's pain was true. Radja followed up with an impressive swoop of strikes that were parried in equal impressiveness. Ryuchi's three-sixty spins and circular movements also proved difficult for Dreanor's size. They were fighting back with all their skill and experience, landing several blows as a team to weaken the shadow warrior. However, Dreanor soon realised a weakness in the band.

He aimed straight for Alicèn himself, knowing that if he were attacked, the defence would prove a little more desperate given his importance. Dreanor managed to gather a few seconds of space and just like that he pointing his palm to Alicèns shield which shattered into thousands of splinters immediately. Dreanor sent every sharp fragment into the spinning, jumping and oncoming Ryuchi like a large cloud of daggers which was impossible to evade, killing him instantly.

Alicèn took the opportunity to strike himself and landed the edge of his blade onto the gauntlet of Dreanor's hands. He dropped his black sword with a familiar screech but quickly found his own face in the palm of Dreanor's other hand as the life was sucked out through his eyeballs. He resisted with all his might and strength but felt his end was nearing. The air, his pulse, his life was being bled out of him, and death was taking its place. An empty loneliness filled him.

The process became inconsistent as he could see Dreanor fend off the remaining members of his band. Despite being unarmed, they were still being warded off by The Drethai's backhands, sending them back one by one. Seyfi was first to fly back into the rocks surrounding him while Radja was sent spinning violently away. The process of death resumed on Alicèn's face, he struggled and heroically yelled with every fibre he had left.

Suddenly Dreanor's grip was broken entirely followed by a horrific cry from Deonrick, whose dagger entered The Drethai's back, sending him to his knees in excruciating pain. The blow was sufficient and substantial. The King of The Ancient Drethai was still on his knees before Alicèn, as he mustered every bit of strength he had left to bring himself to stand, sword in hand. He had never been so exhausted in all his life. Every muscle ached and spasmed, which he struggled to control. Dreanor's frozen eyes stared straight up into The Durgeon of Durge Helm in defiant resignation, as Alicèn turned his sword upside down and with all his remaining strength, plunged the tip and following body of the sword straight into the top of Dreanor's skull. A fourteenth sword to add to his crown!

The painful and deathly screech echoed as Dreanor's body started to implode once more, sucking the air right into his heart. When there was nothing left to absorb, he once more exploded in the same fashion and enormity as his spawning. Alicèn fell back, blowing his body along with the carnage of Icarzbolden as everything else turned into a desert of mountainous rubble.

Fatigue and exhaustion took over Alicèns' body. He was broken. He had nothing left. No strength, no air, no life. He was well and truly resigned to whatever happened next. He could hardly think as the weight of exhaustion took over. He couldn't even spare a thought for his dead. He consciously knew that his eyes were open, but he could not process what they saw… Until the moment his consciousness told him something was happening. The approaching of footsteps.

He gently turned his head to process the information, but his blurred vision could not see exactly who was coming for him – but he knew. Through the enormity of his fatigue and draining of life, he could not care that The Banamie had come back to take him away.

The Extra Journey

The mildens were fed, watered and saddled with provisions enough for the band of Pippersby and The Durge curtaining their sides on route. The swords and armour of The Durge were not a calming sight to see for the people of Pippersby but they understood precautionary measures had to be taken.

The town gathered amongst the cobblestones of the street to send their gentle farewells to the men, waving them off as heroes encouraging their swift and safe return. The weather was overcast with soft streaks of sunlight piercing through, mirroring a slightly odd atmosphere amongst the town.

Garrison, determined and organised as ever to get things moving, spearheaded the band. Joined at the head by Joric, they all filtered out of Smithwins. The town folk shook the hands of the band as they left with gentle thanks to services to the town. Children followed the band as the sight of adventure seemed to light up their eyes before being whisked back by their parents. Other children played with sticks on the side of the road as seeing The Durge in full militia gear inspired their playful nature.

As the band made their way out to the edge of the town, they passed Alex's house. Amba was standing in front of the cottage with a bouncing Jàque in her arms, and aunt Gràcene by their side. Alex veered off to hug his boy, ruffling his hair, which brought a smile to Jàque's face before lightly kissing Amba.

"Be safe," she said.

"I will. Look after them," he said to Gràcene as he hugged her too.

"No need to tell me what to do. Just look after yourself, and the rest will follow. We'll be fine," Gràcene replied.

"I promise to bring you back something nice, okay son?" Alex said as he started to walk away.

"Don't come back without my protecy stone father!"

"I'll bring you back a clip round the ear if you're not careful!" His son groaned dramatically as he concealed a smirk. "Be a good boy."

"Bye, father! See you soon!" They all waved goodbye.

The band turned into a corner of the street. Before disappearing behind the bend, Alex looked at Amba a final time. A streak of sunlight brightened the moment, no need for words, but that instant acknowledgement of what Alex needed to find bore into their minds before a cloud covered the warmth of the sun and just like that, they disappeared from sight.

The band journeyed across the province of Landonhome, a rural plain vastly powdered with trees and greenery with hills covering the landscapes. The band would sing old songs on route, some funny, others with a more sorrow tone. Alex, Bran and Brody banded together the whole journey through, keeping their distance from Jacklatoro and his minions. He would often give Alex a cruel stare. *Just you wait, Alex. Just you wait.* As usual, Alex calmly shrugged him off.

They were lucky the weather was clear for the first few days, but the closer they got to The Gurken, the closer and more humid the atmosphere became. They would travel for several hours before stopping off to give the horses a short break. Night time came on the second day of their travels, and the band cooked their meats of bacon, stuffed sausages, thick soups and potatoes on the budget pots and pans.

"Only one more day lad," said Brody. "Then it's nothing but chipping away at rocks, stone and the depth of Mother Nature for our lives."

"I doubt it's changed much since last year," Bran said. "Going to try and not fall down a cavity this time around."

"Thank The Blessèd they blessed you with that belly of yours. Without it, you would have fallen right down to the bottom, you fat lump!" The comment was met by a familiar right fist to the arm by Bran on Brody's arm. "It took us an hour to dislodge you!" Brody laughed. Bran whacked the bottom of Brody's plate which sent the remains of his supper into his face, bringing more laughter.

"You're such an arse, Brode," Bran said. "Go and kiss that horse."

"Not quite my type. I like them clean, well kept. You know what I'm talking ab- actually on second thoughts you probably don't."

"At least I go for actual women Brody. The shock on your face when what's-her-face told us all she had a big secret! I never laughed so much in my life!"

He howled with laughter at the image. The memory of Brody's catastrophic mistake in identity for one of the *women* he tried to court, only then to realise she was a little more masculine than he thought… It even brought a smile to Alex's face.

"I thought we agreed never to mention that again." The laughter started to wade in from the other men too. "I'm a man of the realm what can I say. Needs must and all that," winking at Alex.

"Go kiss that horse before you explode, Brode." Joric interrupted. Brody made his way over to the milden, confidently jibing on route. They all knew he would do it, just for a laugh.

"Come here, ya beauty!"

He puckered up to the horse, but the horse evaded several advances before shying sideways with a snort and trotting off to safety.

"Setting the standards high Brody," laughed Garrison along with the rest of the other men.

A bolt of lightning flashed the scene, followed by thunder several seconds later, which stopped any laughter immediately.

"Rest up, lads," Garrison said. "When we arrive tomorrow we are full on and flat out mining. Get your rest. Brody, try your luck with the horse later when he's asleep!" Brody crudely muttered something inaudible in retaliation.

The band packed away their provisions and readied themselves for lights out. Alex, throughout the night, wanted to ask Joric the big question. But no real opportunity arose.

He ventured back to his tent, blew out the fire before letting his thoughts drifting around his head, replaying once more the conversation he had with Amba on their last night…

"It must be the stone! It's the only thing that makes sense. 'Time in the Water.'"

*"After everything, I just hope that it is. She would have served the High King,
and he must have told her about it. But why didn't she say what it was?"*
*"She might not be aware that it's a stone that she is telling us about. She says
I'll know it when I see it. The Time Stone is real; it has to be. I know it."*
"If you don't come back with that stone, I'm going there to find it myself."
"I'm coming home with it. I promise you."

The morning after, the band readied themselves for the final stretch before The Gurken. The rumour of Rawblers roaming the land made everyone tense, keeping all eyes and ears as sharp as they can.

Rawblers naturally hunted in packs. Not the most intelligent of creatures, often predictable and not very discreet. However, when provoked they were a dangerous opponent even for skilled warriors. Their sheer numbers were a daunting sight when confronted.

The afternoon passed with a mixture of tropical rain and humid heat, making the journey less pleasant. They arrived at a clearing where the clouds overtook the usually familiar sight of the cold, grey and stoney mountains of The Gurken. But the clouds were so thick; some barely recognised they had reached the mountain unscathed. Alex felt a small weight lift off of his shoulders as he thought that he now had a chance to find the stone and save his boy.

The closer they got to the mountain, the more they could see how tall it stood. Before them sat a small lake between themselves and what appeared to be the opening. A dark slither carved into the stone which they knew was the entrance. A small wooden man-made bridge arched over the lake which the band made steadily across, going one horse at a time. Joric went first along with Garrison and several other Durge members. Almost disappearing out of sight, they cautiously scanned the area. The brothers convened together which brought an anxiety to the smithies and other Durge members on the other side before Joric waved to the rest of the band for them to cross. They sheepishly trudged across, continually looking to the lake as they know Rawblers could swim also.

"I can't believe this is happening," Bran said.

"The sooner we across and get set, the sooner we can go home," Alex said. "We'll be fine."

"How are you so confident?"

"I'm sure they know what they're doing mate. Keep your head on our jobs and let them do theirs."

"But what if they're wrong? Or miss something?"

"Then we're screwed," admitted Alex with a sly smile.

"Okay well if Rawblers do come I'm shoving Garrison in front first, then his brother, then that pillock Jacklatoro!" Bran panted.

"I'd shove you if your butt cheeks were smaller," Brody joked.

"Bastard."

They all made their way over the bridge to the wall of the stoney mountain.

"We set up base here," Joric stated, which followed with the setting up of tents, fires and food for the horses and men.

Alex was keen to get his gear on and start straight away. He was sworn to secrecy by Mirabella and couldn't let on the real reason for his motivation. He confronted Garrison to speed up the process.

"Shouldn't we get going now?" Alex asked.

"We need to figure out just how long we are going down there for," Garrison said. "I want to bring extra torches and oil. I have a good feeling about this year, but we need to be brave and venture further in."

Alex was sure the stone he needed to find wasn't placed anywhere near the entrance, and he had more chance the more he prepared to delve deeper. However, the weight of anxiousness clouded his head once more when he reminded himself that actually, the chances of finding this stone were slim at best.

"'Time in the Water.' How strange this all was."

The band were finally ready. Half of The Durge guarded camp outside; the other ventured in with the smithies. Pickaxes, food, water, torches and oil were the main components of the men venturing in. The rocky entrance slithered into the mountain, darkness loomed in front of them, against the overcast weather topping the mountain. Torches at the ready, belts and buckles fixed, backpacks on. Spearheading the band were the brothers, closely followed by Alex, keen to get on with it as they nervously entered the skin of the mountain.

The torches lit up the aesthetic of the inside, nothing so far that wowed the men. Just stone and rock surrounded them. Not very generous in terms of the room they had to manoeuvre, often travelling two-by-two.

"Now if I remember correctly, which I always do, we'll come to a slope, leading down into four paths." Garrison explained. "Last year we split into two. This year we're splitting into three as planned at Smithwins. Myself, Bran and Taryn will be accompanied by Dariel and

Broma, we'll take the first tunnel. Brody, Nerrick and Ramir, you'll be accompanied by Thaniel and Hiero, you'll take the second and Alex, Iestyn and Reyga you'll be accompanied by Joric and Jacklatoro who will take the third."

The smithies knew the other smithies who would accompany them, but they were unaware of the members of The Durge that accompanied them. Alex felt more anxious the further they went in, Joric was fine but knowing Jacklatoro who would love to bludgeon his head at any moment, was also coming made things more difficult. Also knowing that if he did find this stone, no way would Joric allow him to walk out without Garrison having it. Alex caught up with Garrison, grazing his arms on the narrow path, desperate for him to reconsider.

"Garrison, you know what happened back at the yard, Jack wants my head! Why on Rèo would you pair him up in the same band as me?"

"You are going down the new route, I have no idea what is down there, and neither do any of us. I need my best fighters on the job."

"Then get Brody with me. He's a better fighter and no offence, but a more efficient smith than Reyga. He'll slow us down."

"Reyga needs to learn from you Alex; he's also a competent fighter should it come to that. You're in charge."

"I seriously doubt that with Joric at the head," he thought.

"What's the matter, hero? Homesick?" Jacklatoro butted in.

"I'm surprised you can remember my name after what happened in the yard?"

Instinctively feeling like he shouldn't have said that. The more confrontation, the harder it would be, but couldn't stop his emotions bleeding through.

"That doesn't help, Alex," Garrison cautioned. "Both of you keep your heads or I'll get my brother to bash them together."

The path got wider the deeper they got in, the only light coming from the torches. The coolness of the mountain did in fact chill their cheeks, but they were well insulated and padded. Should they have to heist, they brought extra padding for their knees and elbows, which aided their warmth. The further they delved in, the more reflective in colour and beauty the walls became. Some even sparkled a gentle flicker as the fires from the torches hit them. Some men picked off the smaller, more beautiful looking stones, but more prominent and glamorous gems laid ahead. The claustrophobic nature waned out some of the men travelling in but was soon relieved when Garrison announced they had arrived at the tunnels.

"Here we part gentlemen. Our jobs rely on this expedition. Go further where you can, and we'll reconvene back here in one day. Good luck."

The band split into three and went their separate ways down the tunnels which seemed much broader now. Alex gave Brody and Bran a nod before parting ways. Iestyn and Reyga awaited Alex at the entrance of the tunnel. Iestyn was a gentle man, a typical nobleman and similar to Alex in many ways but slightly older. Reyga was only eighteen. A nippy kid who had a fascination for smithing. He was more excited to be on this expedition than anyone; he took it as an adventure rather than work. Joric led the way with Alex.

"Seems pointless all of this, don't you think?" Alex stated.

"Why's that?" Joric replied.

"Well, if in the event of an attack, how are we ever going to defend ourselves if we get outnumbered?"

"We won't. Which means you boys will have to do your jobs quicker."

Alex's band journeyed through the veins of the mountain. That particular path was completely different to the one Alex went to before. He was with Garrison, Brody and Bran last year going down the first path where they had found a record amount of amethysts which made profits soar. However, this new path was relatively dull. Not even in the walls were the twinkles of gems which the other bands would have been bored of by that point. Alex grew increasingly frustrated with the lack of excitement the path entailed.

"Trust you to lead us down this wonderful experience," Jack smirked. His face was painting a picture that Alex would happily ram his fist down.

The light from the torches was relatively sufficient, but the sound grew increasingly sponged, which heightened the more eerie tone. Reyga's face turned from a fruitful nature to a glum and hopeful picture.

Suddenly the light dimmed, not because of the fires burning out but because they had exited the tunnels into a large chasm. Still no sign of a gem but instead the light came from what was now a moonlit sky, a crack in the mountain's roof where its lunar shone through to reveal a vast lake, surrounded by other tunnels and walls. The sight of the lake had even Joric nervous. Rawblers could swim, and his heart started to beat a little faster when he realised that they might well have been led straight into the beast's nest. Alex noticed Jacklatoro's confidence dislodged somewhat before staring back at him with eyes that could pierce skin.

"If you get me killed Alex, my ghost will come back to haunt yours for the rest of your days!" Jack harshly whispered.

Alex, on the other hand was not listening, and felt disorientated standing before the weird discovery of water inside a mountain. He experience an odd sensation of his mind slowing down. His eyes were scanning the lake vigorously. The palms of his hands and brow were sweating profusely at the prospect he had potentially found hid goal.

"'Time in the Water.' Could this be it? It seems too easy to have found it if so. I'll know it when I see it Mirabella said."

Alex's optimism clouded his judgement. The banks seemed new and more like a flood than a lake. The general formation around the lake suggested that the height of the water regularly changed.

"So if I'm to be guessing correctly, The Time Stone should be somewhere in this lake. Am I really to scan the bed of this lake, with my hands scanning for a stone? And what if there actually are rawblers in-"

"Alex!" Joric purposefully whispered. "I think we should turn back and go the other way. I don't like this."

Alex desperately wanted to explore the lake and had a feeling it was there. He almost felt some connection to it running magically under his skin. However, should he find it now there would be no chance of him taking it for himself.

"Joric I think there's a reason why we haven't found anything yet," Alex cautiously said as he ran his fingers against a wall improvising an excuse.

"Why's that?"

"They've already been found. Take a look at these markings on the wall. These are man-made, too sharp and polished to be natural forms of rock."

The band examined, relatively perplexed. Iestyn was perhaps the only one who could potentially disagree with the formation of rocks over time but trusted Alex's judgment.

"Whoever was here sure didn't leave anything behind. I think this whole route has been wiped out. Let's go back and check out the forth tunnel tomorrow."

The band quickly formed out, as quietly as they could just in case. Alex planned to come back when everyone rested and search for the stone. Which he felt was in that lake somewhere.

They got back to the meeting point empty handed where the other two bands were there, sacks full of gems and several protecy stones. Alex's band stopped before them as they in turn, paused as well.

"Couldn't find anything?" Bran asked, bringing laughter to the men.

"A complete waste of time," Alex acted. "Tomorrow we're going down the fourth tunnel."

"What was down there?" Garrison asked.

"The sky. That's it. It looks like we were too late, the walls were chipped and skinned already. And no one fancied me to go for a skinny dip."

Joric pulled Garrison to one side and lowered his tone.

"I fear we need to speed up our expedition. We have one more scout, and then we leave tomorrow, my orders," Joric commanded.

"What did you see?"

"Nothing for sure, but I fear the longer we stay, the more risk we take," Joric whispered.

The band made their way out of The Gurken to camp outside. The feeling of anxiety crept in as Alex prepared his mission of sneaking off in the middle of the night to find out what it was he felt near that lake.

Night fell and the band sumply tucked into their suppers of pan-fried sausages, bacon and stews cooked on cauldron fires. Garrison put Jacklatoro on night watch. Luckily the camp was based around the corner from the entrance, and the wet fog had not cleared, luck was so far on his side.

The lights doused out in the camp, the tents tied shut. Everyone had been quiet and asleep for at least a good hour before Alex, who was sharing a tent with Brody and Bran, made his move. Slowly he made his way out of the enclosed tent, grabbing his sword while stepping over Bran. He lost his footing and dropped the sword right onto brans foot, which made him freeze. Bran's reaction was a small murmur and shuffle before snoring back off again. Alex made sure Brody's face was very much still and asleep before safely resuming to slither out of the tent and into the cold outside.

He peered around the corner to see Jacklatoro smoking his pipe. Alex has no chance of just walking straight through to the entrance unseen; he needed to be smart and discreet. He waited to see if an opportunity would reveal itself, which it didn't. The misty river lead right round the bend, under the bridge and out of sight to where the entrance was. The possibilities became a little ambitious in Alex's mind.

"Am I mad? I'll freeze to death in there!" he argued with himself. *"I really have lost my mind."*

He made his way to the bank of the river, keeping in line of sight of the tent where he couldn't be seen. He dabbed his hand in the river, and the feeling of glacial temperatures rose, icy spikes pulsed up his arm as the water was biting cold. He drew a breath before sliding into the cold water feet first, followed by the rest of his body and head. The water wrapped a spikey iced hug round Alex's body which made him resurface immediately. The cold was unbearable as stabs of frost pierced his skin. He struggled to swim through the river, which felt like he was working three times as harder not only because it was unbearably cold but also to keep movements to a minimum to not draw attention. Through the struggle he kept as close to the bank as possible not to be seen.

So far so good, he made his way through sandy, wet ground trying hard to keep ripples to a minimum. The mist helped his disguise as he reached underneath the bridge for a bit of respite where he couldn't be seen. As he tried to elevate himself above the water grabbing the bank, his hand slipped on the wet grass, creating a rather loud splash and whirling of water which radioed out into the river.

"Idiot!" he peered around the bridge and saw Jacklatoro creeping forward to see what caused the splash. Feeling like he had no other choice, he took a huge breath and sank into the water, grabbing the vines on the riverbed to hold himself down. The moonlight bled through the clouds as he looked past the surface of the water to see the silhouette of Jacklatoro peering in.

"Keep calm, keep your breath."

Annoyingly Jacklatoro was a bit more thorough in his investigation than Alex hoped. The only thing he could feel other than his skin freezing over was his heart beating rapidly against the water, thumping harder and harder the longer he stayed down. He couldn't hold it much longer but had no choice.

Luckily Jacklatoro's attention was drawn away back to the camp where he made his way back to resume his post. Alex rapidly resurfaced to balloon his lungs back up with life, his heart resuming again to fast rather than racing. When the white spots of his vision had cleared, he peered over the bank to see that Brody had joined Jacklatoro.

He resumed his way round the bend, and with a burst of relief he made it out of sight of Brody and Jacklatoro. He slithered out of the water quickly and made his way to the entrance of the mountain once more. He knew he was leaving a wet trail behind him, which quickened his steps to vanish before anyone notices. The familiar winding path of rock and sparkling walls were reflected from his fiery torch. Alex felt the weight of his task getting heavier on his shoulders the further he delved into the mountain. He thought he had until the morning at least before anyone noticed his absence but knew getting back would prove equally challenging so had to move quickly.

The memory of the conversations he had with Mirabella and Amba kept ringing and replaying in his head. He was travelling much faster than he realised as before he knew it he arrived back at the lake. Even more luck was on his side when the moon stared straight into the cavity, illuminating the pool and its surroundings, which made visibility much clearer.

He approaches the lake with caution, the air much cooler than it was before, and the prospect of Rawblers lurking put him on edge. He crept slowly towards the lake, and a drop of rain hit his nose. He looked up to see that clouds had started to form from up above and reduce the white of the moon to a struggling grey light which was followed by heavy torrential rain into the cavity. The ripples of the water started to circle out, smashing into each other, causing the lake to look as it was moving.

Alex was hit with that same feeling as earlier when he approached the edge of the water. So strange was this feeling he dropped to his knees feeling as if something was leaving him. He stared into the rippling water which reflected his face, before shortly seeing the face of his son staring back at him in the water. The feeling reminded him of what could potentially happen, a similar feeling of loss which caused a tear to well in Alex's eye. His tear dropped in the water and suddenly the rain stopped where his reflected face showed. The rain continued around his untouched reflection, until the rain started to stop all along a small trail in the water, leading into the heart of the lake. He studied the path that wound into the raining lake, noticing that the raindrops in the path didn't stop to fall into the path; instead the rain reversed and headed back up to the sky, creating a clearer path in the lake which Alex was inclined to follow.

The bed of the lake became more visible the more the rain reversed itself back up into the clouds, creating a parting way to the heart of the lake. The excitement of that moment made him sure this was it. Staring down the path which was now clear, Alex noticed the very slow movement of several small balls of light ahead of him.

He did not hesitate when he felt the desire to head towards them, not even looking at the walls of water beside him. His eyes started to light up at the small balls of light encased by a see-through stone on a low plinth of rock. He felt the energy almost evaporate around him before the feeling intensified, almost as if time was slowing down.

"The Time Stone..." Alex whispered.

He was stunned - completely amazed that he had fulfilled his desperate task. Hope filled him. He couldn't believe such a rare phenomenon lay so easily at the edge of his fingertips. He slowly extended his hand to pick up the stone and with an almighty breath, he felt the essence of time completely leave him. Before he knew it, the stone was in his hands.

His head completely in a world of his own, a dream world. His son's survival was in his destiny – in his hands. The happiness he felt in that moment filled him up and his eyes once more filled with teary joy. The sensations and tingle in his fingers travelled down his hands and arms and all over his body. He didn't know why any of it was happening and how easy it had been, nor if any of it was fate, but he wasn't complaining. He needed to get back to camp as discreetly as possible.

Before he could regather himself, he felt a much more intense feeling in the back of his head which didn't feel quite right. It became very hot very quickly followed by delayed pain and wet drips which he knew was blood from the back of his head. He tried to turn to inspect what had struck him but before he could turn, time seemed to stop entirely as the black curtain of unconsciousness took over.

Alex could hear the hum of someone speaking, gradually getting louder. As the numbness of his body began to leave him, he began to control the response of his vision and opened his eyes to a blurry sight of the band beside him. He laid on the trailer which was being pulled by one of the horses before reality hit him, they were on their way back home. Quickly realising the situation, he scanned his body urgently for some sign of the stone which wasn't there.

"Alex!" asked Joric noticing his consciousness. "Are you alright?"

"What happened?" Alex dazed.

"Found you going for a bit of a swim this morning. What on Rèo were you doing!?" Joric's harsher tone would usually intimidate Alex, but his focus was purely on other matters, the opportunity he had, literally in his hands seemed to have been swiped away. "Talk! You risked the safety of our entire band looking for you! Why did you go back to the lake?"

"I was attacked," he said, still coming around.

"Yes, while you were at the lake, I need to know why you were there in the first place!" Despite Joric's pressing, Alex had no intention of letting on the real reason, instead just rubbing the back of his head where he was struck wincing as he did. "Perhaps a few months in the bard will clear your head."

The horror of the stone no longer in his possession frightened Alex as now any hope that was in his hands, had slipped away forever unless he found whoever it was that attacked him.

"Joric, please!" Alex pleaded. "We need to turn back. If not all of us just let me go back."

"No chance. You're still under my watch, and I will not have anyone placed in danger."

"Joric-"

"ENOUGH ALEX! Not another word!" Alex struggled to escape the cart and get to his feet. "Bind him!" Joric ordered. Brody, Dariel and Broma seized Alex to the cart and bound his hands behind his back.

"Don't be a fool mate!" Brody impelled. "Just make it back home and explain. It'll all be alright. Just keep your head on!" Alex felt utterly lost. The feeling of betrayal loomed within.

"Why was I able to part the ways in the lake? Who struck me? Who has the stone now, and why? Someone must have been following me the whole time!"

The many questions replayed in his head, but perhaps the most daunting one being that if he does not find the answers to these questions, *"how long does my son have?"*

He scanned the band, believing it must have been one of them. Who could have known his plans? The plethora of questions and potential culprits in his head became more and more numbing, almost like an anaesthetic slowly spreading in his brain, the more questions he had. He looked at some of the members of The Durge and didn't connect any dots until he looked over towards Jacklatoro who quickly looked away, keeping very quiet. And without hesitating in his assumption, Alex's heart sank, the pieces of the puzzle placing perfectly, he knew who took the stone.

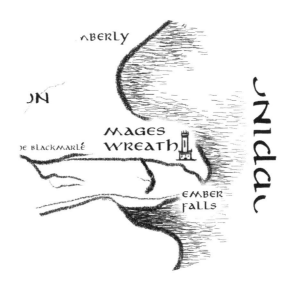

A Touch of Sentimental

Ramalon celebrated his sense of accomplishment by paying a visit to The Opey Deary. He was greeted by many of the professors and Màgjeurs whom he knew when he was a member of the faculty. When he announced his participation in the games, they all wished him well despite how much they would miss him. He never felt a sense of family but The Opey Deary was the closest thing to it. As he never had a family, he never missed it.

"Haldane!" Ramalon smiled as he approached him in one of the corridors.

"My dear friend! How are you!?" his zany voice replied. Slightly older than Ramalon, eccentric and utterly bonkers. His matted black hair mopped his head while his excessive consumption of black coffee as thick as syrup made him continuously fidget. Not to mention his regular scratches of the head and occasional ticks. His musty smell of what seemed like wet wood was also not to be missed. A competent earth Màgjeur. With the exception of the smell, he was Ramalon's ideal friend.

"Exceptional. You?"

"Better now for seeing yourself. How did you do it?" he smiled with

97

his slightly yellowed teeth.

"Do what?"

"Beat Pierro! It was an amazing trick you cast. No one saw it coming! Except for me of course, nice to see you learn something I showed you, eh!?" He chuckled to himself. It wasn't true, and they both knew it but any chance to enhance their camaraderie he would take it.

"How are the students?"

"Very ordinary," he quietly said, leaning in. "But they are young. I do, however, enjoy the oldest year that you would have taken had you not left. I have them this afternoon. Why don't you come and be my honoured guest? They will have many questions, I am sure."

"Of course. Would love to."

Ramalon felt obliged to take up the offer. His passion for the school and caring of students there shining through.

"Excellent! Come, come!"

That afternoon Haldane ushered him along the corridor, filling him in on the new academic year of students coming through. Legally a student had to be eighteen to enchant The Protecy. The numbers in each class would differ. One year could have ten students, another forty. Ramalon taught The Protecy to the only year in the school allowed to partake in the enchantment. They would all have been over the age of eighteen where he would guide their choices, making it clear to them that once they had made up their mind about what affinity they chose, there was no going back. Of course, they would have learned about this all the years leading up to their eighteenth. The familiar feeling of brown woods and bark that decorated the walls reminded Ramalon of his years of enjoyment there. His sense of pride and achievements at bringing young Màgjeurs through and into the world.

The class knew Ramalon from the earlier years as he entered with Haldane. A class of forty students, young Màgjeurs dressed in floppy robes dangling by the ankles and wrists, occasionally slipping to the elbow when they raised their arms to question. They all sat on curved benches, with several levels in the barrelled auditorium. Ramalon indeed knew the students by name in turn and knew of the ones who showed more significant potential. Celebrity status was slapped onto his head as they all were desperate to ask questions relating to his experience in the tournament. How he did what he did, what he planned to do next, who he was facing, how he was feeling etc. He loved not only answering the questions but also extending the information, still defaulting back to his old teaching ways and passion for passing on knowledge and wisdom. Haldane let the questioning happen as it was very productive for the students to know that anyone could be where he is now.

There was however a trio of students in the corner of the auditorium who Ramalon knew and noticed didn't seem interested in asking any questions, instead fidgeting and looking relatively anxious. Haldane also recognised the suspicion.

"Corey? Lenk? Cleverson? Have you nothing to add?"

The attention of the auditorium brought even more nervousness to the trio, as they hesitated under the question.

"We have someone here who walked these halls as you have done. And look where he is now! You could follow in this great Màgjeurs footsteps! And you have nothing to ask?"

Ramalon sensed that the trio did have questions inside their head but seemed afraid to ask.

"Come on you must have some sort of - "

" - It's okay, professor," Ramalon interrupted with a smile. "As you remember when I was their age, I was as silent as anything. I feel it's important to embrace who we are. All of us are different. We bring different qualities. Different ideas. Different ways of life. Never change that. Embrace it. It's what makes us all different. Makes our magical world stay magical. You may find that when you enchant The Protecy for the first time, the process can often bring upon memories or dreams you may have that help you find your identity. For instance, when I enchanted my stone, I had visions of The Dragadelf swarming Felders Crest, which gave me a fascination for them and confirming my choice in fire. You three are still young. You will find your feet in time. As did I. But make no mistake. My journey is not over and I am still striving. One victory does not make me powerful."

"What does make you powerful, professor?" a freckled fresh face from the middle row asked.

Ramalon took a long, absorbing pause to contemplate his answer. His body was still as he thought on his response.

"Power is subjective." Most of the room seemed a little confused at the answer. "But I have come to the conclusion that true power is when you answer to no-one. Power only exists because there is someone below you that answers to you. Would you agree?"

"I... I guess so?"

"And my advice to you all. Follow yourselves. Follow your interests. And follow your journey! And when that happens, power will come," he said the last part to the trio who seemed more interested now that he mentioned power.

Haldane led the applause which the students very quickly followed. Including the trio which Ramalon had his eye on as their praise was very much genuine. As the class filed out, Ramalon stopped the three students. The rest of the class exited while Haldane remained.

"Excellent. Really excellent, my friend." He approached as he shook his hand. "So useful for them. So inspiring. Blessèd, I am inspired myself! You three wish to ask him a question now?" They sheepishly looked at one another again.

"We do," Corey said.

His bleach-blonde and slicked back hair presented a pale face of a perfect complexion. His bright blue eyes also gave his look a grace and air of charm. Well aware of his good looks it was perceived as borderline arrogance.

"Well. Go ahead."

"Do you mind Professor Haldane if we asked him alone? It's a little personal to us all."

Haldane was taken aback a little that they could not ask him.

"I assure you I will keep anything in the strictest of confidence -"

" - It's okay, professor," Ramalon cut off once again. "I'll meet you in the staff room."

He could sense Haldane was now almost a little offended through the hesitation.

"Not to worry. I will see you shortly. *You know to be careful of these three!*" Haldane silently mouthed.

Ramalon knew exactly what he said as he spent years developing lip reading through their friendship. If ever they needed to help one another, they felt another way of communicating could prove useful. And with that, he swiftly left the students and Ramalon to convene.

"I was more nervous than you when I was your age!"

"We're not nervous, Màgjeur!" Lenk abruptly said. His younger complexion bore several spots beneath his greasy dark blonde mid-length hair. His eyes as dark green emeralds.

"No?"

"We're very disappointed we didn't get you this year," Corey assertively said. His sky blue eyes turned from curious to satisfied in a matter of seconds since Haldane's departure.

"What's wrong with Professor Haldane?"

"Well," Corey said, looking at the other two. "He's not exactly you."

"Indeed. No one is me but me."

"We've been waiting to see you for some time, Màgjeur." He sounded much older than a typical eighteen-year-old. "You can imagine our disappointment when they said you were leaving."

"Is there something I can help you with?"

"I hope so. But I'm afraid this is slightly off the book. We know you appreciate us being who we are, and following our own paths as you've said before. Which is why you are the only one we could ask."

"Ask what exactly?"

"You must promise not to tell anyone? This is something we can entrust you with is it not?"

"On the life of my paper dragons, I swear it."

The three looked at each other once again. Corey took a closer step before lowering his tone considerably.

"Could I ask...? Have you ever delved into conjuration before?"

Not much startled Ramalon, but this question did. Conjuration was considered a darker practice. However, it wasn't illegal. Instead, it was majorly frowned upon by all Màgjeur orders as it was a pathway to other darker practices. Even though the essence of conjuration was used to call on The Protecy, the art of conjuration was entirely different. Ramalon didn't flinch, instead, bearing his eyes onto the trio, slowly darting between the three.

"And what makes you ask such a question?"

Lenk and Corey looked at him. But Cleverson seemed to carry the sheepish nature with him. Slightly plump around the belly which flabbed throughout the rest of his short body. His chubby cheeks swallowed his mouth, making it seem rather small. However, it was his white-blue eyes, which was the more noticeable feature. His curly hair gave more suggestion he had little care for his appearance. His eyes did not at any point, meet Ramalon's.

"Because you are the only one who we thought could entertain the idea of conjuration."

"Entertain? You understand what conjuration is, correct?"

"We do," Lenk said.

"And you understand its potential?"

"We do. Would you believe it if we told you we've been studying it for quite some time now?"

"Strangely enough... I do believe that. You three have not gone unnoticed throughout the years."

"So have you!?" Lenk eagerly asked.

"No, I haven't."

"But surely you have at least studied conjuration at some point?"

"Perhaps." He took his time to respond, cautiously aware of what they were getting at. Corey and Lenk seemed more enthusiastic at the response.

"Our main question is, can you help us?" Corey asked.

"No."

"Why not!?"

"I do not believe the route of magic to be beneficial to anyone with sound minds.'

"We do!" Lenk strongly said. "We have seen how powerful it can be if you've mastered it."

"It takes years. Absolute years to get it right, and even then the route of conjuration is for life. The practice will never leave you. It will be a parasite in your life!"

"Yes, it will. But that does not sway us."

"It should. There is a reason no Màgjeur in The Magikai and this year's tournament have the affinity with conjuration. I have a duty to protect you. You are all young. You remind me of myself. I once dreamt of winning the tournament. And I remember thinking of ways in which I could do it. And believe me when I tell you. I thought of many ways to win. Ways much darker than conjuration."

"What kind of ways?" Corey slowly asked.

The trio seemed even more intrigued at this reveal. Ramalon stopped short before realising he had said too much.

"For another time. I promise you. You cannot go far with this fascination of yours."

"I respectfully disagree," Corey said. "How about for yourself Màgjeur? Imagine if you had that ability, to help you in the next round. And the final round after that when it's helped you get there…"

Corey's manipulative tone landed on Ramalon with some directness. He felt strange that he actually imagined it. Fighting reason with right.

"I am sorry to you all. I cannot accept your request."

"We're disappointed Professor. But perhaps this can change your mind…"

Lenk indicated towards Cleverson who took off his bag where the straps were slung over one shoulder. Corey extended his hand towards the door where the sounds of it locking immediately were heard.

"Just a precaution," Corey said.

Ramalon didn't know whether to feel worried or excited, feeling in constant conflict with himself. Cleverson delicately placed his bag onto the floor. As he opened it up, Ramalon noticed how delicately Cleverson lifted whatever this thing wrapped in several linings of cloth was. He placed it onto the pedestal in the middle of the stage with the same delicacy as if he was holding a new-born baby for the first time, carefully unwrapping strip by strip. It got to the final layer before Cleverson revealed what was wrapped inside.

"Graceland save us...!" Ramalon whispered as his mouth immediately came ajar in the shock of what he was looking at.

Ramalon's under-pits started to sweat immediately. He felt the warm heat rise to his face, and the glisten in his eyes sharpen as the moisture grew.

Revealed under the material laid a dead baby Charzeryx, a smaller spawn of the dragon family. There were many types of dragons which lived mainly in the east of Rolgan in the pits of Dragonsnout. The most fearsome of all is said to be The Dragadelf, but a fully grown Charzeryx had its competition. It's scaly, skinny dark green body was starved to the ribs. Its snapped brown wings and sharp head gave it a much gaunter look than its typical bulkier cousins. It laid lifeless.

Ramalon had no idea why but he felt an instant attachment to this creature as if it was his own child. A sadness, an overwhelming regret that something so beautiful, was living no more. A pity that he could not accept. His philosophy for the smaller things that life holds was coming to the forefront of his mind. How can something so small, so young, so innocent have not lived out a beautiful life? Baby dragons were not known to die young as the wrath of a mother would prove too fierce for most. Something must have gone very wrong for the baby Charzeryx not to survive.

"Where on this good land did you come by this?" Ramalon producing every word with additional weight.

"I found it a few years ago," Cleverson nervously said. "My family and I went to Rolgan as we have family there. My family are obsessed with dragons and took the same journey that The Dragadelf were believed to have flown down from thirty years ago."

Ramalon's heart grew fonder by the second of the Charzeryx and indeed of Cleverson. He could tell he too shared the sense of sadness for the baby dragon. Unlike his two *friends* who Ramalon felt were just there on the coattails of Cleverson. A vulnerable and suggestible teenager, finding his feet in life. Bereft of friends and taking any opportunity for companionship. Perhaps the only difference Ramalon felt between himself and Cleverson thus far.

"Where did you find him?" Ramalon asked, causing Cleverson's chin to gently shake, which rippled and wobbled out onto his cheeks. His eyes too began to shine more and more.

"We journeyed through a large portion of rocks and gorges. My parents went climbing to the top while I explored my own route. I came to a huge hole in the ground. I was too scared to go in at first, but I managed to pluck up the courage to venture in. It didn't smell too good, but I started to explore, hoping to find something valuable. And that was when I found this little one. Buried under rocks and rubble. I was terrified. But I decided to take it. I didn't tell my parents about it because they might have taken it. So I kept it for myself."

Cleverson fought back the urge to embarrass himself in front of Corey and Lenk and cry at the thought.

"It's okay," Ramalon gently consoled. "Are you aware of what might have happened? In relation to you finding this creature?" Cleverson shook his head. "I think you have found something that is very unusual and exceptionally rare."

"Charzeryx's aren't rare in Rolgan!" Lenk scoffed. Corey seemed to smile in agreement arrogantly. "Okay there's not many, but there are some."

"And can you tell me where its mother was?" The smiles were wiped off their smug faces.

"Probably off hunting somewhere?" Lenk said.

"You have much to learn of the nature of dragons. They are the most protective and possessive creatures ever to exist. They would never leave, let alone abandon their young unless in the very dying of circumstances. This youngling was not killed... It was scared." Ramalon and Cleverson instantly grew sadder at the thought. "Scared to leave the rubble without its mother. It died because its mother tried to protect and conceal him under the rubble in that cave you found. It died because its mother evidently never returned."

Ramalon was focused on educating a bit of compassion to Corey and Lenk. He felt annoyed and irked by their naivety and felt responsible for trying to make them sad and learn how to feel.

"Why didn't it return then?" Corey quickly asked.

"The decomposition and remains of this youngling is many years old. I'm going to take an educated guess and say thirty years…"

Ramalon looked at the boys to try and prize out an answer from them as to what happened thirty years ago. Corey and Lenk shrugged while Cleverson was clearly thinking.

"This is no coincidence. And there is only one realistic thing on this land that could have killed its mother."

"The Dragadelf…" Cleverson whispered, his eyes gently darting upon the realisation. The other two looked at him relatively surprised

"Correct."

"I was going to say that," Lenk said.

"It must have waited and waited beneath the rubble," Cleverson said, "hoping its mother would come back. It must have been so scared. So hopeful. So alone…"

They all stared at the poor Charzeryx and how horrible it must have been for this one.

"No life is small enough to deserve such cruelty," Ramalon said. "An injustice and imbalance to this world. Something I can never accept myself."

The way Cleverson looked at Ramalon was such a tell as to how much he looked up to him. He connected with every word as if they were his own. Ramalon could understand Cleversons love for this dead creature as he felt it too. Contrast that to the opportunists of Corey and Lenk, it was clear what their agenda was.

"And what is it exactly you are asking of me?"

"Well… We were hoping you would bring the body of this dead thing back to life."

Ramalon felt angered Lenk referred to this beautiful sadness as a *thing*.

"Let me be abundantly clear!" he said forcefully. "You cannot bring anything back to life."

"Yes, yes we know that, but with conjuration, you can share your soul with it and essentially give it a life of its own! We've read it all up and know you can share your soul multiple times, but if that happens each host gets weaker as a result. Once you share your soul, it belongs to you! To control, to nurture, to use to whatever you want it to do. Is that not fascinating in itself? Imagine watching this thing live, Màgjeur. Does that not appeal to you?"

He felt annoyed to agree, knowing what they were getting at. Although he could not deny the vision, they were setting out despite how dark the situation was turning.

"We want you to show us how we can do it," Corey said. "How we can share our souls with it."

Ramalon's stillness spoke volumes. Corey and Lenk both could tell he was bouncing the thoughts back and forth in his mind, debating whether to agree to show them.

"Imagine your hands on that trophy, Màgjeur. Even you could use him to help in your battles."

"I would not use him for me."

"Okay fine but it could help in some way surely."

Ramalon again looked at Cleverson who was not partaking in any persuasion tactics, instead looking very sorry for himself with the Charzeryx in his hands.

"Would you like me to?" Ramalon asked to Cleverson.

He looked up at him with the glimmering shine bouncing off his eyes. He looked to the other two, swallowing the build-up of saliva in his mouth. He looked back to Ramalon and nodded his head.

"Very well. I will help."

"Yes!!" Both Corey and Lenk clenched their fist, giving them a small fist pump.

"However. There will be strict conditions for this."

"Name them, name them!" Corey ecstatically said.

The excitement in them both made Cleverson stand out like a sore thumb as he pretended to smile to please his friends. Ramalon felt a duty to protect Cleverson from them. But he felt unclear whether he did want to see this baby Charzeryx be given a shared life or not. Something he wanted to find out, but considering the similarities he felt with him, Ramalon felt that if the roles were swapped, he would want to raise and nurture this innocent life. Albeit the creature would not be living by its own accord, instead it would be sharing the soul and life of the conjurer which appealed to Ramalon. The conjurer can choose to terminate the connection at any time and therefore leave it vacant for another caster to use which makes the situation appeal to both Corey and Lenk as they would have some arrangement to potentially share the usage of the Charzeryx which Cleverson would also have to agree to.

"First and foremost. This is to be kept in the strictest of confidence." They all nodded their head in agreement. "Second. I will teach you how to do it, but if I am not satisfied with the progress levels and practices we shall use on other examples, you shall not use it! Not until you are ready."

"Okay...?" Corey didn't take too well to this. His eyebrows furrowed, seemingly annoyed at the stipulation. "What if - "

" - No exceptions."

The excitement indeed died down, which brought more life into Cleverson. His general demeanour seemed happier.

"Thirdly. As the body of this Charzeryx belongs to Cleverson, he shall have the final say as to who can use it and for what use. I will not have it's constitution so rationally abused. I will teach you how to care, how to nurture and above all, how to love this creature."

Corey and Lenk slapped their dissatisfied and ugly looking faces back on. Clearly disapproving and not what they hoped.

"Those are my terms. Do you agree?"

Cleverson nodded his head emphatically. The other two hesitated to answer.

"Show us!" Corey demanded. Everyone, including Lenk, snapped their eyes toward him. "I want to see if you can do it first. For all, we know you could just be saying all of this to steal the creature away."

"You think I would do that? You have much to lear-"

"Do it then!" Corey spat.

They both stared off. Corey's smirking eyes were retaliating to Ramalon's relenting stare. The other two shuffled at the awkwardness. But it was Ramalon who broke first, indicating to everyone to stand back.

The Charzeryx laid still and lifeless. The students looked toward Ramalon in anticipation. They could not wait to see what was about to happen, all of their teeth shuddering and clattering into each other as the nerves of anxiety set in.

Ramalon bore his eyes onto the creature, and with a big deep breath, he slowly extended his left hand, palm facing toward the body with fingers apart. All of a sudden, the reflection in everyone's eyes started to turn purple and black as the colours of conjuration lit up their eyes. The temperature in the room swept cool, frosty shivers down their backs which felt like freezing their insides. The colours swam around the Charzeryx as Ramalon intensified the energy. His increasingly stronger breaths drew out steam from the cooler air. The body was lifted into the air slightly as its wings were drawn apart, exposing its dragon-boned body. Suddenly small balls of purples and blacks started to shoot itself through the body and out of the other side continually. The students were scared this might be hurting or damaging the body before reminding themselves that it was already dead. After several shots flew through the body, some started to settle inside the Charzeryx before one final, more significant pulse of magic flew straight into its solar plexus. The skinny body contorted into an unnatural pose, the sound of cracks and splintered snips of the thin bones of its wings were heard. The students wanted to intervene but resisted when they saw the body slowly return to a normal position, cricking in mid-air. As the colours started to fade and disappear, the body was lowered back onto the pedestal before the mouths of all the students dropped along with the widening of their eyes in disbelief as to what was on the seat.

"Do you believe me now?" Ramalon asked breathlessly.

They all silently nodded their head as they witnessed the baby Charzeryx staring at them all with the cutest of wide smiles, which captured Cleverson and Ramalon's hearts immediately. Somehow the typical almond-shaped eyes became more circular, giving it a kinder and endearing look. The sound of a small crackled purr was heard as it immediately approved of its spectators, circling itself to greet them. All the students bent down to be on the same level as the happy Charzeryx. Its scaly body suddenly had some fat to it, its head had a less gaunt look, and its wings were restored back to full flow which had the colours of purple and black gently clouding off of its sails as it moved. Ramalon could tell Corey and Lenk were a little more humble now that they had seen it come to life.

"Please! Teach us," Corey said.

"I will!"

And with that, he looked at Cleverson whose eyes were heavy with tears smiling wider than the creature as he just could not take his eyes off of him. He looked back at the Charzeryx before slowly raising his hand to the ceiling. The baby dragon spread its wings before flying up and around the circular lecture room leaving coat tails of purple wisps behind it. It's elated smile, and happy crackling cries seemed almost thankful to its new master as it enjoyed to freedom of flight.

He had never performed conjuration before, despite always knowing how. The thought of sharing his own soul with the creature didn't know whether to make him feel afraid, excited or anxious. But one thing was certain. He felt satisfied.

Honour Obliterate

The sensation of intoxication and extreme dizziness made Alicèn nauseous. In his semi-unconscious state, he could sense his body was being carried through time but his mind was completely pillaged from the exhaustion of defeating Dreanor. He was conscious enough to recall that the Banamie had come back for him. Cowardly running from the scene only to then return when the main threat had gone. Typical of a Barkler's backbone, he thought. But how would he try and get out of this one?

It was clear to him that Draul would interrogate him. How much strength did he have? He would never give in, no matter how much torture and pain they put him through. His honour and pride were far too great to resign to pain and wrongdoing. Either way, he prepared what he could to give himself the best chance to stay alive as long as possible.

His eyes occasionally opened through the drowsiness to reveal the moving of footsteps and shadowy figures in the night. The glow of torches bounced off of their faces, but again, his sight was too blurred to make out many details before his fatigue took over once more and his body and mind rested.

The next thing that came into fruition was the comfort of a soft mattress hugging his back and buttocks while a fluffy pillow cuddled his head. Such a strange contrast in feelings from what he felt before his fight. Before any notion of sight came to his vision and much to his surprise, his body was feeling the euphoria of restoration. A warming feeling came over him that during his unconsciousness, his body had gone through a process of recovery.

As his vision cleared, he noticed the hospitable environment around him. Not chains and feelings of thirst and hunger he had braced himself for. Early morning sunlight pierced into his straight forward room through the slatted blinds. No one in sight. He couldn't figure out what was happening. He certainly wasn't dreaming, or hallucinating. He slowly pulled apart the thick duvet to reveal several bandages around his abdomen and various parts of his legs. Slightly reddened in the middle, but a sense of well-being was a comfort to him.

He gingerly got up to walk out of the room. A sense of humbleness and peace radiated from the walls. Tranquillity and calm. Peaceful and slow. He looked down the hallway to view a man in loose fitted clothing sweeping the wooden floor. It seemed clean enough already but swept with precision and dedication. He was on a veranda which Alicèn looked out from, viewing several pagoda-like roofs made of wood and clay, curving elegantly to protect the wooden exteriors below.

"Where am I?" he whispered to himself, genuinely perplexed. "Begging your pardon," he said to the sweeping man.

The man stopped and turned slowly to him, revealing an old plain face. He bore slanted eyes and jet black hair with fading greys mixed in. His complexion was scarred and dishevelled.

"Where am I?" The man did not respond, instead standing there with the same blank expression. "Do you speak the common voice? Can you tell me what I am doing here?" No reaction. Alicèn huffed and turned. "I'll find my own way then."

The older man slowly pointed to his right. Alicèn limped across and started to smell a strong aroma of incense before peering into the hall the old man indicated. Candles situated in perfect form either side, leading up to a large statue of a warrior with linen covered loins, sitting cross-legged with a sword lying in front of him, staring out of the hall. This position was mirrored by a lone man whose eyes were closed as he silently meditated. Alicèn was encouraged to step in with a nod of the head by the older man who continued his regimented sweep.

He did indeed enter the hall which had an eeriness about it. What on Rèo was going on? He approached the trancing man who took one large inward breath before opening his eyes.

"Welcome. Alicèndil. Durgeon of Durge Helm." His head was bald while his eyes shared the same slant and angry stare with his thin spiking moustache below. Unlike the statue behind him, he bore thin linen, wearing it like a toga which covered his knees as he sat.

"Who are you?" Alicèn breathed.

"My name is Hiyaro," his light and soft common voice was a little unpolished but easy enough to understand.

"Where am I? What just happened?"

"Just happened? You have been resting for almost two weeks."

"Two weeks?"

"Yes. Your body was ready to pass to The Gracelands. One could argue we have incited an act of evil by stopping your soul from reaching it."

"Something tells me you are not evil."

"Indeed. Quite the opposite. You are quite safe here."

"How do you know who I am?"

"You will learn much here, I assure you. Come."

Hiyaro led Alicèn out of the building which, despite a busier nature of men and women concentrating on private studies, the atmosphere was that of pure stillness and concentration. They walked the gardens of beautiful colours flowering in every corner, gentle streams and small waterfalls aplenty. Certain parts of the gardens had archery targets being fired at truly in the bullseye with remarkable accuracy by Knights who radiated a similar stillness and focus. Other areas had different scenarios of men fighting with one sword against three others and managing to overcome the odds with simple and impressive moves.

"Welcome, to The Reinhault."

"The Reinhault? Are we in Septalia?"

"Geographically? Yes. But we do not associate with a realm. We are our own state," Hiyaro said with a smile.

"Why have I never heard of this place? It isn't on the map."

"Our existence is kept hidden from friend and foe to preserve what we do. We are the true shield of Terrasendia."

"How is that so?"

"You are fully aware that through all of the good on this land there are evils just as powerful."

Alicèn was a little surprised as it was a similar line to that he said to

Meryx back in Durge Helm.

"In all your experience you don't honestly believe that the evils have been prevented by your efforts alone do you?"

That had indeed crossed Alicèns mind on several occasions.

"We are a legion of warriors sworn to secrecy to protect our work. There are very few on Septalia who know of our existence. You will find many paths to learn here. Strength, wisdom, magic are all but a few."

"I didn't think Septalians agreed with magic."

"As I said, we are our own people," he said as they continued their walk.

Hiyaro looked around with a sense of pride. Alicèn noticed beyond the village that they were high up in the mountains, surrounded by green hills and fresh air sweeping in from below.

"We have moved with the times, Durgeon. The Protecy has become one of the most important inventions known to Rèo. So much so that its usage almost governs us. Rather than remain stubborn to man's preference, we accept its invention as a way to further our knowledge and help protect the land of Terrasendia from those who would harm it."

"And what have you done to protect us from The Banamie?"

"The Banamie? A band of vagabonds and fanatics led by a blind ruler?"

"A rather large band of Vagabonds and fanatics. You clearly have not been doing your job if you do not consider his threat to be real." Hiyaro stopped and sharply looked at him.

"His powers will fade. His ideology is flawed."

"Not if the hundreds of thousands of vulnerable minds carry on being inspired by his faded ideology."

"Hundreds of thousands!?" Hiyaro incredulously replied, smiling. "What gives you these figures?"

"My entire life's work!" Hiyaro stared with a little more intensity. "The population of our people have diminished rapidly over the last thirty years. And not just deaths, but the missing are the ones who worry me. Combine that with six realms on Terrasendia and more in Rolgan, and you acquire quite a force. Where else could such large numbers disappear to?"

"Draul is not at the top of our priority."

"He should be! And if I were in charge of the amount of power that I'm beginning to understand is here, I would order every effort in stopping Draul, before its' too late."

"Too late for what?"

"… His retribution. The extinction of all that support The Blessèd and oppose his ideology."

"What makes you so sure his power is growing at this rate? Where could you hide such numbers?"

"That is something I do not yet know. But strange things are happening. Things that I fear."

"Such as?"

"Before Dreanor spawned I had received from a man named Rya Al Asharad a bone. A bone that was undeniably that of a Dragadelfs."

"A Dragadelfs?"

"Yes. I had my analysis double checked and was certain it to be Delfenclaw. And clean. It hadn't just been laying there for thirty years. As it turned out, it was all part of a trap, luring myself and my band into their imprisonment."

"Sounds very much like a deficiency of wisdom on your part. How did you not consider the fact that you could be set up?"

"Trust me, I did. Were it not for the bone I would not have believed it. But what worried me tremendously was how he obtained it. I have a theory which compelled me to go in the hope that everything he said was true."

"What theory?"

"I still need time to come to any definitive conclusions. But let's just say I strongly believe that Draul is not alone in this fight against us. When Rya said, a Dragadelf had escaped and attacked Icarzbolden, I did not think that was impossible."

Hiyaro's eyes became more concentrated but no more worried than before.

"But that is impossible," he confidently replied. "Nothing can breach the walls of that spell."

"Then how do you explain a Dragadelf's vertebrae to have ended up outside The Dragasphere?"

"I cannot explain. But I am not concerned with this theory. The razing of Icarzbolden as you now realise was staged and man-made by The Banamie, to capture you. Which does not prove it had escaped."

"As I said. My theory is rather new, and I need time."

"In addition, were The Banamie to have allies in his fight, he would not be in any position of strength to challenge."

"How about if he somehow did manage to ascertain the power of a

Dragadelf…?" A sharpness arose in the air between them.

"You believe this to be true?" he replied bluntly.

"It is worrying me the more I think about it."

"Then, good. But I would counsel you not exhaust too much effort in this theory. It is illogical. And above all, impossible. The Dragadelf are not beasts you can tame. No power on this land can control them."

Alicèn's eyes suddenly lit up. As if he had just heard something which gave his theory a significant boost. He chose to try and downplay his revelation as he wanted to think about it first.

"Place your energies into something more productive."

Hiyaro calmly walked away but Alicèn did not follow.

"Without seeming to be rude, I have a realm to protect myself. I must be going-"

" - Oh, you cannot leave."

Alicèn's face turned sour, feeling a little bit more agitated.

"No? And why is that?"

"Every man who we take into our service cannot leave for a minimum of two years."

Alicèns eyes narrowed while his lips sharpened in intuitive anger.

"Two years!?" he said in amazement.

"Two years. Most stay after that."

"That is simply unacceptable. You know who I am, yes?"

"I do."

"And you know my responsibility?"

"Yes."

"And yet you want to imprison me knowing that the realm of Septalia is in grave danger."

"You are not imprisoned. Grave danger or not, you cannot leave. That is law."

"I am the Durgeon of Durge Helm!" Alicèn became angrier the more he spoke. "I will not be held captive here. Send a Bluewing to Luanmanu at the capital."

"We do not use birds here, I'm afraid. Nor do we adhere to any titles or prestige you may have. We are all equal. The laws here are our own."

Alicèn's rage began to really seethe, upon hearing he was trapped.

"Are you out of your MIND!!!?"

Several guards dressed in well embroidered baggy robes approached the rising tensions. However, Hiyaro stayed calm.

"I demand that I am released immediately!"

"Not until you are ready."

"In two years there might not be a Septalia to go back to!"

"As I said. We will ensure that will not happen."

"You clearly do not know them. Too preoccupied with other threats when the real threat has been slipping right under your noses!"

"All the same. You are here. You must learn. You must respect. What drives you, Durgeon?"

"I am driven by honour."

"As am I."

"I have never been so insulted in all my life! Why on Rèo did you bring me here?"

"You are not the first to be angry at how we preserve our secrecy. Nor will you be the last." Hiyaro grew calmer the more frustrated Alicèn got.

"You should have left me there! You risk the paramount of safety if I am not released. Who will warn our lands from Draul?"

"Share what you know. And we will run our own investigation."

"I do not trust you."

"So be it," he quickly said as he sharply turned and walked away. "Akiko and Hirotada here will escort you to your chambers. You will be well looked after here, I assure. Good day, Durgeon Alicèndil." He bowed and walked out of sight.

Thick steam harshly blew out of Alicèns nostrils as they flared with anger, like a raging Grozler. He felt every part of his honour completely disbanded, he had never been so disrespected. He was in charge of Septalia's defence and yet he had no power to defend it. He began to think he stood more chance if he was captured and taken to Draul. He did not accept or understand why The Reinhaults secrecy was more important than his work. Nevertheless, his mind was in complete overload that entire night.

Alicèn talked to no one, even after several days. Too enraged, constantly planning how he could escape. He would wander the village regardless and took in the ethereal nature that The Reinhault had to offer. He did admit to himself, the training here was beyond that in Septalia. Much more advanced, a legion completely fearless and dedicated to their chosen craft.

"You must eat," Hirotada urged, for which he would often refuse. He wasn't starving himself, but he lacked the appetite.

Several waterfalls splashed amongst the lower grounds within the mountain. He hadn't explored the lower grounds as of yet, sticking to the main parts as that was where most of the direct combats took place.

"What's down there?" he asked Akiko, directing his question to several houses around the lakes and ponds below.

"Màgjeurs." Akiko was not fluent in the common voice. "Magic."

"How many?"

"Few."

"Good. Perhaps I'll get some peace and quiet."

He made his way down the steps elegantly carved out of the rocks. The air grew cooler as the spray from the waterfall moistened Alicèns cheeks. He wasn't followed as he walked around the rather large lake below but noticed Akiko watching him. There were a few wooden boats tied to the docks with the lake slaloming out into Septalia. Despite the splashing of the waterfall, the air grew silent as he approached the biggest house around the lake. The wooden doors were closed, the windows seemed as if they were made of paper, while the roof protruded out of the entrance above the veranda, steps leading up to the door.

He tried to venture inside, but the door was locked. He stepped back out to the lake and noticed Akiko was no longer watching him. He was alone. Alicèn felt strange down there. He felt in his element surrounded by militia as that was his forte, but magic was most certainly an area where his knowledge was sparse.

Unknown to him he had a sudden urge to explore that part of the village, more so than before. He knew he had to stay there for a long time, despite his frustration. Continually worrying about Draul and The Banamie and how soon it would be before he realised Septalia was vulnerable. Durge Helm was perhaps the only place in the realm which could potentially hold off an invasion. As for the other strongholds, they would not be as well manned nor strategically placed to hold off the sheer power of Draul. Brackbannen, Chelsern, Denmill, Helsenor, Arinor, even Ragabastion and Winstanton would not be strong enough. Durge Helm, however, was carved out of the mountain, its several layers of legendary circular walls were tough to penetrate, even with the use of siege towers and trebuchets.

This all was assuming, however, the worst in Alicèn's theory was not true. *No power on this land can control them,* he remembered Hiyaro saying. He couldn't help his mind wander off as it occasionally did, what if something could control them? What would that mean? He doubted if there was another soul alive who would think this was possible. If someone or something had indeed acquired the right of

The Dragadelf. Even just one that would certainly change things. Perhaps this was the reason he felt compelled to explore the Màgjeurs here. But no one seemed to be around.

After an hour of peacefully contemplating his situation by the lake, waiting for any activity, he gave up and began to make his way back up the steps.

"I thought you would have more patience," the familiar voice of Hiyaro suddenly came from behind him.

"And what exactly would I be waiting for?" Alicèn bluntly replied.

Hiyaro smiled before making his way to the waterfall, which fell from a stream above. Alicèn felt inclined to follow, what else was he going to do? The rushing water covered the rocks behind before Hiyaro indicated Alicèn to peer into the water. He noticed a typical underground slit into the rocks with Hiyaro parting the water to guide their entrance in.

They made their way into a large cave which was manned by only a few Màgjeurs dressed in typical floppy robes. Steps led down onto the main floor of the cave which they went down, lit by candle fire alone. It was almost a library by the plethora of books and parchments littering the surrounding. One Màgjeur conjured a small flame mid-air which another froze with their own magic. The reaction gently steamed and evaporated quickly.

"As I said. We are our own state. The Màgjeurs you will see here all use The Protecy. You will be wise to embrace it."

"Does the council know of your existence?" Hiyaro merely looked at him before continuing his way down the steps. "Why wasn't I informed?"

"Your responsibility as Durgeon was the protection of Septalia. The members on the council swore an oath never to discuss our work. Preserving our secrecy and maximising our purpose."

"You should have mentioned. I could have used you all those times my life was in danger," Alicèn sarcastically said. "Not to mention just recently when I lost some of my best men!"

"You will not hate me forever. You will learn much here."

"I won't have much use for it when Draul wipes out the realm for which I am now powerless to protect."

"As discussed, The Banamie do not have the strength." Alicèn shook his head in denial. "However. Out of respect for your position, I will investigate."

Alicèn still did not want to share in such detail. But reluctantly felt that he needed this closure.

"Razing Gellows. That is where the Barkler said they were gathering."

"The Barkler who deceived you? You're going on the words of this man?"

"Strangely enough, yes. Despite his trickery, I do believe something is happening there? If he lied, I would have been able to tell. I was only deceived because the information he did tell me about was largely true, forming a believability. It makes sense."

"In that case, that is where we will go."

"Thank you," Alicèn reservedly said.

"Anywhere else?" his tone changed to a more inquisitive pitch.

Alicèn didn't want to share such detail about The Draughts, his worst fear, with a man he did not entirely trust at this point. He had no idea why but whenever he thought of that place, his heart began to thump. The amount of evil said to exist there had been enough to drive him away from his own investigations. A growing fear that The Draughts somehow was very important in the recent suspicions. But he could not deny that something lurked down there since Melcelore's capture. A festering of malice that he wished he knew. It was perhaps his worst and only fear.

"No."

"Very well. Use this time wisely. We will report back when we have concluded. Empower yourself, Durgeon."

Hiyaro bowed his head once more and left him in the hands of the watching Màgjeurs, who quickly resumed back to their studies. Alicèn sighed with heavy resignation.

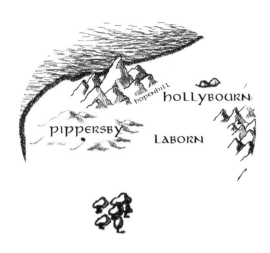

Unexpected Arriving's

Garrison's band were approaching Hopenhill, the final hill before home. The long-awaited return was a relief for the men, with Alex being the only exception. The night sky bore beautiful stars which soon became clouded over the closer to home they got. The anticipation of what felt like a hero's return warmed the hearts of the band. But the real satisfaction was in their desires to go back to their families and loved ones. Alex, on the other hand, was focused entirely on Jacklatoro.

"Brody!" Alex harshly whispered. "You need to help me."

"You don't look too great pal." A genuine concern for his friend cautioned his response. "You need to calm down. Ever since you went bandying off, you've not been yourself."

"I am myself! You need to check him."

"Who?"

"Jack! He has something he shouldn't have. It's dangerous!" Alex lied in desperation, hoping it would alarm his friend to help. Brody couldn't help but feel sad for how he has become.

"Alex, I don't think you're quite right. I say this as your friend, and I don't have too many. You need to calm down and wait till we get back. I promise whatever it is you need we'll get it sorted."

"We won't have time! It will have gone by then!"

"Brody!" Joric firmly said. "Come away from him. Need I remind you, Alex, that you are held in the bard till further notice. Whatever has gotten into you must be sorted. Your actions at The Gurken have been entirely unacceptable and will await trial."

Alex couldn't rest for a moment. Too angry, too betrayed and too ashamed that he was failing.

Shortly after this exchange, they began to ascend the gigantic slope of Hopenhill, a sign they were nearly home. The tilt in gravity Alex felt as he sat with his hands bound in the carriage felt ironic that even though the band were going uphill, he felt as if he was going down.

Suddenly a sense of alarm amongst the men snapped Alex out of his daze. He peered around the ascending trailer to see that the night sky which had been clouded over, tinted orange and brown glow. Riders of the band rushed to the top of the hill to inspect what this unusually bright glow was. When Joric and Garrison arrived with several other Durge members.

"MEN! QUICKLY!" Joric shouted.

The alarm raised panic, and the panic set in. Something was not right. Hearts began to race, the men who had a horse galloped over the hill as quickly as they could, disappearing over the horizon of the hill which resembled a red sunrise. The men travelling on foot raced on behind the horses and carriages, swords and weaponry were drawn, leaving Alex still tied to the cart. The horses were still pulling the wagons and the closer they got to the top of the hill, the more he could hear the chinking of swords clashing, the screams and wailing of the people of Pippersby, all the while he tries to wriggle himself out of his bonds. He tried to see what was going on, the only man he could see was Reyga, who was manning a few horses pulling carts. The rest of the men forgot about Alex in their pursuit of what was going on.

"Reyga! What's going on!?" Alex demanded. A somewhat nervous and frightened Reyga didn't respond. "Untie me!" Reyga shook his head. His youth was coming through and wouldn't dare disobey an order from Joric. "Reyga please, I need to see what's going on!"

Reyga hesitated for a moment before dropping the reigns of the horses and fleeing into the nearby woods, his youthful fright overtaking him. Alex felt angered he was now by himself, tied on a cart being pulled helplessly into a potential doom just before Reyga disappears into the darkness of the woods.

"I'm sorry, Alex!" he cried, before turning and running his body into a sword through his heart, stopping him dead in his tracks.

The sound of his sternum cracking followed by the squelch of his heart bursting as the blade raced through him. The holder of the sword bore thick clad armour, rags underneath and well prepared for a battle, scars made up most of his complexion, angry and almost mad in his intensity towards his newest killing. A sense of enjoyment overtook the warrior as he did not withdraw his blade from the boy but instead used his muscular strength to waltz the boy backwards as he marched forwards. Keeping Reyga suspended on the guard of his sword like a bit of skewered meat, he looked over to Alex, who was well bound.

"Well well well, look who we've found here," his common accent and armour was a huge indication of who these people were.

Another warrior very similar in size and appearance appeared just behind the first as they both approached Alex sinisterly.

"Easy pickings for me."

"And for me!" the other warrior said as he swiped the head off of Reyga with his sword. "One more for me, I guess!"

No longer requiring the body of the headless Reyga, he thrust his sword upwards and withdrew his blade quickly, and the teenager's trunk flew off, crumpling to the floor like a rag doll. Alex watched on helpless. His heart was trying to escape his rib cage as the two men approached.

"This one's mine!" said the first of the warriors. "Show him the head of the boy you just took to show everyone just how much of a tough man you are."

"Maybe I'll add yours to my collection if you mock me again!"

Both men withdrew a smaller blade, looked towards Alex and gathered slowly around the cart which was now feeling more and more like his coffin. The smaller blade suggested this was more sport for them, rather than a battle. This was it, the wriggling and intense pressure he put on his bonds made Alex's wrists bleed trying to escape, but when they looked on, several feet away they just smiled as if this was fun to them. Alex gave up trying as it was useless. He felt hopeless, ready to part ways with the world.

"Noblemen. I feel so sorry for them, don't you?" said the second warrior.

"Not in the slightest!" he growled through gritted teeth. He leaned in aiming to stick his blade into Alex's gut.

Suddenly a huge clump of steel belled into the back of the first warriors head sending him splattering, blood, bone and brains on Alex's body. Alex looked up and saw Bran coming to his aid. He head-butted the other warrior which only warded him away from the cart. Bran's Warhammer was an exceptional craft he created, flat-sided on one half with a cruel and jagged edge on the other. He was bigger in frame than the warrior but not as muscular and probably not as quick. Nevertheless Alex felt he needed to help his friend if he was to stand any chance. The two giants locked horns in their duel.

Bran set the tempo of the fight as his hammer was stronger than a sword, however, if he was to miss-time a move or allow the warrior in, he would not be able to stop the blade from entering him. It was a fight Bran had never had to fight before, a fight to the death. But he held his ground firmly. Often taking big circular horizontal swipes in a three-sixty motion stepping through as he did to ensure maximum safety. The bandit could not get near but instead was almost biding his time.

Alex looked on and saw that Bran's footwork was actually in grave peril on the slope. It was easy to miss-time a swipe and for gravity to make him slip. He felt the blood of the other bandit seep into his clothes before noticing the blade was underneath his dead body. He reached under and grabbed the edge to try and cut his bonds.

Bran went in for another swipe, but that time went too far and predictably slipped on the hill. With his footing lost and body exposed, the bandit took the opportunity to strike, aiming his thrust into the stomach of the gentle giant of Pippersby. Bran's only form of defence was to quickly drop his hammer and parry the thrust with his arm. The flesh of his forearm spilt open causing intense pain and a battle-cry from Bran, plummeting to the floor.

Unarmed, disabled and accepting fate, the bandit stood over the giant.

"One big head for me!" he claimed triumphantly as he lifted his sword, going for the stab to the heart.

As he did, he felt a yank to the back of his head before feeling cold steel slide into his throat from the back of his neck. The relief from Bran was true, seeing a bloody blade erupt from the mouth of his impending killer made him wail with desperate relief. Alex held his position upright for several moments, left hand firmly tight on the bandit's hair pulling back, while his right hand forced the blade to the guard against the back of his neck. Confident that he was now dead with the lifeless sway of the bandit's arms, he released him to the side of Bran.

Alex helped his friend to his feet, the irony of giving Bran a shoulder to lean on giving their size difference showed just how much he appreciated his friend in his darkest time of need.

"You okay?" he breathlessly asked the giant.

"I can't move my hand Alex," he cried, clearly in a lot of pain. He examined the wound, which was indeed severe. The blade had sliced both major muscles in Bran's forearm, which controlled his hand, he could now not use it.

"Let's thank The Blessèd you still have your legs! Come on. We need to find out what's going on."

"Who are these people?" Bran winced.

"Barklers," he replied as he carried his friend shoulder to shoulder to the peak of the hill.

The orange glow on the horizon of the peak brightened the closer they got. Bran was not only very heavy but exceptionally awkward to carry given his size, which doubled Alex's workload. They arrived at the top and horror struck their faces. Pippersby was burning. Plumes of smoke and raging fires littered the town, sounds of swords and cries echoed throughout and the one thing on Alex's mind was to get home as quickly as he could, to protect his family, god forbid if they hadn't already experienced the danger. The likelihood of that happening shook him, he wanted to race off down the hill like a madman but having Bran on his shoulders pinned him down.

"Alex, take the horse and go!" Bran indicated to the cart catching up. "You have to go now. I'll catch up!"

"You can't use your hand!"

"I know, but they come first, and you know it. I won't tell you again, GO!"

Alex resisted very little if any. Torn between owing his life to Bran and potentially coming to his family's aid hurt him as there really was only one choice. He patted his friend on the chest in recognition, unhooked the oncoming horse from the cart and jumped onto it, gripping the reigns and galloping down the hill as quickly as he could.

His heart raced. Sweat profusely streamed over his brows as his eyes stung from the salt. Approaching the town, he witnessed some of The Durge fighting with the Barklers, prevailing in some but falling in other duels. Absolute chaos as he rode through the pebble streets, avoiding conflicts and taking the back routes to his home.

He eventually made it to his family home and his heart leapt into his mouth as he took in the fiery scent before him. Flying off his horse with his sword drawn, he crashed through the door. Thick black smoke hit his face, which made him crouch to avoid the poisonous fumes. Scanning his home to see it had already been used as a battleground. With no sign of his family, he raced upstairs to Jàque's room. He too was not there.

"AMBA! JÀQUE!" he shouted to no reply.

Coughing his way through the house, he made his way outside, the battles seemed to have stopped. Jeers of raucous laughter could be heard at the town hall, but not the sound he wanted to hear. Should The Durge have prevailed, they most certainly would not be laughing. He struggled against the natural panic setting in versus the strength he needed to conjure should his family still be alive. As he started to dash towards the town hall, he took another back route, which was narrower with houses on one side and a raised bank on the other.

He made a move into a clearing, and a flash of wood sped past his eyes before stopping him in his tracks. He looks over to see a Barkler, bow in hand, smiling as he missed his aim.

"You're sharp. But not as sharp as this next one going into your skull!" the Barkler announced as he drew another arrow from his quiver.

Nowhere to run in time, nothing to shield and certainly nothing to counter with, he was perilous to stop it. A large black shape in the form of Bran jumped in from the raised bank. His bloodied arms tucked in, he cocked his head as he descended from the height. The Barkler felt his presence, turned his head and with another almighty battle-cry Bran smashed his skull into the brains of his assailant, chunking off the Barklers skull in the process. Blood sprayed from their heads. The explosive impact from which brains and blood erupted into the air ricocheted and sent Bran crashing into the wall. Never had Alex seen such a demonstration of the fragile nature of a human body. He rushed over once again to his friend. Not once but twice, his friend had come to his aid. He crouched down to examine the damage himself.

"BRAN!!!" Alex cried, as quietly as was possible.

"At least I'm a use for something," Bran dozed.

"I swear this if I have another son I'm naming him after you!"

Truly touched by Alex's comment, a smile spread across his drowsy face.

"Oh... Oh, that's not right."

Alex inspected Bran's complaint after noticing a faint red line on the giant's forehead, followed by an ebb of blood. Alex ripped off a portion of fabric from his garment and applied the faintest of pressure to his forehead to reduce the bleed. What followed made Alex feel like this was to haunt him for the rest of his life. The gentle pressure had moved that portion of Bran's skull transforming it into what looked like a lone island of bone raising it slightly on the opposite end of the fracture. Alex froze. His saviour was surely on his way to The Gracelands. Blood streamed out now like a scarlet river.

"I'm so sorry! I am s-so s-sorry!"

Not even Alex's brave face could hide his building tears. It was too much.

"Find them…"

And with that, Bran's eyes froze dead, resting his head against the wall.

Alex had never lost anyone of significance in his life, and the plethora of feelings he was going through in that moment branched a new twig of pain. Pain which he certainly did not want became even more severe. He gently curtained the giant's eyes shut.

"Rest in peace. My good friend," he sobbed.

His strength had waned significantly. He took a deep, life-restoring breath into his lungs, willing them to carry him once more into the fray and off he went through the back streets to the town hall.

He accelerated through the streets, determined to find his family. With so many thoughts running through his head, he couldn't help but wonder why a small isolated town in the corner of Terrasendia had come under such a slaughter. Forget the talk of Rawblers. This was much worse. He stealthily made his way through the town, going between houses when he found lying in front of him, Jacklatoro on the floor, an arrow in his chest. If he had The Time Stone on him, maybe there was a way he could reverse time to ensure this tragedy never happened. He noticed Jacklatoro moving very slightly and rushed to examine.

"Jack! Where is it!?" he urged.

"Huh?" Jack struggled with his reply.

"I know you took it. You took the stone, where is it?" he started to pat down his wounded body, checking for the stone.

"OW! What are you doing!? I have no idea what you're talking about."

His searching livened up the defendant, but it was in vain as he found no sign of the stone.

"Are you telling me you have nothing to do with the stone?"

"What are you talking about!? What stone!?"

"The stone you stole from me at The Gurken!"

"Alex I have no idea what you're talking about. I promise, please help me - "

A gush of blood spurted onto Alex's face as Jack faded into stillness. Alex knew he was telling the truth. He knew he was going to die and would have no reason to lie. But if he didn't attack him, then who did? He heard talking from two men around the house. He peered around to listen in.

"Have we got what we came for?" one man said, older and more impressive in armour.

"He says he has it but is for the King's hands only. No excuses." His stature wasn't as impressive as the older man's but still struck a feared presence.

"We'll see about that."

They both faded away into the crowd, which gathered at the foot of the steps leading up to the town hall. This wasn't a random attack. This was a planned slaughter. There must have been three hundred Barklers who paved the way for the two. They led themselves through the crowd, up the stairs before addressing their band.

"I Thog, dedicate our victory today to our King! Rightful and just! King Draul, leader of The Banamie!" A huge cheer erupted from the crowd. "May his ways guide us to justice and freedom from this terrible constituent. May the powers of The Blessèd wain and our people brought back from their wrongful death! Noblemen and all who support them on Terrasendia must be sacrificed in honour of our heroes. Continuing with these three."

Pushed up the stairs Garrison, Joric and Amba side by side with several other town folk, all bound. Not fighting, knowing their fate in what they believed to be their last moment, stood tall and proud. Alex wanted nothing more than to run into those three hundred Barklers and take all of their heads. But he felt there was nothing he could do.

"Where is my son?" he thought, perhaps the only thing stopping him from committing his suicide and in the hope that he managed to get away.

The world sank beneath his feet. Gracelands only knew what he would feel if they brought out his son, he would have no choice but to try his best and save him. He looked around for any sign of comrades, any sign of life, any sign of hope… It never came.

The commander of the band chose Garrison first. He kicked the back of his legs, forcing him to kneel in front of his crowd. The cheers could be heard a mile away as an axe was presented to Thog by one of the Barklers. Garrison looked straight ahead. His intense stare was surely an acceptance that this was it. However, Thog pulled out another weapon, a dagger but with the blade no longer than a few centimetres. Just like the blade Alex saw before when tied to the cart. A sporting blade purely designed for torture and painful death.

"May those who suffer now, feel the suffering of our glorious dead!" Thog announced.

And with that, he repeatedly thrusted his gripped blade, punching it into Garrison. Occasional thrusts to the back, a few into his rib cage from the side often pausing for everyone to enjoy the spectacle. Garrison was tough, but even this was too much for him as he struggled to the best of his ability to wriggle free wincing and trying not to wail and give his enemy the satisfaction.

Thog grabbed the axe at last and Alex couldn't bear to watch another of his friends pass. But with absolutely nothing he could do, no chance of a rescue mission working, he closed his eyes and rested the back of his head against the wall... An even louder cheer erupted from Pippersby. And with that, he knew the fate of the owner of Smithwins. He didn't need any confirmation. He opened his tearful eyes and, determined not to let this happen to the mother of his child, he rummaged around his surroundings desperately searching for something that would not allow Amba the same fate.

He saw Jacklatoro's bow and quiver still attached around his body. The weight of acceptance stared down Alex in his face. If Amba was going to die it would be him to deliver the blow. He refused to have his final memories of her suffering in death.

Before he knew it, he heard her screams of pain as the torture began. Time had run out. He quickly took the bow and arrow and peered around the corner. Thog had indeed struck several blows into the side of his lover. Alex almost felt those blows himself when he heard her tortured screams.

Cries of Joric shouting, "take me! Let her live, please! I beg you!!" only added to the entertainment and laughter of the Barklers.

Thog sheaved his dagger and picked up the axe once more. Alex, angry and determined, aimed his arrow into her heart. He winced, not believing what he was about to do, but feeling like he had no choice. If she was going to die, it had to be him to release her from the pain. Thog thoroughly enjoying the theatre he was creating, finally got into position. Before she raised herself, Alex took aim and whispered "I love you…"

Thog drew back his axe, Alex took a deep breath in, and suddenly a hurricane of arrows flew into Barklers from the other end of the street. Followed by the thundering sound of hundreds of horse hooves, Alex quickly looked to see The Knights of Rombard Hill galloping towards the band, war-crying as they raced passed into the melee to wipe out their assailants.

Thog had restarted his swing, which made Alex quickly change the direction of his aim but the distance was too far for him to reach in time. Thog down swung his axe into the back of the incoming father, saving his daughter in the process. Alex released his arrow with all his might, travelling over the Knights and Barklers into the solar plexus of Thog, instantly dying on the spot.

Alex rushed over towards Amba, taking out several oncoming Barklers in the process. The rescue of what remained of the town was no battle. The Knights of Rombard Hill were well trained, and the remaining Barklers were fleeing for their lives, many fell while few escaped. Alex arrived and knelt beside his loved one, holding her in his arms. The extent of her wounds was grave, too weak to see.

"Amba!" he whimpered, trying to inject any form of life back to her. "Come on, talk to me!"

"A-Alex? Is that you?"

The loss of blood was draining the life away from her, spilling onto Alex's knees from the side and back of her body. Alex tried to compress the wounds as much as he could, but the number of entry wounds once again horrified Alex with reality. Her disorientation was becoming stronger. Enough strength however, to open her eyes to meet his. She smiled the longer their eyes met.

"Am I dreaming?" she softly said, a small tear trickling down her face.

"No, you most certainly aren't. You're going to be fine!"

"That's… That's funny," she faded.

"You are! I - " he interrupted himself as he couldn't bring himself to promise her as they both knew her fate. That weird black hole inside Alex's throat grew bigger. "Where is he? Where is our boy?"

Her eyes dimmed, and her breathing had shortened significantly. He sobbed as he touched her face with shaking hands. He kept telling her that he wouldn't let her go, he couldn't let her go. As her eyes glassed over, he pleaded and begged her to come back. To come back to him. To move her eyes. To speak. To breathe… To live. When all his praying had been exhausted, when all his hope had faded, the life that remained of Amba's existence turned slowly into stone. The love of his life, the mother of his child, had passed.

He could almost feel the freeze from her lifeless body accelerate. In total disbelief, he kissed her forehead hoping it would bring her back to life, before resting his forehead onto hers.

The fighting had stopped, several soldiers examining their dead. The Durgeon of the knights approached the scene but respected what he saw. Alex held her lifeless body, not quite believing any of this, or how this happened. Turning to stone himself, he just stared at her. Excruciating pains slicing his heart to shreds at the memories he had with his family. How much more could Alex take? His whole world had turned upside down in such a split second of his life.

"Sir…?" The Durgeon respectfully approached. "My name is Relian, Durgeon of Rombard Hill. What happened here?" His words were met with no response from a gormless Alex. "I respect this is not the best time to ask, but we need to ascertain what happened here. Do you require assistance?"

Without reply, Alex lifted Amba himself and carried her straight passed Relian, down the steps, keeping his gaze on her lifeless eyes at all times. The gathered knights at the bottom of the steps parted ways to allow him through. Soldiers boring impressive armours and bloody swords paid their respects with a small bow of the head. Relian allowed this and tended to Joric who he realised was severely wounded.

Alex felt like he had no more tears to give, replacing emotions with his determination to lay his lover to rest as he makes his way back to their home. Keeping his eyes focused on Amba the whole way, he stepped into his house and upstairs they went. He wanted nothing more than her closed eyes to wake like they had always done, every day since the day he first loved her, since the first day they met.

He laid her onto their bed. Arranged the pillows so that it was comfortable for her lifeless body. Drew the duvet over her, neatly aligning it on her chest and carefully placing her hands over the duvet onto her stomach. He wiped away any stray hairs from her face and neatly tidied her beautifully coloured red hair to one side. He stood back and looked upon her.

"I love you. With everything I have. I will see you again," his voice trembled once more.

That weird feeling in the back of his throat got more prominent again as he leaned in and kissed her on the lips one final time. He hoped in vain for them to respond to his, for which they did not as the reality sank in further, sobbing his heart out. He laid his hand on the side of her cheek.

"I promise..."

Alex laid Amba to rest. He closed the bedroom door, resting his head on it for several moments before making his way sombrely downstairs. He looked around what was his perfect home, along with memories of his perfect family, seeing the ghosts of Amba and Jàqueson in their happiest times. Instead of experiencing the gut-wrenching feeling of loss, it brought another sense of motivation and determination.

"Where is my boy!?"

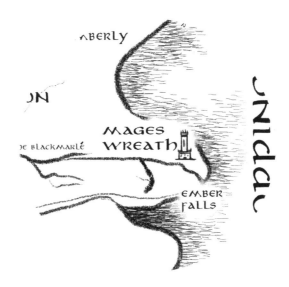

The Fall

The sound of jubilant explosions echoed throughout the white marbled walls on Mages Wreath to announce the beginning of the second round. Once more, colourful and intricate fireworks rippled through the skies above. However, not all could be seen as the sky was much greyer than usual, lighting up balls of light inside the thick clouds. A sight Ramalon gazed upon in wonder from his open window, perched on the side of his bed.

A strange feeling of confidence started to grow within him, not at all fazed by the uncertainty of the next round, he took courage knowing other competitors perhaps were apprehensive about what would happen next. In many ways, he felt it was an advantage to him as it took away their security of preparation. He was the inferior Màgjeur in the tournament, so by taking away the idea of forward preparation, only the skill of intuition and quick thinking remained.

His focus for the week leading up to the next round was twofold. The first being how to defeat Pyros and Allaremsah. The second being his nocturnal activities in relation to the Charzeryx he was sharing his soul with. Not to mention the regular trips to the peak of The Skyurch to understand what was going on with his protecy stone. Davinor would keep the sessions short in his findings and say he still did not understand why his stone was behaving like it was. He returned the stone the day before so that Ramalon could focus for his next round.

He had left the creature under Cleverson's supervision, strictly instructing him to keep it hidden when not in lessons. Were they to show off the creature, The Magikai would surely start asking questions. The Charzeryx would indeed exist and flitter about as if it was alive, seeing that Ramalon left the connection passive. The students would enjoy the hype that they have a fire breathing dragon to share. Corey and Lenk enjoyed the more destructive things they asked it to do, like burning a few books and plants. Cleverson was more conservative and more interested in teaching the Charzeryx how to do things. He constructed hoops in the air for it to flitter through, trying to make its flight more elegant as it was still flying relatively inconsistent and bat-like. Corey and Lenk were predictably not interested in the slightest in its development. Almost more impatient that it wasn't doing the things they wanted to do more efficiently. Occasionally they would laugh when it flittered into one of the hoops before crumpling to the floor.

They had managed to find one of the rooms below the ground floor of The Opey Deary where he was sure it was quiet enough to teach. The room itself was lit only by the fires Ramalon cast into the torches on the nearby walls. No natural light escaped at all and the cellar-like room was floored with sand, much to the complaints of Corey and Lenk.

The first couple of days were focused mainly on the connection the conjurer must share with the object and how to relax and find a way of connecting soul and body. Although the conjurer was sharing part of his soul, he has the choice whether to control or leave it passive so that it could be free to exist as it pleased. This was the case with the Charzeryx as Ramalon had no intention to use it for his himself. Should he want to control the Charzeryx, he would have to intensify his focus on the bond they shared. He stressed how the connection could be terminated at any time and the body would resume back to its deceased originality.

He set up various scenarios where they all would practice on dead animals, mainly birds and rodents which were much more straightforward given that they were smaller subjects. They all struggled to grasp the concept initially. They grew increasingly frustrated after several days, having not been able to achieve their goal. But Ramalon urged them to persist, stressing that it would take some time to master, especially as conjuration was very difficult if The Protecy had not yet been enchanted, for which they hadn't yet. The relaxation needed to find and establish the connection was very similar to that which was needed for The Protecy to flow. Ramalon did not expect that to happen any time soon.

"Have you thought of a name?" Ramalon asked Cleverson as he tried to connect with a dead Bluewing, the smallest of birds with the exception of chicks.

"I hadn't given it too much thought."

"How about something close to you?" Ramalon suggested.

"I dunno," he shrugged.

"Have a think. Everything needs a name."

Cleverson had a think before his eyes seemed to brighten up a little.

"Arinane!" Cleverson quickly said. Ramalon furrowed his eyebrows in confusion.

"Arinane?"

"Definitely."

"What makes you suggest this?"

"Arinane is the place just after the Rolgan Waste and before the Lands of the Neverseen! It's said to be the most arid and deserted place on Rèo!"

"I don't see the connection."

He looked toward the other two, and they were far enough away that they weren't in earshot. "It seems to fit."

"How so?"

"It's a very lonely place…" Ramalon picked up the connotation that being lonely was how he was truly feeling.

"Very well. Arinane it is." And on cue, the sound of flittering wings grew within earshot and landed on the stone pedestal Cleverson was working on. Its radiant and almost cheeky smile made Cleverson smile in return.

"Arinane," he quietly said, lowering himself to the same eye level.

"Arinane? You named that thing, Arinane!?" Corey and Lenk scoffed.

"What have we said about calling the Charzeryx *a thing!?*" Ramalon barked sharply.

"Alright, I'm sorry, I just forgot," Lenk said.

"You forgot? Maybe this is why you are struggling so much, you cannot see the beauty and significance in other living things."

"I'm not struggling, I'm just, you know, not getting it as quick.'

"Which means you're struggling.'

Lenk naively rolled his eyes.

"So how are you going to do it?" Corey asked.

"Do what?" Ramalon replied.

"You know. Win you're next round? You set off at noon, right?"

"Indeed. The other competitors and I are meeting at The Skyurch, where we will find out what the next round is. And then straight in."

"Are you excited?" Cleverson asked.

"Excited isn't an emotion I register like you. But yes, I guess you can say I am."

"Nervous?" Corey asked.

"No."

"Oh come on you must be a little bit."

His sideways glance was aimed to get him to say he was nervous. But Ramalon genuinely did not feel nervous, nor anxious. Upon reflection, he often wondered why he wasn't. The biggest day of his life thus far, and he didn't even seem to realise the weight of the day. His sleep was not disturbed out of its regular pattern, and his morning routine did not change.

"Your minds are young. Nerves come from when you feel you have something to lose. What have I got to lose?"

"Good question. What have you to lose Màgjeur…?"

Feeling a little stumped at the question he searched for the answer. A week ago he would have just said his paper dragons and The Opey Deary itself. But now his growing attachment with his protecy stone and the happiness he felt sharing his soul with a Charzeryx gave him more fulfilment. However, the nerves were still curiously absent.

"I must get going."

"Do you think you will win?" Cleverson asked.

"I am not sure."

"Because I was thinking. Well, we all were thinking actually. Whatever format the next round takes place, Arinane could help you?"

"Absolutely not!" Ramalon snapped at him perhaps for the first time.

"But - "

" - Under no circumstance must you instruct it to help!"

"I don't understand. It might be able to help you defeat Pyros and Alleremsah."

"No! I am forbidding you to do this. I am placing my trust in you

Cleverson. I allow Arinane to live by your wishes, but you would put me at great risk were they to find out my soul is being shared."

"But it would help right?" Lenk intruded. "What if they were never to know?"

"I do not like what you are suggesting."

"Why? Its fires are strong enough to cause harm."

"You do not see the point here. Conjuration is hugely frowned upon."

"But not illegal."

"Indeed. But to demonstrate it in front of thousands would be most unwise."

"I thought you would have done anything to win this tournament?"

"I would. But not this."

"This makes no sense - "

" - Not another word! That's final. I take my leave."

Ramalon stormed out of The Opey Deary and headed straight to The Skyurch with haste.

He felt angered with what his students had suggested, suddenly feeling a little apprehensive leaving Arinane under the vulnerable care of such small impulsive minds.

"Ah! Màgjeur Ramalon. There you are," said the crisp voice of Ronovin, standing upon one of the levels of steps above where the rest of the competitors were already gathered. "We were wondering if you would make it."

"My apologies."

Time had slipped by him before he suddenly appeared on the famous wide stairs leading up to The Skyurch. Crowds began to gather at the very bottom of the stairs to glance a look at the remaining champions.

"Welcome to the next round, Màgjeurs! We had hoped for a clearer day than this, but not to worry. Let's not waste any time. I am sure you are all eager to find out what it is you will be doing in the next round. As you will be competing in your three's, you will know that the winner will proceed to the final round. Please, this way."

Ronovin led the competitors through The Skyurch and through to the square gardens. Icy silences and awkward sideways glances consumed the short journey. Ramalon began to understand the notion of what desires and goals did to people, and what they would do in return to achieve them. Anything. No one spoke, and tensions were high. An experience Ramalon once more felt comfortable in.

They approached the beautiful green square garden in the middle of The Skyurch, surrounded by the familiar white marble of the building itself. The garden was seen as the heart of the premise that the common folk were not permitted to view without permission of The Magikai. Radiating light colours of greens, yellows and oranges, an array of butterflies and bees collecting their nectar. But the most defining feature that separated it from other common gardens was the presence of a number of elegant winged horses grazing on the lawns.

"Mildens of the sky!" Ronovin announced.

Not many had ever laid eyes upon such rare horses. It was said that most of them resided in this very garden. The Magikai used their near extinction as a symbol of defiance and the ultimate form of freedom. A symbol of The Magikai in the form of a statue was placed in the middle, rearing and with both wings attached from its scapula's spread like eagles, representing the freedom of flight. While boasting exceptional intellect, their eye for judging characters was also a wonder. They could sense the good and evil within people which no one had ever worked out how or why it was possible. The symbial was also seen on many banners and flags around the city with white backgrounds and a silver horse in full spread.

"But some of you may know these by another name."

"Windermares," Ramalon quietly said, in absolute admiration of their beauty as they playfully frolicked and neighed at their arrival.

Once again, the small things in life came to the fore for Ramalon. The only species protected by a royal decree of King Thorian Mijkal, preserving the integrity of their provincial treasures. But he saw them in a different light.

"Feeling sentimental, Màgjeur?" Pyros whispered into the ear of Ramalon as they all continued the journey to the statue.

"Yes," he replied bluntly not looking at his competitor, irking him in the process that his insult didn't land.

"Please, all choose a milden to ride," Ronovin said with a smile.

The competitors seemed to liven up drastically. The energy was put into all of them finding the best horse they could before Ronovin put them at ease.

"Do not fight over them! Fighting is for later. They will not be helping you in any way in this task."

Nevertheless, the Màgjeurs still were looking for the biggest or strongest one, often taking a look at one before moving onto another. Ramalon did not move. Instead, he merely observed the others as he took a different approach.

"This one seems to like you, Màgjeur."

A Windermare came up from behind Ramalon, rubbing its forehead on the back of him, temporarily budging him from the spot. Ramalon smiled as it did. Its white coating was flawless. Not a speck or blemish on its entire body. The white only faded below the knees where even then the greys and black hooves were a beautiful sight. Its bold black eyes stared at him from one side before gently blowing its lips to acknowledge and accept Ramalon. The white feathered wings brushed its circular side before its right wing opened to welcome its champion.

"Fitting," Ramalon said smiling.

"How so?" Ronovin replied.

Ramalon looked once more at the other competitors.

"I like the idea he chose me." This drew a smile from Ronovin.

The others had indeed found their mildens and reconvened around Ronovin.

"Please, mount your horses."

Most of them did so without hesitation despite many never having sat on a horse. Màgjeurs did not like the idea of riding horses for fear of feeling too much like a nobleman or Septalian. Their apprehension of never riding one before was beginning to show.

Ramalon placed one foot onto the wing that the Windermare lowered and with its help thrust himself onto its bare back. The comfort he felt on his buttocks was remarkable. The construction of the horses back seemed to fit like a well-fitted glove. Ramalon's comfort and perfect-fit onto the milden's back seemed to breathe confidence in to him. Especially when he saw the others looking relatively uncomfortable and unable to control their mounts.

"There's no way I will be getting on this *milden!*" Pyros sourly said. "I quite like the ground I stand on!"

"Feeling sentimental, Màgjeur?" Ramalon mocked as he leant over from his horse. Pyros' dissatisfied prune of a face puckered to stone-faced anger, before reluctantly mounting his horse.

"Excellent!" Ronovin said. "Now the moment you've been waiting for! The second round is simple. It's a race!"

Some of the Màgjeurs' eyes lit up, especially Chloen and Allenade who were air Màgjeurs. The summons of air would definitely put those with the affinity at an advantage. The ability to propel one's self would prove a useful tool in a race. Poor Ildrèan, the water Màgjeur being in a race with two of them.

"However, you will not be racing on your Windermares in case you were wondering."

"So what are they for?" Lauru nervously asked.

"Well how else are you going to get up there to the starting ring?"

Lauru's face struck horror which couldn't be hidden with a brave face. Along with the others, they were apprehensive beyond what they had imagined. Not only did they have to confront the idea of a competitive race at a height where most, if not all had never reached before, but also the idea of flying a Windermare into the skies knowing one slight slip of the grasp could all but end their lives. It felt like a task in itself but Ramalon once again found himself growing in confidence. He knew that because of the caring nature of a Windermare and that it was impossible to fall off unless deliberately choosing to. He decided to keep that one to himself.

"They will be taking us high above the city and the clouds, to where you must begin... I hope none of you are afraid of heights."

Unfortunately for Ramalon, Pyros didn't seem scared one bit. Neither did Alleremsah who confidently straddled his horse like a Brackbannen knight. Reigning it with one hand to back up his smug look. Typical.

"Indeed you will start from the peak of our atmosphere where you will all need to produce some type of air preservation to keep you breathing. We assume you all know how by this point. If not, we'll be asking questions as to how you made it this far." A few nervous laughs were heard. "It's simple. First one to the bottom wins!"

"It's that simple?" Peter Palgan asked.

"Well. The simplicity of such a task is, of course, subjective. As visibility today is poor we have organised the orbs of water to be in aplenty on your journeys for our entertainment, best try to ignore them. Any questions? Yes, Xjaques."

"Without stating the obvious. Once we get to the bottom and for me, celebrating my win, how would I avoid smacking into the ground?"

"The winner will be the one who passes through and into the stadium first. Upon which point you will be slowed down by members of The Magikai for your safety."

"And if we miss the stadium?"

"Why would you do that? Next question."

"Can we still use our protecy to harm others?" Lazabeth asked.

"Of course! What good would this tournament be without you all showing off your amazing talents in your own unique, destructive and clever ways?" Ronovin sensed the tension among everyone grew to a point where any further questions would just be more awkward. "Without further hesitation. See you up there!"

He raised his arms and the herd of mildens started to clomp their hooves on the slabs leading up to the main building as they prepared their ascent.

"Hold on tight!" Ramalon leaned in with a smile to Pyros once more as his horse set off.

With a scowl, Pyros leaned into the back of his horse's neck gripping the mane tightly, clearly unaware that he couldn't fall off. Another small victory.

And just like that Ramalon's Windermare was first to go and found a runway of patio for it to blend quickly into a gallop. The growing coolness of air skimmed his cheeks as moisture squeezed from his eyes. The sheer power of his horse was extraordinary to him. Adrenaline burned through his veins as the speed grew, wondering how much faster they could go. As the runway came to an end the milden dipped before leaping into the air, spreading its wings as he ascended well above the ground and over The Skyurch walls. His weight sinking ever heavier into the milden's back but knowing it was more than strong enough to take his weight. The confidence he found allowed him to indulge a little in the view over the city before slowly fading, heading into the grey mist of the nubes.

The solemn moment of peace amidst the clouds. A tranquil. Beautiful stillness. The freedom of flight. He felt free. Free from the chains of society. Detached. A place Ramalon felt deeply accepted. Alone. For some reason, he marvelled in the feeling of isolation. An individual flying into the lonely sky. As the grey clouds faded, a feeling that he was in his element came to the fore of his mind. He gazed upon the white of the moon. The lonely moon. Not a brother in sight. Companionless, but full of wonder and misunderstanding. In this moment he could not understand how under-appreciated the moon was to him. Ramalon could not hide the similarities. Companionless. Alone.

He only just grasped how high up he was. The sense of vertigo started to kick in. So high was he that the blue sky above the separating clouds had started to turn dark, allowing the speckles of the stars to become more apparent. The curve of the world was in full view. The clouds below shrouded most of Terrasendia, but they dissipated northwards to the lands of Rolgan and the south in The

Gracelands. The seas and islands off land made Ramalon feel in awe of the beauty the world of Rèo had to offer. So in awe was he, he had almost forgotten about the terrifying drop below - almost.

The other competitors cleared from the grey clouds below. Everyone seemed like they were getting the hang of it, bar a few. The air thinned dramatically the higher they got, and Ramalon produced a bubble which wrapped itself around the top of his nose to his chin, allowing him to breathe easier. A bubble could typically last a couple of hours before he would need to replenish. All of the other competitors followed suit.

Very shortly afterwards Ramalon could see ahead of him a circular ring made of stone, floating in the sky. Ronovin overtook Ramalon as they approached the halo in the sky and he was first to land on the wide ring which was half the size of the stadium below in diameter. The Windermare adjusted its wings to slow them down before the smoothest of landings onto the stone. The sound of hooves clopping was heard as the gallop turned into a canter on the circular runway, before slowing to a light trot.

Everyone followed suit and Ramalon saw how struck in confidence the rest were. Lauru was shaking like a leaf, probably from the dramatic drop in temperature. Xjaques Croller closed his eyes, still clinging to his horse while others weren't too bad. Ramalon however, felt empowered. He was ready. The cold was indeed terrible. The icy bite started to eat away at everyone's insides. Their robes started to crunch as the sheer frost crumpled the fabric. Luckily everyone's cloaks were lined with pyrovines on the inside to keep them warm.

Ronovin invited everyone to step off their horses while he remained mounted. Also meeting everyone up there was the regal Màgjeur Anelene still on her Windermare. As they all shivered off, the mildens galloped and jumped off into the middle of the circular stone, spreading their wings on their descent and out of sight into the white and grey of the clouds below.

"Let's not wait. We shall go in the order that your groups were called out. Once one race has finished, the next one will immediately begin. Good luck! Lauru, Rybon and Lazabeth, please find an area around the ring. You will go on Anelene's mark."

As they found a space Ramalon looked into the ring down below and saw the orbs floating aplenty. He knew the whole city was watching.

"Contestants are you ready?"

Ramalon felt nervous for them. The first ones up. The torture was incredible. The drop struck fear, which was barbaric. The anxiety of free falling took everyone's stomachs away and replaced it with an almighty black hole. None of them looked confident as they crouched over the rim, preparing to dive. They struck determined faces to hide their utter horror. The tension, stress and pressure of the games could not hide the notion of how fragile life was. Anelene raised her hand and held it there while the three took a massive deep breath in. Everyone else just stood in awe as to how tense this was. A knife cutting into everyone's soul as they were powerless to stop. She seemed to enjoy making them wait. Who was bravest? Who was mentally strongest?

"GO!" Anelene lowered her hand.

"NOOOOO!" Lauru wailed as Lazabeth and Rybon nose-dived straight into the abyss!

She cried profusely as the fright and horror got the better of her crumbling to the floor of the ring. Her sobs of defeat were understandable, given the fragility of life. She would not take part in the race. Below they could see in the clouds flashes of lightning and fire, as Lazabeth and Rybon were trying to take one another out on route to the bottom. And then nothing.

The wait was killing the rest of the competitors. Ramalon wondered who had won the race. Ronovin meanwhile went over to Lauru and comforted her as a Windermare came and escorted her safely back to the city.

"Right, next up! Allenade, Chloen and Ildreàn. Please, find a space along the ring." Ronovin still keeping formal and regiment in his demeanour.

Ramalon struggled to watch. He was preparing his own mind for the race ahead. He distracted himself by reminding himself of the calm and ambience of the journey up, which held despite the nerves. He knew Ildreàn stood no chance against the two air Màgjeurs as Ronovin set them off. All three descended into the chaos that ensued. Ramalon noticed that the clouds had gotten considerably darker since the first two went down. Most likely because Lazabeth used some form of lightning to help her down, which disturbed them. Six down. Six to go.

"Next three up you come!"

Enzo, Xjaques and Peter Palgan formed around the circle, and they set off once more… Until there were three. He felt the clouds would help Enzo expel his lighting just like Lazabeth. He tried to snap out of his mind racing a million miles an hour before the nervous wait was over.

"And to our last three. You're up!"

As his name was called out, his heart began to race. Ramalon took a step forward before Pyros cut him up by walking in front of him.

"You've had your fun and games. Now let the big boys play!" Pyros said as he walked backwards and away from Ramalon.

He tried to refocus himself and muster the courage, conjuring the bravery. He stood on the very edge of the stone. His toes hanging off the edge. The terror of the fall was too much, even for Ramalon. He looked up to try and distract himself from his fright. Momentarily, he thought it wasn't too late to back down and not go like Lauru, but then he quickly snapped back to remind himself that this was what he wanted. He looked at Pyros and Allaremsah who were staring intensely at each other. Both assuming the battle was between them only. Ramalon closed his eyes and they crunched shut amid the freeze. He took a breath and felt the fire within him starting to furnace. He was ready. Anelene raised her hand, and Ramalon peered into what felt like the gates of The Understunde.

"GO!"

All three leapt off with a powerful thrust, leaving the ghost of their souls behind.

The force of gravity was immense. Amid the horror, Ramalon used it to focus. He found himself trailing the others as Allaremsah fired several lightning bolts towards the second-placed Pyros, missing its target as it zigzagged towards him. Pyros replied with a few fireballs of his own, which Allaremsah evaded as he exploded lightning bursts between his hand and bolts from the clouds to propel him in different directions. It almost felt like a two-horse race within the dark surroundings. Ramalon chose to build up his own fire in preparation to go for Pyros. But before he could release, Pyros sneakily aimed his attack at Ramalon as he started to spray his fire into him. The rippling of wind made the blows dissipate and scatter before missing his target.

It was then that he realised just how far behind he was, and despite firing a few fireballs towards the other two, he started to understand every time he did that he slowed down dramatically. He needed to change things up, either by landing one of his blows or speeding up considerably, or the race was going to be over before he knew it. He couldn't let that happen, not while he had enough fight within him... But he was running out of time to make his move. The black of the clouds became fainter until they cleared to reveal the full view of the city below. He still had some way to go until he got to the stadium. It gave him hope, despite his confidence waning.

Suddenly he realised the other two had knocked one another out temporarily with their spells leaving them afloat and slowing down. Ramalon continued to conjure fire with his right hand pointing towards the sky, which gained even more momentum as he sped towards the bottom. He overtook the dazzled duo as Pyros came to. Ramalon was winning. He was in the position he wanted and now all he had to do was deflect incoming attacks which would increase his descent.

"Come on hit me!!!" Ramalon urged, seemingly giving him an open target to his chest.

Pyros accepted the invitation and released a mighty spread of continuous fire which Ramalon warded off with his own firewall. Pyros' protecy was much stronger than Ramalon's. The only thing he had going for him was the fact that if he could hold it for another minute, he would be sailing into that arena in first place. There was nothing Pyros could do except hope that increasing his protecy would overcome Ramalon's shield and knock him out. But in doing so, he would be sending Ramalon further away from him. He was so close. Ramalon gasped as the fires burst his air bubble which was no longer needed. The burning pain in his arms was becoming more apparent, but the more he fell, the more determined he became. The more he could picture himself in the final round. This was it. He was going to win.

Suddenly a flash of white light hit Ramalon straight in the chest as the shocks rippled violently through his body. Allaremsah's blow had landed successfully. So violent was the bolt, it knocked Ramalon way off course and away from Pyros' fires as he saw the other two resume their duel to the bottom. As Ramalon was not earthed, the shock had only dazed him, but it was enough to cause considerable damage to Ramalon's body and mind.

There was hardly anything left of Ramalon to fight back as he started to accept his fate. Just like that in a single moment, he was going to lose. His dreams were fading as he drifted lifelessly. Spent and defeated, he resigned himself to the beautiful freedom he was experiencing at the end, as he veered back on course. He closed his eyes to fully enjoy the freedom of flight. He felt angry and sad as the emotions started to take over, which somehow empowered him – refuelling the fires within him. They were too far ahead, he thought to himself. There was no way...

When Ramalon opened his eyes once more, he noticed something very strange below. A fire. A blast which encapsulated both Pyros and Allaremsah.

"What in Rolgan is that!?"

Pyros did not cause it. It didn't look like his particular signature of fire. He could not understand the nature of that fire as it whirled around them in a very specific and malicious way, striking them and causing them both intense and severe pain. Whatever it was, whatever had happened to them both... They were no longer conscious. Free falling uncontrollably.

Ramalon's eyes lit up with opportunity. Angered by his stupidity that he gave up too soon, he used the power he was experiencing through his emotions to charge up his protecy, which happened more quickly and more powerfully than Ramalon could have ever imagined. Even more so than what happened in the first round with Pierro. It channelled through his whole body much more intensely that time to the point where even his eyes lit up with the internal inferno passing through him.

"WHAT! IS HAPPENING! TO MEEEEE!!??" Ramalon screamed through clenched teeth as the feeling was so strong.

He channelled his protecy of fire through both hands and suddenly an explosion of fire blasted from Ramalon's feet as he rocketed down from the sky!

White, red and orange trails of the fire were left behind him as he aimed to catch up to the other two who were still so far below him that they could still win despite their unconscious state. The speed at which he was descending was so unimaginably fast he felt he could pass out. The land was no longer circular to him and became more flat, telling Ramalon just how close he was. The oval shape of the stadium was perhaps only half a mile away, and he could not care anymore for his safety.

Whatever was happening to him, whatever he was experiencing was certainly not right. That amount of power should not belong to anyone. It was not from this world. He couldn't quite put his finger on it, the exact feeling that it was. It was almost like he was...

"Invincible," he said aloud before intensifying the emotions and heat, making him fall even faster toward the stadium. Through awe and wonder, Ramalon risked his life to not only get there before the other two but also to enjoy this incredible feeling. He didn't know whether this power scared or excited him. But perhaps more frightening to him… He didn't want it to stop.

He was unsure that he was going to beat the other two so gave it one last pulse of power to his absolute max.

"AHHHHHHHHHHH!!!" Ramalon screamed like a primal animal.

The rim of the stadium was within a few hundred metres and he was on the coattails of the other two. The last hundred metres lasted a mere second which seemed to last forever. He wondered how on Terrasendia anyone was going to be able to slow him down safely. He noticed the many Màgjeurs in the middle of the stadium, ready to slow them down and control their landing. The sounds of the crowd were heard, in awe and excitement of anticipating who would win. In that brief moment, Ramalon felt exhausted but still pushed as hard as he could. The finish line was right in front of him. He was so close to the other two. He drew in one last breath in the final moment, before suddenly he could feel no more, see no more, hear no more. The fright was no longer as the darkness took his mind. And then nothing…

The quiet sound of cheers and rapturous applause gently grew louder as a thudding pain in Ramalon's back became more apparent. He was surrounded by members of The Magikai dressed in their dangly brown robes as they helped him regain his consciousness. He noticed they were also tending to their own as they had clearly been affected by stopping Ramalon's flight. He was coming round from being completely wiped out himself. The blackout seemed to last an age. When his mind and body started to swim back to the surface of consciousness, he only had one thing on his mind as he asked the closest Màgjeur.

"Did I win?" Ramalon panted.

"Win!?" An older and much greyer Màgjeur rhetorically asked. "I have never seen such astonishment!"

"Màgjeurs and all on Mages Wreath." The voice of Anelene was heard as it echoed throughout the stadium. "I give you your final winner. Màgjeur Ramalon!"

Even more cheers and chants erupted the arena. Cries of *"Ramalon! Ramalon! Ramalon!"* were heard around the arena.

"I won!?" Ramalon couldn't quite believe it. He had passed Pyros and Allaremsah and he was going through to the last round of the Màgjeurs Open. The elation, the euphoria, the relief he felt was so true to him. Assisted by members of The Magikai to stand, they allowed him to appreciate the applause in the middle of the stadium for everyone to see.

He couldn't explain how happy he has. He was the fan favourite. Against all the odds, the underdog was going through to the last round. While nursing his arm which was severely burnt from his warding shield, he waved his hand gently to the crowds in acknowledgement and appreciation of what they were giving him. The greatest and most magical feeling was felt, before he was escorted through the stadium exit.

As he exited the arena, the other competitors were all gathered in a large room. Medimages were attending them all as they examined both their physical and mental state after the event. He could tell how much of a rollercoaster ride this was for everyone involved. Ramalon wasn't too bothered at this point who else had won. Still shocked at the whole event he tried to process how on earth he was in the final.

Pyros and Allaremsah were both unconscious and only they could have known what harmed them. The questions aiming towards Ramalon by the other competitors were how did he manage to attack them from being so far back? He had no answers, only sheepish looks and downward stares.

How could they both have lost so stunningly? But when Ramalon started to think about it more and more, the alarm bells began to ring, and he knew exactly what it was that attacked them. After being given the all clear from the Medimage he marched straight over to The Opey Deary with the looming realisation with what he felt he had to do.

The Charzeryx had to be destroyed.

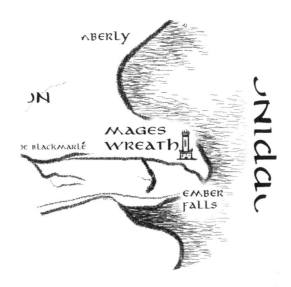

The Repercussion

Ramalon made his way through some of the quieter streets to speed up his march to The Opey Deary. The sting in his burnt arm fuelled his anger further. Angry that the students had completely ignored him. Somehow Arinane managed to attack Pyros and Allaremsah, allowing him to win. Not at all what he intended when he agreed to take them under his wing. He was in constant fear that when they both woke up, they would tell The Magikai and his position in the final would be under threat.

He scanned the torch lit basement beneath The Opey Deary to find it was deserted. He didn't know why, but he couldn't control his anger. He felt impulsive. Impatient. He wondered for a brief moment how long he would have to wait before quickly seizing the moment. He needed to see his students immediately.

He closed his eyes and opened up the connection between him and Arinane. He felt the flow of energy through his body as he latched onto the Charzeryx's movements, wherever it was, controlling them for the first time as he summoned him.

It wasn't too long before he could hear its typical flittering wings fly down into the room. As he opened his eyes, its small bat-like shadows flickered around the room. Ramalon started to feel sudden darkness in its existence. A feeling that something wasn't quite right.

As it landed on the pedestal, it beamed its cheeky smile to its owner. His love for the smaller things overwhelmed his conflicting thoughts. He looked upon its wide circular eyes and found it very difficult to imagine its destruction. A war in his mind raged on.

The voices of Corey and Lenk were heard above. As they ran down into the room, both were jubilant on their approach. Cleverson was trailing behind as usual not looking as happy.

"That was amazing, Màgjeur!"

"You did it!"

"What were you all thinking!?" Ramalon barked. His voice started to shake in an attempt to suppress his growing anger. "Do you have any idea what you have done!?"

"Calm down Màgj-"

"DO NOT TELL ME TO CALM DOWN! You are boys! Living in a dream world! Full of fantasy!!"

"Is that so?" Corey smirked. "Then what are you doing teaching us?"

"You are so ungrateful!" Lenk spat. "Without us, you would have lost! Where would your dreams and fantasy be then?"

"Do not test me!"

"Is that a threat?"

"We mustn't scare the finalist of The Màgjeurs Open, Lenk," Corey jibed. "He might blow raspberries at us and expect us to fall."

Ramalon did not expect to be insulted this way. However, it was not in his nature to fight back, despite the growing rage inside his mind, which felt new to him. He just observed the naivety of the two students. Even though they couldn't control it directly, they still had the means to influence its behaviour and somehow told Arinane to attack.

"I don't think you understand the situation. Màgjeur," Lenk smirked.

"We own you right now! Imagine what would happen if our tongue just so happened to slip to The Magikai…"

Ramalon could not believe what he was hearing. Was this their plan all along, he thought? This time his rage could not be suppressed. He needed to release his emotions, his anger, and his despicable hatred of the two monstrous young minds.

All of a sudden, his ability to control the surge of emotions crumbled entirely. An almighty charge festered within his body. It felt strangely familiar to The Protecy even though he could not recognise the intense feeling.

To everyone's surprise, the Charzeryx on the pedestal started to behave strangely. As if it was in pain. Its skinny wings snipped and cracked as its elegant neck started to crick and protrude. Its innocent wails were heart-breaking to hear as it shrieked, especially for Cleverson who rushed straight over to Arinane.

"What's happening to him!?" Cleverson shook as everyone's attention drew to it except Ramalon's, whose anger continued to manifest towards Corey and Lenk.

He almost felt embarrassed that kids so young had threatened him, which turned into hatred. He never felt so far away from himself than at that moment. It didn't feel like him, but he couldn't stop the surge of anger.

"MAKE IT STOP! MAKE IT STOP! PLEASE!" Cleverson's desperate voice grew higher in pitch. Ramalon didn't stop.

He couldn't. But more frighteningly to Ramalon, he thought that even if he could, his anger that was almost certainly the reason for Arinane's torture, he wasn't sure that he would. That similar feeling of power hooked and plunged him into poisonous addiction. He didn't even spare a thought for the love he had for the smaller things.

"MÀGJEUR!!" Corey shouted. "We're sorry!!! Just stop!"

But before he could accept any apology, the contortion of Arinane suddenly started to make the dragon's limbs grow rapidly. The sounds of stretching and cracking were heard as flakes of its scaly skin dropped off. The bones of its skinny wings started to thicken up before the sails of its wings grew to almost four times the size. Its body bulged even bigger to the size of Ramalon. Its tread on the sandy floor was much heavier as it found its larger and bulkier feet land onto the surface while its longer tail became sharper at the end. But most uncharacteristically, its neck grew much longer and almost snake-like, which looked out of proportion compared to its body. The cute circular eyes it once bore, turned sharper at the sides like an almond, serpent-like. The cheeky smile however, was still there although it was no longer cute. Instead, it was more sinister and wicked. No longer in pain through its growth and transformation to what appeared to be its adolescent phase, but still experienced discomfort as Ramalon's trance continued.

The students looked on in horror before Arinane stood at Ramalon's side and stared upon the students with its nostrils flared. They dared not move or speak, looking on, petrified. Finally, Ramalon managed to regain control of his emotions before a calmness radiated from both Ramalon and Arinane. He closed his eyes as he regained his regular breathing pattern.

"… Whoa," Ramalon panted.

"… Okay. What The Blessèd just happened?" Lenk slowly said.

Ramalon couldn't quite believe what had just happened either. He didn't even know it could happen. The Charzeryx's growth was undoubtedly down to Ramalon's anger, fuelling the connection, but for the life of him he couldn't figure out why it had happened. It was…

"Unnatural," he quietly said to himself.

Arinane turned its back on everyone to reveal its bony spine as it disappeared into the darkness of the underground hall.

"Are you okay?" Cleverson asked Ramalon.

The others did not have the bravery to move, let alone converse. Even they had enough brain cells between them to know they had triggered the events which shocked them all.

"Actually. I am… I've never been more okay in my entire life."

"Do you feel okay?" Cleverson asked, wanting to make sure it was still him that was talking.

"Yes - I mean… I'm not sure. Maybe, I don't know."

That invincible feeling once more made Ramalon's heart beat harder, but not faster. He had calmed down enough to know that if he were honest, it would scare them. He gazed toward Corey and Lenk.

"We're really sorry! We didn't mean to go that far!"

"Please! We won't do it again, we swear!"

"Please just don't hurt us."

Their pathetic squeals of apologies hardly registered to Ramalon as some of the anger carried over. He said nothing, instead just bearing down his gaze onto them as they continued to sob and grovel.

"Hear this," Ramalon slowly enforced. To which they nodded their heads in horrified silence. "If you ever threaten me again… Your end will come. To my liking. In fire. In burning blood. In. Your. Death!"

Cleverson's life left through his eyes, terror-stricken as he looked at Ramalon. Even more scared than the other two whose tears drenched their faces. Ramalon's eyes squeezed shut.

What did I just say?" he thought. He relaxed his gaze as he saw he was clearly distressing everyone which didn't sit right with him. Something had taken over him. A disturbing malice invaded his mind.

Was it his addiction to his newly found power? Did he want it? Did he enjoy it? He had no idea what was happening to him.

"Be here. Tomorrow. After hours," he said, backing out and up the steps, disbelief at what had just occurred.

He had never been so unsure of his life than at that moment. Uncertain because of how he felt so alive and at home with such strong emotion. He left his petrified students to quiver as he marched straight to The Skyurch once more to find out just what on Terrasendia was happening to him. But he felt something entirely new which came to him on his travel, utterly scaring him... A love, for this power.

"A surge?" Davinor enquired, as Ramalon explained the feelings he experienced during the second round. He dared not tell him of the events with Arinane as he was never to know.

"Yes. I have no idea why, but it came to me when I needed it most."

"It is not the first time either. Similar to when you faced Pierro?"

"Yes. Very similar. Although much stronger. More powerful. I felt the connection much smoother this time. I don't know why."

"That is because I purified part of your stone for you. That would make sense to me."

"And to me. But what really is happening to me?"

"I sense worry in you?"

"Yes. More importantly... I'm frightened."

"Frightened? What of?"

"Myself. And what I'm capable of."

Davinor's mood shifted into something more uncharacteristic of him. He started to speak with a little more care.

"What's brought this on? I would have thought this much power would make you happier."

"We both know you're wiser than that, my lord." Davinor cocked his head as he was right. "I feel frightened because I don't know if I can control it."

"Has there been something that has triggered this?"

"... No," Ramalon lied. "But when the connection goes into that state, it's hard to control."

"I see. I need to teach you how to control it."

"No!" He started to shake his head, gradually getting more frantic.

"No?"

"I don't want it anymore. I don't want it, please! Just-just make it go away."

"Ramalon," Davinor soothed, "you're scared. I can understand that."

"No, you can't! You really can't, no one can!"

"If you just let me - "

" - Do what!? Teach me how to control it? You seem to know more than me if you think you can help me control whatever this is! If that's the case, then you're going back on our agreement! If you really are keeping to your word, then how can you help!?"

He could tell his outburst made Davinor uncomfortable. Continually trying to get a word in but failing as Ramalon continued the barrage.

"You can't change my mind on this. It's over! I don't want to do this anymore."

"What if I helped you harness this power?"

"It's the same thing!" his reckless responses almost became shouts of desperation. "You have no idea what it's doing to me. I'm not myself, it's not right, and with the greatest respect my lord, you have no right to force me to do this any longer. I am sorry for wasting your time."

Davinor's expression hardly changed. But Ramalon could sense he was deeply disappointed in his decision.

"I take my leave."

It took him several moments to actually turn his back on The Blessèd Mage and walk away. He felt nervous as he turned his back. Half expecting a bolt of lightning to stab him in the back as that was Davinor's chosen affinity.

"Ramalon," Davinor called. He turned to see Davinor return to his impressive chair, looking relatively relaxed. "You might want to reconsider your decision."

"I'm sorry my mind's made up."

"That wasn't a proposal," he said with a hint of malice.

"What are you talking about?"

"We will continue our little agreement as planned."

"Or what?"

"Or I will have you compelled to live out the rest of your days in the bards of Lathapràcère..."

Ramalon felt like his ghost just left him. A sheet of heat surfaced in his face. The threat of imprisonment for once scared him.

"Do you take me for some Elcarian fool!? To think you could have outsmarted me. Davinor, The Blessèd Mage of Protecy. Outsmarted by a Màgjeur from the slums!"

"I don't know what you mean."

"DON'T MAKE A FOOL OF ME! You and that Charzeryx have disgusted the term, Màgjeur!" Ramalon's heart sank. He had no chance of denying it. "Conjuration yes? Dark. Very dark!"

"How do you know?"

"There's a lot more to your stone than I thought. Somehow I could sense there was something else at work here. Which led me to your little excursions with this creature."

Ramalon searched his robes for the stone which he brought with him but was now no longer there. His search became more frantic before noticing his stone was now in Davinor's grasp.

"Give it back," he pleaded. Davinor gently caressed the stone with his fingers in the palm of his hand, contemplating what to do next. He had carefully stolen it upon entering the room using the most seamless of magic. Ramalon noticed a sense of possession in his eyes. Almost a look of greed and wonder.

"Please."

"No," Davinor quietly said.

"You must."

"Listen here. And listen well. You will leave our agreement in place. We will pretend this conversation never happened. And you will never mention this to anyone."

"Please, please! I do not want to do this anymore."

"That is unfortunate."

"Why are you doing this?"

"Because I can!" Davinor's intensity rose even higher. His stare became more deliberate and cold as Ramalon felt trapped. "This is a truly exceptional scenario. The study on your stone could unravel things we never knew about The Protecy. I will not risk the study being ruined by your inability to hold it together. You will not mention this to anyone, or I will make your life truly not worth living. That I assure you. I couldn't care less that this is too *hard* for you! All I care about are answers. You should be thanking me. A Màgjeur, who hasn't even got their wreath, being in the same room, let alone being able to talk with the great Davinor!"

Ramalon couldn't decide whether he was distraught or angry at the entrapment he was now under. He didn't have a choice. If he didn't continue, he was worried what his life would become in prison. But the alternative, being the continuation and exposure of that poison was, to him, equally as terrifying.

As Davinor continued to barrage him with terms, his voice was reduced to a blur as the emotions started to rise once more and take over him. The toxins began to bleed into his mind as the poison took over. A hatred. An evil in its early stages, manifesting again. Building to a point where he was struggling to contain the surge. It appeared that Davinor was unaware of the growing power burning within. With his protecy of fire secretly charging, full of malice and ready to unleash onto The Blessèd Mage.

Suddenly, Davinor dropped the stone as if it had burned him. Davinor's eyes connected with Ramalon's fiery gaze and he realised what was taking place before him.

Ramalon looked at him with eyes that could pierce skin. A sharpness that he was hoping would rip him to shreds. He wanted nothing more in that moment for his eyes to burn, for his ripped skin to melt, for his bones to incinerate. He wanted his screams at the top of the tower to echo for all to hear. All the while somehow keeping him alive for as long as possible to preserve the pain of torture. It terrified him. That imagination. The addiction. The invincibility.

The intensity of the charged atmosphere caused every window to shatter into thousands of pieces. Colourful glass shards whirled and circled Ramalon and more noticeably to them both, the stone on the floor too.

"MÀGJEUR!" Davinor forcefully said, now standing and fully aware of Ramalon's intentions. Ramalon's hand slowly raised toward him to release the build-up of fire "You must resist!"

"I CAN'T!!"

"YOU MUST!"

"THAT STONE IS EVIL! IT'S CURSED!!!"

"IT'S NOT THE STONE! IT'S YOU!!"

All he wanted to do was thrust every shard of broken glass into the heart of The Blessèd Mage. Davinor readied his own ward to fend off the danger. As soon as Ramalon made up his mind to unleash, the shrieking sound of Arinane was heard in the distance. Ramalon's mind turned to flashes of the Charzeryx. His charge was still high, but the pressure was no longer building. He was about to unleash once more but stopped when he heard the dragon again, this time much louder. Before he could recharge again, Arinane entered the room with its purple and black sails trailing behind, circling as it flew with more guile. It landed at Ramalon's side and looked up at its master with those sinister almond-shaped black eyes. Almost as quickly as it appeared, the urge to strike Davinor faded and faded until the charge finally died.

Ramalon closed his eyes to refocus on his breathing. Arinane made him remember the things that mattered to him. The smaller things in life. He'd brought him back to reality amid the intensity of what just happened. He continued to picture the happiness he had shared with everything he held dear. Arinane, his paper dragons, The Opey Deary, his rose teas.

He opened his eyes. The shards of glass did not disband. Instead, they orbited around Ramalon and the stone very slowly. Glittering and sparkling, twinkling like a constellation of galaxies mid-air, until he completely relaxed. Exhausted. The glass started to gradually descend onto the stone floor, like feathers floating down to the ground, gently clinking when they hit.

"What is happening to me!?" he thought as he looked passed the floating shards to see Davinor. His face full of anger and hatred. Ramalon had resumed back to his usual self.

"You are unstable," Davinor said.

"I am."

"Do you realise the repercussions of your actions?"

"I didn't strike you."

"No. Fortunately for you. But the fact you cannot control your protecy is of great concern to me."

"Please. Please. You cannot make me do this any longer."

"Unfortunately for you. I can. However… I offer you an alternative. One which would make your problem go away. You must sever your connection with the stone. And give it to me."

"What!?" Ramalon gasped. "But you only get one connection as a Màgjeur. Once you break the connection, you cannot go back. I will lose everything."

"… I know."

Ramalon couldn't quite believe the alternative. It would mean the poison of this stone would surely go, but he would never again be able to use his protecy again. He looked at Arinane as he gently spread his wings and flew out of the room, sweeping glass around the room as he flew into the sky.

"This is the only way you can escape. It is a sacrifice. But one which you need to weigh up."

"But Arinane will still survive, yes?"

"I fear it might not."

Ramalon became worried. Which was worse? Continuing to delve into this black hole or risk losing Arinane and the future use of protecy forever? He started to realise a new found fight in him, which wasn't there before.

"I will not sever the connection." His dejected words made Davinor breathe in a sigh of relief through the nose. "We will continue as planned," he resigned.

"Fine. We shall forget this ever happened."

"Yes."

"Also. That beast of yours is to be destroyed."

Ramalon's heart sunk further. Having just made a conscious choice to keep Arinane alive, he was now being asked to do what felt impossible for him.

"My lord. Please no."

"You must."

"I cannot. It will go against everything in my nature."

"You can Màgjeur. And you will. You will disband your connection and incinerate its carcass! Or you leave me no choice but to do it myself. Much better for that bat to go on your terms rather than mine I assure you, don't you think?"

Ramalon did not answer. The term *bat* irked him. But he didn't have a choice. Instead of answering, he reluctantly nodded his head. Heartbroken. Knowing deep within himself, he had to do it.

"Good. I will trust you to see it through on your terms. Do I have your word?"

"Yes," Ramalon whispered

"Do I have your-"

"YES!" Ramalon barked. That familiar icy silence ensued once more glared at each other.

"Go now!"

Ramalon turned to go down the steps, leaving the stone with Davinor once more.

"Màgjeur!?… You ever threaten me again. It will be your last breath, I assure you."

Ramalon finally turned and walked down the steps. The final image he saw was the deep fright in Davinor's eyes as he threatened him… It didn't look convincing.

"Is he frightened of me?" he thought.

A question he asked himself over and over again when he finally sat down in his armchair in front of his fire. The only thing he could think of was how he could muster the courage to kill Arinane forever. He pictured many ways of doing it and how grotesque, and horrible following it through would prove. He just couldn't do it. Thinking of alternatives and how to get around it the best way he could.

His eyes stared into the fires of his hearth like every night before. As they grew heavier and heavier, they squeezed shut, wishing he knew what on Terrasendia he was going to do.

Tales Unfold

A few weeks had passed since Alicèn had heard anything from Hiyaro. Their own investigation into Razing Gellows put him on edge, hoping that they would find something that would vindicate his fears and hopefully release him from what he felt was a stupendous restriction.

He barely spoke as he continued to explore The Reinhault. He stayed mainly near the peak of the mountain but consistently received hidden urges to venture and invest his time with the Màgjeurs in that cave. Only respect and honour for Septalia's ancestors stopped him from going and learning about magic, which he did not believe in.

Only in the last few days did he join in and spar with some of the warriors using wooden swords. He was stunned at not only how quick they were, but how sharp their minds were at reading certain moves. It infuriated him even more so than he was already, as they took turns to take him apart. They did so with pure dignity and not a smile on their face. It seemed to him that they didn't take pride in making another feel small, instead relishing in the self-pride of beating another, always learning as they went.

He tried to think of ways he could escape. Could he slip off into the night when no one was looking? What happened to Deonrick and the rest of his band? He still could not believe that he would be there for two years. Nevertheless, the acceptance got easier as time went on. He did indeed begin to understand the purpose of the place and he secretly admired the dedication the warriors took in their work. Inner strength and spiritual guidance seemed to be the heartbeat of the entire place.

Inside his chambers were several popular books and parchments. *'The Tales of Cèrean and The Understunde,'* a man so evil that Sarthanzar, the mythical god of The Understunde threw him back out. *'A Rivalry in Perpetuity,'* the book delved deeper into Felder and Melcelore's rivalry. But the one that did strike his mind was one he had never seen before by an author, Elver Susmees, *'Tales of The Ancient Drethai.'*

He heard stories about Susmees and how he came to such detailed knowledge of these spirits which have haunted Terrasendia. Nevertheless, he was compelled to read it, sliding the book out while sitting on his bed. The spine crunched slightly upon opening as it was clear it had not been opened for some time. It was not a very large book but contained many diagrams and illustrations alongside very detailed descriptions.

On the first page, before detailed explanations of each thirteen members of The Ancient Drethai with several pages dedicated to each of them, there was an overview of their existence:

'Deceit. Knowledge. Masters. Seldom would you find a greater foe in the collective members of The Ancient Drethai. Residing in Drethai Halls their home haunts the northern scape of The Farrowdawns. Each member focusing on a single path of not only magic but also concepts to enrich themselves in the one thing they desire above all. Power. Not just in power itself, but also knowledge and the benefits it brings. They possess the art of clairvoyance. The magical ability to see things which have happened both past and present. However, their main desire of the art of true clairvoyance alludes them - the ability to see the future. That power to the knowledge on Rèo lies with only two on this world. Together with all their expertise combined, none would have the courage to challenge them... None but one.'

Alicèn couldn't help but try and link his theory of The Dragadelf with The Ancient Drethai. Could it be them who somehow ascertained the power of the Dragadelf? It made sense to him, the more he thought about it. If they desired power above all else, there was nothing more significant than The Dragadelf. The only question is, how? He turned the page:

'The Drethai were once great Princes and Princesses of Royal families. Many years ago, before The Dragastone and the construction of The Dragasphere, Melcelore, once a friend to Felder in the very early days decided in secret to forge a mighty council, made up of royal bloods to avenge the pain he once received from Felder. He offered the young monarchs promise of overwhelming power should they help him which most of his recruits accepted, fully aware of their treasonous choices. They were powerful in themselves, but their younger minds were turned from what they knew was right to the poison of Melcelore's promise.

After swearing their loyalty and fealty to Melcelore, he gave them a home for themselves - Drethai Halls to enhance their work and enrich in all powers. Over time their bodies became shadows due to the darkness of their work, and by this point, they were banished and declared enemies of Terrasendia which angered them. Outcasts. Rejects.

However, one day, Melcelore saw an opportunity for himself once more. He betrayed the loyalty of his newly acquired protégé's and attempted to steal their powers for himself. But over time The Drethai had built up their own resistance in secret. Melcelore took on all members of The Drethai in a gripping battle in Drethai Halls. Melcelore prevailed against the thirteen members he had ascertained but was not considered a victory. Upon their defeat, they collectively were strong enough to cast a spell of preservation. The conditions of the spell were that every member of The Drethai's souls would be preserved and impossible for Melcelore to touch and galvanise their power for himself. In exchange, their bodies would become a shadow for all eternity. Such dark magic seldom existed. It was unnatural and with utter consequence. It was ancient magic they manifested and was at that moment they declared the name that they would be known for. The Ancient Drethai. They did, however, manage to consulate the sacrifice of this spell by allowing the body and constitution of one of The Ancient Drethai to exist one at a time, forever or until their purposes were fulfilled. When one body dies, another will spawn in its place.

Melcelore felt defeated in victory. He himself desired power above all and was seldom outwitted. In their exile, The Ancient Drethai continued to empower their knowledge of the work they created with Melcelore, mainly focusing on the empowerment of the art of clairvoyance, hoping one day to learn the ultimate goal of true clairvoyance, vowing above all that they would never rest until two purposes were filled. First, the avenging of Melcelore which they were relentless on fulfilling as their ultimate desire. But also to avenge the families who exiled them for making choices they felt they were in their rights to make. As a result, they would wreak havoc and murder onto the *land of Terrasendia in retribution for their unjust exile.'*

Alicèn was gripped at how The Ancient Drethai came to exist, surprised that two evils of such power were each other's sworn enemy. He was equally intrigued with Melcelore, in constant connection with his fear in The Draughts which he created when he was at large. His utter ruthlessness and determination to stop at nothing. No boundaries, no loyalty and above all, no fear to achieve his desire. Alicèn, knew of what happened to Melcelore and with every piece of knowledge ascertained by Terrasendia, was certain that even though he was very much alive, he would never escape from the tombs under Felders Crest. So he kept his primary focus on The Ancient Drethai.

He read on and first up, of course, was Dreanor. The description and pictures were impeccably accurate to his recent experience. It goes on to mention that The Ancient Drethai did not believe in ranks and unequal leadership and to enhance their power collectively, they were all considered equal, bar one. They elected Dreanor to be their King as he was the most prestigious of them all. In addition, they did not believe in building armies to extend their arm of power. Instead, they would conjure Grigorians which were statue-like militants for their dark deeds.

They all changed their royal names when they were banished in defiance of their exile. He read on with compelling interest of the remaining Drethai. Drethain, Dreadath, Dreathitus and Dreazor stuck to the sovereignty and likeliness of their new names while Orbow, Graudling, Orthorn, Donasus, Malumpire, Vamprancer, Karnane and Draxina chose their own based on their desires. A collective of such dark power convinced Alicèn that could be enough to provide a capability to control The Dragadelf.

"Hirotada!" Alicèn called. Still following him around like a loyal dog, he entered his chambers.

"Yes?"

"Are there any books here about The Dragadelf?"

"There are many."

"Many that I have probably read myself. But are there any books or even parchments which would not be anywhere else on this land? I'm talking about knowledge kept only here."

"I believe so, yes. Only one."

"Can you retrieve this for me? Please," he felt a little sheepish to ask. "I am here to *learn* apparently. This is where I want to start."

"I will have to gain permission for you to access such material."

"Do what you have to do."

Hirotada bowed his head and went away. Alicèn stayed in his chambers for about half an hour, contemplating the possibility between The Dragadelf and The Ancient Drethai. Throughout all his years of learning about the evils Septalia was faced with, he was beginning to learn the importance of The Reinhault. If by chance The Ancient Drethai would somehow come to full power, he would ultimately be thankful for their efforts in disbanding... If they were powerful enough themselves of course.

"Durgeon Alicèndil!" Hirotada rushed back. "You have been approved and gained permission to read this."

He presented a small brown book which he could tell was genuine and not copied by forms of magic, the ink was original on the outside which had several parchments stuck to the pages inside.

"'The Arcadelfs.' What on Rèo are they?" Hirotada bowed his head and left once again.

He perched on the end of his bed as he began to read.

'By Max Meigar. The Blessèd Mage of Earth.

Thousands of years ago, in a time before The Protecy, the world of Rèo seldom bled. Its peaceful foundations echoed throughout the lands, the need and want for power was far lesser than the world today. Magic still existed as it always has since the dawn of time. Back then magic was conjured through wands and staffs which over the years faded out since the invention of The Protecy. It is rare in the modern age to find followers to the point they are now named in the common term as 'Wandlers.' Magic then was more to entertain rather than influence. None entertained more so than seven of the most famous transformational Màgjeurs Rèo was blessed to see. The Arcadelfs. People from all over the lands and distant seas voyaged to witness spectacles they performed which wowed the hearts for all eternity.

In the modern age, transformational magic is not so common. There indeed are those who, like 'Wandlers,' still follow its allure and continue the practice. However, back then, many Màgjeurs loved the idea of morphing into animals and different species. All that was needed was a portion of blood from the animal or constitution the Màgjeur wished to transform into, twinned with the magical knowledge learnt over many years and voila! The Màgjeur would have full control over one's newer self and could turn back to their original state at any point.

The Arcadelfs would put on shows in the warmer climates of Rolgan and Terrasendia for all to see, morphing into elephants, horses, lions etc. Their reputation and knowledge got that great they decided to venture deeper into the practice and began to revolutionise between the seven of them how to improve this path of magic.

Over the coming years, they developed ways of splicing two different animals together for them to transform into with some funny effects. For example, they spliced an elephant and a primate together, which turned out to be a hairy elephant!

Some experiments, of course, did not work but they accepted failure just as much as success. They mellowed out the idea of splicing two constitutions together to something simpler and decided to splice their own blood with that of an animal. To their growing amazement, it began to work. They shared their knowledge with the world, and despite the difficulty of mastering the craft, many tried and with some success. The most popular of splices were called 'Mions.' Half man, half lion, giving the man greater strength, faster movements and a more ferocious look. Others tried with insects such as spiders and praying mantises, morphing their arms into sharper tips for their desired use.

Known very much by this point as the celebrities on Rèo for what they gave to the world, they were loved and lauded the accolade, until one day their arm grew too long...

Between the seven of them, they all agreed they wanted to further their knowledge of transformation. And what better way to do it than attempting to splice from a dragon. Many had allayed specific fears over this and over time, they lost their appeal. The people feared that if they could, in essence, become a dragon, they worried what consequence that could have. Despite the realms coming together to dissuade their growing lust for dragon blood, they defied the realms wishes very strongly. As it was not considered illegal, there was nothing Terrasendia could do to stop them, but in the process, they lost all of their love from the people.

Their minds grew darker, and their want for power grew ever deeper. They ventured northeast into Rolgan, up Dragonsnape right to the tip of Dragonsnout where dragons famously lurked. No one sane ventured here. Dragons are indeed possessive creatures. The mere presence of anybody venturing there would be considered a threat to their young.

Somehow, between them, they managed to take down a Drogadera. One of the more elegant and feminine families but no less powerful of dragons. Suddenly in their growing madness and love for desiring power, they stumbled across the idea of splicing the blood of not just one dragon... But several. Their greed had overcome reason, and so between them, they took down a Dralen, a more typical dragon with a tyrannosaurial look and a Charzeryx, a more slender and quicker cousin.

By this point, their madness was beyond control. They all combined the bloods of all three families to create one more powerful version of dragon.

However, they stumbled across a problem in the process. The power was so great to morph into, not even The Arcadelfs had the knowledge to overcome the final hurdle and transform completely. They knew nothing else by this point than to become this legendary power, and with one last idea to transform, they cast the bloods of the dragons into the fires of the biggest volcano on Dragonsnout and together they all fell into the inferno!

Their bodies, bloods and souls boiled, fused and manifested for thousands of years, brewing their strength and building their constitutions in the flames. The world of Rèo over the thousands of years forgot about The Arcadelfs and most believed after their expedition that their efforts in acquiring dragonblood got themselves killed in the process as no one ever saw them again.

Indeed over such wait, the intense fires brought everything together, combining: blood, bodies and souls into the ultimate transformation... The Dragadelf.

However, what they did not see through their insanity was the sacrifice that would take place. A trap they did not foresee. Because of the amount of power their souls and blood now inherited, they could not control it. No longer would they have right over the body they now possessed. Instead, their souls were consumed by the constitution of each Dragadelf as they were born once more, only this time, more fierce, more volatile... and more powerful.

The fires of Dragonsnout provided everything they needed to exist. An additional theory is that perhaps this was what they wanted since the madness set in? Maybe they knew they would never return to their former selves and was happy to live out their days in ultimate legend. It was the only thing on this world they were drawn to... Until one day, a higher power emerged.

Smashing into Felders Crest the twinned phenomenon in what later became known as The Dragastone, spawned these legendary beasts back into the world to utter devastation. Drawn to the only power greater than them, their re-birthing from the furnaces saw the beginning of a dominion Terrasendia heeded to. Rèo was not ready for such mythology crashing into Monarchy Halls and the swarming of The Dragadelf, which in conclusion was why The Dragasphere was created, which is common knowledge.

The Gracelands saw thousands of souls pass into their lands that day. The concealment was complete, and Rèo mourned over their loss. All while The Dragadelf claimed The Dragastone for their own, revelling in its power. Their *possessive nature got the better of them, and despite their unnatural creation, their enhancement of strength was made even more unnatural by the presence of The Dragastone. So much so, that they rely on its presence for their existence. To this point, they are by far the most horrific and terrible creations to ever exist. Their one real purpose now lay entirely with the protection of that stone.'*

He had to lower the book and think about what he has just discovered. His breath felt heavy while his mind rained with a number of possibilities. How The Dragadelf were born was not common knowledge even to Alicèn and all his years of studying the constitutions and makeup of dragons. He had never heard of The Arcadelfs before and as Meigar explained, over thousands of years they were forgotten about. Perhaps that's why no one knew of how they came to galvanise into such mythical beasts. But to have read about their beginnings written by a Blessèd Mage gave him the confidence this was all genuine. He instinctively tried to link connections with The Ancient Drethai and The Arcadelfs to see if there was any real link between them. His frustration grew with his struggle to bridge any connections they may have, which led Alicèn to delve further into what seemed like an impossibility. After all, this way of thinking was what he was heralded for.

An hour must have passed just sitting in his element in endless thought. He had no idea why but the urge to go down to the Màgjeurs in that cave became more pressing. Without further hesitation, he made his way down.

He slithered around the waterfall and entered the candle-lit cave to find only one Màgjeur dressed in baggy grey robes.

"Have you had enough of us yet?" The Màgjeur's deep, strong voice hit Alicèn like a stone. His back was turned while etching his quill onto a piece of parchment. He turned around to reveal a well-chiselled face with stubble coating his cheeks. His fierce look alone struck a commanding look.

"I believe I am in need of some help."

"That must be painful to say. Surely a man of your calibre can work out the impossible by yourself?"

"You know who I am?"

"You are famous, Durgeon Alicèndil."

"Then, you know I cannot stay here."

The Màgjeur bounced a small laugh, "they all say that, until they realise here is the only place they can be."

"This is an exception."

"I'm sure it is. But may I ask, why has a man of military who must leave imminently, wander down to the magicians? Want me to show you some card tricks?"

"I have questions."

"And the Màgjeur can help? It seems like we're more useful than Septalians think."

"I have a theory about The Dragadelf. No doubt you've heard of our recent excursion to Icarzbolden."

"Indeed," The Màgjeur said assertively.

"I believe someone or something is controlling them." The Màgjeur approached him with interest. "But I don't know who. As you are probably aware, they heed to no one. It is common knowledge that there is no power on this land they obey. But something is telling me that may not be true. And I have no idea why I am compelled to believe this. It's like an addiction I have with this theory that I cannot shake."

"An obsession?"

"Yes. It's most strange. So first I think what power on this land could *potentially* rival that of a Dragadelf? I recently read *'Tales of The Ancient Drethai'* and having come face to face with one of them I believe they could potentially have the means to do it."

"Interesting," his response was not entirely convincing but entertained the theory nonetheless.

"Then I read this book by Max Meigar about The Arcadelfs and how they created The Dragadelf. So I try and link them together, but I need a little more guidance. I was wondering if you could help me with this theory."

"Your theory could well be just." Alicèn's eyes lit up at someone agreeing with his concerns. "As it happens, I too share a similar view. But the power of The Ancient Drethai would not be anywhere near enough to command the respect of even one Dragadelf. I believe some more investigation is needed."

"So you don't believe they are strong enough to command their respect?"

"The Ancient Drethai are exceptionally powerful. So much so that I myself have learned from their techniques of survival and Soul Preservation. I can teach you if you like?"

"Maybe another time."

"But they would not command the respect of the seven."

"Something that also concerns me was how the knowledge of The Arcadelfs has almost been forgotten save the information in this book," he said with his frustration growing a little. "Why has this not been in many prints and become common knowledge? How do we even know Meigar's information is correct?"

"You do not like what I wrote...?" Alicèn raised his head and his eyebrows furrowed at the realisation of who he was talking to. "Not the most insulting thing a Blessèd Mage has ever heard."

"You're Max Meigar?" The Blessèd Mage of Earth nodded his head with a slight smile. "My apologies. I did not realise." He quickly bowed his head in recognition.

"No need for formalities here I assure you."

"It is an honour to meet you. Why are you here?"

"I am one of the founding members of The Reinhault. We have not existed for too long, but our work and preservation justifies why we must keep secret and hidden."

"As a founding member surely you have a say in how long I am here?"

"Perhaps. But ultimately it's Hiyaro's decision and so far he has no reason to believe you will keep our secrecy. Despite your name and title."

"So you're saying it's possible for me to leave?"

Meigar paused and struck a relatively frustrated look as he knew what he was getting at.

"Possible? Yes. Realistically? No. My advice, empower yourself here. I promise you, it could be the difference in all good this world has to offer."

Alicèn did not know exactly what he was talking about but felt a personal comfort knowing there was a possible way out.

"Do all members of The Blessèd Order share similar concerns?" Meigar's face turned a little less responsive.

"When we created The Dragasphere, we knew of the sacrifice that needed to be made. We also knew that in the process of casting that spell, we would lose all knowledge of the inside. That was one of the conditions. Nothing could go in, and nothing could go out. If we created paths of looking in, so could others powerful enough on Rèo which could use to find ways out. We could not take the risk."

"But do you agree with me that it is possible for them to somehow escape?"

"No. We made sure of it."

"And what about their influence? Can they be controlled?"

"Anything can be controlled provided something more powerful can control it."

Alicèn became a little excited at the prospect of his theory. That made total sense to him, which simplified his plethora of variant thoughts.

"So you're saying should there be something more powerful than The Dragadelf, they could be controlled?"

"Correct."

"Who? Or what?"

Meigar became more interested in Alicèns theory, the more they started asking questions. His general tone suggested he was more keen to have the conversation.

"I can only think of one thing. Common knowledge tells us no power on this land can control them… But what if it didn't come from this world? What power do you know of that is not from this land?"

"The Dragastone," Alicèn quietly said in mid-thought. Meigar gently nods his head in agreement.

"The Dragastone. Rèo was not prepared for such mythical power. As a result, it is the only thing on this world that The Dragadelf would have been drawn to. Its mere presence birthed them back into Rèo. When they sensed its existence, they were drawn to it. It is the only thing they could accept as greater than themselves. Over time, not only would they have manifested from its power within The Dragasphere, but by now they would have built up a reliance on its power."

"Hold on. Are you saying that if someone, somehow owned The Dragastone, in effect, they could command the respect of The Dragadelf…? All seven of them?"

"In theory? Yes." Once again, Meigar nodded.

Alicèn's breath became short while his heart thudded faster.

"Okay, I need a minute…"

He held his hands out to stop Meigar from saying anything while his mind ran with the possibilities.

"Wow."

"You are right in your theory, that there's a possibility that someone or something has ownership over that stone. That much is possible, yes. Should someone or something have possession and outright ownership of The Dragastone, all seven Dragadelf would see the owner of this power greater than them, as their master."

"Gracelands save us…"

The overwhelming of this theory made Alicèn lean his weight on a boulder nearby.

"It would appear that should that be in the wrong hands, we may one day need The Gracelands to save us indeed."

"Who? Who on this world could own that stone?"

"I am not sure. It cannot be any remaining members of The Blessèd I assure you that. There is, however, one that comes to my mind," his voice became more inquisitive. "And it is not the collective Ancient Drethai. Their combined power alone would not come anywhere near the respect of even one of these legendary beasts!"

"Who?"

"I thought the potential answer would come easily to a man who does not rule out the impossible…"

Alicèn felt a white sheet curtain over his face. He began to shake his head slowly.

"No… No it can't be him."

"Is it really impossible?"

"Melcelore!?"

He could not quite believe it. All of the stories filtered down from Felder and The Blessèd Order assured the whole world that the tomb he was buried in was simply impossible to break into.

"That cannot be! You and the other Blessèd Mages said it yourselves!"

"We told the world it was impossible to break in, which is true, but we did not tell the world it was impossible to break out."

"Tell me you are not serious."

"We no longer possess the sight to see. But there could be some connection with Melcelore and The Dragadelf should he have escaped."

"I have a good idea who could have helped him."

"Who?"

Meigar looked at Alicèn with an interest that they were unravelling between them something which has never been thought of before.

"Draul!"

"Draul!?"

"That makes complete sense to me. He was positioned high up in Felders Crest at that time. His betrayal would make sense knowing what he has become now. You say it was impossible to break into his tomb, but what if he helped break him out from within?"

"You're suggesting Draul was in that tomb as well?" Meigar sarcastically suggested.

"No. At the exact time of Melcelore's imprisonment, wasn't Draul close to Felder!?"

"He was."

"So, what if he betrayed Felder? What if Melcelore ensured him some sort of deal if he gave him the means to one day escape? Is that not possible?"

"Unlikely. Melcelore would not have given in so easily."

"I believe he might. In fact, the more I think about it, the clearer this becomes. Draul must have given him something in secret before he went in, maybe a spell to release his binds at the right moment."

"Possible. But again, unlikely. In order for that to be true you're saying that Melcelore would not only deliberately have imprisoned himself, but also planned and seen this whole event - …"

Meigar's mind just exploded at the revelation, stopping short as the impossible thought seemed to have crashed like The Dragastone. Alicèns eyebrows were raised at the apparent revelation they were making.

"I am the man who thinks the impossible, remember?"

Meigar's eyebrows furrowed, his face was screwed up but not out of defiance to the theory, but more that it was now entirely possible.

"I can't believe how this all is making sense," Alicèn said, "of course, he could have seen The Dragastone obliterating Felders Crest! That was one of the paths of magic he was legendary in, the art of true clairvoyance. Only he and Felder possessed the knowledge to look ahead of time!"

"This cannot be!"

"Don't they always see each other's plans? That was because they were masters of the foresight and true clairvoyance. Maybe this was a step too far for Felder to see. Maybe, after Melcelore's eternal imprisonment, Felder stopped looking into the future as there was no further rivalry between them. Maybe, just maybe, this was Melcelore's ultimate move to win. I mean not only did this event kill Felder… But if Melcelore somehow escaped, wouldn't that have been Melcelore's plan all along? To have finally beaten his greatest rival once and for all?"

"Alicèndil. What have you done?" he asked after a long pause.

"Of course, it's still a theory."

Meigar became a foreboding presence as he slowly approached him.

"You may have stumbled upon a theory that could change the path of our world."

"A theory that if true, Melcelore could be the true ruler of that stone!"

"Gracelands, I want to punch you right now!"

Alicèn smiled at how he managed to think of something a Blessèd Mage could not.

"Of course, there is the small matter of how he would own that stone. Any ideas?"

"Màgjeurs could enchant ownership runes onto anything they chose. That process is relatively simple. If Melcelore did somehow escape, and somehow managed to avoid being torched alive by The Dragadelf before his enchantment of ownership, he could have ascertained full right and control over their existence. Then and only then would The Dragadelf recognise Melcelore's power and righteousness through The Dragastone, and heed to his demands. And more worrying than that, nothing could stop him if The Dragasphere somehow collapsed…"

It took a while before either of them spoke again. They both breathed heavily while their eyes darted along the floor having just revealed the strongest of theories imaginable. Finally, their eyes met with such intensity one would think they both would faint.

"Let us learn, my friend."

"I'll try not to run off in the middle of the night," Alicèn replied sarcastically.

"Keep focused. And keep this between these walls."

For the first time since coming to The Reinhault, he felt enriched and lucky to have stumbled here. Meigar smiled back at him.

"Durgeon Alicèndil!" Akiko's voice was heard from outside the cave while entering, drenched from the waterfall. "Durgeon. The master has summoned you. He would like to report to you their investigation."

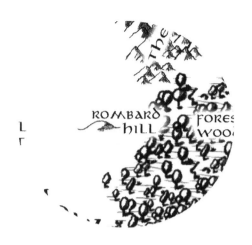

Help in Unexpected Places

Alex rode hard across the plains of Landonhome, the wind running through his unkempt hair and wispy beard, travelling so fast the moisture in his eyes squeezed out onto his temples.

Accompanied by The Durge of Rombard Hill Alex was one of the very few survivors of the attack. What remained of Pippersby was ruckus and rubble which without the vast population of the now charcoaled, murdered town was more of a cemetery. A ghost town. A relic of destruction for The Banamie.

A few days had passed since the onslaught. Alex did not eat, nor did he sleep. Running on fumes, he searched every room, every crevice, every possible trap door that his son could have hidden. Even if the worst had happened, his body would have been found by now, alas he was nowhere to be seen. Neither too was his aunt, Gràcene. What could have happened to her? Was it possible that they both escaped? What had happened to The Time Stone that was taken from his grasp? He hadn't even given a thought about Brody. And that conversation between Thog and his sidekick, something about coming what they were looking for? It all seemed far too coincidental. Luckily a few families were able to seek refuge in the catacombs of the mountains which the Barklers did not reach. Mainly women and children had ventured there with most of the men being killed or wounded. Alex had doubled his search amongst the survivors and into the depths of the mountain to no avail.

Alex and Joric, who was gravely wounded and unconscious through the severe loss of blood, had both been summoned by none other than King Romany himself, the King on Landonhome. Alex couldn't help but feel he was travelling in the wrong direction in the search for his son, but having conceded the fact his son was not in that town, he searched for a new possible way to find him. Alex dedicated his life to this one purpose, to finding his son.

The band approached the open plain leading to Rombard Hill which they could see for miles. A huge city built on the foundations of a mound in the middle of a vast plain. The sun shined brightly across the land leading up to the capital. A fortress of thick reinforced stone circled the city with turrets crowning the walls. Alex had never been to the capital, but he had heard of its legendary structure. Never had the walls of the old fortress been breached. It was well manned and prepared for any ground invasions. They approached the huge steel gates which opened upon their arrival. The sound of metal grinding echoed as the heavy doors swung open.

The band trotted inside and one of the first things Alex noticed upon their arrival was an impressive statue of the King driving his sword into the heart of another King. The band were met by horse masters looking to take reign of the mildens as soon as the Knights needed to travel on foot. The city was busy. Merchants of all trades scattered as they walked towards the peak of the hill.

Relian led the way to the great hall with other Knights while Alex followed. Church-like windows paned the walls while several soldiers guarded the entrance. Long sharp spears gripped by plated knuckles. A large comb of hair mohawked finely crafted helms. Smooth and refined gold breastplates were shouldered with white pauldrons. White and gold made up the colours of Rombard Hill, to signify freedom along with wealth. Their symbol of a white eagle spreading its free wings behind a darker golden background stencilled onto the heart of the armour. These were soldiers. Real soldiers with the training of those in Septalia. Even the way the guards stood radiated with pride and honour to protect their land.

The wooden doors opened to allow the band in. Alex walked into the clean and polished throne room which was lined with even more impressive Knights down both sides. At the far end of the hall, sat on an imposing throne of gold and white, was King Romany.

A large belly throbbed his stomach and his huge black beard had wisps of white speckled throughout. The famous golden crown with the white eagle at the forefront sat upon his head as a symbol of his authority. It was said that the crown was forged by the same smith that crowned King Felder.

To the side of him sat his wife, Queen Cathany. Fair brown hair and gentle in her demeanour. But strong and very capable of holding her own and giving wise counsel to her husband. Not much was ever rumoured about the Queen, other than that sometimes her council was so wise, many believed it was her that truly ruled Landonhome.

Standing to the side of the King stood a much older Màgjeur, cloaked in purple and lined with white. He was a proud member of The Magikai on Mages Wreath, his green wreath draped around his shoulders. As Alex and the band approached, the Màgjeur raised his hand to stop them before Relian led the kneel which Alex followed along with the band.

"You stand in the presence of your King and commander on this land," his slightly odd tone and accent unnerved Alex. "He has requested your presence to explain the events that unfolded two days ago in the town of Pippersby, West of Hopenhill on the land of Landonhome."

"With great thanks, Màgjeur Dalarose," Relian said. "My King, my Queen. I bring you a survivor of the Pippersby invasion. My band received word from several Bluewings, all flying in around dusk two days ago, hence the swift exit from our gates. We rode into the night as we were informed the town required military aid."

The King's chin almost was touching his chest, as if he were looking over the top of invisible glasses. He stared at Relian intensely. Alex wasn't fazed in the slightest of his stare. Passive was a feeling Alex had rarely felt. Like a tree in the woods, he just let the conversation develop while images of the event haunted him.

"During our ride, the town put up whatever defence they could muster. Sadly, the sheer numbers of the enemy overpowered their defences and the city had to be temporarily resigned. On our arrival, we were indeed too late to save everyone, but managed to save those who fled inside the mountain who, had our rescue not been there, would not have survived. This man is Alexandao."

Alex did not look at the King directly. His forlorn expression dragged his gaze down as if he was looking at the monarch's feet.

"Step forward, sir," Queen Cathany calmly said. "Let us know what happened."

"… My Queen," Alex, almost at the point of choking, took a deep breath. That feeling of life into his lungs he seldom felt, placated him somewhat.

"It's okay. Take your time nobleman," she calmed. His exhaustion slowed down his breathing.

"Our band returned from our annual expedition - "

" - Look me in the eye, sir!" Romany instructed.

Startled and encouraged by a nod from Relian, Alex raised his gaze to the King.

"Apologies, my King. The journey has been rough."

"I need to ascertain the severity and numbers of this band. So, how many were there?"

"No less than three hundred."

"Three hundred!?"

"Yes."

"You're absolutely sure?"

"Yes…"

Romany took a deep breath. "If there was one thing you remember about them, what would it be?"

"Romany!" Cathany interjected. "My apologies, sir, your King does not mean to antagonise. We have to understand who this was and their motive."

Alex warmed to Cathany straight away. He sensed her understanding and she immediately gained his respect.

"I remember how he tortured the mother of my child in front of the audience he'd mustered. That man's name was Thog." Romany's concerned look towards his Màgjeur gave Alex the impression Romany knew who he was. "He publicly executed the head of Smithwins after torturing him for sport. After that, he began torturing her. That is when Durgeon Relian's band arrived to save what they could."

"This man Thog is known to us. Was there anything else you noticed?" asked the King.

"Apart from him enjoying every moment of it, he dedicated their torture and beheadings to someone called King Draul, leader of The Banamie?"

The concern in the room rose dramatically. He gathered there was much more going on than he was aware of, but for the King of Landonhome to be concerned about such an event did not put Alex at ease.

"Thank you, sir," said the King. "I believe that will be all."

Alex's shoulders dipped with relief that the statement was over.

"There is just one question I have for this nobleman," interrupted Dalarose. "How came the slaughter of so many men in the town, including those who returned from your expedition, and yet you survive to witness this? Uncanny how you can remember it all in such detail while others fell."

Alex did not like the accusatory tone of the Màgjeur. Suddenly feeling on the back foot, Alex tried to remain calm as the gathering had turned into an interrogation.

"Upon our return, I was placed in the bard for my behaviour on our expedition."

"So your behaviour compromised the safety of your band?" Dalarose pressed.

"My behaviour had nothing to do with our band's safety. The attack would still have happened - "

" - I'm afraid I disagree nobleman. One chink in the armour and the whole pack falls. Were that chink not there, the chances of the band's survival would dramatically increase."

"Apologies for the interjection, Màgjeur," Relian stepped in, "but the sheer numbers of the enemy would have overpowered them all the same."

"But you don't disagree it would have bought more time? Time enough, perhaps to save more people?"

The exchanges unnerved the room and a frosty silence followed.

"The fate and safety of these noblemen were not down to one man, Dalarose-"

"-Just out of curiosity, what was it that compelled your own band leader to banish you to the bard?" Dalarose mused wickedly, digging for a justification of his accusation.

Alex searched and scrambled his mind for an alibi. Sworn to secrecy about the primary motivation to find The Time Stone, he felt under pressure to divert the main reason.

"I was too drunk…" Alex lied. The King rolled his eyes.

"Such a pity. Well as far as I see it my King, I believe that his imprisonment has not yet been uplifted and therefore he should remain in *our* bard until we clear up this misunderstanding."

"Agreed," said the King as he rose from his throne.

"Forgive me, my King!" pleaded Alex. The whole room turned to look. "My son was in that melee, and I cannot find him. I have come here answering your summons but also to ask for your help! Not put me in chains. Please."

"You are aware of the possibility that your son may not have made it out alive?" Romany's cautious tone was rare, it even surprised Dalarose.

"My King, dead or alive, I have to find him. For closure. Please…"

"Nobleman you are confined to the bard!" Dalarose enforced. "Once we have decided the severity of your actions, we shall determine whether you are to be released."

"And what if my son is alive? What then? Who else on Terrasendia is going to be looking for him, you Màgjeur?"

"Careful of your tone - "

" - His mother passed away in my arms in that town. My aunt, too I cannot find. Now are you to let another one of your people, a child, potentially die because you deem my actions to be somewhat responsible for this catastrophe?" Dalarose was a little flustered at Alex's tearful outburst. "My King, I am all he's got left now…"

His desperate tone moved the room. Romany paused to think about Alex's plea, before Cathany leaned over and gently whispered counsel in her husband's ear. Alex's nerves started to tick at the silent conversation they were having. A disagreement was clearly being played out. Alex looked towards Dalarose who was looking at Alex with disgust. The King peeled away from his conversation looking slightly peeved.

"Nobleman, we shall not condemn you to the bard." Alex sighed with relief. At last, a flash of good news for a change. "However, we cannot actively help you find your son. We have a duty and responsibility for those on our land and we shall do everything we can to broaden awareness for those who are missing, but there are hundreds missing all over the land. Hundreds. Unfortunately, I cannot put the value of your son's life above the lives of other parents, sons and daughters." Alex felt that drifting feeling again. Alone. Almost like he was in a small boat, in the middle of the sea. "I wish you luck, nobleman. By the Queen's request, you are permitted to stay for one week. Learn what you can with the city's resources. I hope it provides you with the information you need."

With that, he turned and bowled out of the throne room to his chambers behind. Upon his withdrawal, Cathany gave Alex a gentle smile before she turned to follow her husband. Alex couldn't help but feel it was her words that kept him out of the bard. He gave a small nod of the head to her in thanks as she left. As Relian escorted him out, he peered back just as he exited to see Dalarose standing tall and keeping a very close eye on Alex.

He felt as if he was back to square one, only this time hundreds of miles away. He felt restless at the prospect of not knowing which direction to turn; he could not rest for a second.

Relian escorted him to The Wendy Mare, an Inn with high prestige. One of the few lodges to have two Knights at the entrance. Relian did not talk much to Alex on route, he felt like asking him for his aid but knew it would not work. Passing through the streets of the wealthy city, he noticed some of the famous streets within.

Merchants on either side were selling heavily salted and chilled meats, clothing and finely crafted armour. Bunting occasionally decorated some of the more full streets where the city just did not stop, even through the night. One of the fruit merchants passed an apple to Relian who accepted the offer as a token of thanks for services of protecting the city. It appeared to be a common theme among the folk of Rombard Hill, proud of their Knights. They were celebrities of the city who were held in high regard. Alex was not in the tourist mood but he took his surroundings in, with his mind floating elsewhere.

They eventually came to a very different merchant who stood out amongst the general vibe. A small and dark coloured gazebo sheltered a very odd character selling weird objects. His stall was full and Alex gathered he didn't get much trade. Nonetheless, the character kept his eyes on Alex. His gaze was somewhat surprised at Alex's arrival, almost instinctively knowing he was was not from these parts. He was pale in complexion and wore black and purple overalls with gold linings weaving a strange symbol on his clothes, one Alex did not recognise.

"Stay away from him," Relian advised. "He's Elcarian."

"What's wrong with being Elcarian?" Alex asked.

"What's right it? Dangerous folk they are. Landonhome has never been at war with any other realm, ever. But we have come mighty close in recent times with the Elcarians."

"Why?"

"They are known for their secrecy and delving into darker magic. Sorcery, necromancy and the like. More alarmingly into Soul Mancing which has grown in activity since Melcelore's capture. Strictly forbidden magic which they claim they do not practice. But recent evidence has shown their delving to be true. Despite our best efforts to seek them out, they always have an excuse." The Elcarian kept his gaze on them both till they disappeared out of sight. "His name is Pirocès."

Alex couldn't help but be intrigued by the mysterious Elcarian.

"When you say darker magic, is it possible that they can find things...?"

Alex poised the question which stopped Relian in his tracks. He pulled him to one side on the street and leant in almost at a whisper's distance.

"You mean clairvoyance?"

"Who's that?" Alex asked.

"What? Clairvoyance is a type of magic...?" Relian furrowed his eyebrows.

"Oh." He could tell by Relian's general demeanour that he did not want to let anything on.

"You're talking to The Durgeon on Landonhome. Clairvoyance is one of the branches of magic which we forbid here in these walls. I'm aware you don't know the rules as of yet, but I cannot support your interest in this purely as it contradicts mine."

"But you're saying it's possible? This route of magic. Can it be used to help find my-"

"-Alex... I know exactly what you're getting at, but please, for your sake, don't tell me anything I don't want to hear. The less I know, the better chance you have of keeping out of the bard, do you understand?"

"Yes, sir," Alex replied.

They arrived at The Wendy Mare, with its pristine decor coloured in marble white and blue colours. The guards greeted Relian and Alex. When Relian spoke, telling them they were there under the Queen's admission, they were let through.

The first thing Alex noticed after the wooden doors opened was not a sight, but more an aroma of beautiful fragrances swimming in the air. He couldn't quite put his finger on one specific smell as there were too many. He walked in and in front of him was the check-in desk. Along both sides were the most eye-catching flowers he had ever seen. Rainbows of colours formed the reception with the occasional bumblebee and butterfly in sight. The brunette lady at the reception wore a delightful green well-fitted robe. Just before she was about to see Alex to his room, Relian bade Alex farewell.

"Where can I find you if I need assistance?" Alex asked.

"Unfortunately, our time has run its course. I will be in between this city and scouts this evening to attend to matters concerning this event. Should you need assistance about locations within the city, Taiya here will provide you with everything you need. I wish you luck my friend." Relian bowed his head and left.

"This way, sir," Taiya sweetly said.

And with that, Alex gormless as ever followed her to his room. They entered, and the room was a little less pleasing than the entrance. Nevertheless, it was a few steps above his room at home...

"Home," Alex thought.

Taiya gave a short description of the conditions of his stay, but Alex was not listening. Instead, he stared at his bed which he had no intention of getting in until his son was found. Her voice was just a muffle in the background as he gazed around the room, beautiful colours seemed to be processed in Alex's mind as grey and dull. He saw flashes of his son and Amba ghosting in the room, happy. Enjoying a getaway. Remembering the promise he made to his son that he'd take him to Gallonea. The sense of home reminded him of a very daunting fact. His home, without Amba, was now not there.

"-Everything okay, sir?" Taiya sweetly asked. Alex just about gathered a question had been asked and nodded his head. "Very well, breakfast starts on the eleventh hour of night, and the buffet..." A familiar fading feeling which he struggled with the longer he realised his son was not there drowned her words out before she left.

The energy it took him just to walk towards the window felt like a five-mile hike. He hadn't slept in two days and knew he needed rest. The possibilities rained through his head again as to what could have happened. There was no chance he was in Pippersby, that much was evident as he would have been found by now. The worst-case scenario was that he was dead, which Alex's heart raced just thinking about. But somehow that didn't add up to him as his body would have been found. Every possible avenue he explored and not one of them gave him any more hope or confidence than the next theory.

He waited until nightfall when the town was still alive and buzzing. The only difference was that most of the markets by this time of night were closed. Alex made his way through the town once more. Orange colours glowed in the city sky. Taverns and public houses were aplenty, occasionally spilling out into the streets.

He turned the corner to where he lost sight of Pirocès in the hope that he would be there. His stall was empty. He walked over casually looking around for any sign of the Elcarian. He stopped by the stand

and started to examine it, looking for anything that may give away information to where he could be, an address perhaps. He continued to look around to check if any of The Durge were patrolling about before going around the back of the stand to see the cupboard below was padlocked. Oddly enough, it didn't seem like there was any key to open it.

"What the hell are you doing?" Alex asked himself.

But feeling desperate, he looked for other ways of how to get inside the stand. He walked around to the front, and then round the back once more... To Alex's surprise, a slip of paper appeared, wedged between the cupboard slat. As if by magic. Slightly nervous and confused as to how he missed it the first time around, he withdrew the piece of paper which he read.

'I see you.'

Alex quickly looked around the windows and down the street from his view, several people enjoying the nightlife. But no one he could see was interested in Alex. He stared back at the piece of paper, and the words vanished. Every single hair on Alex's body spiked up. Spooked and gut-wrenched, he had no intention of walking away. Instead, he indulged in this peculiar scenario. He had never experienced magic before of any kind which unnerved him. He placed the piece of paper back where he found it and circled the stand again. He picked up the piece of paper once more which to his delightful fright, read another message.

'I know what it is you desire.'

"I doubt that. But tell me," he quietly said to the paper. He placed the piece of paper back and walked around once more.

'Your son.'

His heart leapt. Indulging in the possibility, he anxiously looked around to see if any knights were watching nearby.

"Can you find him?" he nervously asked.

'No.'

But before Alex could repeat the process, the words vanished and quickly reappeared.

'But I can tell if he's alive.'

"Where can I find you!?" Alex asked impulsively.

"Sir!" Alex turned around to see a member of The Durge inspecting him. "May I ask what you are doing sniffing around the markets at this hour?" asked the stern soldier. "Stealing are we?"

"No sir, I was just - " he interrupted himself as the piece of paper was no longer in his hands.

"Come with me. I saw you take something from that cabinet which is quite clearly closed for business. That looks a lot like stealing to me."

"Sir Knight, I was not stealing. I - "

" - You can explain everything once we get to The Durge."

"Sir Knight it's the truth! I am no thief. I require an item from this man that could not wait."

"The Elcarian does not trade anything of value. Anything you desire could never be so urgent. Now come with me before we make a scene."

Alex reluctantly followed the Knight. They passed the empty market, down several streets and past several public houses again, getting quieter the longer they walked. The Knight turned into a side street and went through a door around the back of a building which Alex followed into.

He looked around the room and noticed no one else present. It looked like someone's house lit with several large candles and no windows.

Suddenly he heard the door shut and turned around to see the Elcarian standing before him and not the Knight. His build much older and frailer which mirrored his wrinkled pale face. Skinnier when stood face to face and much greyer too. His drooped grey hair slithered against his wrinkled cheeks as he looked straight into the eyes of Alex.

"I would say my name, but wisdom tells me that you already know who I am," Pirocès mysteriously said with a surprisingly baritone voice.

"Wisdom? Or magic?" Alex asked with similar coolness.

"I guess the answer to that is subjective depending on how one obtains information."

Alex was not wise enough to answer back with such philosophy.

The orange glow of the candle fire lit Pirocès' pale face which looked gaunter under the shadow. His Adam's apple was also poignant in the flickers of the fire.

"You're Pirocès?"

"Yes."

"How do you know about my son?"

"If you knew who we really are, you'd understand more than just you're own questions." Alex was way out of his depth with what seemed like a philosophy lesson. "These are no riddles nobleman. You're probably wondering why you're here, in my chambers?"

"Yes, I am. You told me you could tell me if he is alive, is this true?"

"It is."

"Tell me, please."

"You understand it will involve a process. A process which involves an act which in the eyes of the men of this city, as forbidden...?"

Alex felt like he was walking on a tight rope. One slip and The Durge will surely throw him away, and any hope of finding his son would be all but gone. But should he get to the other side, through the perils and substantial risk, he could almost see his son at the other end.

"What do I have to do?"

"You're far more courageous than others."

"Not courageous. Just fearful," he thought.

"Fear can show you a lot about fate. Fate which is the orb of the world."

Alex snapped back to look at him. How could he read his mind? Pirocès snapped back another wry smile. Alex did not seem phased by this. He somehow just had this urge to take on a raging bull head-on by the horns. A growing eagerness festered within.

"And what does fate tell you about me finding my son?"

"It says you will see him again."

"Alive?"

"... Let's find out."

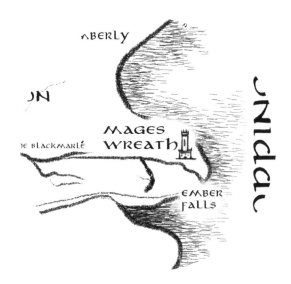

A Hello and a Goodbye

Ramalon felt a rare sense of calm while perched on the side of his ordinary dull bed. The windows were wide open as the cold swept in, staring out onto the regular view of the same old houses.

His paper dragons were flying from furniture in the room but his eyes did not take anything in. Instead his mind was in constant overload, thinking about the events that happened several days ago in the second round, the entrapment of Davinor and the looming realisation of what he had to do with Arinane. Still contemplating ideas of how he could avoid incinerating its body, which he knew deep down was perhaps the right thing. This whole situation with his students and teaching them about conjuration was a mistake. He should never have done it despite his best intentions.

He repeatedly thought about breaking the connection with Arinane temporarily just while the whole situation blew over. But he couldn't bring himself to do it. It wasn't fair on the creature to continually bring it to life and decease it when it suited him; it didn't sit right with him and went against his principles for the smaller things. If he was to terminate the connection, that was it. No turning back.

The last words he heard from civilisation was the unconvincing threat from Davinor. He had not left his house since. Not even for the session with his students, which he felt no guilt about not showing up for. He was at the tipping point and felt the only place he could be at peace was at home. Alone. Away from the world.

He didn't even know who he was facing in the last round. He couldn't care. The biggest fear he had was his concern with his protecy stone. Why was it making him feel this way, and only him? No other Màgjeur has ever had this problem with their stone in this manner. Was it cursed? And if so, why? He never wanted to use his protecy again.

It frightened him because when he did use it in combination with his emotions, he loved it. He admitted to himself he was addicted to the feeling of such power, hence the reason he did not want to use it, because when he was not using The Protecy, he was in fear of what he may become. In fear that he would want to use it again, and again, and again.

Suddenly several loud knocks rapidly thudded onto the door which he went to open.

"There you are!" said the breathless Haldane. "No one has heard from you since The Fall, why have you not been to The Skyurch?"

"I have been resting my friend," his croaky, tired, weary voice was a surprise to him as he had not spoken in days.

"May I come in?" Haldane was perhaps the only person on Terrasendia he would have accepted into his house at this moment. "How are you?"

"Yes. I'm okay."

"You look bloody awful!"

Ramalon looked into the reflection on one of his windows, and indeed, he looked exhausted. Not even a few days of rest made the bags under his eyes go.

"You must be exhausted. Here sit down. How many roses do you have? I'm going to put on some rose tea for you. We always ran out when you were at school. Could never produce enough roses in time-"

Haldane stopped short as he went to the plant pots near the stove where they were kept to see every one of the plants had wilted and died. The colours of oranges, purples and scarlet reds faded to black as the stems curved and touched the surface. Haldane's expression could not understand how Ramalon allowed this to happen.

"What's happening to you?"

"I don't know," he quietly said. "Honestly, I don't know." His arms hung by his sides in utter resignation as his gaze fixed on the floor.

"Sit, sit." Haldane ushered him to sit on his armchair as he perched on the pouf. "You do not look well. Please tell me what's happening. I can tell something is not right with you, ever since you started competing."

"I can't tell you."

"You can. I promise your words are safe with me."

"I am sorry, my friend. You mean well I know, but for your protection, I can't."

"For my protec- dear Blessèd, what are you talking about? I do not need protection, I assure you. Protection from who?"

"… From me."

Haldane slowly leaned away from Ramalon as he was concerned.

"Why?"

"You're not safe here. No one is safe."

"Ramalon! You have been my friend for many years. I am not afraid of you. I know you better than anyone, and I know you will never hurt me."

"I know that too. But what if I am not me?"

"Not you? These are some dark words you speak."

"They are. You say I'm not myself. You're right. And when I am not myself, nobody knows how much danger they are in."

"Does this have anything to do with your stone?" Ramalon looked at him as it became difficult to lie to him. He nodded his head. "I thought so. You're worried about the power of your stone, aren't you?" He nodded his head once more. "It's no secret. In both rounds, what you have done has stunned everyone on Terrasendia. But I guess the main question is why? And how? How would a Màgjeur like yourself be able to defeat others more experienced? Whom for many years would have trained for battles such as these, yet you surpassed your opponents with such colossal magnitude. It's a mystery."

"I'm scared, Haldane."

"With the power that you possess, I would be too."

"But that's the thing. I possess this power, but I am not myself when it happens."

"What, you turn into someone else?"

"No, not like that. I can still control my body and my actions. Only when it happens, it's like the power is influencing my choices."

"You love this power, don't you?"

Ramalon looked at Haldane straight in the eyes before lowering his gaze once more.

"I think I do."

"If I told you-you could use this power and be completely fine after, you would take that wouldn't you?"

"I think I would, yes."

"Hmm… Well that explains it."

"Explains what?"

"Secretly, behind those eyes, my friend, you want this power. Beyond anything, you want this. The low Màgjeur from the slums, becoming the most powerful on Mages Wreath."

"No. No. No! I do not want that."

"Yes, you do. If there were no risks, you would not hesitate to use this power."

"You do not understand. It's such a poison."

"A poison? Really? Then why would you use it again?"

"I would use it if it didn't make me feel like that."

"Exactly! And that's my point. It is not the power itself you fear. It's what happens when you feel like you can't control it!"

Haldane was hitting the nail on the head, he was right. Ramalon did secretly want this enormity of power but was too scared to delve into using it in fear it would take him to dark places.

"My friend, I do believe you know me better than myself!"

"Yes. I do. My advice would be to find out whatever it is that is making this power toxic to you. And stub it out! Imagine that. This much power, risk-free!" Haldane's voice was becoming increasingly excited. Even more so than his usual jittery self. "Ramalon. A Màgjeur from the slums, to being the most powerful Màgjeur on Mages Wreath. Perhaps even on Terrasendia… Perhaps even the world… Some story, eh?"

Even to Ramalon that appealed. In fact, to him, it would be a dream come true.

"That's the plan, my friend."

"Make sure when you are, I will get a few perks! Perhaps maybe a wreath for myself, eh?"

"Don't push it!"

Haldane laughed. "You will be loved. I promise you."

"Will I be the people's champion?"

"Oh, yes. Everyone loves an underdog. You win this tournament, and I think every Màgjeur would adore you. Powerful Màgjeurs would turn to you. Younger Màgjeurs would aspire to you. That I know you could not resist the chance to take."

Haldane's visit certainly put Ramalon in a happier place. Calmer and focused on getting his mind back on track. He wanted the love of the people so much now and was determined to see that they did.

"Who else won in the second round?"

"Good Gracelands, you're saying you don't know?"

"Does it look like Bluewings visit my house every day, Haldane?"

"The whole event was brilliant! We all loved it as a spectacle. Shame what happened to Lauru of course, but apart from that, such a spectacle! You, taking all of the headlines once again," he said with a silenced wink. "Lazabeth won the first race! Completely zapped Rybon to shreds amid the storm she'd created. Who do you think won out of Allenade, Chloen and Ildreàn?"

"Must have been Allenade. He was strong."

"Nope."

"Chloen?" Haldane shook his head with a smile. "You're kidding me!?"

"No one gave Ildreàn a hope! She managed to do it! They both didn't think she was in the running, took their eyes off her and she beat them by collecting the orbs of water in a massive ball and essentially drowned them both in the skies. They were trapped, and she got down first."

"Impressive."

"Of course, she left a few up there for us to see."

"And who was the other?"

"Once again. Another surprise. Well, not really when you think about it. Peter Palgan!"

"I knew it."

"Yes. He turned himself to rock and stone! He became much heavier and descended much quicker. Also gave him more protection, especially when Xjaques tried to hurt him with ice. The glacier around him just made him descend even faster. And Enzo's bolts weren't strong enough to penetrate!"

"Xjaques was too naive. That's why I wanted to pair up with him."

"And then, of course, yourself. The star of the show, literally crashing down like the bloody Dragastone!"

"I didn't expect to that's for sure."

"You know, many people are asking questions. As to how exactly it happened."

Ramalon's concerns grew once more. Were anyone else to find out about the Charzeryx it would be devastating to Ramalon's chances of continuing the tournament. All the more reason to have Arinane destroyed.

"I mean you were behind, by some considerable way before releasing such power to win eventually. But everyone was questioning how both Pyros and Allaremsah both lost so stunningly. What happened?"

"I managed to hit them with a fire blast of mine," Ramalon lied.

"You did? That was my initial thought. But then others started to point out that the manipulation of the fire onto both of them was certainly unnatural. More violent and cruel, which is why they both are still unconscious. Alive of course."

"I told you. My stone is behaving strangely. That must have been what it was."

"Hmm, I see. Well, I'm sure you will think of a way to convince everyone what had happened. I will let you rest. I think that is the best thing for you right now."

Ramalon did need rest. But more immediately to him, he could not until Arinane was put to rest one final time. Only then he could start a journey to recover his mind and refocus.

"Haldane?" he said as he was about to exit. "Thank you."

Haldane nodded his head in appreciation. "Rest well, my friend."

He waited until Haldane was away from his house before he grabbed his robes and headed straight out the door himself.

He made his way west to the outskirts of the city where he thought of the only place he could lay Arinane to rest in peace. The forest of Valencère. He knew with a heavy heart it was the right thing to do. If he buried him then there was no real way to prove his use of conjuration. Even if the students did go blabbing, it was his word against theirs. The only real danger came from if both Pyros and Allaremsah had accurate memories of seeing the Charzeryx. Their concerns twinned with the students could prove problematic, but even then there was ambiguity and no real proof. It was the only way.

The stars above the forest could hardly be seen as the white of the moon covered their gaze. Ramalon entered the forest which was aesthetically beautiful. The bark of the trees was smooth and symmetrical. The height of leaves all was consistent and high while the ground was also flat and cushioned with fine grass. He delved deep into the forest to make sure he wasn't followed.

He knew Arinane belonged to Cleverson and telling him what he was about to do would break his heart. But he was sure he would understand. He couldn't care what the other two thought.

He came to a large clearing where the trees grew around the circular space before him. It was rather large, about a hundred metres separated the open plain. He was alone. The perfect place to bury Arinane.

He perched himself on a fallen tree all the while telling himself procrastination wouldn't help. The sooner it was done, the sooner it was over. Ramalon knew that Davinor wanted the creature to be incinerated, but that was too much for his heart. This was a better way to go. He laid out his hand onto the ground, and suddenly swipes of fire started to carve into the soft soil, digging out Arinane's tomb in the process. He made sure the grave he dug out was deep enough for it never to be found again. It must have been about twenty metres deep. Deep enough that the light of the moon did not reach the bottom. He felt ready.

He closed his eyes and summoned the Charzeryx wherever it was. It took several minutes of feeling his presence before he heard its playful voice. He looked up and saw its silhouette against the full moon. The black sails swimming in the air as it swooped down and brushed its wings against every tree in the circular clearing, spraying leaves and branches as it landed smoothly next to Ramalon.

He held out its hand and laid it on Arinane's bony cheeks. It gave a small cackle of appreciation at his touch, sinking Ramalon's heart further. His head became heavier the longer he prolonged the situation. All Arinane did was smile back at him. He didn't deserve this. He didn't understand what was going on. He deserved a better life, one he never had because of The Dragadelf.

"I am sorry. I am so sorry," he tried to fight back the tears as he knew Arinane couldn't understand. All it did was smile back and want more attention, like a dog, always wanting to be stroked.

He led the dragon to the hole he had made, and Arinane suddenly got a little frustrated at the lack of attention he was receiving, making him spread his wings and get airborne above its grave, still looking rather playful and gently bouncing in the air.

Ramalon stood before him and looked into his magnificent eyes. He wanted one last feel of the dragon's power and gently produced small flames from his hand which Arinane returned with gentle fires from its belly. The two met in the middle, creating a delicate ball of fire, whirling slowly and elegantly in the space between. Ramalon knew just how lucky he was to have had this opportunity to feel the dragon's power one last time.

The fires continued to meet, and a tear rolled down the side of Ramalon's cheek as he knew the time had come. He closed his eyes and felt that connection with Arinane once more. His pulsing heart. His fires. His breath, before latching onto the crux of the connection, and severing it entirely.

He opened his river-strewn eyes, finding his vision more blurred through his tears, relaxed his protecy as Arinane's fires gently slowed to a simmer, diminishing smaller and smaller and smaller… Before its breath was no longer. He watched on as the life in Arinane's eyes waned until they were still and lifeless. As Ramalon's heart sank, so did Arinanes body as it gently floated down into the dark abyss. He felt empty. He could no longer feel his warmth, his breath. His life. It was nothing but a beautiful carcass once more. He promised to himself in this moment he would never share his soul with anything else again.

He buried the body with the earth he had dug, and as a symbol of respect, he lit a small fireball above the grave which simmered gently before turning to leave with heavy regret. He looked back one last time at the grave before the small flame dissipated into a wisp of smoke. A sign that he was now, truly at rest.

"What!?" Cleverson said as the waters grew heavy in his eyes.

Ramalon had told his three students that he buried Arinane. Corey and Lenk's response was indeed angry and full of hate and spite. And for the first time, Ramalon sensed a little bit of that anger in Cleverson as he tried to come to terms with what happened.

"And as a result, it is time that our lessons come to an end," Ramalon said, emotionless.

It was the right thing to do, while also covering his tracks. He was so close to winning the tournament and all he wanted to think about was preparing for the final round.

"Where did you bury him!?" Lenk spat

"It was not your decision to do that!" Corey said in equal aggression.

"I have every right to have done that. The whole thing was a mistake, our lessons were a mistake, allowing that poor creature back to life only to take its life away again was a mistake. You cannot meddle with something so fragile."

"Coming to you was the mistake!" Corey said. "You underestimate us, Màgjeur!"

"Do I?"

"Yes! Because of you we now have lost something so rare. And you will tell us where-"

"Corey, no!" Cleverson interrupted as he struck nervous looks between the two. He looked frightened at angering Ramalon again. "We mustn't. The Màgjeur is right. He must be at peace."

"Stand up to him, Cleverson! For once in your life, stand up for yourself!"

Cleverson didn't know what to do. Scared out of his wits. "I can't," his small words caused a laugh from Lenk. "I am sorry to everyone. I really am."

"You have nothing to be sorry for," Ramalon consoled. "The only thing I regret is you losing something so beautiful. Something you cherished and nurtured for yourself. It was not to know of its end, but if there is something good to have come from this, it is how you have grown, Cleverson. I look at you now, and I am reminded of my own purpose in life. To inspire. To learn about the value of life. No matter how big, or how small, how loud or how shy, a life is a life. And no value should be placed upon it, as it is priceless. One day, whether it would be today or tomorrow or in the years to come, you will remember this and remember how you gave joy to something which you loved. I only wished the better for you two. Whom despite my best efforts, I largely failed," looking directly at Corey and Lenk who glared at him with intent.

"We will find that beast!" Lenk said.

"NO!" Cleverson said. "No, we won't. We must honour the Màgjeurs wishes on this."

"But Clever-"

"Lenk! Trust me. We will not do it. Bringing it back to life and taking it again and again, just isn't right. It's principle. I learned that from you, Màgjeur."

Ramalon gave a small bow of the head in recognition.

"Fine! It's your call Cleverson as it is yours, after all." At last. Corey's tone had changed to something a little more comforting. Most unusual for him. "Very well, Màgjeur. Have it your way." And with that, Corey and Lenk stormed off and out of the cellar for the final time.

Cleverson was left, and Ramalon could sense he was trying to hide his nerves. He avoided eye contact whenever he could and tried to hold his tone.

"I am very proud of you."

"Yes."

"Yes?"

"I mean, thank you."

"No. Thank you, Cleverson. Carry on as you are and you'll be who you want to be."

Their eyes met, and a nervous Cleverson scurried out of the cellar and out of sight.

Ramalon's worry seemed to alleviate somewhat. Two major problems in such a short space of time were now gone. He could now solely focus back on achieving his dream.

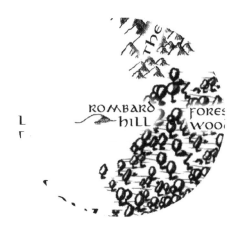

ROMBARD
hILL

FORES
WOO

Blood Monarch

Inside Pirocès' chamber candles were lit and placed in a pattern symbolic of two triangles, one upside down inside the other. A wooden bowl was set on a stand in the middle and underneath laid a single candle roasting the dish, with Alex and the Elcarian outside the candles at opposite ends. But Alex couldn't help but look at Pirocès with suspicion.

"Shall we begin?" asked Pirocès.

"Why are you helping me?" Alex furrowed.

"Are you sure you want to delve into questioning now? Surely finding out if your son is alive is more urgent."

"Of course, it is. But I find it hard to believe helping me is a hobby for you. What do you want in return?"

"Maybe we should discuss this after the ritual."

"No." The Elcarian looked a little stunned. "I need to know now what it is you intend me to do. Should my son be alive, there's not much I can do to help you as you know I will have to find him. But if he's not, I've got nothing left in this world than to pay you back. Please."

Pirocès took a breath, almost resigning to Alex's plea.

"Help me!" demanded Pirocès.

"How?"

"I was banished from the realm of Elcaria since the new King took power eleven years past. Since then, I came here to Rombard Hill. To be studied, in purgatory."

"Do they harm you?"

"Only my pride. They do grant me access to live here away from harmony in return for what I know about the Elcarian ways. Durgeon Relian is kind to me, although he does not see eye to eye with things I have done. I am bound here by the King's orders never to leave. But I am dying. Not because of any disease or anything materialistic. But I have no purpose here. I need to return to my home."

Alex began to feel a little sorry for the Elcarian. Having his home stripped from him felt like a parallel he could relate to.

"And you need my help specifically?"

"Yes. No one I have ever met would try to get me out of these walls. No one has fought for me. No one. Especially when they hear me say that you need the King's permission."

"You're telling me I need Romany's permission?" Alex asked, almost rhetorically.

"I'd understand if you did not want to proceed. But I need someone who also needs to venture into that realm."

"You must have the wrong man. I have no desire to go there."

"I disagree. I know of your journey, Alexandao."

Confused as to how this man, who he had never met, was claiming to know all about him, he continued.

"Enlighten me. What is it you think I need to do?"

"Make no mistake. When I picked up the notion of your arrival, I sensed an opportunity for us both. I am not your foe. Embrace reality. If your son has not yet been found, I fear he is either dead which you are aware, or that he cannot be found without the help of magic unknown to the nobleman. But times in my realm have grown more dangerous compared to the days of old. We can trust few save my kin."

"And you're certain your kin are people who would help a nobleman?"

"On my life, yes! There are still those who still revel in the ways of old. And in return for helping me back to Casparia, he will grant you your wishes and help locate your son! Should he be alive."

Alex was gradually warming to Pirocès.

"Tell me why you were exiled," he asked.

"Let's start with why I want to return home. It's simpler," he said with a smile.

"Okay...?" Alex pondered the order of priorities the Elcarian ordered the conversation with but went with it.

"Have you heard of the wonders of Casparia?"

Alex had indeed taken Jàqueson to the library on casual occasions. Professor Gregrick would often give his young students impetus to study *'A History of Terrasendia.'* Perhaps the most important and relevant book in recent times. The authenticity of the book was genuine having contributions from The Blessèd. The importance of the book was well regarded in juniors as it encouraged respect and gratitude for life on the land. Alex had read this book and found it an excellent read. It had detailed maps of all the realms on Terrasendia, basic knowledge of Rolgan above in the north, and only references to The Gracelands below in the south. A place enshrouded in such beauty it is said souls who have earned it through good deeds on the land venture there when their bodies die.

In contrast it is rumoured north of Rolgan, to The Lands of the Neverseen, they take those who are worthy through the acts of evil deeds. To go one further, few fanatics believe that both lands do this to build their army and that one day they both will unleash on each other in war with the certainty of Terrasendia's extinction, being sandwiched in between the two mythical lands. But to many, this was all just rumour...

"I know of Casparia only through the descriptions and the illustrations."

"Oh, you should see it Alexandao," he said with a hint of ecstasy. "A city tombed inside a mountain so thick, the Dragastone would not have pierced into its halls. The haunted forest of Aspari tops the mountain, which makes getting in and out very challenging. Such a beautiful wonder built by my ancestor's thousands of years ago. No war has come to that ancient city because no power on this land could penetrate its defences. Defended by some of the cleverest magic of deception the land has ever seen. I loved my home, Alex. I loved my city. I loved my people for who they were. Not who they now are." His tone started to drop slightly. "The experiments I have practiced for many years were largely my own. That was the Elcarian way, and still is to some extent."

"Changed how?" Alex asked.

"The old way did not ever delve into the darker practices. I remember a time when we invented ways to help. Those days are long gone." One of the candles extinguished by itself, wisping its way slowly into the ceiling. An ethereal haze clouded the room which they both recognised. "How relevant. Let's take it as a sign."

"A sign that you're telling the truth?"

"I have no means to trick you. I have waited for some time for someone to come to me and help me get back."

Alex gently sighed.

"Tell me about what is happening in your city now," he said. Pirocès relit the doused candle with a slight wave of his hand.

"The new way is to invent paths of magic using darker sources. The old routes of magic were a symbol for our people, of how proud we once were. Now that has changed. Now, the new routes are poison! Unrecognisable. There are those who believe in the old ways still, but I fear the lure of the darker magic's are too strong for the young and the vulnerable in my city and forth in the whole of Elcaria to resist. It's temptation to revel in this magic invokes greed into my people."

"I'm assuming that's why the men here are on edge about Elcaria. These new routes of magic," Alex said with genuine intrigue.

"King Caspercartès was not like his predecessor, Dianarcès. He is rash, selfish and takes things for his own. It all started with him."

His tone suddenly dropped several notches. His eyes saddened as he stared into the fires of the candles. The mention of Caspercartès gave Alex the impression he knew the King.

"He came to me when he rose his rebellion to ask for my advice. Advice on darker magics which I studied as part of my learnings. He led me down into his chambers, and I could not believe what I saw."

Alex saw the horror that laid within Pirocès eyes as if he could almost see the scene play out by his narration.

"What did you see?" Alex cautiously asked.

"… Everything. I saw everything! The beginning of a new era. Experiments were going on beneath the cities floors. Experiments on men, animals, dwarves. Experiments using dark magic! Illegal magic on Terrasendia! Causing victims pain, suffering, transformational experiments, cross-breeding lifeforms, rapid growth of any lifeforms you name it! Conjuration and preservation magic, all very unnatural stuff. I even saw something else that I could never have imagined existing in those walls… I saw practices of Soul Mancing!" His eyes were horror-struck.

Soul Mancing was the form of magic, invented by none other than Melcelore himself and considered the top crime on the land of Terrasendia.

"Let your imagination run wild, and it will probably land on something very close and similar to what was going on in that chamber!"

Instead of Alex reacting, he just observed, in shock as he tried to hide his growing fears.

"Durgeon Relian mentioned they have proof of Soul Mancing to be true."

"Indeed. However, your King does not have a spine!" Alex struggled to disagree with that. "Even though I act as an informant to him, I am still and forever will be judged as someone who they will never trust fully. I have urged him to take up arms against them before their cancerous delving spread too far, but would he heed the advice of a foreigner? I think not."

"I fear a war would not benefit anyone."

"For many a year, this must have been in the making. Right underneath Dianarcès' nose. No way could this all have been established in Caspercartès' short tenure at the time. By now, the learnings would have festered within that great city. It may even be too late now."

"What did you do when you saw all this?"

"He asked me what I thought. He apologised for never mentioning this to me, and when I asked how long this lab had existed, he walked away."

"You knew he was hiding something."

"Yes. But I didn't expect what came next. He asked me to be his chief mantrancer. Because of my prestige, I was regarded as one of the most important Elcarians in the high order. One whom he could trust seeing as we were very close."

"I sense that you knew the King well?"

"Very well. One of the reasons why he chose me was because I shared my learnings with him. But he saw them as something I did not. He wanted to base a revolution of dark magic based on the foundations of my own, which I could never in a millennia accept. He offered his hand... I protested and said that this coincides with all the ancient laws of our ancestors, laws built upon the very foundations of our existence. *"My friend, the world, has changed!"* He said. *"Too long have we been resided to ancient laws. We must move on and take back our power. Not be held to account by Terrasendia and The Blessèd any longer! We need to protect ourselves, my friend."* And with that, he offered his hand once more with confidence I would accept. But when I said I would have to think about it. His face turned very sour, and so I left."

"You didn't seriously think rejecting his offer would go down well did you?"

"No. I most certainly did not. In fact I thought I would be killed that night. But instead, something much worse happened."

"Worse than death? Bloody Rolgan!"

Keeping your enemies alive and living in complete cruelty was seen as a much worse punishment than death ever since Felder did the same to Melcelore. To live in cruelty, purgatory and pain till the end of their days to utter self-ruin. Alex was very aware of the story of Felder and Melcelore as it was one of Jàque's favourite stories that he would read to him before his night bathing. On seldom occasions, he would get into it so much, he would start impersonating the characters in the story which had his son in stitches as to how bad his impressions were.

"I rushed back to try and protect my work so that he or anyone else could not use it. But I got there too late. By the time I had got back, it was gone."

"He stole it?" Piroçès starred at Alex before lowering his eyes.

"He did."

"And you need my help somehow to take it back?"

"Oh, dear Blessèd no! Never take it back. I need to destroy it!"

His impetus put Alex on edge. He could suddenly feel that he was essentially getting into even more troubled waters. But did he really have a choice?

"How in Rolgan will you manage that!?" Alex asked.

"Easy. When you didn't quite tell him everything..." he said smiling.

"You're confident you can destroy your work if we get there?"

"On my life, certain! You understand now. I started this. Now, I must finish it!" he said passionately.

"And your kin, what can they do to help me?"

"My brother Dancès is the one we need. He possesses the art of clairvoyance. A rare talent that very few save The Ancient Drethai possess."

"I've heard about them."

"Yes, terrifying spirits. The art of *true* clairvoyance takes decades to master. It involves tapping into the dimensions of many senses: sights, sounds, smells etc. However, what sense is greater than them all? The sense that binds the information?" Alex shook his head. "Time. A sense of time is the greatest attribute to clairvoyance as it pieces the senses together and also when. Dancès is one of the very few people who understand the intricacies of time." This reminded Alex of another weight on his shoulders, having just lost The Time Stone. "I promise you, when we get inside I will take you to him first. He will be able to find your son and locate him. I then will run my own errands and get out of there."

"So your plan is to sabotage your work and simply walk straight out of the front gates of Casparia? That doesn't exactly fill me with confidence," Alex queried.

"The process of destroying my work will involve planting a timer in the foundations of my rune. We will be long gone by the time comes." Alex's brain felt well and truly fried from the questions he had. But he was starting to lose patience and just wanted to get on with it. "I promise you. On my life, this will work. We find my brother, we find your son should he be alive and I drop my rune before our timely escape. What say you?" Piroces asked.

Alex considered his options and came to only one conclusion. The conclusion that had already subconsciously been made before he sat down with Piroces.

"What is it you need from me?"

Piroces exhaled in happiness that he finally found who he was looking for.

"Thank Blessèd! Thank you! Once we perform this ritual, you will need to talk to Relian and try to persuade him to get the King to release me."

"What if he says no? And more importantly, what if he says yes? How will you get in if you are exiled?"

"If he says no, then I've helped you free of charge. If he says yes... Let's say if my cover fooled you, it would fool anyone," he said, smiling again. "They would let you through on visitation no worries at all. I hope your King persuading skills are up to scratch," he said humourlessly.

"They're excellent."

"Good! We will need that. We will need all the luck we can get. So you're saying you'll do this? For me?"

"For us." His tone suggested that he gained the Elcarians trust.

"Thank you, Alex. You have no idea how much this means, even just to try." He started to shake a little at the thought someone was helping him. "Now. The ritual we are about to perform requires your blood. A lot of it."

"How much are we talking?" Alex asked. Pirocès looked and indicated to the bowl which wasn't large, but big enough to cause concern.

"That much," The Elcarian nodded.

"What are we waiting for?" he quickly said.

They both sat opposite each other, and Pirocès handed Alex the knife. Alex held his hand over the bowl with the blade placed on his palm. He looked to Pirocès who gave him a nod, Alex squeezed the knife and withdrew quickly, slicing the spongy flesh. Alex winced at the pain, clenching his teeth as the warm blood started to trickle below his now-closed fist. The blood began to drip very quickly into the bowl. It hissed as it hit the burning hot dish, wisping and evaporating some of the drops. The influx of blood started to fill the bowl, which made the blood boil slightly.

"How much more do you need?" Alex winced.

"Much more," he replied.

Alex's heart started to race around his body a lot faster, expelling more blood into the dish. To accelerate the process, he clenched and relaxed his fist to increase the blood flow. The bowl was nearly three-quarters full before Alex's head started to lighten up, his head floating from existence as the blood left him. He managed to keep his focus before the blood slowed down. The platelets in his body started to congeal up, eventually stopping the blood.

"Is that enough?"

"Yes."

"What now?"

"Now, you watch."

They both waited in anticipation before the blood in the dish started to boil again. The Elcarian began to murmur some incantations which Alex did not understand. With his words intensifying with every sentence, it peaked, and Pirocès picked up the bowl and began to drink the boiling hot blood.

"What are you doing!?" Alex demanded.

He got no reply. Instead, Pirocès finished every drop before quickly dropping the bowl, heavily breathing at drinking the scorching scarlet-hot blood. The Elcarian stopped still and appeared to relax and breathe normally. He took in his surroundings calmly and started to gentle laugh.

All of a sudden, the bumbling of laughter turned inside out, almost to a constricted groan of pain before he started to shake violently with a panicked expression on his face.

"Something's not right! GIVE ME THE KNIFE! I CAN'T TAKE THIS! IT'S-S T-TOO M-MUCH!" he panted.

He took the knife from Alex and cut the candle underneath the dish stand in half, dousing it in the process. He placed the bowl back onto the stand and placed both his hands above the dish. He took a deep breath in.

"*Midi-Carcerous!*" he quickly whispered.

Immediately two slits carved their way into the Elcarians palms as the bowl started to refill its dark red colour quickly. Alex watched in anticipation, not sure of what was happening or how to help. The dish continued to fill much quicker than Alex's. Pirocès immediately started to calm down, his breathing turning from gasps of air to loud panting. His hands were still over the bowl as he bowed his head, keeping very still, almost in recovery for what just happened. The blood in the dish had been replenished to the exact amount that he had drunk.

He fell backwards onto the candles behind him, stopping short at his breath. His robes caught aflame on the candles on the floor, and Alex rushed over to try and extinguish the flames. Something didn't feel right at all. He sensed the Elcarian was in trouble and started to rip the clothes off of him as no water was available. He placed his hand on his bare back, which was one of the coldest things Alex ever touched, colder than the freezing lake he dived in days ago. Luckily his robe was off, and the pale skin of Pirocès was shown.

Alex saw tattoos all over his back and skinny chest. But the tattoos were not of ink, but scars. Sentences and phrases were all over his body. '*Our mind, our bodies, our souls, forever entwined,*' was the most significant phrase etched onto the top of his back. Alex knelt beside him and tried to comfort. Pirocès sat back up, panting still but slowly recovering.

"Are you okay!?" Alex asked with heavy concern.

"Look…"

They both looked over to the bowl. The blood started to vibrate a two-beat rhythm which repeated itself with a mini-break, that symbolic of a heartbeat.

"What is it?" Alex asked.

"That, is the heartbeat of your son…" Alex snapped his head towards Pirocès.

"My sons?" he gasped. "You're telling me- "

"-Yes. He's alive!"

Alex's heart wept and skipped several beats with overwhelming relief, he couldn't stop staring at the dish.

"Are you certain!?"

"I am certain! Having your blood run through my veins, I was able to latch on a spell which mirrored the movement of blood within your sons. That is how we know he is alive."

"I must find him!"

"Yes. You must. *Ramerick*..."

Alex furrowed his brows at hearing the term Ramerick.

"What?"

"Ramerick."

"Why are you calling me, Ramerick?"

"Who would have thought it...? I don't believe in coincidence but this I cannot ignore. I did not expect this."

"What did you not expect?"

"I'm guessing you have no idea who you are."

"My name is Alexandao."

"Yes? And who's your mother. Who's your father?"

"I never knew them. My aunt Gràcene raised me."

"And this aunt Gràcene, she never told you?"

"Told me what!?"

"That you are the son of King Felder..."

Alex felt as if a ghost just walked through him. Taken aback, he stared into Pirocès to see what kind of spell this was.

"King Felder?" Pirocès hummed in acknowledgement. "The high King on Terrasendia?" he asked sceptically.

"Is it so hard to believe?"

"Just a little, yes."

"This is no trick. What good is it to me to lie, I have no use to torment or antagonise you. This is real. Your blood is true. Your blood is royal! You are the lost Blood Monarch!"

Pirocès ascending excitement of the realisation gave him the strength to stand to his feet and address Alex.

"It's impossible," Alex calmly shrugged off. "You're mistaken. How can I be, if I lead a nobleman's life?"

"Impossible to you. You only perceive the world as it's presented to you. No books were ever written of this. They say that when The Dragasphere was created, Felders new-born never made it out. Not many knew he was expecting in the first place, and even then it was a rumour. I am now one of the only ones to truly know."

"So I take it you have had a lot of monarch blood run through your veins in your experience," Alex said with heavy sarcasm.

"Believe me, the power that just ran through my veins was something I have never felt before. Something I just could never have imagined was real. Blessèd, the power nearly killed me. But most importantly, I heard a voice. The voice of Felder himself. He spoke and said the name, *Ramerick.*"

Processing the feelings that his son was alive twinned with the information that he was now the son of the high King on Terrasendia, caused a mini explosion in Alex's mind, asking himself if this really could be true. No, was the practical answer he felt.

"It's a mistake."

"Many questions I am sure, questions that I cannot answer. We must keep this between us, Alex. Or I should be calling you Ramerick now."

"Save the breath. Does this put us seeing your brother at risk?" Alex asked.

"No. It won't," Pirocès answered.

His eyes were finding a bit more life back. As balderdash as Alex felt this new discovery was, he could not help but indulge in the impossible revelation.

"Did you know Felder?"

"No. But if you were alive at the time, you would know who he was. Such a powerful Màgjeur! I believe in the equality of life, Ramerick. For many years Elcarians have not seen eye to eye with the world. But I know the corruption within my people. Since his death, we have lived a divided world. But the news of the heir to the throne of Terrasendia could bring a just world and end the corruption of my people, uniting them once more!"

"That is no concern of mine right now with respect. I only have the interest in finding my son! And we need to get going now!" Alex attempted to gather his things. "If what you say is true, the power of that seat lies in the swarm of The Dragadelf. I won't even have a throne to sit upon."

"A united Terrasendia could challenge The Dragadelf Ramerick, and take back the real seat of power. But only your blood would be enough. A true high King!"

"But what of my- wait," Alex's interrupted himself, his eyes lighting up in fright. "If I am as you say, of monarchy blood, that means that Jàque would carry it too?"

"Yes. He most definitely does!" Alex's body suddenly felt tighter as

Pirocès slowly approached. "I think there may be a reason why you couldn't find your son. Someone may have known about your blood and taken your son for their use."

"DON'T SAY IT!" Alex snapped. "I don't believe that! I can't believe that!"

"Believe what you will, but blindness to the truth will not help you find him. We must hope that is not the case. Embrace reality. And answers will flow. So far, every question you've asked doesn't seem right or make sense until now. Now suddenly after knowing about your true identity Ramerick-"

"-Stop calling me that!"

"You must see that the questions you ask now will make sense. Embrace reality."

The rising temperature in Alex's body simmered. His imagination wondered, and as horrified as Alex felt, he sensed an element of truth that he could not deny. He was so eager to ask him about The Time Stone, and the idea was on the tip of his tongue before remembering Mirabella's promise, from which he withdrew the urge to reveal his secret.

"So. Shall we begin?" Pirocès asked.

"Begin what?"

"How to get me out of this city!" Alex had briefly forgotten about his promise to the Elcarian in the melee of everything that just happened. "You are a true nobleman, yes? True to your word."

"Of course."

"Good. There are answers for you there, I promise, from my brother. But we must leave now."

Alex started to believe that maybe a trip to Casparia was in his best interests. Even though it was a risk of wasting his time should nothing help him, he felt that all options considered, it was his best chance.

"Let's go!" he said with an enthusiasm that brought a new found energy to his body. As Pirocès had the strength to gather his things, they stood by the entrance of his chambers, pursing his lips and with a gentle blow into the room, every candle slowly extinguished. The thin black smoke slowly clouded the room into an air of mystery.

Alex's world started to spin slower than it had back in Pirocès' chamber. So many things ran through his head like water skimming past pebbles in a shallow stream. The news of his son being alive, the venture to Casparia and perhaps the most bizarre notion that he had monarchy blood ultimately compelled him to his main priority, to find his son. Not that he believed he was the son of Felder, but of course when you're asked not to think of something so abstract and bizarre, it's impossible to shake it. It just wasn't possible, Alex thought.

Pirocès had gathered what possessions he could, not much by the looks of things as his small sack didn't seem full. They made their way to The Durge of Rombard Hill. Weaving through streets and ascending the mound. It was still the early hours of the morning and yet the night sky was still glooming white from the crescent moon.

"A sign," Pirocès happily said. "Thank you, my friend. For doing this."

The term *my friend* caught Alex a little off guard. This was by far and large his deepest darkest moment, and the thought of friends seemed so far down the pecking order of priorities to have. But after hearing that he appeared to have admitted to himself that he could not do this alone. With Bran dead, Brody and his Aunt Gràcene missing, Garrison killed, and Joric gravely wounded, he needed a friend. On top of that, the Time Stone had slipped from his grasp and now a potential war loomed with they who call themselves The Banamie. Pirocès reminded him that hope was not lost.

"Don't thank me yet, old man. I've done nothing yet," Alex replied.

"Oh, but you have," he said genuinely smiling once more as they came to the thick doors of The Durge.

Two knights stood on guard with finely combed Mohawks and impressive armour. The white moon reflected from their breastplates with spears in hand, they halted them both on approach.

"State the nature of your business," one of the guards said.

"I need to talk to The Durgeon. Its matters are private."

'The Durgeon is currently sleeping. Leave us your message, and we shall notify you when he has received."

"We need to talk to him now. It's a matter of urgency," Alex impulsively said.

"Wake the Durgeon of Rombard Hill?" he rhetorically asked as the two guards shared a laugh in how ridiculous that sounded. "Go back to your chambers and we shall-"

"-Alexandao?" said the voice of Relian, approaching them from behind. He was in no armour but instead his leather tunic which was well fitted. "Stand down soldiers."

"Durgeon, you are up early today."

"Yes, these warmer nights of late are a nightmare for me, Cedric. An early start, however, improves the day," Relian replied. "What business do you have with me? Not to mention why is the Elcarian by your side!?" he asked slightly peeved as he glared sideways at Pirocès.

"That is my business, sir. I need to talk to you."

Relian looked at Alex with a sense of disapproval.

"Come with me. Both of you."

Relian led them both inside the thick wooden doors of The Durge with the bright blue of the moon beaming through the doors.

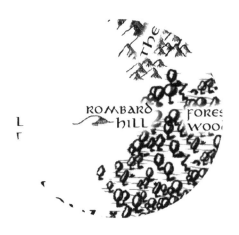

Flaw in the Law

"It's out of the question!" Relian answered. "I cannot help you. The only way this could be possible is by a royal decree. He cannot leave these walls without it."

Pirocès and Alex stood side by side in The Durgeon's quarters, with the former looking down looking somewhat dejected. The room itself seemed very organised and medieval. Swords, scabbards and helms decorated the room. The hour was early, only the ninth hour of night and still lit by candles and a gentle fire from the hearth, not to mention the blue moonlight which shone through large windows showing a view of most of the city and beyond. His perfectly crafted table was peppered with documents, ink and waxes.

"Why the sudden interest in the Elcarian, may I ask?" Relian queried. "You remember me specifically telling you to stay away from him?"

"I do," Alex replied.

"And yet you chose to ignore my counsel?"

"With respect," Pirocès interjected, "it was I who found him."

"I see," his tone suggesting his disapproval. "Are you aware this is not the first time he has come to me asking the same request? Why is now any different?"

Alex honestly had no answer to this, and neither did Pirocès.

"What more can you learn from me?" his voice sounded beaten like a prisoner confessing to a crime. "I have taught you everything I know," Pirocès pleaded.

"And I believe you. But we cannot risk you leaving right now. Tensions have never been this high between us and Elcaria, and I fear your knowledge of our city will aid their cause. I'm sorry, but this is just not something I can even entertain the idea of. You will have to find another way of finding your son, Alex."

He stayed silent as he had guessed that Relian knew why he took an interest in Pirocès.

"I will hear no more on the matter. My decision is final."

Relian led them to the door. Alex and Pirocès looked at each other with a sense of regret. A smiling Pirocès could not hide the hurt behind his eyes.

"I'm sorry," Alex said. "I'm so sorry."

Pirocès couldn't conjure a word. Instead, he nodded his head and prepared for life as it had been for the last eleven years. The Durgeon looked at them both with a heavy heart, turned the circular doorknob and pulled the door open. Upon opening the door, all three men stood in shock with their mouths slightly ajar at who was on the other side of the door.

"My Queen!" Relian said, bowing his head immediately after the initial shock had sunk in, with the other two following suit.

Queen Cathany radiated such beauty, dressed in the finest clothing on this half crescent night. She wore a hooded cloak with her red and brown hair sliding out the side. Her garments were flawless made up of intricate woven patterns. Clothing fit for a Queen.

"How can I be of service?" Relian asked.

"May I enter, Durgeon?" she calmly said with her pure and soothing voice. The simple tone of her voice bounced sweetly off the eardrum, like nectar to a bee.

"Of course, please. That will be all gentlemen," indicating to Alex and Pirocès it was time to leave.

"Actually," Cathany interjected, "my reason for being here involves them."

Their forlorn expressions turned into hopeful intrigue. Almost like school kids being let off detention.

"My Queen?" Relian asked.

"I know the purpose of these two being here at this hour and what they ask of you, Durgeon. I am here to tell you to honour that request."

Both Alex and Pirocès again looked at one another with growing hope.

"My Queen, how came you by the information they seek?"

"It doesn't take too much to work out. I lost my boy years back, you remember?"

"How can I forget? Prince Selbey was warm to all our hearts."

The Queen had indeed lost her son when he was two. The death of Prince Selbey caused extreme trauma between Romany and Cathany, and caused the whole city to mourn for months. One never recovers from the death of a child. A loss so unbearable, irreparable, it strips a piece of humanity, a part of a person's purpose away that forever is lost. The King had become a changed man ever since and for the worst with many silently questioning his ability to lead because of it. However, Cathany had grown stronger over time as a result.

"Durgeon, please tell me you have the release documents in this room."

"I do my Queen."

"Then, please find them."

Relian hesitated, caught between a world of right and law.

"With the greatest respect my Queen, I must remind you I am a man of order. A soldier of the law and regardless of my intentions, I must exercise restraint to my heart."

"Yes, of course, you must. But need I remind you, as you have reminded yourself that I am your Queen. And as your Queen, by law you must obey my command."

She calmly waved through the conversation as she walked the side of the room. Her tone did not change or escalate.

"My concern with your demand is that it directly conflicts the law. The documentation you require is only valid with the King's signature. However, let me find that for you."

Relian went over to a draw and scanned through several documents. The Queen nodded and stood patiently by the window.

"How old is your son?" Cathany asked Alex.

"He is ten," Alex replied.

"Such a tragedy, the events of Pippersby. And your wife?"

"She wasn't my wife. She was my… Well, she would have been," he bravely answered, holding back the urge to collapse at the mention of Amba and his child. It reminded him of the regret he had that he never proposed to her in time.

Queen Cathany walked towards him, her eyes sorrowful.

"I apologise sincerely. I loved my only born more than anything.

Were I in your position, I too would do everything I could. You say our friend here can help you?" indicating to Pirocès.

"Yes," he confidently replied. "When every answer to every question leads to nowhere, I've come to believe that any help, is help you should take."

He swallowed the influx of saliva building as his nerves started to take over, carefully keeping one eye on Relian searching through his papers. Cathany slowly smiled as she took the hands of Alex.

"I can't tell you how dearly I want to help you."

"Your words are kind my Queen."

"If every man were more like you, I would die very happy. My husband is an unfortunate man. Once fierce and mighty. I once thought he would rule the world. But that was when I was a naive princess. When I learned the politics of how to rule, I learned that there are things that can and cannot be done. But the one thing I truly hold dear to me, and something I will never forget to live by, is that your people are what make you who you are. Look after your people, and they will look after you."

"A noble philosophy."

"Indeed," she smiled. "I do however, have a question to ask. And please forgive the nature of the question." She released Alex's hands and held her own. There could not possibly be any question Alex was afraid of right now.

"Ask it, my Queen."

"How do you know your son is alive?"

Alex immediately turned his head toward Pirocès who in turn looked toward Relian who still had his back turned, scrolling through yellowed papers. Pirocès turned his grey and white head back to Cathany and confidently nodded to suggest he is most definitely alive. Cathany figured out that Pirocès must have used some form of magic to give them the information. And with that, she nodded back to the Elcarian.

"Here! I've found them," Relian interrupted. "A bit dusty I apologise, but they have been here a decade and probably the last time were touched were when I placed them here last."

The Queen extended her hands to ask for the papers which she took from Relian. She scrolled through the documents and immediately smiled.

"As you can see my Queen, every signature the document requires regarding his release clearly requests the signature from the King."

Relian's voice felt edgy and unconfident. "The relevant sections on page two and three do specifically state - "

" - Durgeon I must stop you there," Cathany interrupted politely.

"My Queen?"

"Please read the title of this document," she handed back the documents to Relian. "What does it say?"

"It says, A Royal Decree of Pardon," Relian sighed.

"A Royal Decree. Indeed. Ambiguity is a wonderful thing I have found. Wouldn't you agree?" her body language oozed quiet confidence. A confidence confirmed in Alex's mind as to who really made the important decisions in the city. "The documents do indeed require the King's signature however the document is invalid to this point. A Royal Decree is indeed for a royal to make." Relian looked a little shunted as he knew the Queen was right. "I will hereby sign the documents on the proviso that they are indeed *mine* to sign."

"The King will never accept this. Nor will Dalarose," Relian cautioned.

"Allow me to deal with my husband. You will not come to pay the price for my decision, that I swear to you. And as for our Màgjeur, he has no jurisdiction here. Look to your heart Durgeon. Look into the eyes of these two."

Relian reluctantly looked at Alex and Pirocès who returned the expression with almost desperation. He grunted before turning his back and looking outside the window from his desk, his fist curling into the wood.

"I never meant to make this difficult for anyone," Relian admitted.

"Of course, you didn't. You wouldn't be our Durgeon if you didn't abide by the law as your sworn duty. But this is a flaw in the law. And I urge you to exploit this, follow your heart as a true nobleman. Demonstrate the courage of our people here, in this moment. They both deserve this chance."

"Believe me, I know they do," his voice was quivering slightly at the conflict in his mind. "The horror you have had to endure, both of you. You deserve better than what you have been given."

"Please, Durgeon," Alex pleaded. "I only ask as a father to his son. Let me go with this man. I believe he can help me."

"So do I, Alex. I will never trust an Elcarian. But you are not like your people, Pirocès." Relian took a moment for himself.

"So does this mean you like me after all?" Pirocès jested. The following silence however, lasted what seemed like a decade as Relian did not respond. "Worth a try, I guess."

"My Queen," Relian diverted. "Based on the information that these documents are as you say, *invalid,* I have no choice but to act with the dignity of a nobleman and do what is right. I will sign the papers and accept the Queen's signature as valid."

Alex could not believe it. At last, a stroke of luck, a sign of what he hoped would be more to come. Relian took the feathered quill from the small vial of ink, dipped the residue back into the ink before scribbling the papers in several parts. He urged the Queen to do the same thing which she did with haste and the most elegant of script. Alex could not thank the Queen enough. She had no loyalty to him, no ties whatsoever. But she put her time and love for her people into him, which gave him confidence.

"And now I urge you both to go. Now! Before my husband learns of the legalities and reverses the decision. Relian. Thank you."

"My Queen," Relian nodded his head. "As always, it is my pleasure to serve you. I shall file these documents first thing after dawn, by which time you both must be gone."

"We will leave immediately," Alex said.

"Go," The Queen urged. "Go with the grace and love of our people. Find your son. Teach him to be like his father and watch him grow as you do."

"Thank you. To you both. You have no idea how much this means."

"I think we do," Cathany said, looking towards Pirocès as a happy tear rolled down and disappeared into the wrinkles of his cheek. He was going home.

They left The Durge at speed to gather what little Alex had from his room back in the Wendy Mare. It almost felt like he was being asked to dive to the very deepest part of the darkest ocean to find a small rock. Only this time he had a torch in the form of Pirocès. Even though the odds were stacked against him, they at least had a chance which provided hope that all is not lost. They walked towards the exit with the tear off of the pardon Relian gave them.

Suddenly an image of Joric's body flashed as he blinked, which stopped him in his tracks. He blinked again, but no image repeated itself. As he walked with Pirocès through the night streets, which started to glow orange as the sun rose into the early morning. It was slightly calmer than before.

"Where are the wards?" Alex asked Pirocès.

"The wards? What do you want with them?"

"My town's Durgeon is there, I completely forgot. I need to see him before we go."

"You realise procrastination won't help? Okay, if you go then I shan't follow, I don't want to get too close to the hill. They might start asking questions. It's the building west side of Rombard Hall. I shall meet you by the gate, but don't be too long."

Alex headed straight for the ward with haste, but not too quick to draw attention. He knew Joric was still unconscious, but despite his time constraint, he wanted to pay his respects in case it was the last time he was to see him as his nobleman conscience shone through.

He arrived at the ward where ivy made up much the decor, inside and out, covering the same light woods which constructed much of the city. Gliding down the quiet corridors, he came up to a room which was guarded by two Knights. Energised by his revelations with Pirocès that gormless feeling was no more. He felt he was now riding the wave of hope. He approached the guards.

"How go you, sir?" asked one of the helmed Knights.

"I am here to see Joric. My name is Ram... Alexandao. How is he?"

He felt strange almost accidentally calling himself Ramerick. True or not it was alien to him, but strangely, he found it difficult to shake.

"Not good. His wounds are severe and have become infected. His scapula is completely cloven in two, and his left lung has been punctured. Mirabella has sealed both wounds and he regained consciousness earlier, but it remains to be seen how his body heals."

Alex's eyes lit up at the prospect of speaking with Mirabella. The Time Stone seemed such a low priority right now but felt he needed to see her.

"Mirabella is here? Where is she?" The Knight turned his head to the door, indicating she was inside.

"One of the finest restoration Màgjeurs on the land. Joric would certainly have passed, were it not for her."

He allowed Alex to enter the room, which he did so slowly. And there she was, by the side of Joric. She turned her head towards him and looked at him, happy to see him. He looked at Joric who looked completely drained. Sleeping and breathing very slowly. His arm was linked up to a magical orange cord which was feeding liquids into his body soothing any pain he had. Alex made sure the door behind him was closed.

"It's good to see you alive, Alex," she slowly said.

"And to you. I didn't expect to see you here."

"My work never ends, here there and everywhere, but when I heard you and Joric were brought here, I had to come. I was beginning to think you weren't going to visit. I hope you didn't mind me flashing your mind just now."

Not that it bothered him knowing it was her that just flashed the image, but more painstakingly he felt the shame of not finding the stone for her, and in turn for Jàqueson.

"Mirabella… It was a stone. *Time in the Water,* it was The Time Stone."

"The stone?" she asked with amazement. "Oh my!"

"I don't have it. Mirabella I - "

" - Don't. I know you don't have it."

"How do you know?"

"You wouldn't have been allowed into Rombard Hill with it gleaming from your satchel."

He felt it was strange that she didn't ask about the attack, but guessed it was because she already knew and pressed the issue on their private quest. The reminder of losing the stone brought on that gormless feeling again.

"I found it. I held it in my hands."

She compressed a shriek. "You're telling me it was in your grasp? And what then?"

"Then, time slowed down. I look back, and I don't know if it was because of the power of that stone, or the fact someone had bludgeoned my head. I have no idea who or why."

"You were robbed?" her concern grew to almost frantic level.

"Yes! And I don't know who took it."

Mirabella's eyes started to dart, her breathing shortened, and her pace picked up.

"Alex, we need to inform The Blessèd!"

"What! Why?"

"I am such a fool! I should never have told you, I'm sorry,"

"Yes you should, why do we need to tell them?"

"Remember when I said that the enhanced knowledge of time in the wrong hands could change the fate of our world…" Alex didn't respond. "This is serious. We need to tell them Alex. Not just for our sakes, but all of us on Terrasendia."

"But you will lose your wreath."

"I will lose more than that if it ends up in the wrong hands. I need to leave immediately!" She went to leave before Alex stopped her.

"Wait! What if I said there may be a way."

"What are you talking about?"

"A way to find it."

"How!?"

"You know the Elcarian?"

"I've heard of him, yes."

"Were on our way to Casparia, right now."

"Alex. No!" she pressed even more than before. "You cannot trust the Elcarians!"

"And why not?"

"You could lose yourself in that realm. They are too dangerous."

"And what more is there to lose?" he whispered harshly. The nature of the conversation made his voice quiver and fail to breathe regularly. "In the space of two days I have found and lost that stone, I lost my home, the mother of my child, and I have lost him! Every avenue I've pursued has led me to nothing, no one has been able to help, until now and every single thing I do is to find my…" His voice broke, making him stop his tearful outburst. "The only thing keeping me going right now is finding the only thing I have left. And all I seem to be doing is getting further and further away. With each day he isn't cured, is a day closer to the day I will never see him smile again. How long till it spreads to his heart now?"

"It's unclear, but yes not long. But you think that going to Casparia will somehow help you find an answer."

"Pirocès is my only hope. No, I don't know him. But from what I do know of him, I believe him. He wants to go home just as much as me. I have to trust in hope now."

The same expression fixed on Mirabella's face again, the same one she had when Alex and Amba pleaded with her to reveal the eventual information of The Time Stone. Mirabella once again felt the weight of what was being asked of her.

"What can I do to help you?"

"Bella…" said the weak voice of Joric. They both turned to him to see his eyes flicker open.

"Joric!" Mirabella said. "How are you feeling?"

"Alive. Just."

"It's okay, Alex. He knows what happened to Amba and your son," subtly stressing on *Amba and your son* gave him a hint that she didn't want the conversation about the stone to go on any longer as Joric was not to know.

"Alex?" he was indebted to Joric for saving the last moments he had with Amba even though the saving was not enough to stop the inevitable.

"I'm so sorry,"

"It's okay, son. It was my job to protect her. Not yours."

"No. It should have been me. I should have done more, and I'm sorry."

"You couldn't, son. You did the bravest thing a man could do. Your heart told you to do something stupid and try and save us, but your head saved you from the same fate. I couldn't be more proud to have had my girl marry you..." Alex's eyes lit up.

"How did you know?"

"The whole town knew, son," they both faintly smiled. "But I couldn't have imagined anyone braver or nobler to have sealed her life with. My girl is gone, but if your son is alive, he has a chance because you made the right choice. Go and find my grandson. Bella?"

"Yes."

"My satchel. And Sythero. It's his."

They both looked over at the corner of the wall where his satchel and legendary sword rested. Joric's sword, Sythero was legendary. Woven into the pristine steel were pyrovines, magic-induced heat which lit up colours of orange and reds when in battle. Being a former militant of The Knights of Rolgan, he was honoured with the magic as a token of his services to their cause. The pommel shone with gold while the guard resembled a flame. The sheer beauty of the sword was a sight to behold.

"Joric I can't take that. It's yours!" Alex said, taken aback.

"I never had a son. But you were as good a son as I could have ever asked for. Take it! And use it with pride and honour. You need every bit of help you can get. I know I won't survive this, and Sythero needs a worthy champion, which it now has."

Alex was lost for words. He couldn't deny his wounds were grave, but the honour and privilege he felt in that moment stunned him. Eventually he managed to nod his head to acknowledge his thanks and acceptance of Joric's words. Mirabella passed the sword to Alex holding it delicately as it was presented inside its beautifully crafted sheath in the shape of flames. Alex took the sword with the same delicacy. He was amazed at how light it was. A newly found motivation followed when he pulled the handle and the sheath apart to reveal the legend of Sythero in its glory. The colours of fire lit up the pyrovines gently, which took Alex's breath away.

"Use it!" Joric implored. "Not just for fighting. But to inspire you, as it inspired me for so many years. Find my grandson."

"Thank you, I will see you again. Don't you die on me. My son needs his grandfather,"

Alex sheathed the sword and took it along with the satchel. Joric watched him as he left with Mirabella following. As they both walked the corridor to the exit, he sensed that Mirabella still wanted to persuade him not to go.

"What exactly will you do?" she asked.

"Pirocès says he knows someone who might be able to use clairvoyance to see where Jàque is. And possibly the stone."

"Alex," she pleaded. "By all means, go, take this risk for your boy. But do not let the Elcarians know about the stone. It's bad enough that whoever took it knew about it in the first place, but were those people to find out about it, people who Terrasendia cannot trust, it would be a disaster."

"What of Jàque? What if I find him, and I don't have the cure?"

"You must promise me this, please. I've risked a lot by sharing the information about the stone, but please. His life is the most important thing to you I understand that, but the lives of millions of others rest on this. We cannot risk it falling into the wrong hands."

"So what do I do?"

"I don't know, I really don't and I'm sorry! I fear if they managed to get a hold of it, there might not be a home for him to go back to. They are very powerful and have been known to extend their hand if it meant they could gain, no matter who suffered as a consequence."

Alex certainly had something on his mind ever since Mirabella told him about The Time Stone.

"I don't understand. If this information was so fragile and the risk was too great, then why tell me in the first place?" Alex had pondered this question for some time which shunted her.

"Alex-"

"I also think it is fair to ask how you knew about such a thing."

"I appreciate you have questions. But I'm bound to secrecy. I believe I have already broken one vow by telling you. I cannot break another."

"Fine."

Alex promptly walked away with Mirabella hastily following.

"Alex, stop!"

"Thank you, but I need to get going."

"Don't use that reverse-psychosis rubbish on me!"

"I'm not. I'm going. Don't worry. I'll do as you wish."

"Just promise me, stay low, get what you need and get out. Don't lose yourself."

"I will, I promise... *Promise I'll try.*"

And with that, he was satisfied that was enough to keep a nobleman's word. He bowed his head and she regrettably nodded back, sighing as it lowered. Alex turned to leave, heading towards the gate of the city. Mirabella felt the world was slowly drifting away from her. Dazed by the prospect of even more disasters unfolding she returned into Joric's room to tend to his wounds.

Revealing Destiny

"Nothing," Hiyaro simply declared as he reported back on their investigation into Razing Gellows.

Alicèn couldn't hide his disappointment that his theory and concerns were not vindicated. There was however a slight reprieve in the sense that his relationship with The Blessèd Mage of Earth had grown stronger with their shared discoveries. Their recent revelation about Melcelore was still just a theory so Alicèn made it his sole focus to find out for certain.

"Well, that's disappointing to say the least."

"Indeed. Unfortunately for you, it does mean you are like all others who are conscripted here, bound for the minimum term."

"Well, I better get learning then," Alicèn threw away his words as he turned from Hiyaro, storming out of the great hall and down to the cave once more.

"You didn't honestly believe they would find anything, did you?" Meigar asked.

"I didn't. If Draul's army is indeed as big as I fear, he would be smart enough to conceal it. But I still believe Rya used Razing Gellows to distract us from where he is truly hiding." Alicèn pulled up a chair to Meigar's table and sat. "But I want to know about Melcelore. Why did he become the most feared Màgjeur on Rèo?"

Meigar sat back in his chair before staring blankly at the table, bouncing heavy sighs.

"Many years ago Melcelore was once a true friend to Felder. He was also very much in love with a woman. Unfortunately for him, Felder grew to love the same person."

"Who was it?"

"Her name was Eveleve."

"The Blessèd Mage of Life?"

"Indeed. She was once Melcelore's. And they loved each other. Fiercely and wholeheartedly. Or so Melcelore thought."

"Felder wanted her for himself?"

"Yes. And Kings tend to get what they want. Despite morality and righteousness, if they want something they get it. So Felder took Eveleve for himself."

"Would it be right to feel sorry for him by now?"

"Oh, no! Not after what he became. But it was not the fact that she was stolen from Melcelore. The thing that really broke him was that she loved Felder back. His heart and world shattered at the hands of a King who betrayed their own friendship for his lust for love."

"I had no idea Felder was that ruthless."

"He was the most ruthless man I've ever known. He was mighty. Strong. Invincible almost. Only one thing could have killed him."

"Love."

"Yes. But not his love for Eveleve… The love for his child."

Alicèn raised his head surprised, "so the rumours are true?"

"There was a reason Eveleve was not seen for such a time before The Dragasphere. She was carrying Felder's child and only a few knew of her whereabouts for the protection of her and the child. Not even the members of The Blessèd Order knew all of the details. In fact, we still do not know if the child was ever born."

"Someone must have known."

"My knowledge stops with a man named Ramavell. He was apparently the midwife to Eveleve. Beyond that, Felder kept it away from common knowledge."

"What do you think? Do you think she had the baby?"

"What a story that would be. But no. I do not. The timings do not match up. She would have had the baby near enough at the same time as The Dragasphere was created and they would never have survived."

"But Eveleve escaped, right?"

Meigar slowly shook his head, "I doubt it very much Alicèn."

"We all know she has not been seen for many years, but The Blessèd Mage of Life cannot die, surely."

"She could if she chose to pass her life onto another, which she may well have done to save her child's life. But we do not possess the sight to see that."

"Gracelands!" Alicèn quietly gasped. "So you're telling me out of all members of The Blessèd order, Felder dies, Aristuto and Eveleve goes missing and The Blessèd Mage of Earth goes into hibernation?"

"We grow smaller and smaller."

"Why don't you share this knowledge with each other?"

"Only in times of peril would we ever convene. We often have frosty differences with one another. If ever the day were to come where you saw the remaining members in one place... That would be the day our end is near."

Alicèn paused in thought as it was all a fair amount to take in before trying to get back to his primary concern.

"So before, I'm guessing this is what sparked their rivalry?"

"Correct. All members of The Blessèd Order agreed Felder was our divine leader, despite the reservations of him marrying Eveleve, making her the Queen. But as their love grew, so did Melcelore's demise."

"I'm lucky I never found love. Look at what it does to people."

"Words of a soldier," Meigar assertively said. "And thus this started the enraging rivalry between the two. Melcelore vanished for many years. In that time he manifested in the unnatural, becoming a pioneer in The Protecy. By the end, there was a theory that Melcelore only loved Eveleve because of her powers of eternal life. But I think that wasn't a strong enough reason for Melcelore to delve into the darkest corners of our imaginations. The only true reason I can think of was that his heart was truly broken. Seeing his whole world reject him and love another. Only that would provide enough self-torture and utter madness to turn one's self to ruin!"

"What exactly did he do to become so evil?"

"He invented the art of Soul Mancing. It's new magic which he devised many years ago. Luckily for us, it is not exactly common knowledge of how to use it. Only those who share darker platforms of magic dare practice it. It's sadistic. It butchers the soul, like ripping the heart from a pig! Since its invention, it was made highly illegal and those who are ever found to practice it are instantly sentenced to death as a deterrent to others."

"What does it do?"

Alicèn could see Meigar grow nervous at the simple thought of trying to explain.

"It bridges the gap between life, death and the purgatory they become trapped in," he explained. "The heinous process is where the mantrancer rips both soul and blood from someone whose body is still alive, only to then absorb it for themselves and use it for their desired deeds. Typically this comes in the form of casting their newly captured soul into a dead body, to manipulate and control them to do their bidding."

Alicèn's growingly pale face shared the same horror. He felt apprehensive to know more in case it disturbed him further.

"And what happens to one's perception? Do they die when their soul is taken?"

"… Oh no. They do not die. When their soul is cast into a body of the dead… They see… They hear… They feel… Everything!"

Alicèns teeth began to grind against each other as he grew increasingly nervous of how frightening the prospect of Soul Mancing was. It sickened him to the bone.

"Everything?" he whispered.

"Imagine you right now, not being able to control a thing that you do. Never resting. Never living. Constantly in purgatory, awaiting the commands of your master. A victim of Soul Mancing would appear as a dead body in possess but the eyes would be that of the poor soul that is trapped inside. The wide-open glare would look as if the soul is trying to say GET ME OUT OF HERE! You can see why we don't want Terrasendia to know just what exactly this is."

"And I thought that fletching was evil."

"That too is just as unimaginable. But fletching is considered less terrifying as you are only extracting the blood from someone once they are already dead, taking the use of their protecy in the process. Unless you have put something in place to preserve the soul, the protecy can be stolen through fletching once the subject has died."

"And that's what you said you practice?"

"Indeed. The art of Soul Preservation is not illegal, nor is it considered dark. It is the manner in which it exists which determines how it is labelled."

"That's how The Ancient Drethai survived from Melcelore, isn't it? They created a spell to preserve their souls while knowing their bodies were going to perish."

"Yes, through preserving their souls Melcelore could not touch them. That is what they desired."

Alicèn was purely fascinated by the knowledge he never knew. Being a military man he knew much about the art and mastery of war, but his knowledge of magic and what forms it could take was limited and lacking, almost making him feel like a school kid with much still to learn.

"I want you to teach me."

"Teach you?"

"How to preserve one's soul."

Meigar looked at him with a curious eye, "you want to delve into the art of Soul Preservation?"

"I do," Alicèn confidently stated.

"May I ask why the sudden interest?"

"Survival. It's the foundation of thought. If you asked the question of why anybody does anything, it will always trace itself back to why we are even here in the first place. To survive."

"A philosopher indeed. You are aware of course, that to do this you need to enchant The Protecy first?"

Alicèns face once more took a turn. "No, I did not. Is there no way around it?"

"Unfortunately not. In order to preserve the soul, you must be able to channel it and cast onto something using The Protecy. Without that knowledge, you cannot hope to preserve."

"The Ancient Drethai. Are you saying they preserved their souls onto something?"

"You don't need a specific object to encapsulate your soul onto. You can indeed cast it out vacant into the world, but you need the use of The Protecy to draw out the soul. It is the only way."

Alicèn paced, contemplating very seriously.

"Do it!" Alicèn impulsively said.

Meigar sharply looked at him, "you want to use magic? Even though you are Septalian?"

"No, I do not and will not use magic! But I think I can justify enchanting The Protecy. Would that seem right to you?"

"It is not me you need to answer to. If you think you can justify and weigh up the sovereignty of your people against the demands of your tasks, only you can make that decision."

Alicèn truly believed that it was the right thing to do. He had no idea why, but it just seemed so right to him. Gravity pulled him to the decision leaving him feeling that it was almost fate.

"How do you do it?"

Meigar stood and went over to the corner of the cave, unlocking a wooden cabinet. As the cupboard doors opened, Alicèn saw a plethora of protecy stones on different shelves. Some were slightly bigger than others, but mainly they were all the size of one's fist. The black and dark green colours were the primary makeup of all Protecy stones. Meigar picked one at random and quickly examined it before taking it and locking back up the cabinet. He placed the stone onto his desk. The brighter lights from the candles and torches revealed certain purities in the stone which were clear and see-through.

"Is this mine?" Alicèn asked.

"It is. Once enchanted you best look after it. If it gets destroyed, you'll lose the ability to use its powers forever."

"Not too worried about that."

"Still, if it's destroyed you cannot use Soul Preservation so keep it safe. I've picked perhaps the clearest stone I have. Not that you will ever use it but just in case."

"You're right. I will never use it. I'm ready."

"I warn you. Enchanting protecy stones is a little strange. It can often cause side effects."

"Such as?"

"It varies from Màgjeur to Màgjeur. Seizures. Flashbacks… Death."

Alicèn grew even more nervous. "Death!?"

"… Just kidding," Meigar chuckled wickedly which released a certain amount of tension in the air. "To enchant, you must first choose an affinity. What's your preference?"

"Not that I have given it much thought, but I think air would be my choice."

"A good choice."

"A sentimental one. Aristuto was someone known to my people. I never met him, but between Landonhome and us he cared much for the poor."

"A favourite of yours?"

"Don't take it personally."

"I'm not bitter."

"Sure, you're not." They both smiled at one another.

"Very well. Air it is. And you are aware that once enchanted, there is no changing once it is done?" Alicèn nodded confidently. "Good. Now every affinity has a different process and enchantment to undertake.

Take the stone in both hands."

Alicèn did feel the pressure of going against his morals, but it felt right. The cool stone was not any heavier or lighter than he expected. "What do I do?"

"Relax. And follow my instruction. For the enchantment of air, you need to feel the affinity around you. Close your eyes." Alicèn obeyed. "Tune in to your senses... What do you feel...?"

"... Nothing. I feel nothing."

"You have to really tune in Alicèn. Feel the air around you. Air will only respond and accept you if you respond and accept back."

He tried as best as he could to feel the air around him, but in the stillness of the cave, it was challenging.

"I can't feel anything!"

"Keep trying. Breathe and don't get frustrated... Relax."

Alicèn breathed in very slowly and then breathed out. Suddenly he tuned into the flow of his breath instead. With each flowing breath, he felt more and more connected with himself and the air that was passing through him. He grew very light headed as he allowed his deep breaths to take him to where ever it wanted.

All of a sudden, he felt a growing coolness around him. The air swept in from outside the cave, circling lightly all around him. Several parchments and books flew off of desks and swirled in the air as he was almost in a trance.

"I feel it! I feel the air around me."

"Good. Stay relaxed and accept the air as part of you. Let it flow through you as if you are one with each other."

"Yes! I feel it now. It's like its mine!"

"It agrees with you. Keep that connection going! You need to confirm and establish this connection. Speak these words. And keep repeating them."

"When do I stop?" he asked with his eyes still closed, feeling the flow of air not just around him but going through him. The Protecy was alive in Alicèn.

"You will know when. Repeat these words and establish The Protecy... *Cassas ala è, protasas iumlai.*"

"*Cassas ala è, protasas iumlai...*" he quietly repeated as the air still flowed around the cave and through his body. "*Cassas ala è, protasas iumlai... Cassas ala è, protasas iumlai... Cassas ala è, protasas iumlai...!*" He did not stop repeating but wondered what he had to do to find this moment to stop.

"Feel it Alicèn! Feel the air and the bond you now share!"

"I am… I am… *I am…*"

Alicèn's head grew lighter and lighter until his mind started to fade out. Just before he lost all consciousness, the strangest of things came into his mind. A paralysis of thoughts soon flooded and ravaged his mind in what felt like a lucid dream.

His mind's eye flew through the dusk sky like a bird keeping watch over the whole of Rèo. His flight rapidly took him over a peaceful Felders Crest, circling it to then gliding through the busy streets of its architectures and elaborate structures before ascending once more.

Suddenly the orange sky turned darker and more sinister as the seven shadows of The Dragadelf raced passed him with their black sails, inflicting their pyro storms onto the city. His flight took him high to view the construction of The Dragasphere, which enveloped the city.

Why on Rèo was he seeing this? he thought to himself. He didn't feel a thing. He knew he should feel empathy for the thousands who died but for some reason he couldn't.

Suddenly within the dream he had found himself in, the world turned upside down and inside out until all he could see was the grey of the sky. The image gentle, calm and still. He started to notice a darkness bleeding in from around the edges of his vision. The sky seemed to be falling as the horizon slipped from his view. He soon realised that he was the one falling, agonisingly slowly, not the sky, as he descended into what looked like a large, bottomless hole. Alicèn's view of the sky slowly grew smaller and smaller as the sides of the hole swallowed up the light.

Suddenly the sound of footsteps were heard marching behind him. As he tracked back, the sound grew louder until the crunch of a boot landed right beside him. It continued its travel until he suddenly saw more ghostly, bare legs plodding either side of him as they waltzed towards the entrance heading out of the cave. The sound of heavy weaponry dragging on the stones chinged and scraped away in his head as he continued to track back. He saw many other legs walk towards the entrance, until handfuls became hundreds…then hundreds becoming thousands.

He tried as lucidly as he could to capture as much detail as he could as to who the marching force was. The cave was so dark it was impossible to make out for certain from his current point of view. By that point the sky in front of him was less than half in comparison to the swallowing cave.

As his sight slowly became clearer, his eyes strained to determine what was happening and started to notice more details of the marching men around him. White orbs of light radiated from their broken chests. The charcoaled skin of every marching body looked burned and torched and was clothed modestly in ragged armours covering their loins and torsos. Alicèn ascended over thousands of animated corpses, all marching toward the entrance before a huge flash of white and pale blue light erupted suddenly, temporarily blinding him.

He wondered what had happened when the blinding light started to move into a single concentrated point – like the sun.

A deathly, hungry growl was heard from the light. Still hovering above the burnt marching bodies, Alicèn saw the spine, sails and shadow of a Dragadelf gliding toward the entrance with an almighty roar. Without warning, he received the hugest pulse of his heart as if someone had bludgeoned it with a steel Warhammer, snapping him out of his dream to black emptiness…

"*Alicèn…? Alicèn…!? Alicèn…!? ALICÈN!!??*" Meigar's words came into fruition snapping him out of his trance.

As he came around, he was fully aware of what he had just seen. His breathing was just as heavy if not more so than what it was before. Not only that, but his heart thudded with such enormity it felt like it was trying to escape. His eyes opened to see Meigar kneeling beside him as he had clearly fallen back.

"What just happened?" Alicèn gasped.

"You're okay. Keep still. You blacked out, but you're fine. Take your time."

Alicèn winced at the stabbing pain in his back as a result of his fall. He slowly got to a sitting position before contemplating what just happened.

"In all my years of witnessing the enchantment, I have never seen someone react so strongly before."

"What happened to me?"

"Your mind just went. I couldn't catch you in time. You've been out only for minutes, but look."

Meigar indicated to the stone on the floor beside him. It's once see through and still insides were now encapsulated with slow swirling winds.

"You are now the proud owner of The Protecy of air!" he announced. Alicèn completely forgot amongst what he just saw of what he was doing in the first place. He wasn't sure whether he felt elated or sad that he was now a Màgjeur. His muted reaction confused Meigar.

"You don't seem happy at all."

"What was that?"

"What?"

"What I saw!? It felt so real!"

"Of course, it was real... The opening up of The Protecy taps into the path of the one enchanting, often giving off memories that have happened. So whatever you saw had to be real. That is part of the process The Protecy needs to enchant... Alicèn?"

His stunned face grew white. "Just to be clear..." he slowly said with a substantial gravitas to his words. "That it's impossible for what I just saw, to not be true?"

"Impossible. The enchantment would not have worked if the by-product wasn't true. Memories can't be fabricated in any way. Are you alright? What did you see?" Meigar asked with growing concern.

Alicèn had never felt so frightened in all is life. His heart drummed so fast it injected a surge of adrenaline through his veins. He tried to scramble to his feet before getting up too quickly. Suddenly the burning sensations of bile started to build and erupt out of his stomach, scorching the linings of his throat and expelling out of his mouth. His vomit splattered over the rocks as he stumbled onto them. Meigar tried his best to help placate him before resting him against the side of the cave once more.

"Alicèn! What is it? What did you see? Alicèn!"

He gritted his vomit-stained teeth as he drew staggered breaths. His intense stare into the distance grew more focussed as Meigar's words seemed to drown out from the horror of his realisation. He tried to gather himself from what he saw, re-piecing the images trying to link them all. When he realised exactly where he was in those visions, he pieced together the puzzle which prompted him to slowly look at a distressed Meigar.

He braced himself, mustering the strength to tell him what was imminently upon them.

A Man of the Realm

"This is most irregular," a confused Hiyaro told Alicèn who barely moved from the spot.

Some of The Reinhault's top officers also were in attendance in the cave. Still spellbound by fright, he could feel his back bouncing off the cave wall as his breathing did not shallow. The stinging smell of dried bile started to waft around the cave.

"This is no lie, Hiyaro," Meigar intervened, "what The Durgeon saw was real."

"How do you know he tells the truth? He could be attempting to escape."

"Hiyaro - "

" - In any case, this was not a memory Max. This seemed like a vision, yes?"

"It would appear that way."

"So he claims that through this *vision*, thousands of dead bodies armed for war, along with a Dragadelf which, coincidentally, he has already claimed has somehow escaped, is now upon the realms of Terrasendia?"

Alicèn confidently nodded.

"Can we at least entertain the idea that this is true?" Meigar advised. "What then?"

"But this is not. You claim this King Draul builds an army here, then a Dragadelf appears there, then more of these burned dead... Forgive me, but this is not logical. Hardly a prelude to war."

"Since when has any war been logical?"

"Max!" Hiyaro's defiance grew stronger. "He cannot explain this. You cannot explain this. How do you expect me to act upon visions and prophecies, especially from the irregularities surrounding his enchantment? You understand our problem here? You are asking us to risk the very secrecy of our work based on foresight?"

"Because if he is right... There will be no Terrasendia to defend. I implore you to seek wisdom here."

Hiyaro sighed in frustration, "and where would you suggest this army was walking out of? - "

" - The Draughts..." Every person in the cave turned their attention to Alicèn. His eyes fixed on a point in the distance. "The same place Draul would have hidden his armies. I feel I've known for many years. Something about that place... The place I feared above all. One day knowing I would confirm what lurked within the shadowy depths. Only now, I'm beginning to understand."

"The Draughts?"

"I felt it. I felt its presence. The Dragadelf's presence as if it were in this room right now. More real than anything I've ever felt."

"You are entering dangerous territory with your obsession with these theories."

"Tell me what's down there and I will take everything I said since being here back."

The reaction to Alicèns words seemed like he had just frozen time. No one had an answer, instead, they looked blankly at Hiyaro.

"It has been dormant for many years."

"Tell me why..." Hiyaro continued his intense stare into him. "Listen to me. Now. All of you. The reason why it has been, as you say, *dormant*, is because that's what Draul wants you to think."

"A spell of concealment would seem the most logical answer," Meigar suggested. "Shielding our eyes from the retribution they wish to inflict."

"And who do you suggest would provide such a spell powerful enough to shield not just one, but two whole armies, my lord?" Hiyaro asked.

"The only one strong enough to imply such complexities to it. The one this world has forgotten. You know of whom I speak."

Hiyaro remained intensely calm. "Impossible."

"No. It is not."

"You believe that Melcelore has arisen from his doom?" Hiyaro asked incredulously.

"The Durgeon and I, cannot hide the theories we have uprooted and we have not the time to explain. It is quite possible this army has already escaped The Draughts and are on the march."

"That brings me to my next complication. You forget that The Dragasphere you were very much part of creating is simply impregnable, is it not? Nothing goes in, and nothing comes out, that is how it was created. How do you explain now seeing a Dragadelf fly into our world once more?"

Meigar and Alicèn's only explanation lay solely on what was unknown to them inside The Draughts.

"Our theory is still raw, Hiyaro. And we have not the time to explain. You must let The Durgeon go. Let him warn his people of what is coming for them!"

Hiyaro paused in contemplation, which made them both feel a little hopeful. "Why him, Max? Why does he see something that no one else can?"

Meigar looked at Alicèn, who continued his train of thought in his mind. "I am not sure. I hope I will find out just why, but that will never happen unless we act. Now. All of us!"

Hiyaro sighed once more. "We will run another investigation - "

" - No!" Alicèn snapped. "We do not have the time. If they are at The Draughts, then The Banamie are ahead of them!"

"Where do you suggest they will be heading then?"

"An eye for an eye. A heart for a heart. Durge Helm. That's as poetic as it gets for Draul. Should he wipe the city out, his retribution will have only just begun."

"Our work has stayed secret for many years."

"You want to protect the lives of the many you start there... Or I will!"

"You are bound here for the minimum term, Durgeon Alicèndil."

Alicèn's determination gave him the power to come to a stand.

"On my honour. As a man of the realm. As a Knight of Septalia, charged with the protection of all on this land, for all things good and green on Rèo, I demand my immediate release!" His passionate declaration did not phase Hiyaro.

"You think you are the first to threaten me?"

"I think I am the first to threaten your philosophy... The very thing that keeps me here."

"Which is?"

Alicèn looked at Meigar who's face turned in the most subtle of ways, to proud and honoured as he knew what The Durgeon was going to say.

"... Survival." They continued to stare off. Hiyaro looked away in disgust, shaking his head looking slightly annoyed. "If the land of Septalia falls, you have failed. That is not the purpose of The Reinhault as I've learned. You all pride yourselves on protecting them and for them to never truly know the horrors that you shield them from. I ask you all to seek out that pride once more. This is by far the greatest threat you will ever likely see. Help us. What does The Reinhault do? Does it buckle under the pressure? Or does it act in the true light of its purpose and protect it from those who wish to harm it...?"

The anticipation in silence grew more awkward as everyone awaited Hiyaro's verdict. He angrily looked away from Alicèn, subtly shaking his head.

"... Go," Hiyaro quietly said.

Alicèn was slightly taken back, not quite reacting in case he didn't hear Hiyaro's word correctly.

"You mean - "

" - Go, Durgeon Alicèndil," his disappointed response relaxed Alicèn's shoulders with pure relief. He had won his case and the relief started to spread and blossom within. He approached Hiyaro with sincerity.

"Thank you," he said.

"All I ask of you is that you never mention us and our purpose here. I hope your honour keeps you to this vow. Farewell." Hiyaro quickly turned and headed for the exit, along with the other knights who followed.

"You will not help me?" Alicèn called to his back.

"I have helped you beyond my remit Durgeon. Gracelands save you if you are right."

The cave emptied of all except Meigar who remained with Alicèn. His jaw slightly ajar as he couldn't quite believe it himself.

"You've just done something no other has ever managed to do here," Meigar proudly said.

"Is that a good thing?"

"Not if everything you envision is truly upon us. There is something about you. Something compelling. That I have never seen in any man living, you are not like the rest, and I have known many Knights. Many heroes. But you don't strike me as someone who wants that. I believe you hold the true values of The Reinhault. Something which he may not like to admit, but he sees in you. Which is why he released you, because deep down, I believe he trusts you. With my blessing, go. Go with the graces of all good men, women and children you were born to protect."

"I will."

"I want you to have something."

Meigar hurried over to a wooden chest and lifted out a long rectangular box which he placed onto the table with delicacy and grace. He carefully slid open the lid to reveal a perfectly crafted longsword which glimmered against the torchlight.

"This is the only remaining heirloom of my family. Forged from the fires in Meigarthia. I want you to take it."

Alicèn snapped his head back to The Blessèd Mage in astonishment. "No! No, I cannot take this!"

"You can, and you will."

"It belongs to your family."

"To serve and protect all those good on Rèo. I have little use for it being a Màgjeur, and I feel the time is right to pass onto another for good use."

"I don't know what to say."

"A thank you would be nice," they both laughed gently. "Take it."

Alicèn grew nervous at the sight of this sword which was sheathed in a black and silver embroidered scabbard. He slowly reached into the box and gripped the tacky leather handle with his steady hand, lifting the body of the sheath with his left. The grip alone stuck marvellously to his mitts.

"How many deaths has it seen?" Alicèn asked.

"None, but now it will. It has a worthy master. Cherish it like your own."

Alicèn felt the urge to pull the sword from the guard which he did so quickly, shinging away as he presented the sword in all its prestige in front of his face. The long tip of the blade seemed to go on forever. The blade was made of perfectly straight steel, the guard curving elegantly at the sides. He felt totally at home with it as the balance was perfectly weighted, sitting in his grasp.

"I shall wield it in honour of your family."

Meigar walked around to stand opposite him. He placed his right hand onto Alicèn's left shoulder as he counselled.

"We did not have time for me to show you how to preserve the soul, but remember this. Should the time ever come where you feel the need to do so... Allow the ancient power running through the veins of this sword help you. You will know how when the time comes."

Alicèn could not believe his luck. After the potential anger at having to stay enlisted for two years he was now free to leave, with not only a beautiful sword and friend in a Blessèd Mage but also with the means to truly protect his people from the impending dangers they now faced. His empowerment in knowledge was the most significant slice of luck he ever had. He could not ignore the disappointment of not being taught how to preserve the soul, but in the balance of things, he felt tremendously fortunate. He knew that his obsession with Soul Preservation would become so great in time, it could well consume him. He almost forgot entirely, he possessed the ability to use The Protecy of air. Not that he ever would do so, even in dire peril he was not wholly convinced using it sat right with him.

"Where will you go?" Meigar asked as he released his hand.

"I will rally as many as I can. The Banamie will strike first. And they will strike hard. I need to get to Durge Helm before they do. Draul's army will travel the northern scape where it's least watched. Despite their presence being shielded by Melcelore, or so we think, the helm will realise in time to prepare."

"Then let us not waste a second more! Warn your people. And if you see him, Draul, give him a fitting end with that sword."

"I shall. What will you do?"

"I shall ride for The Draughts. We have put this off for far too long. We need to find out for certain what is down there. If what you say is happening, there are many more questions we need to answer. And I fear above all if Melcelore has indeed returned, The Blessèd Order may well be gathered in that one room after all."

Alicèn felt nervous for Meigar entering The Draughts alone, but nonetheless, he had more pressing concerns with the salvation of Septalia.

"Prove us wrong my friend. Farewell."

Meigar could tell how much Alicèn appreciated him as he exited the cave. His gratitude could not be misplaced as he proudly hurried back to his chambers to gather what little he had. Luckily The Reinhault gifted him one of the shire horses to aid him in his cause. He rode upwards along the freckles of the valley where the main entrance was. He looked down one last time at this place, feeling a portion of guilt for the very first time. He could see with the speck of his vision Hiyaro looking up at him from the great hall with his routinely intensely stare, before slowly raising his hand, suggesting goodbye.

The race against time grew ever more pressing. With each thudding rhythm of his galloping horse, the window to ride to Septalia's aid diminished. He had to naturally assume that Durge Helm would receive information of the impending attack in good time to organise its defences, despite the apparent smokescreen from Melcelore. While it would not be enough Alicèn imagined, he prioritised the rallying of who he could muster over riding straight for the capital. Should he raise the alarm in good time, he may have a chance to muster enough of a force to defend the city.

He slithered his way around The Draughts and rode to every stronghold, city and fortress on route in southern Septalia.

"Send every Bluewing you have," Alicèn ordered to Osgrey, The Durgeon on Winstanton, which was the first fortress on his journey. "Order every man and milden with the strength to bear arms to meet at Brackbannen before the sun sets tomorrow."

"Yes, Durgeon," the younger red-headed Durgeon obeyed at once. Everyone knew, of course, Alicèn's prestige. And his plan was for his men to rally at Brackbannen, one of the largest strongholds on the realm closest to Durge Helm. It would be a twelve-hour ride from there to the capital. "Forgive me. But every man? Not just Knights?"

"Yes. Every man you can spare."

"Of course," Osgrey obeyed, understanding the weight of the situation being asked to rally men who weren't even considered fighters. Hundreds of Bluewings rippled out of Winstanton's watchtowers, sending word to raise the alarm.

He swiftly rode to the next locations, by which time they were already saddled up and ready to go, moving as one with The Durgeons from location to location.

Amid the intense panic and urgency, Alicèn managed to find a moment of peace in the morning ride as he rode the misty plains of the realm which he has seldom really appreciated. He wasn't sure if he had the capability to love, being a man of regiment and militia but found a hidden beauty in the land he was entrusted to protect. He gathered this was the closest thing to loving something he was ever going to get.

His next location was Ragabastion. It only really dawned on him then that his closest band members on Durge Helm were not there to help him with his fight. He explained Xjazen's death to Fenrir Flent, The Durgeon on Ragabastion who Alicèn felt compelled to honour his memory. With the little time he had, he took a white rose into Xjazen's chambers, lit the fires he would never light again and gracefully dropped the flower into the flames, sparing a thought for his band member. He had no family and no real purpose other than to aid the protection of Septalia. When the flower had quickly wilted and dissolved to ash, he journeyed out once more to Brackbannen.

To his surprise, not many of the strongholds had responded to his call to arms when they arrived through its tall, thick gates.

"We made every effort to raise the alarm to the whole of Septalia, both north and south!" Osgrey explained to the great hall in Brackbannen.

The many Knights there were arrogant, but brilliantly poised for a fight. The Itranir as they liked to be known, was the home of Alicèn's band members Falcone and Athrempitritus who also fell fighting Dreanor. He paid his respects in the same way as he did for Xjazen when he had the opportunity.

Only a handful of Durgeons representing their strongholds appeared in the cold cobblestoned hall to discuss their plans when they arrived at sunrise. Alicèn stood at the head of the war table with a map and crafted wooden figures to help with the geography. It was impossible to say just how many Barklers there were, but as a precaution, he anticipated a lot more just in case.

Osgrey and Fenrir were also in attendance along with Conway Gallaghan of Brackbannen. Also, Thaniel of the smaller towns of Sunkern and Semberly were there too. And lastly, Anique, charged with defending the even smaller but plentiful villages on the district of The Blackmarlè, as south as Septalia goes.

"We have less than half of the men on the south side of Septalia," Osgrey explained. "Why has no one else come? Chelsern? Denmill? The Denishales? Where are they?"

"Could it be conceivable that the Bluewings never made it to their destination?" Fenrir suggested.

"Bluewings fly higher than anything else. It's unlikely that arrows could reach that high," Alicèn said.

"Something else that may be relevant," Conway said. "We had word from Landonhome to say there was an attack in the village of Pippersby not long ago."

"Pippersby? Why on Rèo would they attack such a precise village?"

"It's unclear."

"An isolated attack?"

"It would appear so. The rest of the Hollybourne district and indeed Landonhome seems unscathed. It seems strange. Could there have been something there we have missed?"

"I think we have missed many things here. Our duty is to put it right. What happened there?"

"The village burned in their pillaging. When the Knights of Rombard Hill got there, it was only too late. Their declaration apparently was for *King Draul*. Few survivors remain but why would they not be concentrating everything they have onto Durge Helm?"

"I don't know."

"What did Romany do to retaliate?" Osgrey asked.

"Sat on the privy no doubt!" Alicèn blankly jibed. "Do we have any cause to believe they could help us now?"

"They would never get here in time," Conway said. "With the force needed they would take more than a week to arrive. So no. We are on our own."

"Then, so be it."

"In any case, if we ride into the night with what we have, it seems like we will not have enough to even make a dent in their front line come the morning."

"And that's if the helm has still not fallen by then," Anique contributed. An eerie sense of foreboding distilled the room.

"Nonetheless..." Alicèn intensely said, "we will not abandon our people. If Draul truly wants to wipe us out, we will open the gates of The Understunde onto him and his army!"

His rallying words were met with convincing nods of the heads from the other Durgeons.

"We are with you, Alicèn!' Osgrey said. "We are with our people!"

"Agreed," Fenrir chipped in. "If we are to die. We will take as many of them as we can!"

The energy in the room was suddenly filled with positivity. Knowing completely how undermanned Alicèn's rally become, he like his fellow companions were braced for the fight of their lives.

HOOOOOOOOOT... HOOOOOOOOOOT!

The attention of The Durgeons was drawn to the sounds of the horns that blew from outside of the walls.

"I know that sound," Alicèn encouragingly announced as he raced with a bounce in his step down to the forecourt of Brackbannen.

A familiar branding of armour bore the torsos of the many Knights riding into Brackbannen. And in good numbers too. Alicèn looked down onto the court from the balcony with an encouraging feeling as he knew how much of a boost the presence of the arriving Knights was. The Helda-knights had come.

As he watched the plethora of Knights roll into the fortress, Alicèn's heart almost stopped as he saw something he forgot was even possible. He raced down as quickly as he could and hastily approached his dearest friend at the head of The Helda-Knights.

"Where on this green land did you go, brother?" Deonrick said with a smile. They embraced with a huge man hug, clunking their armour together.

"I thought I lost you!" Alicèn gasped.

"Same to you. It takes more than an Ancient Drethai to take me," Deonrick yelled to his men, which was met with a raucous of cheers.

"How did you survive?"

"Not just me, brother…" Deonrick gestured to the two men walking toward them. Both Radja Gahani and Seyfi Alamori slapped cheeky smirks on their faces as they approached to embrace their Durgeon.

"Takes more than dark magic to defy a Rolgani, I tell you that," Radja said.

Alicèn's mood lifted dramatically. He knew his band would never be fully repaired, but gluing together some of the broken shards proved to be a sign of encouragement.

"We received a Bluewing," Deonrick said. "Well, several actually. After Dreanor attacked us, we thought The Banamie had got to you. I rode straight for Helden-Arma to recuperate with Radja and Seyfi. That is when we discovered them Alicèn."

"You saw The Banamie?"

"We only saw their tracks. Something is concealing them, though I do not know what."

"I have an idea."

"But something else too. Sharwings Alicèn," he said with a hint of gloom. Sharwings were skeletal-like birds, but ten times the size and with wings as sharp as razors. Their bony legs were curved in an ugly fashion, with sharp tails to aid attacks on their victims as they flew toward their targets. Dangerous and lethal.

"Maybe they got to as many Bluewings as possible. That would explain why others have not come," Osgrey suggested.

"What's your plan, brother?" Deonrick asked.

Alicèn looked around Brackbannen. "This is it."

"No one else?"

Alicèn shook his head. "If you saw Sharwings then we have more reason to fear what else they could have."

Deonrick placed his hand on Alicèn's shoulder as he did the same. "We are with you, brother. Shoulder to shoulder."

"Shoulder to shoulder. Stand with honour."

"Stand with honour."

Alicèn walked up to the balcony, prepared to give a speech to inspire the men, but as he looked into the eyes of every soldier he could, he realised an address was not needed. Their eyes were already filled with the same desire and motivation as his. It filled him with the strongest sense of pride.

"Men! Stand with honour!"

"STAND WITH HONOUR!" They all roared back at their Durgeon, before saddling up and lining in formation, out of the gates of Brackbannen with what little force they had, riding hard into the night sky.

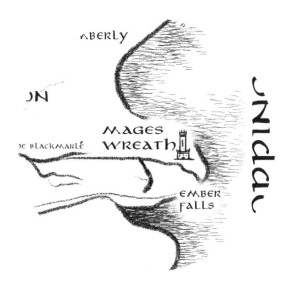

ABERLY

JN

)E BLACKMARLÉ

MAGES
WREATH

EMBER
FALLS

Surviving Instinct

Ramalon entered The Skyurch for the first time since The Fall. The explanation for the next round was delayed until now to allow for the recuperation of the remaining competitors, both mentally and physically. Ramalon, Lazabeth, Ildreàn and Peter Palgan. Fire, volts, water and earth. Ramalon felt strangely nervous the more he told himself that he had a chance. It gave him something to lose, which was strange to him and he didn't like it.

Ronovin, accompanied by Anelene and Dorovir, approached the pedestal in the great hall. Several other Màgjeurs from The Magikai were also in attendance.

"Gather round, gather round!" Ronovin called out to the four. "Well, what can I say? A huge congratulations to you all for making it to the final round. You have already done yourselves, and Mages Wreath very proud. Regardless of what happens in the final round, your credit will take you far in your careers as Màgjeurs I assure you. Before your event, you will be meeting a few honoured guests of ours..." Ramalon's glance was taken away to one of the side alleys down the great hall. He noticed a very weak and faint Pyros being helped by one of the Medimages as he walked gingerly back and forth. His consciousness gave Ramalon a sense of unease. "Màgjeur Ramalon! Do I have your attention?"

"Yes. Apologies."

"Good. Now as I was saying greater revenue this year has contributed greatly to your winnings..." Ramalon's thoughts trailed off again, continually worried about Pyros and Allaremsah, anxious about how much they saw of what happened. "The final round will take place tomorrow afternoon at the peak of Ember Falls."

The contestants seemed excited at where the battle would be taking place, however none more excited than Ildreàn. Ember Falls was a large waterfall on the very eastern part of the city overlooking The Chopping Sea, with its drop a little less than a mile deep. Before that, there is Ember Lake which is overlooked by a large portion of the city on the higher ground. No wonder Ildreàn was excited.

"The theme of this round is survival. Very simple, the one who survives will be crowned the champion of The Màgjeurs Open! Not that I can release details as you know, but make note, it will not just be your competitors that you will have to survive against. I will leave you with that."

Ramalon thought Ildreàn would surely be made the favourite to win, given the natural advantage of the location. Nobody knew how this was going to play out but being surrounded by millions of tonnes of water would surely favour her. Again, another situation where Ramalon's fires would prove mostly ineffective against her water affinity.

Ronovin concluded the formalities and wished them all good luck for the final round which would take place the next day. Everyone dispersed from the hall and Ramalon made his way straight down the hallway to confront a very weary Pyros. He was startled as Ramalon called out his name.

"Keep away from me!" Pyros barked. "Take me back. Please!" he ushered to his Medimage.

"I mean you no harm."

"Is that so? What-What on this land did you d-do to us?"

"I don't know. I really don't."

"Liar! Allaremsah cannot yet walk. The-the f-fires! They weren't yours! Whose were they?" His frightened voice suggested a monumental shift in Pyros' mentality. It wasn't him at all.

"They were mine I assure - "

" - STOP! Just stop! Cheat! You had an accomplice!"

"I did not."

"There's no way you could have won I'm told. No way."

"If that's so then how is it that I am not disqualified?"

"Good question," Ramalon was secretly relieved at how the conversation was going. At no point thus far did Pyros give any notion that he knew what had struck them both which was the only thing Ramalon cared about. He was sure if Pyros didn't see it, neither would Allaremsah.

"Very well. Tell me what you saw and I will explain what I did."

"You do not deserve this!"

"Tell me what you saw, Pyros!"

Ramalon cranked the pressure up a few notches to gain assurance and closure that he did not see Arinane. Pyros resumed his shaking as his black beaded eyes attempted to pierce Ramalon's skin.

"I saw... I saw... A monster," he whispered.

"A monster? Where?"

"I don't know..."

"In the skies? On the ground? Where did you see it?"

"I-I c-can't remember. It was not on the ground."

"In the sky then?"

"... No."

'What kind of monster?"

"... You! All I saw as the fires scorched through my flesh... Was your face..."

"I thought you said you saw a monster?"

"You are a monster, Màgjeur Ramalon!!"

Ramalon's heart pinched. Not that he cared for the words of Pyros, but to be called a monster with such intensity was the polar opposite of who he felt he was.

"I do not think I will ever meet someone as evil as you!"

"I am not evil."

"You. Are. Cursed!" Ramalon shook his head in denial. He was speechless. "Never. Ever. Speak to me again."

"Pyros - "

" - Please! I beg you! Take it! Take it-take whatever you want. Please just never come near me again!" Pyros's final words as he turned away seemed so desperate, Ramalon was convinced he was genuinely scared of him.

He was almost tearful as he scrambled away clinging to his Medimage, shell-shocked, frightened and spooked to his core.

Ramalon got what he came for. He felt confident Pyros didn't see Arinane. However his one problem was almost replaced by another. He had never thought in a millennia he would be called a monster. A realising horror that bothered him deep in his heart.

As Pyros and the Medimage bumbled around the corner and out of sight, Ramalon slowly turned around and walked back to his home, locked in a trance all the way. Even in constant denial, he could not stop the words, *"Monster. Monster. Monster!"* replaying in his head over and over again and did not stop until his head was forced to bow in front of his fireplace, tired, weary and with the weight of the voices mellowing out until he could hear the voices no longer.

When he awoke, the embers from the doused fireplace warmed his cheeks. He did not prepare one bit for the afternoon's event. He couldn't. Too preoccupied with what Pyros had said. Words like *cursed, cheat, monster* and *evil* rained inside his mind as he perched routinely on the side of his bed.

He tried to focus and charge his energies as much as he could but knowing it would take more than that to win the tournament. His dream was within reaching distance. He never wanted something so much. He didn't like what it was doing to him, but every time he thought about the accolade he would receive should he win, his body would shiver with excitement. He could almost feel the people's approval, their warmth, their recognition of his achievements, it would mean the world to him.

He made his way to Ember Falls, raising his hood over his head to avoid attention. He noticed magical banners of the remaining four competitors on his journey which warmed his heart, but every time he had thoughts of jubilation, sights of Arinane would flash his mind. When he tried to shake them and go back to lifting the trophy, other images would flash of him teaching conjuration to his students, let alone the situation with Davinor which deeply disturbed him. He had agreed to give back his stone for this last round which Ramalon hid in a place he was certain it would not found.

Ramalon had seen Ember Lake many times before as The Skyurch directly overlooks it on the perch of the cliff. As he made his way to the edge, he could see the lake in full view. Ramalon's eyes widened at its complete transformation.

"What is this?" he thought.

It was completely frozen over. An eerie chill ghosted off of the frozen lake as the steam lightly hazed. Cold. Crisp. Fresh. He made his way down the side of the cliff where giant steps and viewing areas had been carved into the side of the mountain. At this point, his appearance could no longer be hidden as several spectators noticed him making his way to the bottom.

The welcome was largely subdued, though few cheers from the common Màgjeurs made him smile.

"Imagine how many more cheers I'd get if I win!"

When he arrived at one of the main tents that Ronovin had instructed them all to go, he noticed a kid, must have been no older than five. He smiled at Ramalon which he returned. The kid held out his hand in the same fashion as if he was using The Protecy and blew raspberries at him, followed by an explosion of the lips to imitate Ramalon's fires. He had clearly inspired this young potential Màgjeur, which meant the world to Ramalon. He quickly held out his fingers and blew raspberries back to engage in an imaginary firefight. When they stopped, the boy was ushered away by his mother who turned a relatively worried look towards Ramalon, as if to ask him not to encourage her child.

"What was that about? Did she not like me? Was I not a good role model for him?"

"Màgjeur Ramalon!" Ronovin called out from the tent. "This way, please."

"Am I in trouble?" he said half startled in a trance of thought.

"No. Why? Should you be?"

"No."

"Good. This way."

He pulled the side of the tent open and ventured in. His jaw dropped as he instantly noticed the guests before him.

"Good Gracelands!" he breathed.

Standing before him was the King of Questacère himself. Thorian Mijkal, also known as The Blessèd Mage of Ice, dressed in his ice cool blue robes tinted with colours of whites and silvers woven into the fabric. But what also struck his eye was the appearance of his idol. Ethelba, The Blessèd Mage of Fire. Ramalon stood there completely stunned.

"I'm impressed, Màgjeur Ramalon," Mijkal elegantly said. "The others bowed almost immediately." Ramalon, star-struck, quickly bent his knee and his head to rectify his actions. He heard the King gently laugh at him. "Rise, rise Màgjeur, there is no need for such formalities here."

"Please accept my apologies, my King."

"No need, I consider myself a guest in your city."

"You are kind."

"Anywhere else mind, I might have you frosted alive." Ramalon swallowed loudly. "I jest Màgjeur, I jest!" he said with another bouncing laugh.

"It wouldn't work anyway. I'm too hot to handle."

Mijkal laughed back. Ramalon did not. He felt it was too true to laugh.

"Well, you did say he was a character Davinor!" Ramalon saw Davinor too was in attendance.

"He's very sharp. I'll give him that. A little too sharp at times." Adding a hidden intensity which only they both understood.

"Yes, yes."

"Màgjeur, may I also introduce you to Ethelba." Davinor took over. "I believe you share an aligned interest."

She was petite. Her head came up to Ramalon's chest and her tunic was covered in flawless fabrics in the style of flames which dressed most of her torso and thighs. Her arms, legs and head, however, were not covered. They didn't need to be. Woven into her skin were the orange glow of pyrovines, gently flowing throughout her whole body. Her uncharacteristic cute tail also dangled behind her. Ramalon had never seen a woman so beautiful. She was perfect. He was aware however that she never spoke. Her beauty almost brought him to tears.

"It is my absolute honour to have met you in person, my lady."

Ethelba's smile gently grew as she faintly nodded her head.

"May I also introduce you to Lestas Magraw."

Ramalon knew who this was also. The Blessèd Mage of the Mind. Ramalon was relatively underwhelmed by Magraw, considering he had just laid eyes on Ethelba, but he was still honoured to meet him. Lestas looked at him with a hint of apprehension however that Ramalon clocked.

"It is fitting to have met you, Màgjeur," Magraw carefully said. His old, deep and gravelly voice matched his much older and greyer self.

"You four are a credit to this city and to all Màgjeurs on Terrasendia," Mijkal said. "May the blessing of The Gracelands be with you."

"Thank you, my King. I look forward to entertaining you all in battle."

He nodded his head toward them and Ronovin guided him back out.

"Could you do me one favour?" Ramalon asked Ronovin, who looked somewhat perplexed.

"It depends what it-"

"Could you produce a boulder and smash my head with it?" he quickly said.

"Dear me, why would you need me to do that?"

"I've just met the most beautiful person I've ever seen."

"Dare I ask you to confirm who that was?" he smirked at Ramalon, trying to put him at ease.

Ronovin showed Ramalon to his private tent where he had a little over an hour before the start. He left him to prepare and focus, wishing him good luck as he went.

The wait was the worst part. He paced around the tent occasionally before realising he was doing himself no favours by allowing the nerves to get the better of him. He perched on one of the wooden chairs, closed his eyes and took a deep breath in which even that was difficult to do and concentrated on his breathing.

The staggered bouncing in between inward and outward breaths evened out the more he focused. He had a hidden motivation to impress. Impress not only Ethelba but also members of The Blessèd Order, regarded as the most powerful of Màgjeurs ever to live. Thinking of impressing them gave him focus. It gave him clarity as to what he had to do. He slowly opened his eyes.

"Win," he calmly and determinedly said.

"Màgjeur Ramalon!" called a voice from outside. "It is time."

He felt ready. He was fully aware the others would have also met The Blessèd and received the same encouragement, but to him, it gave him hope.

The cheers started to come more into fruition as he was led toward the frozen lake. He found himself side by side with the other competitors as they looked out onto the vast open and white plain, which was reminiscent of a frozen wasteland. The cliff curved around the frozen lake before them and turned into a gigantic viewing area.

"Màgjeurs, one and all. I give you, your finalists!" Anelene bellowed out using some form of magic to amplify her voice. The cheers erupted around Ember Lake which shook the ground so much, the ice threatened to crack and shatter.

"How on Terrasendia am I to survive this?" he thought.

"Màgjeurs! Take your places."

With a deep collective breath, they all wandered out onto the frozen plain, carefully treading as they did. All four competitors were all too focused and occupied on the battle to acknowledge the crowd. They all found random spaces onto the lake. Ramalon thought about who he could attack first. He knew he needed to stay away from Ildreàn as her water was perhaps the worst affinity to face. She was about a hundred metres to his left. Lazabeth about the same distance to his right while Peter Palgan was directly in front of him. In a tactical mind game of who would strike first, Ramalon made up his mind as to who he would go for. That similar tension built up again, even more so than when they were on the circular ridge from The Fall.

"You will begin when the fires hit the lake."

"The fires hit the lake?"

Anelene's last words were met with an anxious silence before everyone's eyes turned to Ethelba's appearance in the royal box, some fifty metres above the playing field. She held out her hand as she stood on the plinth and suddenly a mighty ball of fire built in front of her. It grew and grew until it was so large it turned into what appeared to be a star, absorbing the natural light of day. She threw the ball up into the sky with such might the whole arena and city lit up, blinding everyone in the process before she sent it crashing down into the middle of the four. They all flew back even further amid the blast onto the ice which cracked a massive hole in the middle. The haze grew so thick nobody could see one another. Ramalon got to his feet as quickly as he could to find the others. It had begun.

He saw through the cloud shocks of lighting and blue colours which told him Ildreàn and Lazabeth had found one another.

"Good!" he thought to himself. But before he could scan to his right, he was blasted upwards by a piece of rock, cracking through the ice. Luckily he was alert to it and smashed it to pieces with his fires in mid-air, still crashing into the ice with a thud which took the wind out of him. He gasped desperately to breathe back the life that left him. He stumbled to his feet quickly to search for Peter Palgan through the clouds. He saw several large shapes, rapidly flying towards him, which turned out to be more boulders of rock. He produced his fires onto them, shattering them once more before expelling random flames into the haze. It quickly dispersed as the heat flew through the air, revealing Peter Palgan. Ramalon launched his fiery attack but was blocked by more rocks coming up through the ice.

Ramalon felt good being on the offensive, it felt right to him to ride this wave of confidence and continue the attacks. However, just as his confidence was peaking, he was struck by a lightning bolt from Lazabeth to one side. He had never experienced such pain. The searing aftershock sliced into him like a hot knife through butter. He was not surprised how Lazabeth had gotten this far. Luckily for him, she was counter-attacked by both a resurgent Ildreàn and Peter Palgan as the roulette continued.

As he recovered from the blow, he noticed something very strange below the surface of the ice. Buildings of rock and stone depicted that of a village, drowned in the waters underneath. Ramalon never knew this was here. And neither perhaps did the others. He quickly hatched a plan. He knew he didn't stand a chance in a duel with any one of the others. They were too powerful and too smart for him. He had to turn the tide, but before he could conjure his fires, he was grabbed by a sphere of water as Ildreàn had caught him. She moved him high and above the hole in the lake as she attempted to drown him. He was trapped. He couldn't use his fires as the waters surrounding him squibbed them down as he tried to cast them. He opened his eyes, and all he could see amid the murky sight was the small blur of Ethelba in the royal box who he wanted to impress so badly.

Another piece of fortune was gifted to Ramalon in the form of even more powerful shocks, violently reverberating through his body. He thought it must have been Lazabeth attacking Ildreàn while her guard was down. He suddenly felt the sheer force of gravity take over, and he fell into the hole with a splash. Smashing into the water, his heart raced and thudded harder as he swam underneath the frozen lake, attempting to scramble toward the surface. However, it was not the hole he aimed for. He felt he had enough breath to execute his plan.

He swam up to the sheet of ice and saw the defeated figure of Ildreàn lying face down toward Ramalon. Lazabeth's bolt had clearly struck her to devastating effect, eliminating her. Ramalon was going to come third no matter what happened.

He quickly placed both hands onto the ice above him and produced a manipulating fire onto the ice. It did not just heat the spot above him but he spread the flames all across the lake. The glow of oranges and reds lit up the village below to reveal another battleground, one which Ramalon had already mapped out the best places to be strategically for the second phase of the battle once his plan had hatched.

The ice began to crack and fissure amid the intense heat before it started to melt into one. He knew Peter Palgan and Lazabeth would not have expected this. The ice thinned out that much that Ramalon punched his way through the ice and rose his head to intake a humungous gulp of air which ballooned his lungs full of life again. His heart was beating so ferociously he was certain he could see the vibrations radiating from his chest in the water. He noticed the other two in the distance struggling to fight the freeze of the water as they attempted to climb fragments of ice that had not yet melted. Ramalon however, was a lot more able to survive because of the warmth of his fires and the pyrovines in his cloak.

As predicted, he suddenly started to feel the waters ushering him toward the edge of Ember Falls. He very deliberately did not defrost the streams leading into the lake for one sole purpose. He needed the lake to disappear. Which it started to do when he melted the whole of Ember Lake, sliding off the edge into The Chopping Sea. The whole lake was sinking lower and lower as the water continued to cascade off the edge of the arena. When it was low enough, Ramalon took a big breath in and blasted his way down under the remaining waters of the lake with a firebomb. He managed to grip the roof of a building at the bottom of the lake which was slippy with algae as he tried to find the low ground to conceal himself underwater. Not out of cowardliness, but out of strategy and to find the right moment to strike.

He realised the other two would have been smart enough to have not fallen off of the edge and braced for the final battle. The main concern in his mind was that actually, the odds had swung in Peter Palgan's favour, being surrounded by natural elements. Lazabeth's chances had reduced as she no longer had the effects of water or ice to aid her volts. As Ramalon held on to the building, he felt the surface of water touch the tip of his hair and descend his face and body. He stayed on top of the building until he could see the other two and their whereabouts… Which he could not.

The village he had reduced to a minor flood was relatively small. Broken walls and slimy bricks decorated most of the village. If populated, it would house no more than a hundred people. He made his way off of the structure of the crumpled house, to go on the hunt. The cobbled street was far too slimy to walk on so he stuck to the soil paths between houses where his footing was better, squelching underneath his boots. His robes started to dry out amid the pyrovines, occasionally brushing the side of the buildings as he tried to stay low.

"Where are you both?" he thought.

An eerie chill blew into the village. It was still. Silent. Reminiscent of a graveyard. Even more so as he peered down what appeared to be the main street. He thought he saw something move around one of the buildings. It must have been one of them. He readied his protecy, knowing the avenue led into a cul-de-sac. Whoever it was, was trapped. If Ramalon could keep his cool and time his moment right, he could strike with fury and if it was Lazabeth, he felt she would not be able to respond in time to deflect any blows. He quietly slipped down the side of the street, keeping a good eye on that path in case they came out and attacked him. He kept his guard on the other end of the street also in case he was to be attacked from behind. The sound of squelching soil did not help his element of surprise but he was ready with his attack.

Ramalon was moments away from stepping around the corner and releasing his strike onto his opponent, whoever it was. The warmth of his charge burned inside him as the adrenaline exploded. He released his fires before he showed himself around the corner and they scorched the sodden debris of the cul-de-sac. He kept them burning to be absolutely sure whoever it was wasn't getting back up. They did not put up a fight, which gave him reassurance his strike had landed successfully. However, when he relaxed his protecy, his face fell. There was no one there.

He had no idea where they had gone. His heart skipped a beat as he realised how naive he had been. It was a trap. His position was exposed but luckily Ramalon's realisation kicked in so quickly, that he was able to ready a firewall to protect himself from an attacking Peter Palgan. He had transformed into a type of golem, taking the form of the stones from his surroundings as he sent a boulder hurtling at Ramalon. His blazing shield was produced just in time to deflect the fatal blow with the collision sending Ramalon flying in a mighty explosion. It knocked nearly every bit of fight out of Ramalon in one hit. His body ended up outside of the village and landed just short of the cliff edge. His body and mind felt totally spent and he knew he was utterly done for. Exhausted and almost paralysed in defeat.

Peter Palgan recognised his opportunity to strike and ran quickly towards him, despite the additional weight of his stoney self. Ramalon tried to scurry toward another part of the edge to escape the coming attack, but was distracted by a bolt of lightning landing on the stoney soldier that was Peter Palgan. Lazabeth had attacked him from behind with a volt of her own. He temporarily crumpled to the floor before raising parts of the cobble street himself to deflect the blows. They raised their duel on the street spitting electricity, rocks, stone and fragments of nearby buildings into each other with such passion, fighting for their lives with everything they had. They both yelled with all their might, but it was Peter Palgan who prevailed. His continuing blasts of boulders and pieces of earth were too much for Lazabeth as her shield of volts failed her. Lazabeth had fallen.

Ramalon meanwhile felt he could have potentially struck one of them with Peter Palgan being in the middle of the three, but his cheek sank in the mud as every part of him was spent. Even if he did have the energy to strike, it would not have been enough. Peter Palgan was going to win. Even after his epic duel with Lazabeth, he had just enough strength to finish off a helpless Ramalon. He didn't even move as a relentless force approached him. A triumph in his eyes and the determination to deliver one last blow.

How Ramalon wished the roles were reversed. He was so upset at his resignation and despite giving it all he had, coming second place felt like no consolation. He wanted to go all the way. He tried to scurry right to the edge to see if there was anything he could do to turn it all around, but when his head hung over the side of the thousand-metre drop... He knew there was nothing to be done.

Peter Palgan courteously stopped before Ramalon as he rolled over to view him.

"We certainly gave them a fight to remember," Peter Palgan breathlessly said. "But you know what I have to do now."

Not even the surprise of his words consoled a beaten Ramalon. In one last feeble attempt, Ramalon raised his hands to attack, but only wisps of smoke fumed out. A sign he was truly spent. He started to shake the more he realised his demise. Peter Palgan in return carved a mound of earth between them, raised it above Ramalon ready to bring down the curtain on The Màgjeurs Open. Desperate to hold onto his dreams, Ramalon produced what he could to shield the attack knowing it wouldn't work. He saw the boulder quickly grow larger as it was heading straight for him. He closed his eyes and produced his shield.

All of a sudden in the darkness, Ramalon felt a blistering surge of heat from below his head. The extreme flames scorched around Ramalon's shield and blasted Peter Palgan sending him crashing into a house. His body made of rock crumbled, forcing his limbs to look like spaghetti before the metamorphosis gradually stemmed down to reveal a very weak Peter Palgan in his normal form. The fires however, were most certainly not his. What followed was something that made Ramalon's guts churn, his teeth clench and caused his eyes to narrow in blistering anger.

The snake-like neck was the first thing he noticed, then its familiar sized wings until the whole carriage of Arinane flew in full view over the village and upward to Mages Wreath. The sounds of screams and horrors were heard above from the spectators. Luckily the Charzeryx flew straight over the city, avoiding conflict and out of sight.

Ramalon could not believe what had happened. He buried Arinane. He was so sure he wasn't followed when he laid it to rest. The anger was seething once more inside his mind before suddenly, the answer came to him. His eyes widened at the realisation and the images of Corey and Lenk resurrecting Arinane from his grave. Not only did it anger him that they revived him once more but a truer pain staked him more. He felt jealous it was not his soul that was being shared with Arinane. All he wanted to do was to wring both of their necks, watch their eyes pop like grapes and scorch them alive. He had never been so consumed with fury. That similar feeling came again to that which he used during The Fall.

His sight returned to normal with the rage still building. Peter Palgan's minimal movements suggested the event was not over just yet. In fact, he started to come to and scramble gingerly to his feet. Ramalon watched on as he began to hone in on his target. Palgan's eyes blurred as he met Ramalon's. His breath heavy as he panted helplessly. A foreboding cloud seemed to hang above Peter Palgan.

"And now. You know what I have to do," Ramalon sinisterly announced.

The horror struck in Peter Palgan's eyes as a resurgent Ramalon found his strength through pure rage and wrath. He charged up his protecy born from white-hot fury, as he felt that invincible energy flow through his stone once more. With one final primal yell, he unleashed a hurricane of fire onto the earth Màgjeur. It was the most powerful piece of magic he had ever seen, let alone felt, which sent Peter Palgans body flying through one wall, and another, and another, completely obliterating everything in its path while turning buildings and houses into crumbles of flaming rubble as the shattering of the village continued. Ramalon felt invincible once more.

Peter Palgan's body ran out of buildings to smash through and ended up plummeting into the side of Ember Lake. It hit with an explosion that rumbled the floor and the entire arena while its trail left behind a decimated village. Fires incinerated any pieces of wood, blocks of stone were shattered into millions of parts, and Ramalon's view of his opponent was clear… Peter Palgan had fallen.

The anger very quickly subsided to jubilation and joy.

"I won…" Ramalon whispered. "I won!" he said louder. "Gracelands, I WON!!!"

He fell to his knees, happy and elated. The euphoric feeling he felt overtook everything else. The exhaustion, the fight, the pain. It was all worth it. He began to shake with joy. The winner of The Màgjeur's Open, his dream had come true. Not one part of him could believe it. Ramalon looked up to the crowd on his knees to seek out the approval of the crowd.

"Màgjeurs. One and all," Anelene announced. "I give you. The winner of The Màgjeurs Open… Màgjeur Ramalon!"

He took in a nervous breath before expecting a wave of cheer and applause… But it did not come.

Ramalon couldn't understand why they weren't cheering his name by now, why the fireworks had not gone off, why there was no such appreciation for his win. He dreamt since he was small of winning this event and for everyone to love him… The quiet jeers and boos started to get louder and louder as the collective voice was made. His dreams began to shatter and break. Every voice he heard booing him tore his heart to shreds. The sadness. The rejection. The loneliness. His heart started to sink to an all-time low. He had nowhere else to turn to until the familiar feeling of hatred began to rise within to him, comforting him in the darkness of his mind.

He looked toward the royal box, and all of The Blessèd Mages looked upon him with great concern and disappointment. Including Ethelba who turned quickly and walked away in disapproval. Others in the crowd looked angry at him. Their spite angered Ramalon. They all clearly heard rumours about the conjuration of the Charzeryx and having seen it first hand confirmed their suspicion and disgust for what they believe Ramalon had done.

He got up from his knees and when the members in the royal box emptied, only one was left standing, staring at Ramalon with such malice. Davinor looked down at him and they both knew this was bad news for them both. He could no longer continue his work on Ramalon's stone which put him in great peril as he knew it. But right now he couldn't care.

He made his way up the side of the cliff where he did not head for the royal box to receive his trophy. Instead, he slipped away through the side of the cliff and had thoughts for one thing.

His embarrassment to ever speak to anyone again could not be understated, he was caught in a terrible situation where he was not convinced anyone would believe him. His uncontrollable shaking and blinking was proof of his genuine anger. His whole life as he knew it was going to be turned upside down and the things he shouldn't have done were to be unravelled no doubt because of this event. He could feel himself changing as the vengeful thoughts for the people of this city who spat upon him started to take over. A sickness in his mind began to bleed through. Uninvited and unstoppable, poisoning his head… And there was not one thing he felt he could do to stop it.

His familiarity of the back streets of the city enabled him to march hastily without being seen. He looked back toward the city and luckily he could not see anyone follow him as the sun set, before entering the forest of Valencère. Corey and Lenk were the only images in his head as he fumed over what they had done. He went to Arinane's grave and as he arrived, the sight confirmed his horror.

The whole grave of Arinane had been dug from the earth. Piles of soil spilt out around the huge hole. He sent a small flame down to the bottom to make sure he was not there, to which he was not. Suddenly he heard the snap of several branches behind him. As he turned to see who it was, his emotions could no longer be controlled.

"What did you do!?" Ramalon suppressed his anger to Corey and Lenk who looked more cocky and arrogant than he had ever seen them.

"What's wrong? Màgjeur!?" Corey said as they both advanced on him.

"Ha! Màgjeur!? Not a very good one if he needed our help to-"

All of a sudden Ramalon screamed as ferociously as he could and released a raging flame of fire onto Lenk. His high pitched, ear-splitting screams spooked Corey to the bone. The burning smell of flesh stunned him as he quivered in unrelenting fear of Ramalon. The deafening sounds of the eighteen-year-old dimmed down to confirm his death as his ashes laid aflame on the burning ground.

Corey did not dare move a muscle. He stood frozen, too scared to do anything to provoke Ramalon who did not feel remorse or show any sign of regret over what he had just done. Just more of the same satisfied feelings grew within.

"Look at me…" Ramalon quietly said.

When a petrified Corey eventually did, he let out a reserved outward cry which brought him to his knees. His diaphragm seized up as the fright took over. The power and relentlessness in Ramalon's eyes was so powerful, he felt like he was looking straight into the black and red eyes of Sarthanzar, the mythical god of The Understunde himself.

"What did you do?" he calmly asked, his eyes as dead as Lenk.

"I-I-I… P-Please!!! D-don't hurt me!!! I beg you PLEASE!" his uncontrollable pleads did not register with Ramalon. "We didn't mean to I promise!"

"All I need to know… Is what happened here… That is all."

"It wasn't me! I promise it wasn't me!"

"Then, who? Tell me now… And I might let you live…"

"It wasn't him Màgjeur!" the approaching voice of Cleverson admitted. As Ramalon turned, he saw him emerge from the blacks of the trees followed by the familiar shape of Arinane, looking toward them both. He had never seen Cleverson look more determined and angry at Ramalon.

"It was me. I brought him back!"

"You? No. No!"

Ramalon genuinely could not believe it. He saw so many similarities in himself and Cleverson and could not have trusted his character more. He was so sure he would have wanted Arinane to finally be at peace and rest, only for him to go behind his back and do what Ramalon felt like a betrayal beyond redemption. He felt hurt, which quickly turned into jealousy again.

"Sever the connection. Right now."

"No. I won't do it!" Cleverson shook his head.

"Please. For your own protection, you must listen to me. Sever the connection or I will not be able to control what happens next…"

Cleverson understood the weight of what Ramalon was saying.

"Where is Lenk?" he asked, before turning to tearful Corey. "Where is he?"

Corey still too petrified to speak could only look toward the burning ashes on the floor. Cleverson began to crumble and shake too when he realised what had happened.

"Do you really care? They were never your friends Cleverson. But I was. I trusted you."

"He was not yours to bury."

"He was not yours to bring back! You can't mess with life so candidly! If there's anything I regret it's not making you realise that."

Cleverson noticed Corey slowly grabbing a rock from the ground. He tried to keep his cool not to bring on any distraction.

"CLEVERSON NOW!" Corey yelled as he attempted to swing the rock into Ramalon's skull.

However, Ramalon was fully aware of the impending strike and quickly turned and blasted him back with a ball of fire, crumpling him to the ground. It was not a continuous flame, but it did set Corey's robes on fire. His screams pierced Cleverson's ears as he attempted to stub it out.

"I see," he turned to a very nervous Cleverson, but more interestingly to him, Arinane stood in front of his new conjurer, ready to attack Ramalon on Cleverson's order. He looked angry and poised for attack, cackling the burn in his belly. Ramalon was not sure if he would win a flame fight with the adolescent dragon, but he had a theory he wouldn't have to find out.

"I do not believe you," Ramalon carefully said, quietly judging him. All the while, the screams of Corey were still painstakingly loud.

"Please. Don't make me do it."

"Sever the connection. And there will be no more pain."

"I swear I will attack you!" Arinane became angrier the more Cleverson got upset. Ramalon however, grew confident.

"Then do it," he smugly said.

A white sheet pulled over Cleverson's face in horror before Ramalon turned back to Corey to finish the job. He released more flames onto the student who was now burning in the same fate as his accomplice.

As Ramalon was doing so, he looked over to Cleverson to frighten him and prove he was well out of his depth. He indeed was correct in knowing what Cleverson would, or in this case, wouldn't do. The Charzeryx remained angry but passive, still waiting for the instruction to attack from Cleverson which never came.

The screams once more died, along with Corey. Once again, Ramalon had that sense of self-satisfaction. He hated them both. They did not deserve to live in Ramalon's eyes and he was happy they were gone. Two mounds of ash burned on the ground before he turned his attention to his final problem.

"Now. Don't put this off any longer. Sever the connection. Let him finally be at rest," he said the last part almost as a plea, closing his eyes briefly to add weight to his words.

A tearful and stunned Cleverson reluctantly nodded his head, knowing this was the only way for him to get out of this alive. He placed his hand on Arinane's head as it cackled in appreciation.

"Goodbye, Arinane," he tearfully said. "Be at rest."

Cleverson closed his eyes and established the feeling and amazing connection between him and the Charzeryx. He felt its sails and its bony spine but most potently, the warmth beating in his heart before severing the link completely, causing the dragon to slowly crumple to the ground.

When Cleverson's eyes opened, a flood of tears fell to the floor as he sobbed profusely over Arinane. He looked toward Ramalon whose face was utterly emotionless, stone-like, watching on. He nodded at Ramalon, hoping that would be enough as he could not bear any words right now. But he did not respond which made Cleverson nervous. He got to his feet and slowly turned his back on Ramalon, hoping by some miracle that he would allow him to leave.

As he slowly and nervously walked towards the trees, he heard perhaps the only sound which could have stopped his heart. The loud snaps of branches were heard, not the sound of twigs. It was more the sound of thicker branches. A more substantial sound. And to Cleverson's horror it was not Ramalon's footsteps.

He turned to see Arinane's body, once again full of life with his chiselled face being caressed gently by a satisfied and relieved Ramalon, who had shared his connection with the Charzeryx once more. The relief came from the jealousy no longer being there, his satisfaction brewed in his warped view of how the world will now suffer. In that moment, his mind found comfort in the darkness, the madness, the companionship of power which Ramalon accepted as a brother to him.

"Màgjeur!? Please. Don't…"

"It's not Màgjeur… It's Ramalon," he declared.

Cleverson's eyes and mouth both widened as he looked upon the Charzeryx whose mouth opened to reveal the glowing light at the back of his throat. Before he could parry the fear, he saw the flames from Arinane rippling through the air at him.

Ramalon watched on, listening to the screams. The more the flames burned, the angrier Ramalon got. He finally landed on the more immediate reason to having burned his three students alive. He loved the power he was feeling. He felt the poison run through his mind but rather than fight it, he let it happen, which made him feel more powerful as the anger grew.

Twinned with his feelings he suddenly saw the flames grow larger and larger while the heat on Ramalon's face got hotter and hotter. Ramalon looked at Arinane, and to his surprise, he heard the sounds of bones cracking, scales stretching and the flames roaring louder. Arinane's limbs started to grow even more gregariously than before, its sails stretched further while its spine grew spikier. Its vicious tail built thicker and longer and the cruel jagged tip at the end sharpened. The last thing he noticed was Arinane's head poised on its neck which grew even more disproportionately snake-like than before. His sinister oval-shaped eyes replaced the cute round ones he once had. His face was chiselled and angular, taunt and hideously ugly. Ramalon admired what the creature had become. The Charzeryx had now grown into a full adult, and it was his, and his alone. Words ultimately left him as he was even more amazed at the fires still erupting from its belly, the infatuation and love set in.

When Arinane was done, half of the forest was burning. Arinane turned to Ramalon and it seemed as if he knew who his master was. Its clawed feet had more gravitas to them now, which rumbled the ground as it moved. Its head alone was much larger than Ramalon's entire body, and they squared up to each other, looking one another in the eye.

"Beautiful. Utterly beautiful."

He reached out both hands onto Arinane's head. It's flaring nostrils growing and relaxing as it drew breath. Just before he made contact with him, he suddenly saw flashes of different lights propelling towards them both.

War screams and shouts were heard as Ramalon turned to see who was attacking them. The lights of proteìc spells being cast toward them were a mixture of water, ice, volts and fires. Ramalon understood exactly who they were. The Magikai had arrived.

"NOOOOOOOOOOOOOOO!!!" Ramalon yelled.

Several blows hit Arinane but Ramalon commanded him to fight back with flames of his own which he did. Several Màgjeurs defended it with walls of water which seemed to boil and steam immediately. As it did so, attacks from all corners of the circular forest started to land on Arinane. Ramalon stared into his struggling eyes as it began to thrash fires all over the place before being continuously attacked from all angles. Its wail was loud as it was being seriously wounded by The Magikai.

Ramalon's anger was turning to sadness at how they could treat something he loved so terribly. It continued to confirm his ideology in now wanting to watch the world burn for what it was doing to him. Ramalon delved into the connection with Arinane more intensely and felt its wings which were severely wounded, but not so bad he could not fly.

He noticed other members charging up their protecy's for one significant final blow. He told Arinane to draw in a massive breath before springing from his knees and thrusting his wings to get airborne. Ramalon observed and judged that The Magikai's spell was going to hit Arinane before he got high enough to clear. He had only one option in mind to potentially save him.

The beast got to about thirty metres in the air when The Magikai were about to release the spell. As their energy built, Ramalon placed both hands on the earth and suddenly two lines of fire rapidly scorched its way toward them, landing directly in the middle. The impact caused the spell to implode and sent the Màgjeurs flying backwards into the forest. The enormous explosion allowed Arinane time to ascend higher and higher to a point of relative safety… Arinane flew the night sky once more. He was free.

The battle simmered down. The clearing was littered with flames as a hundred or so of The Magikai seized Ramalon who did not resist. When they surrounded him, they all angrily glared toward him with potent hatred. Ramalon returned the disgusted looks before seeing the reason why it all happened.

Clearing a way through the people, Davinor made his way to confront Ramalon. He squared up to him with those intent-filled, cruel eyes attempting to burn a way through Ramalon's soul. Vengeful hatred ensued on his face… But Ramalon did not back down, nor did he feel intimidated.

"Màgjeur Ramalon. You've been busier than we thought," he said, smiling with a hint of rhetoric anger. "Bind him."

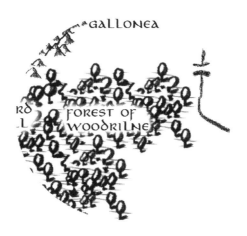

Companion

The feeling of wind rushing past Alex's cheeks and cold moisture from his eyes squeezing onto his temples was becoming a regular occurrence.

Accompanied by Pirocès, their two mildens galloped towards the realm of Elcaria. Racing through the fading green forests, turning greyer the closer they got to the border. The whole journey, Alex kept reminding himself of the blood in that bowl, his son's little heart beating away, which gave him definitive hope at last.

They eventually came to a clearing inside of the Woodrilne forest where a gleaming lake reflected the dusk.

"We shall camp here tonight," Pirocès said.

They gathered the dry wood to make a fire, tied the horses to the trees and shuffled the earth with leaves clearing any branches so that it would make a more comfortable cushion for their mildens to sleep on. Alex removed two small blankets as one wasn't enough for the chilly autumn night. Pirocès on the other hand, didn't have a blanket at all.

"Would you like mine?" Alex offered.

"My dear friend, we do not feel the cold as you noblemen do. Our blood is cool. You need not worry about me."

"It'll be freezing two hours into night," Pirocès took a sideways glance towards him.

"Believe what you will, but I raise you a golden hare you won't see me shiver this entire night."

"I'll see you to that."

"Done."

Alex laid his head back and looked towards the fading sky. A nervy silence existed between them before Alex flicked a golden hare into the body of Pirocès.

"It's not yet dawn," Alex looked over to his new gift from Joric, Sythero with its glowing dark orange vines shining across the blade as it sat perched on a tree next to him.

"Don't think I don't know what pyrovines are now. I saw them under your cloak earlier," Pirocès looked a little surprised.

"I thought you were a nobleman."

"I am. Through and through," Alex said, assertively.

"Then why would you deliberately lose a bet?"

"It's on my list of things to do before I die."

"Lose a bet? You people are strange."

"To outsmart an Elcarian..." Pirocès' mouth slightly opened and was in slight disbelief.

A famous old saying amongst the two races was that as Elcarians were naturally smarter, they would never be outshone by what was deemed the simple mind of the nobleman, which provided a challenge for both races to upend or overturn that saying if ever an opportunity arose. For the Elcarian they would always be alert to being tricked or outwitted. For the nobleman, they looked for those opportunities to puncture that superior attitude. Not that it would mean much should it happen, but gave the nobleman a sense of bragging rights should it occur.

"Don't go spending that all at once now."

"Bloody noblemen!" Pirocès muttered under his breath. "Relish this moment. It won't happen again, I assure you."

"It will," Alex assertively said, smiling genuinely for the first time since the events at Pippersby. Despite the odds stacked against him, he had reason to be optimistic. However, his smile did not last long and slowly turned back to his default gormless expression.

"Tell me about your son," Pirocès asked. Alex looked at him before staring off into the lake.

"His name is Jàqueson. We called him Jàque, Amba and I. He was a good kid. Loved his books. Loved his riding. But he's very sick. Suffers from Malerma."

"Ooph! Nasty disease. Rare, very rare if I'm correct."

"Yes."

"I am very sorry to hear."

"We have absolutely no idea how he came to such a disease. Mirabella couldn't figure it out and neither can we."

"May I throw something in here?" Alex nodded. "Let's pretend for one second that you are Ramerick, the son of Felder - "

" - Dear Blessèd! Which is impossible but continue," Alex interrupted.

"If you are, your life has been protected by secrecy. There must be those on Terrasendia that have known about your existence and made a choice to keep you from harm. I fear that your identity has finally been unearthed and that there are those on this land that sought after your blood. Which in turn, is why your son cannot be found." Alex just listened to the theory, not reacting in the slightest, in fear that a reaction could prompt him to believe it and make it real. "And I believe that for the past thirty years since the death of your father, that they have some notion that you survived The Dragasphere and got out in time, but because of the advanced spells and magic hiding your identity, they could not find you. Until now. Maybe, just maybe, it was only a matter of time."

"A matter of time?" Alex thought.

He wanted to ask him if his theory was correct, would that explain his association with The Time Stone?

"But of course, if you are the lost Blood Monarch then that means that you will need to inform The Blessèd."

"Seeing as I'm not, I don't think I'll be doing that anytime soon," he stubbornly retorted. "I've heard enough. I don't want to think any more about why I can't find my son."

And with that, he rolled over to try and get some sleep.

"I apologise," Pirocès said. "I am your friend, Ramerick. I don't have many I grant you, but I feel that when someone has their life snatched from them, it is only right to help. I hope you see that until the days we depart."

Alex felt angry, but strangely not at the fact that Pirocès once more had brought up the theory, but because actually, the theory wasn't the most impossible thing to believe. He sensed a caginess in the Elcarian's voice, which made him feel that Pirocès had gone through something similar.

"Who is the woman your scars refer to?" Alex asked as he peered back round. Pirocès gulped the rushing saliva to his mouth, turning completely expressionless. "Pirocès?"

"She was mine. The one I loved," he slowly croaked, continuing to avoid the eye of Alex as he stared into the distance. "The very first moment I saw her, I knew. I knew then that my heart could belong to no other. She was my inspiration for many years. I loved her. So much."

"What happened? Do you still love her?" he felt embarrassed to ask. Not that Alex could see any tears, but Pirocès looked away from him to hide his feelings. Alex respected his privacy and asked no more. He felt sorry for him. It had quite clearly stained his life. The connection of shared loss was felt between them both and brought them on level terms once more.

Alex stared into the lake, reflecting the white of the half moon, rippling its shimmering light onto him. He missed Amba every day since that fateful night. Every spare moment he had when it wasn't filled with worry and horror at never seeing his son again, he remembered her beautiful face, curtained with that bright red hair that dazzled and those magical gleaming blue eyes which had him buckling at the knees. Her soft angelic voice, enchanted him, casting him under her spell of love every time he heard it, sending butterflies around his stomach. He loved her then. He loved her since. He loved her still. Maybe Pirocès was just the same.

"Maybe it's time you told me how we're going to do this," Alex proposed. Pirocès looked back over, still no tears, just reddened eyes.

"Very well," he said. "The help I need from you is to vouch for my cover if required. They will ask you questions, and you will have to deflect as much as you can. They will grant us access into the city on visitation and allow you to keep your weapons just in case you wondered. And then we see my brother. As I am exiled, I of course, would not be welcome. So I will take the form of another. You will have to excuse my personality as the more I react, the more chance I have of my cover being blown. Elcarians are experienced in transformation and will know the signs should they arise, but I am confident my cover will work. My brother is the one we need. I take you to him, you find your son and after I run my errands, we leave. It's as simple as that."

"Will anyone get hurt?" Alex asked.

"No. Not unless they try to stop us. By which time we will, of course be long gone."

Alex didn't care about the potential risk should he get caught. Only the reward. He resisted the temptation to think of the consequences of their plan. The less he thought, the better he felt.

"What could possibly go wrong?"

"We shall arrive in Casparia in a few days. This will work, I promise."

"Funny thing promises. I keep to mine and have done all my life. But maybe that's a sign that times are changing."

"Then how about my word?" Pirocès suggested.

"The word of an Elcarian?" Alex asked with heavy sarcasm.

"You have my word. On my life. I know what it's like for your world to be turned upside down and need you to believe that if this is going to work." This was met by a gentle nod of the head by Alex. "What did you promise your son?"

"So many things. I promised that when I return, I'll take him to Gallonea. To see the city where his favourite Màgjeur had lived. I said I'd start sparring with him, teach him to be a better rider. Read some of my favourite books before his night bathe that he had never heard. *'The Tales of Cèrean and The Understunde'* which he was too young for, but he loved an adventure. That was him. Full of life..."

He stopped short before that tight feeling in his stomach returned along with that weird empty feeling in the back of his throat as he started to well up.

"Today perhaps has been the hardest day since." Alex said, as a slight tear squeezed from his eye.

"Why?" Pirocès replied.

"Today was his birthday."

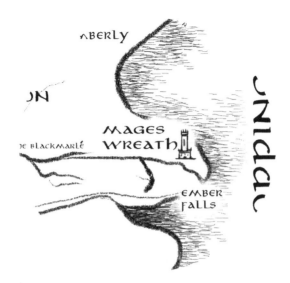

Turning of the Tides

The occasional drips of water provided the only comfort in the darkened dingy cell that imprisoned Ramalon. His damp cloak sat heavy on his shoulders as he sat on the cold stones for what felt like days in the bards of Mages Wreath, purposefully placed in the middle of the cell staring with malice and hate at the door.

So intense and purposeful was his stare, that it was as if he was trying to burn a hole through the door. A stare born out of vendetta for every Màgjeur that in Ramalon's reality hated him. His wrists were bound by a magical blue shining bracelet, chaining his protecy so that he could not use any form of magic while imprisoned.

The bold notions of the last couple of weeks replayed inside his head. More happened within this time than the whole of his life. His euphoria at being chosen to compete in the games, Davinor's interest in his protecy stone, his foolish teaching of conjuration to students he found out he could not trust, the love he felt for sharing his soul with such a beautiful creature in Arinane, his infatuation and addiction with this power through his stone which was clearly poison. To now, where he finds himself having won the biggest prize on the land only to despise the world that gave it to him.

One would have hoped that the short time in prison would have given him the chance to feel remorseful and reflect upon his heinous crimes. For which it did not. In actual fact, the more time he spent thinking about chargrilling his students to a roasting end and setting Arinane free, the more he felt righteous in his actions. They betrayed him and all he could think about was how justice was served.

The sudden sound of chains rattling and keys jangling was heard outside the door before swinging open. Ramalon did not move one bit, keeping his stare in the exact spot. The familiar shape of Davinor appeared in Ramalon's peripheral vision as he slowly waded into the cell.

"So. Murdering children are we?" Davinor inquisitively asked.

He was clearly angry at how someone could go so far down such a twisted path. Ramalon did not respond, keeping his trance transfixed, his silence creating an air of mystery. Davinor shook his head in embarrassment.

"Why? Why choose to kill those with such promise? Màgjeurs just like you at one time... They were boys, Ramalon. Only boys. Whatever they did, there was no crime on this land to justify what you have done. Tell me why..." Ramalon again did not show any sign of responding to Davinor's questions. "Tell me. I have the right to know."

Ramalon turned his head to Davinor. His smugness could not be overstated.

"You have every right to know," he slowly and carefully replied.

"Then tell me. Why murder the students?"

"Amazing... Just amazing," he whispered, tailing off back into his trance.

"Answer my question!" Davinor started to blink more rapidly. "Very well. If you have no intention of answering my questions, we will declare you a Rògar of the State. You will be asked to give up that stone of yours and you will forever be held in the bards. If you refuse, you will die... Unless you talk."

Ramalon heard every syllable Davinor spoke. But his response was a mere smile in the distance.

Rògars were the title given to those who the realm considered had performed acts of such evil, that they had dissociated themselves with the principles of Màgjeurs, hence the term *rogue*. As a result any Màgjeur who was imprisoned was given this label. There are indeed Rògars all over Rèo who have not been captured and still perform their darker deeds. They are included on *'Terrasendia's Most Wanted List.'*

"Very well. Death it is. Let's just thank everything we hold dear to us all that you will never see the light of day again." He turned to walk out of the room.

"Oh, I don't think so. My lord," his sinister response spooked Davinor to the point where he stopped and confronted the rogue once more.

"What did you say!?"

"In fact. I think I will be seeing more light than you will for the rest of your life... Which will end much quicker than you think."

"Threatening me now? The great Davinor? Your mind is clearly descending into madness!"

"No. Not descending... Descended. The darkness has welcomed me with open arms. The darkness you have thrown me into. And I am free. Free!" Ramalon smiled and grew happier the more he was realising his freedom.

"You blame me for this?" an incredulous Davinor said.

"And you still don't realise it... The blood... The guilt... Their screams do not lie with me. Their deaths have seared three scars on your heart, my lord."

Davinor tried to hide his harrowed look. "How dare you blame me for this? For your madness!"

"The fault and the stain of these adolescents is solely on your hands."

Davinor's jaw tightened at the sheer unbelievable accusation while Ramalon kept his tranquility and calmness.

"In my hands, you say?"

"You killed them. It was you! Every ember, every flame! Was your doing. I wanted to walk away from this. I told you I did not want this power. Imagine how people on Mages Wreath would react once they find out. Imagine what The Magikai would say... Even better still, The Blessèd Order! When they find out it was you that allowed this to happen."

"The reason behind your sickness and your addiction is with your ideology."

"I fear for you, my lord."

"Is that so?"

"My concern for you is how many more scars will be etched onto your heart any second now..."

"You will not scare me with empty threats!"

Ramalon suddenly started to laugh hysterically. Wheezing

uncontrollably.

"Empty!" shaking his head. "Oh, my lord. You are mistaken if you think my threats are empty! There is a sickness coming for you. A cancer in the wind. And what's worse… Is that there is nothing you can do to stop what is coming for you. For all of you!"

His smile turned sterner and more malicious before suddenly, the ground shook. Sprays of dust fell from the roof of the cell as Ramalon watched a surprised Davinor.

"What is this!?"

"Don't worry. I can't hurt you with these on my wrists. But he can."

"MY LORD!" a cry from one of the Màgjeurs running down the hallway shouted. "My lord! He's back. The Charzeryx!"

Davinor snapped his gaze back to a satisfied Ramalon. "What have you done!?" he demanded. Ramalon just smiled back. "Sever your connection! NOW!"

"You better get back to work, my lord… I can hear those scars scratching onto your heart. Scratch. Scratch. Scratch…"

Davinor clenched his jaw and stormed out of the room, furious at what was happening. He knew Ramalon had no intention of severing the connection and thought it would be quicker to tackle the beast head-on. As the heavy doors slammed shut on Ramalon, he closed his eyes, feeling the warmth of Arinane once more.

The rumbles and vibrations of the puddles in Ramalon's cell continued to reverberate. Every pulse filled Ramalon with joy as his vengeance had started. With his eyes closed, he felt the sails of Arinane as he instructed him to descend with fires onto the city. He felt confident that its power and its flight would prove too strong for The Magikai. The people of the city were instructed to take refuge deep underground to minimise casualties while The Magikai attempted to take down the beast. However, some were not so lucky.

Many Màgjeurs of the city who were not members of the order also tried to help, ultimately against The Magikai's instructions to not get involved. Some wanted to be a hero. Others wanted to stand for what was right. But Ramalon felt no shame in torching them alive through Arinane. His enemies. Their existence was a symbol for his retribution.

Arinane did not lay siege constantly to the city under Ramalon's instructions because in doing so, it would expose him and would be more likely to be attacked. Instead cleverly choosing his moments for him to lay fury.

However, during his latest attack, the connection did not feel so strong. In fact, he felt a particular weakness in Arinane that he was unsure of. Arinane presented Ramalon with his only real hope of revenge. Being locked up in solitary, it was impossible for him to escape. Were Arinane to die he knew it really would be his end. It wasn't as if he could rely on the unpredictability of his protecy stone as his binds stopped all protecy. Winning The Màgjeurs Open seemed like such a distant memory. One he was quite keen to forget.

The familiar sounds of keys jingling and bolts unlocking ruffled the steel door once more. Davinor entered looking calmer than he did on his last visit. Ramalon continued his stare out of the door which was left open.

"So our kill count is rising?" Ramalon sneered. "Thirty-eight is it? Or is it thirty-nine? I can't tell... Oh! Apologies. It must be forty-one or forty-two when you count the students, of course." His coy smile did not provoke a reaction from Davinor. "I must admit. I'm glad we share this burden. How is he by the way...? Hmm. You want him gone yes?"

"Yes," Davinor calmly replied.

"Ouch!" Ramalon theatrically clenched his heart. "That pains me to hear. Really? You give up this easily? I expected more from you! Don't you admire me? Look at what I've done? I've brought a whole city to its knees!"

"Sever the connection now."

"You seem upset. Was it me?" Ramalon gently laughed. "Okay, okay enough now. I can see what's happening. You want a deal."

"Deal?" Davinor furrowed his eyebrows. "Deal? No. I do not want a deal with you."

"I see. It's going to be very difficult to stop him then. Unless you're prepared to - "

" - There will be no deal. No negotiations. There will only be a condition."

"I see. And what condition is this?"

"The condition that you sever your connection with the beast. Right now."

"Or?"

"... Or its death will scratch an almighty scar on your own heart."

"Really? That's the best you have? Haven't you tried killing him already?"

"We have. But I don't think you know yet."

"Know what?"

"You're telling me you don't feel it?"

"Feel what!?"

"I didn't realise it was that minimal."

"Minimal?" Ramalon grew a little agitated. But not by anything Davinor had said. But actually at how comfortable he was right now.

"Minimal, yes. I am surprised at how minimal the poison I placed onto him actually was."

Ramalon's palms started to sweat at the revelation. His arrogant confidence began to wane on his face.

"What?"

"The poison. That I placed onto him. That treasonous spite will die... As will you!"

"I don't believe you," Ramalon shook his head in disbelief.

"Yes, you do. Feel it. Feel the poison eating away at him right now."

Ramalon moved his attention to his connection, and indeed he was hit by a wave of pain. It struck his chest, which made him instinctively back off. His eyes shot back to the smug Davinor and he made a run for him with his fists curled. White hot rage induced him to attack with what he could.

"You monster!" Ramalon screamed.

Suddenly another searing pain lashed inside Ramalon's head which forced him to cry out in pain. So painful was it that he was sure his head was going to split wide open. His eyes felt like they were going to pop out of his sockets as he crumpled to the floor, writhing and clutching his head, his vision wholly blurred as a result. He turned and noticed standing at the door was the figure of a much older Màgjeur with his hand held towards Ramalon. He seemed to be the one controlling this episode of hurt onto him.

"That's enough," Davinor said. The wave of relief paralysed him as he lay a helpless figure on the ground.

"What did you do to me!?" Ramalon angrily asked.

"You should feel honoured. You have brought the attention of two Blessèd Mages onto you."

Even though Ramalon could not see, he knew who attacked him. The Blessèd Mage of The Mind, Lestas Magraw.

"Would you like something for the pain?" Magraw slowly said.

"So this is your plan? To torture me to submit? Well, guess what! I will not yield! Every second you cannot break me is a second more that he is out there!"

"Ramalon! Arinane will die!"

"So will you!"

"You do not understand. Very slowly, the poison will eat away at his body. We cannot destroy him by force, which means this was the only way. It will be a slow and painful process - "

" - His ghost will haunt you! Will haunt all of you."

"Is it not more right to sever the connection now? Is it really you? To allow something you love to die in such agony. All while you know you can put him out of his misery? Surely that is not your philosophy, Ramalon. Surely the killing of innocents whom you do not even know is not as valuable as putting the only thing you hold dear out of its growing misery. You can end this, Ramalon."

He started to shake as his vice over Davinor was loosening by the second. He did not want to admit it, but he believed the poison had already set in and Arinane's condition was now terminal, accepting that he will soon die. He felt lost.

"How long?" he quietly asked.

"Judging by the mass and the tough constitution of a dragon, I give it several weeks."

"Weeks? To be in pain for that long? And you call me the monster!?"

"You gave us no choice! You must do this."

"And what if I refuse?"

"Then Magraw here will personally see to it that your pain is the same as his so that you can be reminded of what you are doing to him. Not even you could live with that."

Ramalon resigned inside. He wanted his whole body to curl up and melt into the stone floor. Embarrassed that he thought he could outsmart one of the most powerful Màgjeurs on the land. Terminating his connection with Arinane was the last thing he wanted. But he knew he could not live with himself knowing Arinane is in pain. Every card Ramalon had up his sleeve, was spent. He slowly stumbled up to his knees as he looked at both of them with such spite. He hated them, Davinor more so than he ever did.

"There is a place in The Understunde. And it has both of your names etched onto the molten stones."

"Then I guess we shall see you there one day."

"That day will be sooner than you think. I promise you that!"

"Sever it now! For your sake. And for his."

Ramalon looked away, wincing his eyes shut. As he regrettably composed himself to terminate the connection, he took a huge breath in as he knew that he was going to feel the pain. As he felt the Charzeryx's warmth and burning fires, he felt the excruciating pain he was in. He winced as he felt the poison. After experiencing this pain, he knew he could not let Arinane suffer any longer. He quickly latched onto the crux of the connection and attempted to scythe it to smithereens.

Suddenly the bond between the two started to evade any attempts to terminate it. Ramalon tried again, but the same thing happened. He began to panic as he tried frantically to break the connection but was unable to for some reason. He felt an overwhelming feeling of defiance within his connection. A strength which worried him. The total opposite of termination came into fruition. It was growing more resistant the more he tried. Amid the pain and frustration he was feeling in both himself and the poison searing in, he clenched his teeth and yelled furiously in the hope that it would end. That explosion of fury sent Ramalon flying backwards in his cell, smashing his back into the wall before he could feel the warmth and flowing poisons no longer.

Both Blessèd Mages approached his broken and ragged body as he came around.

"It didn't work," he panted. "It didn't work."

"What happened?" Davinor worriedly asked.

"I tried. I tried to break it. But I couldn't."

"Why?"

"I don't know. I really don't. But I don't like what I felt."

"The poison is exceptionally strong-"

" - I'm not talking about the poison. The connection. It's too strong for me. I can't sever it!"

"What?"

"I swear to you I tried! But every time it evaded any attempt. And when my scythes did land, it only grew stronger... I cannot terminate the connection," he said with growing fear. "Did you hear me!? I cannot destroy him,"

Both Blessèd Mages looked at each other as they shared the concern.

"He is telling the truth," Magraw said.

"How could this happen?" Davinor asked.

"I think he is too strong now. Being a fully grown adult, he is too powerful for me to break. I can't even control him any more."

"Then there is only one choice. We wait."

"What? No. No! You cannot do that!"

"I can. And I must! We cannot take him by force, you cannot disband him, and so we have no choice but to wait it out."

"You cannot do this! You must cure the poison, he is in pain!"

"Which is of absolutely no concern of mine!"

"It's barbaric!"

"What's barbaric is that you have in cold blood killed innocent people," he angrily spat. "And make no mistake about it, once this is all over, you will suffer. You will suffer the same fate as him. We would have allowed you to live out your days without the pain in these bards, but you have condemned yourself to a painful end."

The threat of torture strangely did not scare him. Instead, he was only afraid for Arinane's wellbeing.

"Please… Do not do this," Ramalon begged.

"The most disgraceful thing is that it was not the stone that has driven you mad. It was you! It was who you are. These chains would have broken you from the effects of that stone, but you choose to act in the same way. You loved what the stone has made you feel. Power. Which is why you could not stop your insanity. You now have the rest of your short life to think about that."

Davinor and Magraw turned to walk about of room.

"Wait!" he desperately gasped before they both stopped and looked. "What if there was another way?"

"If you cannot sever the connection, there is no other way."

"Yes. There is."

The Blessèd Mages looked at each other once more with growing concern.

"Enlighten us."

"What if I destroyed him…? Directly."

"Directly?"

"Yes. Directly."

"Are you suggesting that we release your bonds so that you can go gallivanting off to your own devices?"

"No, I will not be going anywhere alone. I cannot control him any longer, but that does not mean to say I cannot feel him. Which means he can feel me. What if I used that to lure him into a trap?"

"Trapping a dragon?" Magraw ironically laughed. "You really have gone mad."

"I still share my soul with him. If we can go somewhere where he will be enclosed, and he knows I am hurt he will come. And there I can destroy his body once and for all. You cannot deny if this happened, we could do this right now, rather than wait for weeks which may kill more people…" Davinor considered the options carefully. He walked to one of the walls, turning his back, contemplating the alternative.

"And when we release your bonds, what stops you from attacking us?"

"Keep the bonds on. Till the last moment. Gather every Màgjeur from The Magikai to stand watch."

Every word of this alternative felt like a blunt dagger to his own heart. It pained him that it was him conjuring this plan. But allowing Arinane to suffer in such agony was more painful for him.

"Insanity!" Magraw growled. "This. Would never work."

"Why not?"

"If our fires and our magic cannot kill him, what makes you think you stand a chance? What power do you possess that we don't?"

"I believe he can answer that one," Ramalon indicated to Davinor, who slowly turned around.

"Judging by the amount of hate, and emotional connection... I believe it would most certainly be enough to kill him," Davinor confidently confirmed.

"My lord, Davinor. The moment we release these bonds, we will be struck by not just him, but by the beast. And if that happens, the whole of The Magikai will be in one place to be destroyed. An easy target if you asked me. We cannot trust him or entertain this idea. It is exactly what he wants, we simply cannot take this risk."

"I won't. There must be something you could do. Control my mind? So that if I do something out of line, you could stop me?"

"Well yes, I could. But I could not stop the beast."

"You wouldn't have to. The powers of all the Magikai in one hit would be more powerful. Especially if he is trapped."

"I agree," Davinor concluded with a hidden air of self-gain. His fascination and obsession with Ramalon's protecy was still at large despite the recent horrors it had birthed.

"Davinor! This is preposterous!"

"Yes it is, but it is doable. I will not have any more bloodshed of my people."

"I have one condition," Ramalon said.

"You cannot be serious."

"I want to be the one who delivers the blow. You've won, Davinor. Now let me be the one to find him peace."

"Done," Davinor quickly said. "I will not have The Magikai engage. Unless of course, you do not carry out your promise. Should you go back on your word I will see to it that it suffers and I will make you watch, before you suffer the same fate."

Ramalon nodded his head to Davinor, almost in shame. "Where would be best to do this?" he quietly asked.

"Funnily enough," Magraw interjected. "I know the perfect place."

Thinking the Unthinkable

The forest of Woodrilne came to a less colourful end. The view from the nose of the woods was certainly different from that from which they entered. In contrast to the green and brown mixtures of autumn, they painted grey, dull and misty vibes over hills. Very uncharacteristically these hills were huge and surprisingly enough weren't classed as mountains but their height suggested the title.

They slalomed through the valleys encountering streams and luckily no rivers large enough that they had to swim across. The steam from horses' breath became more noticeable as the journey went on but strangely didn't feel any colder than before.

"It's typical of this land," Pirocès said, referring to Alex's intrigue at the weather. "So much unnatural magic has taken place that it's interrupted the natural process of life. Almost an imbalance if you will. You will find the realm very strange. Most noblemen never venture here and for a good reason. It makes them feel uneasy, unsafe, and in certain cases, they have been known to lose their mind."

"Is that a warning?" Alex asked inquisitively.

"Not to you with your blood. Only to the more vulnerable of people."

The enclosure of the valleys certainly did feel very close and rather sick. Alex had no doubts as to how noblemen could lose themselves here, feeling claustrophobic due to the opaque low clouds and disappearing hills.

"So if I lose my mind will that confirm that I am not this *Ramerick?*" he asked rhetorically.

"I'd know you would be faking it," to which Alex just smiled. "Are you ready for this?" Pirocès produced a vial from his robes. It had white wisps inside the water, swirling gently.

"What is that?" Alex asked.

"A portion of my life's work," he smiled.

He raised the vial almost toasting to himself. He drank the water which slithered down his throat and into his old belly, releasing a gentle burp at the end. He turned to Alex.

"And? How do I look?"

"Ugly," Alex replied.

"I've changed appearance already?"

"No," Alex said slightly higher pitched. "Just more the same."

Pirocès look took an angry sigh as he started to walk around his horse.

"Hmm. The air must delay the reaction somewhat."

"Will it not work-"

Pirocès reappeared round from the other side of the horse completely transformed into another.

"There we are," his older and croaked voice had newly turned.

The Elcarian's hair turned from murky grey to lilac-white, his complexion dried up like a dying spiders legs, his eyes started to cloud white with suspected cataracts, his hands and fingers turned frailer and longer. Overall he certainly did look much older. He attempted to speak again, but no words came out. He adjusted his throat with a few light coughs which manage to hit the vocal cords before he tried again.

"How do I look now?"

"Still ugly," Alex said again.

He couldn't notice a reply from Pirocès as his face was so wrinkly it covered nearly any expression. Despite taking the form of someone much older, he was still strong enough to stand, walk and mount a horse.

"Let's ride."

They cantered as fast as they could to their destination. A gallop was perhaps a little too much to ask of an older Pirocès, but they rode as hard as they could, ascending the valleys until they came to it at last.

They reached the capital of Elcaria, Casparia. A sigh of relief came from Alex as they arrived over the valley to view the humungous stone carved archway. A long bridge separated the entrance to the nearest height of a hill. Enormous in size and crowned by woodland, the haunted forest of Aspari, so he was told. He could very quickly see how this city was truly impregnable. They rode towards the point where the bridge met the archway and slowly walked the mildens across.

"Remember, allow me to do the talking," Pirocès frowned.

As they crossed the narrow bridge, they could see several guards at the open stone entrance. The Elcarian guards wore no armour. Very pale in their complexion and wore only black, slim fitted robes with flared sleeves on the arms. More characteristically, they looked more or less how he envisioned. The intense stare with their cold eyes tested Alex's confidence on his approach. The three guards formed a line across the entrance. He could see the main light that came from within were that of torches and flames. It seemed very well lit from out front. One of the Elcarian guards laid out his hand upon their coming.

"*Qual!*" he instructed, to which they came to a halt. "Please state the nature of your business."

"On visitation," Pirocès croaked.

"And to whom are you visiting?" drawing a slight pause, which made Alex look sideways at Pirocès.

"Jzahozai."

The guards took a little look at each other, followed by a longer pause.

"Wait here, please."

Two of the guards went inside to check a rather large book, which Alex imagined was the book of alias. The third guard continued to inspect Pirocès and his accomplice before addressing him directly.

"You're from Landonhome, yes?" he asked in a slithery tone.

"What makes you say that?" Alex replied, nervously.

"These mildens were bred on Rombard Hill. What purpose can a nobleman have to enter our city?"

"I am bringing a friend of mine to see the wonders of this city," calmly interjected Pirocès. "He is very much looking forward to it."

The guard inspected Alex a little closer. Fully aware he was being examined, he tried to deflect the inspection.

"Been here, long child?" Pirocès slowly asked.

"Child?" the guard replied, taken aback. "Who are you to call me a child?"

"Oh, I meant no offence. I-I'm old you see. Old eyes and all."

"You have a sharp tongue for someone on your deathbed!"

"How rude," Pirocès played the part of taking offence rather well.

"He meant no offence sir," Alex's said, all while his complete focus was on the other two guards.

"Sir? Do you think I'm some foolish Knight? Do you see pathetic armour surrounding me?"

"No," Alex accepted. "You're far too wise to be a Knight, my apologies."

"We're not doing very well here are we?" Alex noticed that the guards inside were having a conversation. The anxiety was killing him. "So when last you ventured here, Elcarian?"

"Many a year. I live by the great waves in Icèria where my family are from. But I've missed this city too much. And I need to look at it one last time."

"I see. And how came you by a nobleman? A nobleman so far from home?"

Alex and Pirocés took another sideways glance, followed by a frosty pause. They hadn't thought too much about their background, all the while trying to stay calm and genuine. As Pirocès started to speak, Alex interrupted before he could say anything.

"I was told that Icèria was that of great beauty," Alex awkwardly said. The guard merely frowned. "My friends in Landonhome sent me there. I work as a reviewer."

"Uh-huh. Is your job a joke?"

"I didn't say I was a good one."

"Icèria has less entertainment than a graveyard."

"Now wait one minute," Pirocès interrupted, "I grant you it has its flaws, especially in the last ten years but we remain a place of great attraction," The guard scoffed at the description sounding like he took great offence. "The waves are the sailor's entry onto our land."

"Indeed, and I've never seen waves," Alex said, playing the part of the clown with surprising new confidence. "I was sent there to explore, nothing more. Which is when I met my good friend here," he tapped Pirocès on the shoulder relatively hard, forgetting how old his body had turned. He groaned rather loudly at the friendly gesture. "Sorry!"

"I see. And if that were true, how came you by two horses from Landonhome and not one?"

They looked at the guard a little perplexed and a little stumped. Luckily the other two guards arrived.

"You will be pleased to know that your visitation has been approved. You may enter the city on the proviso that your host reports back to us as soon as possible to let us know you are here on their responsibility. You may pass."

With relief, they ignored the previous question and attempted to pass through with the horses.

"*Qual!*" the guard said, bringing another heart in mouth moment. "Have you forgotten the laws, old man?"

"Which laws are you referring to?"

"The laws regarding equine? Your mildens are not permitted passed these walls. However, your sword, nobleman, we will permit as we see it is of enchantment."

Under Casparian law, weapons of any kind were strictly prohibited, however as Sythero had pyrovines woven into the blade, it was seen more of a relic in which was admired and almost honoured within the walls and therefore accepted to carry only.

"Oh. Forgive me. Old mind and all."

They were forced to tie the horses outside the city walls and enter. Pirocès leant on Alex's shoulder as they struggled in. The guards watched on and to their surprise, slowly closed the stone doors after them. Not something that seemed welcoming to them both.

"Good work," Pirocès whispered.

"Thank Blessèd."

They walked the Casparian halls. Alex had always wondered how the decor inside would be. The way Pirocès talked up the city made Alex anticipate beautifully crafted archways lit with intricate fires as no solar light ventured through the thick stones. Busy Elcarians trading in wagons like that in Rombard Hill, the expectation was built up to be something he would live to remember. He felt hugely underwhelmed to say the least. The great city he heard about looked more like a cave which was very much untouched. They walked past a huge opening which went down what must have been half a mile deep, several levels to the city which looked ugly and made Alex feel the furthest away from home he had ever felt. Bristled and coarse walls which were not maintained added to the sinister surroundings.

The Elcarians appeared to be dressed very similar as they walked through, the slim fitted black robe with a touch of purple. A very unwelcoming contrast of colours, Alex had thought. Most of them stared at Alex as they were probably bewildered as to why a nobleman had ventured past their walls. The lack of natural light certainly explained their pale complexion and shadowed eyes. White blonde hair crowned their heads. Very difficult to distinguish a difference between them, similar to twin siblings. Nonetheless, they did have giveaways to their faces, which gave them their unique identity.

They made their way down several levels of the city, the concerning looks among the Elcarians did put Alex on edge. He would have gotten used to it provided they were just a few looks, however, the further down they arrived, the more populated the city became. Suddenly Alex's heart became noticeable again, beating out of his ribcage, his palms began to sweat. Not because of the nerves and anxiety of being in a new place which felt intimidating, but actually because of the theory Pirocès presented him with. If he really was the son of Felder, he was truly in a vulnerable place.

"Don't be so stupid!" Alex thought. The constant war raged in his mind.

"We're nearly there," Pirocès said, bringing some reprieve.

They walked away from what seemed to be the central part of the city, descending several levels to which they began. Alex was led to a path which had as much appeal as the tunnels he had walked when he was venturing into The Gurken. The doors down this tunnel however, were indeed made of wood. Most characteristically these doors were all different. They were the doors of homes. They had built these doors as a symbol of their philosophy that Pirocès explained. Creating their own paths of magic which were unique and individual to them. So dangerous Alex had thought but in some capacity, admirable.

Pirocès knocked on a door which was met with a peculiarly long wait. He knocked again.

"Go away! Off!" the voice behind the door shouted.

"Oondespi Chindouzi!" Pirocès said.

All of a sudden, the sound of footsteps, bolts and shackles rapidly came into fruition. The door opened to reveal a similar looking man to Pirocès, or at least as similar as you can get with an Elcarian. His hair was slightly curlier than that of the others. His grey robes flopped from his arms and dangled above his feet, very different from the sleek and slender norm.

"Get inside!" he said frantically before closing the door shut, followed by every bolt attached to the door.

The room they were thrust into was well lit again by candlelight.

The only furniture came from wooden tables and chairs. Unique ornaments similar to that Pirocès was selling in Rombard Hill peppered the room while a large hearth timbered very lightly which shared its warmth within. The most striking aspect of the room were the number of clocks this man had.

"What on Rèo are you doing here!? Do you want yourself to get killed?"

"It's good to see you too, brother. Alex, may I introduce you. This is Dancès," Pirocès said.

Although he needed no introduction, it was not difficult to make out who he was.

"Pleased to meet you," Alex replied and Dancès nodded in his direction.

"Brother. What are you doing here? I have not had word for many a year. I thought you were dead!" his voice was crisp and well-spoken as he calmed.

"We need your help."

"We? As in you and your friend here?" he lightly scoffed.

"I have errands to run. And my friend has a particular aligned interest."

"What kind of errands?"

Pirocès paused, which was not welcomed by Dancès.

"Brother, I'm not a nobleman. I'm not as stupid as you think." Alex tried not to be offended. "I know what it is you intend to do and I - "

" - Brother, you think and worry too much!" he tried to diffuse as he walked away into the room. "That has always been your problem."

"My problem is that my exiled brother who I have not heard from in years suddenly shows up to my door aided by a nobleman requesting my help!" He didn't even look at Alex when mentioning his name.

"Listen to me. One day I will tell you all about my travels. But Alex here I think you'll find has more to him than meets your eye…" he said tailing off with intrigue.

"How so?"

* * *

"It cannot be!" Dancès said in amazement.

"Trust me, I said the same thing," Alex replied, a hint of irony in his voice.

Pirocès had explained everything to Dancès. Alex's encounter with

The Banamie, the disappearance of his son, their ritual and Pirocès' theory that Alex was the son of Felder, to the Queen on Landonhome offering their help. Somehow Dancès was not concerned with the information. He almost felt privileged to hear the theory. Pirocès had left the room to run his errands. Despite Dancès' caution, his brother still proceeded with destroying his work. He couldn't have been more confident in saying that he could do this and get out in time, which was why Dancès who shares similar views to his allowed him to do it.

"The son of the high King in my chambers!"

"Bizarre isn't it?" Alex shrugged off.

"And you say you need my help to find your son?" Dancès asked.

The moment Alex had been waiting for. "Yes. That is why I came. Can you?"

"I can."

Relief sank into Alex's heart. Hope was confirmed. The room itself was very much similar to the rest of the city, no windows and pure rock which had been carved out. Candlelight bounced off lighter woods to improve sight, airtight and the feeling of claustrophobia, this was not the great city he had pictured.

"My brother has already performed the blood ritual, which confirms your son's heartbeat. Which I can confirm was done correctly and that he is alive. Clairvoyance is complicated, however. And the reason for this is because it requires the knowledge of time. All the senses required are useless if they are not bound together. Time is the vehicle that does this and is something very few people delve into as it is very challenging. My brother, I assume, has told you about The Ancient Drethai?"

"I know of them, yes."

"They are masters in their own right. I have taken a lot of knowledge from them. And then you have Felder and Melcelore who possess the art of *true* clairvoyance, the ability to see that ahead of time. That is what made their rivalry so great, so fierce. How they saw each other's plans, trying to deceive one another, outsmart one another."

"I heard that Felder defeated Melcelore and imprisoned him in a tomb so deep into the heart of Felders Crest that it was impossible to get out."

"He would never be able to escape. During the creation of The Dragasphere he was indeed left behind and good riddance if you asked me."

"And there's no chance of his escape?"

"No chance. And even if there were he would not survive the wrath of The Dragadelf. They heed to no one. Their loyalty is with no one. And even though he is exceptionally powerful, he could not stop their destruction. And on top of that, he would need to escape the most powerful and strongest containment spell ever to exist. It is simply impossible." Alex hummed in agreement of Dancès' logic. "But anyway, let's find your son shall we?"

"Thank you," Alex replied, a deep gratification in his voice.

"And more importantly to me… We will also be finding out if my brother's theory is correct."

Alex did not know what to make of that. Having thought about it a lot, it was almost as if he did not want to know the answer. It would potentially explain Mirabella telling him about *'Time in the Water,'* it would explain somebody wanted to steal the stone once it was found, it would explain his son's disappearance for either his blood or his protection, it would explain Pirocès' reaction to having royal blood running through his veins. But surely, the son of the highest King of the land?

"*Come on,*" Alex repeatedly thought.

Dancès went over to his bedside and grabbed a clock which not only told the time but also had those slow swirling white wisps inside the glass protecting the hands. Similar to the ones which were inside The Time Stone. He walked back over to Alex and looked at him.

"Let me guess. You need my blood again?" Alex asked.

"Oh, no, no. This time, I need your mind."

After a long pause, his response was nothing short of assertive.

"Of course, help yourself," Alex indicated, making Dancès smile. "What exactly will happen?"

"I will tap into your mind and the past and present of your life. As soon as I have identified your blood, I will be able to trace the same blood you share and its location to him." Alex hoped that of course, he saw his son and where he was, quietly hoping not to see Felder. "I will warn you. In certain cases, clairvoyance can also cause the mind to spiral out of control. I will guide you through this experience as best as I can, but there might be a scenario where you lose yourself. If that does happen, you must listen to my voice as I try to bring you back."

The caution did worry Alex somewhat, but he felt strong. If he were able to get this far, keeping faith in his strength, he would be able to get through this.

"You will have an urge to ignore me, I guarantee it, but failure to pull out of this trance will result in you potentially being lost in time, from which I cannot get you back. Is that understood?"

Eager to get on with it and without even a second's hesitation, Alex assured himself he was ready.

"Let's go."

"Good. By the way. Thank you," Dancès humbly said.

"For what?"

"For bringing my brother back to me. We are the last of our family, and I am grateful to you. Please accept my help as a token of my gratitude."

Alex nodded his head as an acknowledgement of his help. However, he knew inside it was he who needed to thank both the Elcarians.

Dancès grabbed Alex by the arm and smashed the clock on the floor. That similar feeling of disorientation instantly hit Alex, like waking salts to bring back those knocked unconscious. His mind floated away from his body, his feet taking off as if the ground disappeared right underneath him. He no longer had any sensations of feeling, sight, sound or smell.

"Am I dead?" he thought. The simple thought gave him confirmation that he was indeed alive but in a different world. As if in a dream which he had no control over. A powerful trance took a hold of his mind.

He was still... Conscious enough to know that he truly was nowhere... Wondering what would happen next... All of a sudden, he started to notice the formations of clouds whirling ahead of him in the darkness, which came closer and closer towards him. He lucidly walked towards and into the clouds as they came near. The entering of clouds took his body backwards, and gravity once again did its work. However this time, he could see with his own eyes, time was being reversed. He suddenly felt more in control of this weird dimension which had surrounded him with clouds and mist. Until he wandered, trying to find something.

It wasn't too long before he started to hear the sounds of clocks ticking faintly, which he followed. It indeed got louder and louder until he finally saw the clouds dissipating apart and portrayed a perfect picture of himself and Pirocès entering into Casparia. He watched on as he saw himself reversing into various parts of their journey on route, quickly to the people he met on Rombard Hill, to the ghostly remains of Pippersby and the fires that existed there just days ago. He recognised that he was going back in time. The sheer sight of the town in pyrosteria made Alex shudder. The view of Amba dead, laying on their bed, to quick flashes of the knives piercing into her, made Alex wince.

No sign of Dancès or his voice but he was confident he could see everything he was seeing. He continued to move through various parts of the clouds, wherever the sound of the clock took him to his venture from The Gurken. He saw himself within the waves of the lake where the rain had reversed, and even though he had not told the Elcarians of this part of the journey he nevertheless was eager to see who had attacked him. He looked at himself from afar in the cave holding the Time Stone, desperately scanning the picture trying to search for his attacker. But before the events unfolded, the picture ahead of him started to wisp away and dissipate.

"NO!" Alex shouted, which echoed several times. "Show me that again!" To which he got no answer to.

The sound of the clock once again had spurned, and he followed once more. They were back at Pippersby. Moving images of himself, Bran and Brody in The Spuddy Nugget to sparing in The Durges yard. More images of Jàqueson reading his books, riding his horse guided by his mother. A time Alex was truly happy. Mirabella then appeared to examine Jàqueson and treated him, his tired body lying on his bed. Uncle Brody attending him with sparring swords as a gift to him, before the cloud dissipated literally into thin air before the image died once more.

The clock had stopped, and Alex continued to walk around aimlessly within this cloud. Suddenly a new sound was fainting onto Alex's eardrums. This time the sound of a heartbeat. His heartbeat, he didn't know how he knew but felt that he owned this heartbeat. He found his vision in the clouds to reveal a woman giving birth. Her presence radiated of purity.

"Ramacès," she gasped to the midwife before he passed the new-born to the Medimage. To Alex's surprise, he pulled another baby from her womb.

"Ramalon," she breathlessly panted, before the second baby was passed to the Medimage again. And finally, one more baby was birthed.

"Ramerick," she panted... And with that, Alex froze in shock...

"It can't be!" he thought. But he started to make sense of it all. Pirocès heard the name Ramerick. And now he has heard himself the title of Ramerick. He found it more and more difficult to deny it, but he continued to search for something more that proved he was this new-born or at least one of them. Something potent, something concrete. It was clear to him that this woman giving birth was the wife of King Felder and that the Queen had given birth to triplets. Three princes, born in a room which was undoubtedly decorated to be fit for a Queen. Not many were in attendance, just the Medimage, a man, a woman and the midwife. The image revealed the mother holding her three newborn sons, all wrapped in toasty blankets as they snoozed their beautiful, innocent faces away.

"Thank you, Ramavell," the Queen panted to the midwife, exhausted from her efforts. "Mirabella, please, take this one. Watch over him."

Alex was amazed to see the familiar Medimage. Mirabella did indeed look younger, more polished and proper. The Queen kissed the forehead of the baby before he was taken delicately into Mirabella's arms.

"Quickly! You must go, before it's complete!" The Queen urged and with that, she walked away in haste as the picture dissipated once more.

Before he had time to process any of the information, Alex was presented with a larger image in front of him in which he saw a huge magical dome, The Dragasphere as he understood. It was in the process of being completed before he was whisked off to several events.

The first was that of a white horse ridden by a cloaked rider whom he couldn't identify, carrying one of the new-borns away. He was then raced around the edge of the dome to another horse and rider with the other newborn before again circling round to the same image. All three horses and riders were fleeing the event in time in different directions. Only the third newborn was being chased by several assailants which he did not see the conclusion of.

He was cast off inside the sphere with hair rippling speed, the adrenaline spiking through Alex's body. He flew through the streets of the great city of Felders Crest. The screams of people running for their lives during the event. The wails of murder and flashes of dead bodies with eyes full of life and terror wielding weapons to kill at will all the while ascending the mountain on which the city was built. Fires being spat by black-winged figures beyond the clouds. He knew what he was seeing, the event of what happened that day thirty years ago when The Dragadelf came. His vision zoomed into the very peak of the city into Monarchy Hall.

A ball of light inside was visible from outside the building, the heart of Terrasendia, until he saw the phenomenon with his own eyes. The Dragastone. The shattered throne that once sat in that spot was in pieces around this mysterious power. Alex felt nervous solely in its presence, but similar to that of his heartbeat, he felt something which he did not expect. He didn't know if the feeling mortified him or made him feel like the most powerful man to exist. He felt invincible in its presence. As if the stone was his. His to use and his to own. It literally took his breath away - the power it held. He had no idea what any of this meant. His connection with this stone was strange but undeniable. Was it really the stone, he thought? Or was it the feeling that gradually approached from behind him in the middle of the clouds.

First came the smell of burning dead dragon breath. Then the sound of heavy footing before the sight and details of one of the legendary Dragadelf bled through the cloud and approached Alex. His bones chilled to the marrow in sight of this colossal creature. Every hair raised from his skin. Its unrelenting eyes bore through him as the beast swayed towards him, mixed in with the surroundings of the clouds. Once again, this invincibility took over Alex's lucid existence and he felt connected with everything going on.

Suddenly an explosion of fire erupted before him which propelled him backwards. He did not feel hurt, and when he recovered quickly from the fall, the image was not lost. A pyro-duel between all seven of The Dragadelf's embers and that of a man, so fierce in power, protecting the stone. Who else could this great King of a man be? Alex couldn't help but feel how revealing this all was. King Felder fended off the beasts while the stone was stuck to his other hand. Until he saw the King's powers wain and wain, he saw the inevitability of his death. But in a magical moment before it happened, the King looked directly into the eyes of Alex.

"… Ramerick," he said as he bore his gaze onto him smiling, and from that moment on, Alex began to believe. The fires consumed the King and lit fire to the clouds around Alex, drowning him in flame. His eyes snapped wide open and he was staring once more straight into the eyes of Dancès, back in his chambers, gasping for air.

Neither of them dared to stray from each other's gaze. Nor speak, nor attempt to break what was very clear to them both, and what they had both seen. A long filled silence existed between them.

"Blessèd save us…" Dancès finally said. His voice weakened at the discovery. "You really are his son. You are Felders… Oh my."

Dancès took himself to his table and gingerly sat on his chair. The loss of breath took a hold of him.

"He spoke to me… Are you sure this all happened?" Alex asked lightly.

"Without a doubt. You are his son. There is no way that I could have clairvoyanced your mind to any other path than to what we have just seen!"

"If that's true… I have two brothers?" Alex said, staring into the middle of the distance.

"It would appear so."

Alex wished somehow that someone would enter the room and claim it was all a massive hoax, and that is was a trick. But he knew that it would not happen as everything started to unfold to him now.

"And more interestingly, three lost Blood Monarchs. Not one... Unbelievable!"

"As overwhelming as this all is. We didn't find him," Alex stated with disappointment.

"No, we did not. We need to go again. When you were at The Gurken I had to break the chain as I could not find the path without your knowledge of who did it. But I think I can adjust that next time around. Let us delve a little deeper, shall we?"

He walked back over to Alex, took a deep outwards breath before pointing his open hand to the shattered clock. It slowly and elegantly found its way back to its original form, the sound of broken glass chinking its way back to being fixed before floating into the hand of Dancès.

"The Time Stone, huh?"

"It's complicated," Alex softly said.

"I'm sure it is. If ever you were to find it again, I would take that as a thank you," Dancès suggested.

"Am I safe here?"

Alex's concern grew more significant by the second. Being the son of the high King placed him on edge. There was undoubtedly a reason why his identity was hidden, and he did not like the prospect of finding that out. He was in a foreign place, well-guarded, and the hostility of the Elcarians made his anxiety worse.

"You are as long as they don't know who you are. But we must hurry!"

He took Alex's arm once more and shattered the clock. The process was the same, the disorientation, the ghost-like feeling of wading through time to the entering of the clouds once more, only this time, the faint sounds of both a ticking clock and a heartbeat were heard together.

He followed his ears where the sound grew louder and louder, until the clouds ahead of him formed the picture of his son once more in his own bed. Mirabella was tending to the Malerma on his neck. He started to wonder that Mirabella must have known all his life who Alex was. He could only imagine she changed his name to protect his true identity, a title only she would have known. But why would she have sent him to ascertain The Time Stone if she knew the potential risk? Bran and Brody entered the room checking up on the Jàqueson, zooming to other members who knew him, Joric, Garrison even professor Gregrick to see him as he regularly slept due to exhaustion of his illness. Once more, the scene dissipated along with the sound.

Instead of him wading through the clouds again, his whole surroundings transformed. He suddenly found himself outside Monarchy Hall standing on a vast marble-floored area with many steps below him leading down onto the central part of the city. The whole picture horrified Alex. A black, dead, wasteland destroyed by fire. He could see a Dragadelf flying in the distance, but where the others were, he did not know.

Suddenly he felt a strange sensation from behind him, an icy chill and the pull of gravity was pulling him gently backwards. He turned around to see the doors of Monarchy Hall creak open amongst the dark of night... Alex was entirely in control now. He could not see anything from his vision. Not wanting to go inside but unable to help it. He didn't know what any of this meant, why he was being shown this? He was here to find his son, but here he was in the most dangerous place on Terrasendia. How can this be relevant? he thought.

He slowly followed his instincts and moved towards Monarchy Hall. The gravity grew stronger, the closer he got. He opened the doors, seeing The Dragastone once more. He wanted to indulge and pick it up. Whether he could or not was unclear to him, but it was his, he felt. He walked across the famous hall which took forever it seemed, the silence was piercing as his footsteps echoed. The gravitational feeling disappeared when he entered the hall. Surely he would see a Dragadelf or something that would jump out and scare him... It did not. Instead, he got within arm's reach of the stone and paused for a second. The absorbing power overwhelmed him.

All of a sudden, the gravity grew even stronger than anything he had experienced before from right behind him, he snapped round, and every hair left his body in fright. The face and shadowy figure of Melcelore appeared right in front of him. His light green striking eyes entranced him, his body literally dying on the spot before his ghost left him and floated into Melcelore's icy hand before the scenario turned once more into clouds.

Never before had Alex been so frightened. That was undeniably him. The one who they buried forever, beneath Felder Crest, impossible to escape. Clearly that was not the case. Melcelore had indeed, arose from his captivity. The description matched the stories about him perfectly. How on Rèo was that possible?

How many more moving parts could he process? he thought. He once again saw an image of himself at The Gurken, the attack and waking up on route back to Pippersby. The scene played itself out to the point where they recognised the town on fire and Joric's band rushing to their aid. But instead of the following of Alex, it zoomed away from him and flew through various parts of the town being attacked, its burning and the gathering of The

Banamie to the execution of Garrison. Once the Knights of Rombard Hill arrived, he zoomed off far away from Pippersby and off into the night.

As he approached a nearby forest, he saw a carriage, accompanied by a small band of The Banamie. He was just outside of the wagon when he slowly peered inside the window of the cart… And there he was. His son lay onto the floor of carriage unconscious. Alex's heart wrenched at seeing his son being transported away. Frightened and scared to his wits, this was his worst fear.

"Shall we speed up?" he heard the horse master say.

Alex was then slowly flown around to the front of the carriage where several Barklers were on foot, and a man Alex recognised leading the band on his horse.

"Aye, I think we should," Brody said, trotting past on his black horse and The Time Stone gleaming from his satchel.

Alex could not believe it. White-hot rage burned throughout his whole body. The feeling of betrayal scorching his insides. His best friend, one who he had trusted his entire life was one of them. How could Brody's heart be so black and dead to have been a part of Jàqueson's nightmare? It was him that attacked him and took the stone for his own. His blood was searing hot as the image of Brody's band started to disappear into the clouds. He began to run as fast as he could towards him. But as he did, his body felt disconnected, as if he was not to do it, but his rage made him continue.

"Ramerick!" he heard Dancès say, muffling in the distance.

He did not respond but instead continued to force his body through the clouds, significantly breaking down, making him feel more disconnected.

"RAMERICK! COME BACK NOW!"

But the image faded more and more the faster he ran. His blood grew hotter and hotter literally, as the clouds surrounding him turned into an inferno of orange and yellow. The illusion was disappearing into the flames. As the fires grew, he felt his body fly backwards crashing into a stone wall inside Dancès' chamber.

His body impaled by the force of flying into rock. Wisps of smoke started to replace the fires around him, and he was back to reality once more. His stunned look saw the door of Dancès' chambers blown right off its hinges and Dancès himself on the floor next to him. Several Elcarian soldiers entered the room and seized both men, who they were powerless to resist. As they grabbed him, he peered outside to see Pirocès without his cover on his knees with his hands bound. He knew this was not right. And another face Alex knew approached and stared into his eyes.

"Well isn't this convenient?" Dalarose said with a sadistic smile.

"Bind them! The King will want to see this."

He double snapped his fingers, and all three were bundled out and down through the levels of Casparia.

The descent of the city felt like Alex was walking straight down into The Understunde itself.

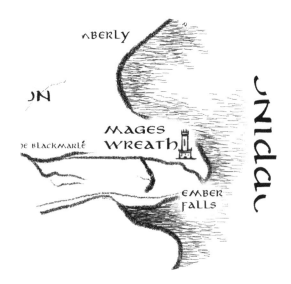

Retribution Unbound

As The Blessèd Mages left Ramalon's cell to quickly put the plan in motion, Ramalon found himself sitting against the cold walls continually thinking about how much he despised everyone on Mages Wreath. But it was Davinor who he blamed for his downfall. Everything that had happened was because he trapped him with the power of the stone just so that he could selfishly learn for himself.

The bolt of the door unlocked and swung open to reveal a familiar face.

"Good Gracelands it's true," said the jittery voice of Haldane. "What on this land has happened to you?"

Ramalon almost couldn't look at his friend out of shame.

"You shouldn't see me like this."

"Why? Is there something I should not see?"

"Haldane."

"They told us that it's all because of you, and that it was your beast that - "

" - Do not call him a beast!" he angrily replied.

"I am sorry. They say it's your Charzeryx that is killing people and that you are controlling it. Is it really true?"

Haldane was perhaps the only person he felt too ashamed to admit it to.

"You do not understand."

"No, I do not! So help me."

"I cannot be helped."

Haldane carefully knelt by his side. He positioned himself so that his back was turned to the door.

"*I do not have much time*," Haldane silently mouthed. Ramalon tried not to perk up too much at their hidden communication. "Well if I cannot help you then I really fear for you my friend, I really do! *I know a lot more than you think!*"

"I am past help, my friend. *How do you know?*"

"*I haven't the time to explain.* I can only hope that whatever it is that has brought you to this madness will not make you forget who you are. *Davinor has put out a search warrant for your protecy stone!?*"

Ramalon looked more worried as it was another knife to his heart to hear. He didn't want the man that had caused him so much torment and evil to ascertain more power by studying his stone again or even somehow taking it for himself.

He had time to think about why he could not sever the connection and how strange it was despite the more obvious reason of Arinane growing too strong. However, he was still confident that was not all that was going on. Somehow, the poison of that stone played a part. He was so sure of it. He desperately wanted the stone to be destroyed not only to free him of the poison but also to sever the connection with Arinane and therefore he could rest in peace without the terrible pain.

"I will never forget! *Please, Haldane. You must destroy my protecy stone! Rid me of this plague!*" Haldane's face struck a more concerning look. "*Only then will I be able to find peace. Dead or alive!*"

"I thought as much. *Where can I find it?*"

"I don't know who I am anymore. *The Opey Deary, go to the pedestal where we used to study. You will know what to do when you see it. And then destroy it! Go now!*"

"You need to find yourself again. *I will! It would be the evil that swallows this city!*"

Ramalon didn't care too much about the people of the city anymore, but had to stop Davinor from seizing the power for himself by destroying it and releasing himself from the poison and evil that it had thrust upon him. Haldane got up to leave.

"What has happened to you will never happen to anyone on the land again. I swear to you." he said, making it sound as if he despised Ramalon but he knew he was talking in code.

"Haldane. Don't remember me as the Màgjeur that is. Remember the Màgjeur that was." Haldane looked once more at his friend in need. *"Thank you,"* he nodded his head before swiftly exiting the cell.

Ramalon painstakingly realised the sudden change in his thought process. Why was he capable of being so kind to his friend but a complete monster to the world? He had no answer. Perhaps he just wanted to be free of the stone haunting his life and when he needed a friend to help the last notion of humanity in Ramalon's soul was exercised. A recognition that maybe there is hope left for things to change. Perhaps he was clinging onto the piercing streaks of light before the darkness swallowed him whole.

Shortly after Haldane's departure, several Magikai stormed into his cell and brought him to his feet. It was time. Still bound by the magical chains, he was escorted to where Magraw had suggested. The high catacombs on Mages Wreath. A tomb built underneath The Skyurch inside the mountain of Ember Falls itself for the deceased Màgjeurs of The Magikai.

Magraw had suggested that place as he was given special permission to examine the minds of the dead that lay there. As unacceptable as that sounded to many on Mages Wreath, it was said that his learnings from the minds of the dead were vital in the research for the preservation of life. Ramalon did not believe that. He knew it was more for personal gain.

There must have been a hundred Magikai escorting him up into the building of The Skyurch and through several hallways. A sea of brown cloaks weaving around the nucleus that was Ramalon. They all seemed angry and determined to see justice and have the Charzeryx killed. Their older complexions and greyer hairs made him wonder if they were strong enough to withstand Arinane's fires should it come to it. He knew that Arinane would not survive the blast Ramalon would lay onto him should Haldane fail. He found new levels of anger and rage bubbling under the surface every time he thought about Davinor gloating with Ramalon's stone and with that, his newly found default of sinister behaviour radiated.

"Do you hear that?" Ramalon asked, cocking his head at one of the Màgjeurs.

"Hear what?" the Màgjeur replied with perfumed disgust.

"Nothing… Absolutely nothing," he whispered as they walked past the entrance of The Skyurch.

The white city was still, calm and tranquil. Just as Ramalon liked it and he knew The Magikai despised him for the city's lockdown. He relished every bit of torment he could find.

"There's something so pure about the colour of white," he whispered once more. This time the Màgjeur did not respond. Ramalon knew it was because he was loathed and they didn't want to warrant his existence with a response.

He constantly thought to himself on his descent that should Haldane be successful in destroying his stone before the event of killing Arinane, would he sever the connection or take the risk of unleashing the fires onto everyone in the hope it would destroy them? However, it would go against everything he stood for. One way or another, Ramalon would be the one to kill Arinane. The question was whether he would die peacefully or painfully? Every hope depended on Haldane's success.

The decor by that point had become less pristine and more sentimental. Statues of ancestral Màgjeurs littered several hallways as the walls became rougher with rocks and stone protruding through. They came to a final set of doors where several torches lit the entrance. The flames did not flicker. The air became cooler and still the more they descended. Ramalon felt the crisp foreboding of the ghosts that resided here and how they would spit on him if they could. When the doors opened, Ramalon did not react to what was inside.

A gigantic chasm with several hundred metres separating the ceiling and ground. The only light was coming from the many large candles and torches floating around the room where statues had been carved onto the walls of more Màgjeurs. Ahead of him lay hundreds of burning flames floating ankle height gently above the ground. Similar to that which Ramalon used to commemorate Arinane's funeral in the forest of Valencère. This is where they buried every member of The Magikai since its formation so many years ago.

Ahead of all the flames stood Davinor and Magraw with their backs turned, standing on an edge, looking down onto a drop which was about thirty metres deep. Amid the fall was a level surface which Ramalon knew was going to be where it took place. Both Blessèd Mages turned to view the prisoner but they didn't speak. Davinor indicated with his hand to make his way down the side of the higher ground to the lower. All Ramalon could think about was Haldane, willing him on to find his stone soon. Not that he would be able to see what was going on, but he would be able to feel its presence should Haldane retrieve it.

He was guided to the lower ground as The Blessèd stood above watching his every move. By that point, all Ramalon could see in front of him was a vast empty space, surrounded entirely by the rock of the underground. The Magikai made a large semi-circle formation around Ramalon. Their protecy's ready as balls of their chosen affinities were conjured gently out of one hand in preparation. Everything was set. He looked up toward Davinor with as much burning hate as he could muster. He would have hoped his intense glare would have haunted and cursed him. Cursed them all.

"It is time," Davinor calmly said.

He indicated to Magraw to initiate the torture onto Ramalon. The older Màgjeur nodded his head looking forward to that moment. With his very deliberate spiteful expression aimed at Ramalon, he raised his hand like before and suddenly Ramalon could feel the extreme pain fissuring his head open once more. The echoes of his wailing cries reverberated around the chasm, clutching his head as he crumpled to the ground, convulsing in the process. For some reason, the excruciating pain felt worse than in the cell. Any more and he felt like his head would literally crack like a baby duck egg. Only this time it was cracking from the inside out. The Magikai watched on with mixed expressions of hate, enjoyment and justified smiles as the soon-to-be Rògar writhed in pain.

Davinor looked on emotionless. He knew that he had played a vital part in Ramalon's demise, but he would never admit it.

"That's enough," he said.

Ramalon relaxed into the hard ground. His body shaken and dishevelled in the aftermath. The sweet relief that he felt was as if the ground he was sinking into was lifting him up.

"Come on Haldane!" he thought. Hoping above all else that he could be free of the stone and the chasm would entomb them all.

The air resumed its stillness with a faint and gentle haze ghosting above them as they all waited patiently. Most of them doubted if Arinane would come to Ramalon's call. Was this really going to happen, or was this part of a trick? The silence went on for longer than was comfortable with the Màgjeurs occasionally exchanging anxious glances with each other. As Ramalon got to his feet, he looked at Davinor as if to say, *"he is coming."*

Suddenly the sound and feel of a deep, monstrous rumble shook the chasm. Even the mist shivered as the vibrations echoed through the air. Everyone reacted, all but Ramalon who was still and silent. The chains on his wrists suddenly broke off, allowing him to use his fires. He wanted nothing more than to use this opportunity to strike everyone around him. He continued to glare at Davinor.

"Come on my friend! Where are you?"

The rumbles soon escalated into minor earthquakes the closer the beast got to the trap. Ramalon didn't have that much time left for his friend to complete his quest. He closed his eyes, hoping beyond anything that something would happen and to his luck, he felt the presence of his stone in his soul. His heart warmed with a slight feeling of joy. Haldane had done it.

"Do it, my friend. Do it!" he whispered urgently, willing him on.

With a deep breath in and the closing of his eyes, he prepared for his own doom and for the poison, the power and the curse to be broken off and exist no more... But no such relief came.

"Do it... Destroy it, you fool!"

The quakes grew so loud that large chunks of rocks were dislodged and fell from the ceiling. Still, Ramalon didn't react. A few members of The Magikai wobbled on their feet, the shocks were that intense.

"Why had he not destroyed yet? Was he stealing it? No. He wouldn't. He was loyal. Was he being attacked?" he continued to ask himself questions but one thing he knew for certain was that Haldane had successfully found his stone, but for whatever reason he had not yet managed to destroy it.

He scanned for answers in his mind before looking directly into the eyes of Davinor once more... His slow smile suggested something that sucked every bit of hope from Ramalon. Without needing any confirmation, he felt confident he knew why it was not yet destroyed. Davinor's vengeful and satisfied face said it all. Did his only friend betray him? Or was he followed and attacked as soon as Haldane revealed the stone? An answer he knew he was not going to find out in that moment as his eyes shut, heavy in the resignation of what he had to do now.

All of sudden an explosion of rocks and fire blasted from the ground way out in front sending debris and rubble high up into the ceiling of the chasm. A defeated Ramalon again did not react even as the resulting boulders and stones landed mere feet from him. The Magikai readied their energies more ferociously this time. Arinane had come to protect his master, unaware of the trap being constructed.

Ramalon's eyes narrowed as he looked up one final time at Davinor. Defeated. Even in that final moment, he was still toying with the idea not to kill Arinane and take his chances. But what if Arinane escaped? It would make everything so pointless, and he would likely die without having the opportunity to avenge any defeat he was now consumed in. As the dust settled, Davinor looked directly at Ramalon with intent. Daggers were spitting out from both of their eyes but Davinor again even won that battle. Ramalon knew he had lost and was forced to give Davinor what he wanted.

"No one living should ever have to experience such inhumanity," he thought to himself as that familiar power of his protecy stone was once more felt the angrier he got.

That invincible flow of energy started to build and manifest for him to use. He turned his body and raised his right hand toward the hole Arinane had blasted open while his left hand lay by his side, calling upon his protecy. He could not yet see the Charzeryx, but through his extreme emotions, he started the produce something no one had ever seen before. A huge sporadic grid of orange and yellow flames suddenly lit in front of Ramalon. Almost like an intricate spider's web with no symmetry, just randomised lines. As The Protecy intensified, the flames started to run along themselves, getting faster and faster in the process. Not only were the flames racing in this pyro-web, but the heat grew hotter the more it built. Waves of heat rippled out of the fires before the vibrant yellow and orange colours turned into a glowing white. The sight blinded everyone witnessing the spectacle. Davinor could not believe what he was seeing. Even his jaw had dropped as he observed the magnitude of the magical phenomenon. Ramalon's anger was peaking once more. Barriers were breaking through his rage and he knew that this was going to be the last time he ever experienced his protecy, which provided him with the notion to give it everything he had. The lines of the grid grew thicker and brighter with more energy tearing through the air, ripping the oxygen and feeding the colossal spell. It got to the point where so much power and energy was being cast through Ramalon, that it started to pass through his eyes as roaring white fires hurricaned behind his pupils, making them glow white in the process.

Very few spaces within this grid could now be seen as the fires grew thicker and it was then that he saw him. Appearing first was the top of Arinane's skeletal wings as they helped lug his huge carriage up into the cave. Its skinny taunt head emerged and the long snake-like neck was followed by its scaly body. It spread its wings dramatically and roared ferociously, observing its new surroundings and the Màgjeurs with raised caution.

Ramalon could just about see through one of the gaps in his grid of light and met Arinane's serpent eyes with his own rushing whites. Every member of the Magikai was utterly petrified as the energy in the room was maxing out. Their protecy's were readied and only awaited the order of Davinor to attack, but he had no intention of stopping what he was witnessing. The extreme heat, the sound of the roaring flames, the burning smell of the fires and the sheer fright at the thought that Ramalon may not go through with this.

"There was still time enough to reconsider and turn the spell on Davinor!" he thought, indulging in one last impulsive doubt in his mind while he still had the chance. Unfortunately for him, his heart was already made up.

Arinane took his gaze away from Ramalon and looked up and straight ahead at Davinor, transforming its gruesome, gaunt face into a fierce snarl as its jaw unhinged to reveal the orange glows down the back of its black throat. His clawed feet and sails clenched into the stone beneath his feet which crumbled like thick sand in its grasp, grounding himself ready to attack The Blessèd Mage. Its wobbly neck turned long and stiff as it rose higher and higher, rearing like a scorpion's tail, prepared to spit its breath. Davinor still had no intention despite the shock and mesmerisation on his face of defending or counter-attacking.

Members of The Magikai panicked at why no order was being given to attack it. They feared greatly for what was going to happen to not just Davinor but to the rest of them after. But Davinor held firm as if he knew exactly what was going to happen.

Suddenly one final rise of energy flowed through Ramalon as the last gap closed itself to reveal a massive wall of fire burning white-hot, blinding everyone. He had no time to deliver a final apology to the last thing he held dear as Arinane's fires flew out of its grotesque mouth. Ramalon finally released the surge of energy, yelling as mightily as he could as he propelled the whole wall, like a solar flare, straight toward his beloved Charzeryx. Their fires met with a titanic explosion and blasted the entire chasm into a descent of eye-piercing light…

Before the light started to fade and the pupils in everyone's eyes turned back to normal, they could hear the weak wails of the fatally wounded Charzeryx. Its heart-breaking cries tore Ramalon's heart. As his vision returned he could see the burnt sails and half ripped open frame that was Arinane's body. Its blood was bursting from its open belly as Ramalon's strike blew him wide open. His exhaustion did not cover up the guilt and deep sorrow he felt as Arinane crashed to the ground, heartbroken at what he had just done.

However, Arinane suddenly started to move, jerking its way toward the hole it had dug for itself in one last feeble attempt to save its own life, slipping and scurrying in the process. Within the desperate cries, he sensed an underlying tone which wrenched Ramalon's heart further. The sound that it knew its master had betrayed him. He could not believe what he had done. His shock grew more as he saw hundreds of proteìc spells flying passed him as The Magikai laid siege to the defenceless, helpless and innocent Arinane in the hope of finishing him off.

"NOOOOOOOO!!!!" he yelled once more. Davinor promised they would not engage unless he did not carry out what was promised. He felt it was his task alone to have finished, and their attacks felt like another attack on him. He did what he set out to do, but Davinor had once again betrayed him and caused what was left of his conscience to descend into absolute mindless fury.

Arinane spread its bony wings, which no longer had sails as they were singed clean off, attempting to fly down the hole amid all of the attacks landing on him. His wounds were fatal enough for him to die imminently, but it jumped high up into the air with the idea of falling down.

Suddenly in mid-flight, several flickers of white and navy blue light bounced off the chasm walls before travelling through the air a lightning bolt landed directly through the exposed and pulsing heart of Arinane. The bolt suspended him in the air temporarily as its croaking wails turned silent. Ramalon quickly snapped his head to the owner of the bolt. Davinor stood poised, his lust for power and sheer pleasure of at killing something so significant and pure, evident in his evil grin. No longer could he control his own impulses.

While The Blessèd Mage's guard was down, Ramalon gritted his teeth and very quickly unleashed a scorching fireball onto Davinor in revenge for that final blow. He attacked with every intention to kill him once and for all as he didn't care anymore what happened to him. It would be a small price to pay to achieve some form of redemption. Some form of justice for all that he had done. Unfortunately for him, Davinor managed to produce a small cloak of electricity to dampen the blow just in time. The resulting strike however, did blast Davinor backwards sending him flying into the wall behind him, crashing and obliterating it in the process.

Very quickly, Magraw regained control over Ramalon's mind in response to his violent actions. His skull was experiencing more pain that carved his head open like a saw running back and forth, opening up his cranium, nicking his brain in the process which sent his eyes rolling back in agony. However, it was not the feeling of crucifixion that his mind was focused on even though he could no longer hear a thing amid the extreme amount of stress and pain. In that moment of madness, he hoped with all his might that his strike did kill Davinor. Everything he stood for sent Ramalon mad. When his head fissured open again and reduced him once more to the ground, he witnessed the final beat of Arinane's heart as it slowly descended into its black tomb, and out of sight. Arinane's body was finally broken.

He realised in that moment that all recognition of good within him had gone. He had nothing left except terminal hatred, no longer holding onto the hope of that light. Instead, he felt as if the light itself had let go and banished him to the darkness. Forever. Never to see the light again.

ARIES HOLL

ᛞURGE
HELM

LIA

•BRACKBᛞ•

The War for Septalia

"LIGHT THOSE STONES!"

Luanmanu ordered to the men at the trebuchets as he rode his huge white stallion along the curved, thick walls of the capital.

In the absence of Alicèndil, he naturally assumed command, organising the defence of the city. He was an accomplished battle commander, only retiring his role to Alicèn out of righteousness for someone younger and better to lead the realm's defences. It would seem his moment to come out of retirement had arrived, much to the confidence and inspiration of all men on Durge Helm.

The orange haze from the city's fires bounced off the night sky, illuminating only several hundred metres worth of vast empty plain ahead of them before a black curtain blanketed the distance. Durge Helm had forever laid in fear of the The Farrowdawns on their doorstep which could be seen, on a clear day, some few miles in the distance. However, on that night, that fear was made even more intense as the darkness smeared their vision. It felt like it was coming for them.

They received word from their scouts in The Farrowdawns and also the Bluewings from Osgrey that The Banamie were marching toward them en masse, confirming without a doubt that the threat was real.

They could only assume in what little time they had, that they were on their own since no one else would have that same confirmation until it was too late. Despite their numbers, Luanmanu was to hold them off as long as possible at the walls until the cavalry arrived.

"ARCHERS!!"

Alexa Greyman was charged with the organisation of her bands of marksmen for long ranged attacks. The archers readied the tips of their arrows on the turrets as commanded.

Other council members such as Nedian and Farooq Manwa led the bands of swordsmen from within the walls as a final line of defence should the walls be breached. The women and children took refuge in the rocks of Aries Hollow. Should the city fall, they were instructed to evacuate and take their chances in escaping through the various mountain paths. Luanmanu made it very clear to all the innocents that Draul would show no mercy to them should he prevail and implored them to do what they could in order to survive.

Meryx Meigar took his best Knights on their mildens and placed them in front of the walls to prolong their defence. The smell of several thousand horses standing patiently was ripe and pungent as they grew anxious, staring into the abyss of darkness ahead of them. Steam gently rose from their warm breath and sweaty saddles as the cool crisp of night grew cold.

The stillness among the capital walls and the men was almost tangible. Eerie as a graveyard, the intensity grew with each waiting moment with each man knowing their role and responsibility to fend off whatever came their way. The sun would rise on the tenth hour of night… They were only on the second. No one knew whether they could hold off the invasion as no one really knew how big Draul's army was. The Knights of Septalia were some of the finest on Terrasendia. Despite their hearts pounding and vibrating against steel breastplates, their fear drove their motivation to protect and preserve all that was good and green on the land.

"Is this really happening?" Nedian asked of Luan as he walked his white horse to the forecourt. "What did we miss?"

"Everything," Luan intensely said through his golden helmet. "I do not believe we are just against the strength of arms."

"What do you mean?" Farooq asked, his heavy Warhammer sat behind his shoulders on two forks that held it in place.

"Something has shielded their presence. A plan in the making for many years."

"Alicèn was right," Nedian revealed.

"It would appear so."

"And rumours of a Dragadelf? Is he right about that too?"

Luan paused as he looked at his comrade. Alicèn had indeed mentioned in his Bluewings message that a Dragadelf was very possibly accompanying them, along with a secondary army which Luan still had reservations about whether it was true but kept that to himself.

"I don't think it's entirely impossible to rule that out now," he answered honestly.

"What do we do if it comes, Luan?" Farooq tried to hide his anxiety.

"We stand! With honour!" Luan defiantly said.

"Stand with honour!"

"Should we surpass the night, I believe this war has only just begun."

Several hours of painstaking silence echoed throughout the city. Haunted by the prospect of death, they all stood waiting, watching, and staring into darkness. After a while some men grew comfortable, in two minds whether to believe if the threat was entirely real or not. Soldiers occasionally glanced sideways at each other as they became more sceptical of an attack.

Alexa Greyman still had her archers in perfect formation around the walls, several men deep to make waves of defence more consistent. Her bands did not draw their bows but were readied nonetheless.

Suddenly, her razor-sharp gaze spotted a small yellow dot in the dark abyss. As her heart began to beat more vigorously, she focused in on the light which slowly grew larger and larger. By that point, everyone's attention became more concentrated. Every band readied their stations as they focused on the fast approaching yellow light which they soon realised was a flaming torch attached to a single horse, galloping with haste towards them.

The distressed pale horse, coated in patches of blood, was clearly frightened as it desperately scrambled its way to the other mildens in front of the fort. Meryx noticed the horse did have a rider, sat atop the saddle bouncing rigidly with the horse's movement. It looked as if it was held there artificially by an improvised wooden frame attached to the saddle. Meryx examined the rider with horror, anger and unresponsive shock that was mirrored by the nearby men as they too realised what they were seeing.

The body was made up of mutilated body parts with limbs stitched cruelly together at the seams, but what horrified Meryx even more was that he recognised the identity of the individual body parts. The torso had bulging chest muscles and huge abdominals with a wide slit in the solar plexus. He recognised the tattoos of The Itranir across the chest that once belonged to Falcone, helping him also to identify the legs. Similar tattoos and markings showed the legs of Athrempitritus, stitched by the hips to Falcone's lower abdominals. He gathered instantly the message that was being sent by Draul. The burnt feminine arms attached to the shoulders and swaying by its flanks were those of Snira and Nutat. The decapitated head of Xjazen was fixed atop the body, his neck still bearing the arrow sticking out of his oesophagus. The final piece of the mutilated remains of Alicèn's band was complete as Meryx's attention was drawn to the eyes which were cruelly pinned open. Sharp shards of wood splintered from the bloody pupils. A crucifixion of despicable imagery that was too strong even for some of the toughest men of the realm as they struggled to hide their revulsion. Some could not look, others looked away squeezing their eyes shut with gritted teeth.

"He is trying to break us!" Meryx attempted to rally to his troops. "But we do not heed to such barbarity! Use the fear Draul attempts to induce, use it! Men of the realm!"

The sickened Knights seemed to take courage and inspiration from their band leader, tightening their jaws and squaring their shoulders as they prepared to retaliate with everything they had.

"STAND WITH HONOUR!" The mantra was repeated by the Knights in the front line and was soon echoed passionately by the men on and beyond the walls behind them as they roared with determined fury out onto the open plains. Meryx raised his sword as his horse reared in rebellion toward the darkness.

All of a sudden, the roaring of the Banamie on the north side of The Farrowdawns was soon heard bellowing back, followed by more yellow specs from the middle and gradually spreading both left and right. With each growing second more and more torches spread, their fires growing larger as they advanced on the capital. The span of fires grew that wide, men of the helm wondered when it was going to stop. It did not. The lights seemed to spread across the dark horizon for miles and miles, as far wide as the eye could see as The Banamie flexed, in great numbers, the strength of their plethoric and absolute retribution.

Luan rallied the helm with huge battle-cries. They were ready to defend their realm with every fibre of their bones, to the very last man. The time it took for The Banamie to approach suggested they were not on horseback, instead running like madmen into the belly of their enemy which every Knight readied for. They were right on the edge of darkness before the city's lights could reveal their identities in more detail.

All of a sudden, cruel screeches were heard in the air behind the helm. The distraction took many of Alexa Greyman's archers by surprise as hundreds of grey Sharwings descended onto the walls of Durge Helm, thrusting their sharp, unnaturally bent claws into the bodies of the soldiers on the turrets. The haunting wails and desperate, ear-splitting screams instilled fear and panic into the men. The Sharwings bloodied legs flexed as they lifted their prey high and above Meryx's Knights below, spraying the blood of their brothers over the helm, releasing the mangled dead onto them without mercy before circling and descending to attack again.

"SHARWINGS! LET FLY!" Alexa ordered to her archers, taking down several of the winged skeletal beasts in the process as they nose-dived into the ground.

By that point, the chaos had already set in. It was a complete aerial fracas haunting the city from above.

Meanwhile, the distraction of the Sharwings proved effective as the charging Barklers, clad in their distinctive armour and armed with jagged axes, were suddenly a lot closer to Meryx's men for comfort. With what little time Meryx had, he commanded his Knights to keep formation and brace for impact without the aid of Greyman's archers to take the sting out of the blow, before the curved advance of the Barklers launched their lunging attacks onto the front line of the helms defence.

Some of the Barklers were immediately pierced by lancing spears, while others slipped through the net, inflicting severe wounds onto the Knights and horses as the cries of war were born with deafening volume. Meryx's Knights were indeed far superior to the Barklers in a one on one fight, but the sheer number of opposition that surrounded them in close quarters overwhelmed them, their talents dampened down as they struggled to maintain formation. It was not an easy battle for Draul's men either as the Knights of Septalia truly fought with their lives, occasionally managing to push their enemies back in small pockets.

Several hours of relentless fighting and chaotic melee felt like many nights had passed. Luan had ordered the trebuchets to unleash their fireballs onto main bulks of the incoming forces, torching many parts of the battlefield. While similar fireballs were indeed sent back onto the city as Draul's siege weapons replied in force. The obliteration of buildings and explosions hit with utter devastation. Some fireballs were aimed directly at the gates themselves which took out many of the Knights in front of them, but the target was too small for a trebuchet to hit directly from long range. Luan noticed an increasing number of Barklers heading toward the main gate with still no sign of Draul.

"NEDIAN!" Luan bellowed to his officer below. "Spears to the walls! Protect the gate!"

"SPEARS!" Nedian ordered. "TO THE WALL! WITH HASTE!"

Nedian's men filed out in perfect order to garrison the walls as the suicidal Barklers did their worst. Draul would have rallied them beforehand making it clear that Septalians would not want to take their lives one for one as they knew they outnumbered the Knights of the realm, giving them freedom in certain moves they may wish to inflict onto their enemy.

By the time the Barklers reached the walls, many of Meryx's men had already fallen as they tried to fortify their position as much as they could around the gate with spears and shields in a porcupine. Meryx's Knights were being warded off from the entrance as The Banamie started to thrust a battering ram which was manned by no less than twelve people into the fissures of the thick wooden gate. The porcupine of spears allowed the Banamie a longer run-up for more of an impact into the wall, provided the men holding the ram were not taken out on their thrust. Luckily for the helm, Greyman's Knights, twinned with Nedian's spears took out several men on the charge which minimised the blows. They wondered how long they could last, growing silently confident that they could hold out for quite some time.

Out of nowhere, a bright orange flare ignited in front of the Knights guarding the gate as a flaming boulder obliterated one side of the gate along with the infrastructure holding that side together. Most of the Barklers surrounding the area fell instantly while Meryx's Knights tried their best to take advantage of the gaps that appeared in their formation, but to no avail.

Very quickly the Barklers picked up the battering ram and began pinpointing the weakened side of the gate which they landed with a squeezing crunch of wood, inflicting severe damage onto the weakened structure.

"Farooq!" Luan rallied. "Swords to the court! Swords to the court!"

"Yes, Durgeon!" Farooq replied, rallying his band in formatted lines behind the gate. "LUAN WATCH OUT!"

A Sharwing was several metres away from swooping its deadly tips into Luan's heart. Having no time to defend against the attack, he winced in anticipation of the pain before the incoming Sharwing was hit and diverted away by a singular arrow. Luan's heart leapt as he looked around for his saviour. Smiling back at him was Alexa from one of the higher turrets some forty metres away. Luan gave a quick nod of appreciation before heading to the courtyard.

They knew it was now only a matter of time before they would have Barklers infecting their city. Some of Alexa's knights flew arrows into the tiny gaps that appeared as the gate splintered open. Bodies piled up in front of the entrance, making it trickier for them to power through.

To Luan's horror, another flaming boulder appeared, this time heading for the men on the front line inside the walls.

"TAKE COVER!!!" Luan ordered.

It hit with a devastating blow that sent the men surrounding the gate flying in all directions. Smoke lightly hazed before silhouettes of the incoming Barklers ran towards Farooq's swordsmen.

They engaged in battle once more inside the forecourt with Farooq's band swiftly taking care of the Barklers that trickled into the courtyard, before more and more filtered through. Luan rode across on his white stallion, swishing his impressive blade into his victims before dismounting and sending his horse away. The milden was no good in close combat which he braced himself for. The main gate had been fully breached on both sides and a more emotional charge was upon them.

As the battle for the forecourt ensued, the Septalians saw a frightening determination in their enemies eyes close up. Almost as if they were enjoying the experience and not holding back one bit. It almost seemed like a relief to them that they were finally avenging the deaths of those who did not make it out of The Dragasphere so many years ago. The look in their eyes was so true and brave, they all believed they were heroes fighting for what they felt was right. Farooq's men were being pushed back further into the city.

The Knights of Septalia were losing this battle. Meryx's men were trapped on the battlefield outside the walls with spears ten men deep they could not penetrate. Greyman's archers remained as active as they could, albeit large portions of her band were being butchered by Sharwings while Nedian and Farooq's bands did all they could to stem the flow of the advancing enemy who was now well and truly inside the walls.

"DEFEND THE WOMEN AND CHILDREN AT ALL COSTS!" Luan ordered which forced his defending army, including the archers on the walls to fall back somewhat into more compacted and defensive positions within the confines of Durge Helm.

Luan looked out of the broken gates to see that the path into the city had very much been kept clear. He would have assumed that after the breach of the city, every man would be filtering in. To his and everyone's surprise, the Barklers inside the city stopped their advance as they held their ground. The sounds of weapons crashing and men crying out died down instantly as the battle came to a mysterious halt. Confusion and stunned silence filled the air as the men looked questionably at each other.

Luan looked through the gates and saw in the distance, a guard of four men on horseback striding calmly toward the city. Mulrek, Slair and Standl rode behind a man whose presence merely vacuumed in every portion of the atmosphere. A man whose unforgiving eyes shone with piercing intensity. A man who compelled everyone around him with respect. Even the black stallion he straddled waded in with pure presence and power, mirroring that of his master. The presence of a King.

"Draul," Luan declared to Nedian and Farooq by his side.

It was clear Draul had brought the advancement to a halt not just inside the city but outside with Meryx's knights too. Luan had no choice but to hold his ground. Every second he could preserve his men was absolutely priceless. No one took their eyes off of the man who created and commanded The Banamie, as he looked around the city with his intense black eyes, looking in disgust at the walls and men around him. He slowly made his way up the stairs of the garrison to view the dying city in its entirety.

Greyman's archers were too far away to inflict any attack in time. His horse clopped its hooves as it ascended the walls, accompanied by spearmen to protect his position. He stopped himself over the bridge which sat on top of the now broken gate as every soldier continued to glare at him. A man hell-bent on retribution. Like an honorary statue, he stood right in the middle of Meryx's band and the rest of the Knights in the helm at the heart of the battlefield, exactly where he wanted to be. Like gravity, his presence commanded everyone's attention.

"… Thirty years," his deep gravelly voice loudly vibrated, resonating from pillar to post. To that moment, no one had heard a voice so potent and spellbinding. His anger grew as he continued the moment he had imagined for so long. "Since our brothers, your brothers. Your sisters, mothers, fathers, children… Murdered."

The passionate anger was almost tangible amongst all members of The Banamie as they wailed and hooted in agreement, which Draul only calmed when their anguish was heard. Marvelling in their voice,

"You hear them Septalia? That's the sound of pain! Hear their pain. Feel their pain. Too long have our voices been swept aside. No longer. You will now suffer the same fate as those who fell. And then maybe, just maybe, you will know how it feels…"

More rallying cries from the Barklers echoed for miles. The women and children hiding in Aries Hollow heard the twisted declarations which induced fear around the innocents as they whimpered and wept.

As Draul turned his attention to Aries Hollow, his face twisted into a cruel smile as the rising sun hit his face. He relished in the warmth heating his cheek, taking it as a symbol from the dead, thanking him for what he felt he had fought for… Before that warmth shadowed and quickly disappeared. Draul slowly turned his attention to the southern side of The Farrowdawns where he could see the rising glimmer of the sun being blocked out by Alicèn and his rallied bands.

The city was well and truly burned as a gentle brown and red haze dusted off of the plains in front of the helm. It was the first time Alicèn had seen the Banamie in its entirety, and even he was surprised at the sheer mass of Barklers Draul had conscripted. His main priority was to take back the city which had been pillaged and to rescue Meryx's Knights trapped outside of the walls. Even with his men he was not sure if they had enough to make the difference, however he grew more defiant that they would try the longer he observed.

The Durgeons of Osgrey, Conway, Fenrir, Thaniel and Anique braced Alicèn on either side, all leading their own Knights on horseback, spreading for less than a mile wide. Alicèn himself kept his own band of Deonrick, Seyfi and Radja close to him. Their mildens reeked of sweat from their night ride, taking a moment of pause to gather every bit of strength they could.

"BROTHERS!" Alicèn bellowed heroically as he rode his horse along the line. "I do not need to share words to inspire your hearts. You are all brothers to me. Standing shoulder to shoulder. I could not be more proud to wipe this world of evil with men who desire good as much as me."

He pointed his Meigarthian sword straight at Draul who still sat on top of the Helm, observing Alicèn with contempt. Many of his Barklers had halted the invasion of the city, instead prioritising the defence of Alicèns impending charge. Their eyes met from afar, staring each other down.

"Wipe the filth of their ideology from this world! STAND WITH HONOUR!"

The men roared their rallying cry which boomed across the plains, but before Alicèn initiated his charge he heard something that he didn't expect.

WAAAAAAAAAAB! WAAAAAAAAAAB! The droning sound of a horn erupted from the opposite side of the plain. Emerging over the hill from the north side of The Farrowdawns was a much smaller band which made Alicèn's heart leap into his throat.

"Who are they?" Deonrick asked.

Alicèn could not hide his booming smile.

"Men of the realm!"

The sight of Max Meigar and Hiyaro leading the smaller band of some two thousand Knights on horseback was hugely welcomed among Alicèn's men. The Reinhault wasted no time as they charged first from the north while Alicèn initiated his battle-cry once more, leading the much larger charge from the south.

The timing from the pincer movement worried the Barklers trapping Meryx's Knights as it was perfectly poised to hit at the same time. Members of Alicèns band rode even faster than he did as their passion and heart overtook caution, riding fearlessly into the fray.

Despite the Barklers forming a spear wall to defend themselves, the Knights grew increasingly motivated as their mildens leapt over the spears and trampled the sorry Barklers. Some mildens were caught grotesquely by the spears but their sheer speed and power blew apart holes in the defence on their fall while Alicèns band wiped out many lines of the enemy before their momentum slowed down, slicing away at their enemies in the midst of battle.

Even with the additional forces, they were still outnumbered at least three to one, but the balance had dramatically turned in favour of Durge Helm with the arrival of reinforcements surprising Draul's army. Alicèn imagined Knights of The Reinhault would have suffered fewer casualties than his own band as he believed they were fighters of much higher quality and training, with their skill in the art of survival much greater than his own Knights. Nevertheless, his men fought with such honour and determination that some of the Barklers tried to turn in retreat.

It wasn't too long before The Reinhault, and Alicèn's band trapped the Banamie themselves, halting their escape and eating away at the main bulk of militants. Some fell to their knees praying for mercy, which the Septalians did not oblige as they continued their onslaught. Too much Septalian blood has been spilled because of their choices over the years as a result of their warped ideology and had caused too much pain to forgive.

Alicèn found himself in a patch of space where he was in no impending danger.

"I know that sword!" came a familiar voice from behind him. "Seems it likes its new owner," Meigar said with a smile.

"It's a little light in the handle," Alicèn replied.

"Sure, it is!" they laughed.

"You came, I did not expect this."

"You were right, Alicèn," his voice took a more worrying tone. "All along, you were right."

"Hiyaro believes us?"

"He does now. I went there. Not all the way inside but..." Meigar shook his head in disbelief. The horror on his face concerned Alicèn. "They are coming. Exactly as you saw. We need to get inside the mountain before they are here. Before *it* comes!"

"A Dragadelf," Alicèn replied. Meigar nodded his head.

"If one can escape what's to say the other six can't?"

"I don't know, but first, we need to take care of him," pointing towards Draul whose gritted angry face was that of a man who was realising defeat.

Even so, Alicèn grew concerned that he had not tried to flee or save himself. He remained exceptionally still. Waiting. Watching. He did not look like a man resigned, which disturbed Alicèn and made him grip his sword tighter.

Max and Alicèn rode towards the main gate which no longer had an isle of spears of the Barklers. The whole battlefield was an open plain as Alicèn rallied both Deonrick and Meryx to his side and the four of them rode toward the gate with Draul snaring at them on approach.

"You took your time," Meryx jibed to his brother.

"Thought I'd leave all the killing for you noblemen," Max replied.

"Bloody Màgjeurs!"

Slair, Mulrek and Standl positioned their horses on the ground in front of the gate, defending their King.

"It's over, Draul!" Alicèn declared. "You've lost."

"Lost?" A perplexed Draul responded.

"Look around you. Your men are spent. The false hope you gave them has worn off. It's over!"

"You think this war is over because of a few drops of blood?"

"You will surrender your men now, or they will die!"

"On the contrary."

"Draul! I implore you, save your men," he pleaded. "What is coming will not stop with us, I promise you. They will come for you too."

"My dear boy... Why do you think I stand here? I know what is coming!"

Just as Alicèn thought. He wanted to confirm his theory about The Draughts and the growing rebirth of its existence, and Draul has just confirmed it.

"Draul."

"And I have seen what will happen. You will not survive this Alicèndil..."

He was not surprised that he knew his name and identity as it wasn't at all inconceivable but the way Draul said his name alarmed him. It was as if he had known him for many years. A delivery which was far more personal and unexpected.

"Mulrek, show these noblemen a taste of what is to come."

Mulrek dismounted his horse and strutted confidently toward Alicèn, drawing his blade in the process. Alicèn was just about to dismount his own horse before Deonrick grabbed his leg, stopping him.

"I do not believe you will fall, my friend. But let me take this man for you. For Xjazen. For Falcone. For all our brothers!"

Alicèn did not believe in letting someone else fight his battles, but it was Deonrick's fight just as much as it was his. He nodded and allowed his best friend this moment as he understood the value of his honour. He was more than confident Mulrek would fall in less than a minute against *Helms Hunk.*

Deonrick dismounted and stood ready against the advancing Mulrek whose grimaced face could not have been uglier. Juxtaposed to Deonrick's calm nature which prepared him, focused and together. Suddenly a glimmer of light flashed towards him as Mulrek tried to sneakily throw a small dagger at him. He caught the blade with impeccable timing in his weaker hand, while his opponent foolishly lunged at him.

"Impressive," Deonrick announced as he quickly stepped aside of his incoming enemy, slicing his own longsword cleanly through Mulrek's midriff. "... Not so now."

His victim's body froze on the spot before it crumpled, cloven in two to the floor. Both Standl and Slair watched on, mortified. Deonrick threw the blade disgustedly to the ground before them before they both cowardly retreated behind the walls and out of sight. Draul looked a little more peeved than before but still remained poised above them.

"You think men will win this war," Draul began to laugh, his deep booming voice harrowed the city.

And this time, it was for a more immediate reason. As Draul continued his evil laughter, the light from the rising sun cooled as thick mist drew in from the nose of The Farrowdawns and over and beyond its rocks, ghosting its way high and wide several miles away from them. The attention and focus of all on Durge Helm was drawn to the descending grey gloom ahead of them. The clouds had not left the mountains since that fateful day thirty years ago.

"Alicèn, what is happening?" Meryx asked.

"Get your men inside, now!"

"I will not abandon my Durgeon!"

"That's an order! Get your men inside the mountain as quickly as you can!"

"Go, brother!" Max said. "This is something beyond the strength of arms."

"I will not abandon my family!"

"There is nothing you can do. Go, now!"

Meryx reluctantly withdrew as many of his men behind the walls as possible. By then, the Barklers peppering the city were dead, beaten back by Luan's command from within and freed up space in the capital for the retreat. Draul still did not move. It was as if he felt empowered on top of the city, looking forward to having a view of what happened next, despite his forces all but depleted. Alicèn extended this commanding retreat to the rest of his Durgeons who too, reluctantly obliged his command.

Meanwhile, the battlefield cleared with amazing speed. The remaining Barklers fled into the mist and out of sight. All that was left in front of the walls was Max Meigar and the men of The Reinhault who chose to stay in front of the walls, led by Hiyaro.

"I am sorry," Hiyaro sternly apologised approaching Alicèn. He placed his fist on his chest. "Forgive me."

"There is nothing to forgive, only honour to share."

"It's what we do when evil intends to harm what's good and green on this land."

They placed their hands on each other's shoulder in thanks to one another.

"You know what is coming for us?"

"I do."

"I suppose ordering you to get behind the walls would be pointless."

"We are our own people, so yes," Hiyaro subtly smiled.

"Then we hold them off. Anything that comes our way, as long as we can."

"I hope you're thinking about using some of that Màgjeur stuff, Durgeon. It could come handy round about now."

Alicèn had completely forgotten he could use the power of air magic. So consumed by what he had seen, he had not given one thought about using his protecy to help him. Should a Dragadelf indeed appear, he guessed he would have no choice but to use it, no matter how futile and pointless it may seem.

"Alicèn!" came the voice of Luan, emerging through the gate. "What is happening?"

"Luan. It is good to see you, brother."

"And you."

"We have been deceived. All of us. Everything I feared is true."

Luan sighed with heavy regret. "What can I do?"

"Save as many men, women and children as you can. They are your responsibility now."

"You think I'm going to leave my Durgeon to sacrifice himself? You know me better than that."

"Who will protect them?"

"Our people will protect themselves. They know how to."

Alicèn reluctantly accepted as there was no telling anyone around him what to do. A Blessèd Mage to his right, a commander of a rogue band to his left and his superior just slightly behind, but yet somehow, Alicèn held more power than any of them. It was a true example of leadership and above all, companionship. He could not do any of it alone. All the while they were being overlooked by the watching stare of Draul, still on the garrison.

"Men of the realm!" Draul gravelled once more. "Our lord, presents… A justice. A retribution. Our vengeance!"

Through the thick veil of the gentle and still clouds ahead of them, they noticed small white orbs peppering the grey horizon, in the same manner as The Banamie approaching the night just gone. They could not make out the source of the balls of light gleaming slowly toward them, but Alicèn knew exactly what they were.

"Behold, The Boldemere!" Draul boomed.

"The Boldemere?" Luan worryingly queried. "What are they?"

Horror-strewn they all looked at Alicèn.

"… The ones who didn't make it out, thirty years ago."

No one could quite comprehend what they were witnessing.

"That cannot be!" Luan gasped. "They died."

"They did. And so did their souls… But the ones before us are the souls Melcelore has manced over the years, and placed into the bodies of the ones who died."

"It's true," Max reiterated.

They were all aware of Soul Mancing and the horrific process it involved. But none could quite believe the enormity of the manced souls before them. It did indeed seem like thousands upon thousands in the clouds, wading towards them.

"What do we do?" Luan sternly asked.

"Has praying ever worked before?"

"How can we pray when there are no gods?" Hiyaro said.

"Then we stand… With honour."

They all repeated back the honorary declaration before watching the white orbs grow more abundant the closer they got. It almost didn't seem real as they could not make out their complexion in the mist. Suddenly their gaze grew sharper, and all became as real as the rusted swords in their grasp.

Slowly emerging into view, the thousands of waltzing bodies spread across the horizon, confirming the utter sadness and dread of what was happening. The first thing they noticed were the piercing white lights gleaming from inside their slatted ribcages, the white orbs of the manced souls which were implanted directly in place of their hearts. Their burnt, charcoaled skin scaling off with many pieces of flesh singed off in various places. Lightly armoured tunics covered the modesties of both the men and women left behind to die in the Dragasphere, but what scared the men most as the corpses drew closer were their eyes... Full of life and fear. Someone was living behind those eyes. They were not looking at the dead souls of those who died that day, they were looking at fully living souls being hosted by the bodies of the dead killed by The Dragadelf thirty years ago, controlled by their mancer Melcelore. The only one on Rèo powerful enough to have manced that many souls for himself and cast onto the dead.

"Blessèd save us!" Luan gasped.

"I shall do my best," Max replied humourlessly, staring blankly at the enormity of The Boldemere.

"Why have they stopped?" Hiyaro asked.

Alicèn looked directly back up at Draul who looked at his approaching army with utter glee and happiness.

"What better way to justify thirty years of stolen life, than for those who died to avenge themselves," Draul's triumphant voice echoed above them.

Alicèn had no time to indulge him with his hatred, he knew his ideology and sense of retribution was flawed. It wasn't even the people who fell thirty years ago that stood before them in these dead bodies. Those imprisoned souls had nothing to do with the warped idea of redemption.

They all stared out along the horizon at the white balls of light that had come to a halt before them, anxiously waiting for The Boldemere to charge at them with everything they had. No one moved for many minutes. It felt like hours to the men of the Helm.

Amid the strange wait, Alicèn began to feel a little light in the head. He wasn't quite sure why. Was it exhaustion, he thought? A lull in energy before the final plunge? A strange sensation began to take place in the tips of his fingers. He felt remarkably unusual as if something was trying to talk to him, exchange something with him. So bizarre was the feeling, the only thing he could recognise was that something was leaving him, but at the same time, something was being put in its place. A foreign exchange which he did his best to ignore and concentrate back on his physical state, to defend his city.

Suddenly amongst the grey advance, the sun was seen trying to burn its way through the clouds... Before the intensity of light suggested it was not the sun that was piercing its way rapidly towards them.

"TAKE COVER!!!!!" Hiyaro bellowed at his Knights.

A huge flash of white and orange fire rippled its way past the clouds and through the skies above them, landing forcefully into the side of Aries Hollow. The men felt an unbelievable heat wave above them as all but Alicèn crouched, shields above their heads. The same sensation in Alicèns body grew rife and strong. He had no idea why, but he did not feel the need to duck or take cover. It frightened him to feel so fearless in such a vulnerable situation. He was not a reckless man and would not put his life in danger needlessly, but something inside him calmed him and told him not to flee.

The sight of black wings, a long tail and a heavy carriage swarmed directly above them, roaring its burning crackle into the sky. Alicèn felt frightfully righteous, he was right all along.

"DRAGADELF!!!!" Max shouted.

The men of The Reinhault really did not know what to do, scattering in all directions. Not even they had the skill or training to match such a foe if it decided to fire its breath onto them. The Boldemere still did not move and watched on lifelessly. Alicèn used the opportunity to turn to his commanders in an almost pleading state.

"Please!" he said, his pupils wide. "Get your men inside. As many as you can."

By that point, they recognised that staying put would be far worse as they would be sitting ducks. It would have been different if The Boldemere had starting charging as that would give them reason enough to stay and fight, but as they continued to stand and stare at them, haunting them, Hiyaro decided to defend behind the walls and rallied his men to fall back. As the Knights began to filter quickly through the gates, Max turned to Alicèn who sat motionless on his horse, staring into the open space between them and The Boldemere.

"What about you?" Max asked to a weary Alicèn. "You are coming with us, yes?"

"... Go," Alicèn lightly said. "You must."

"Alicèn!"

A deafening roar from the sailing Dragadelf flew directly above them, before swiftly landing directly in front of them both. Despite being a Blessèd Mage, Meigar was certain the wrath of a Dragadelf would prove too much even for him. He reluctantly listened to Alicèn's command to retreat behind the walls, leaving The Durgeon of Durge Helm to stand alone against the beast.

Its snaring unforgiving eyes stared Alicèn down. The learnings during his time at The Reinhault of how The Dragadelf came to exist, was confirmed with his own eyes. The fusion of the three dragon families formed its constitution. Its elegant wings were that of a Drogadera's, while its spine was clearly that of a Charzeryx. And lastly the tyrannosaurial look of a Dralen, made up its terrifying head as one of the legendary Dragadelf.

He felt that strange feeling once more as if something was trying to connect with him. Letting the feeling guide him, he dropped his sword and slowly laid out his right hand towards the Dragadelf to open up his protecy. Not to attack, but to attempt to explore the connection he felt radiating from the beast.

The air gently started to flow through his conjuring left hand, feeling the crisp air flow through his body and expelling it out of his right, sending a gentle but concentrated breeze to circulate the Dragadelf. The sensation of The Protecy running through his body felt euphoric to him. No wonder Màgjeurs loved using this magic. The beast did not stir, nor feel threatened but continued to watch Alicèn intently.

"What on Rèo am I doing!? This cannot be real!" Alicèn thought.

But it was, more real than anything. Nothing frightened him more than in this moment. He had no idea what was happening, why he was feeling this connection with the Dragadelf. It was odd, a beast of such legend to be in his grasp. An ownership. A possession. An invincible feeling. As if it was his to control. To cement the idea, the Dragadelf stretched its skeletal wings and embraced Alicèn's air around its rippling sails as its clawed feet stayed rooted in the earth. It let out a gentle breath of fire, catching the whirls around it and encasing itself in a ball of searing fire which extended its way down the line of Alicèn's flume of air. It was not hot enough to burn him but instead, he felt the warmth of the beast flow through and inside him. Not a thing on this world could have convinced him that this was not real. The Dragadelf accepted his protecy and in turn, he accepted the Dragadelf's power.

Alicèn and the Dragadelf's mutual fires whirled slowly to a close, before embracing their connected stare... A mutual understanding somehow existed between them. The world of Rèo stopped and looked upon the event unfolding middle of the battlefield. Alicèn did not believe he was himself anymore.

"It must be some mistake!"

The watching men behind the wall could not believe what just happened either. Why was the beast not roasting their Durgeon alive? Why was it somehow able to communicate and connect with Alicèn? The Boldemere stayed rooted to the spot, still glaring ahead in the same horrific fashion.

Draul, still sitting on top of Durge Helm, clearly did not conceive this was at all possible. He had imagined the city burning to rubble by now but alas, it was not. He finally started to realise the vulnerable position he was in, as his panicked eyes were fixed on the impossible scene before him, the approaching Knights were making their way to seize him at last.

Alicèn slowly approached the legendary winged creature, still unsure if he was going to get burned alive. He did not. With every nervous step, he grew increasingly powerful and confident the beast would not strike him down. He was within metres of the colossal framed head, its unrelenting eyes bearing him down. Confidence ran through him to the point where it was most unnatural. Within touching distance of its flaring nostrils, he decided that physically touching the beast was not necessary, instead concentrating on their connection and mutual acceptance of one another. He paused for a moment, feeling deep into that connection before indulging in a stupendously outrageous silent request that he believed would be fruitless... He could not have been more wrong.

The Dragadelf responded instantly to Alicèn's telepathic request, slowly turning, snaking his long bouldered spine around to face down The Boldemere in all their mystery and horror. The power Alicèn felt spooked him in every fibre of his core as he realised that it was his to command. His possession. His responsibility. He experienced an almost a paternal feeling, at its acceptance that Alicèn was its master to protect at all costs.

All of a sudden, every burnt body of The Boldemere sprang into life and began sprinting wildly towards Alicèn, the Dragadelf and the Helm. Alicèn gritted his teeth and delved once again into the connection he had before. The Dragadelf obliged once more, unhinging its jaw and unleashed a devastating plume of fire onto the many oncoming bodies. The true death of the imprisoned souls were confirmed with the splintering sounds of smashing glass, followed by the escaping white smoke of the orbs themselves as they floated above the pyro-storms before dissolving high in the air. Their souls were free at last. No longer in the possession of Melcelore. Free from the purgatory that encapsulated their existence.

Alicèn continued to issue commands to his new weapon as The Boldemere continued to fall under the intense fires, their chests bursting with exploding souls as they were freed on the battlefield.

However, the sheer number of racing bodies meant that some slipped through the net. Although The Dragadelf did its best to swipe them with its muscular tail to protect his newfound master, he could not stop them all as they continued to run straight for The Durgeon. Alicèn lost his concentration at the incoming threat and before he could reach down and grab his dropped sword, a Boldemere launched itself at him, flying through the air with unnatural thrust. Luckily for Alicèn, a single arrow landed directly into its bright ribcage, smashing the soul in the process causing the body to shatter instantly into dust. Knights of The Reinhault and every member of The Durgeons of Septalia flocked back in all their numbers and bands, swiping and killing their assailants, protecting their Durgeon at all costs.

By that point, many Boldemere had escaped around the Dragadelf's fires, but their numbers dwindled with each passing moment. The relentless Boldemere did not retreat, fighting with incredible unnatural strength using their jagged swords and even teeth to attack the men of the realm... But their efforts were waining. The battle was coming to a close. A mixture of falling Knights and escaping souls slowed down Alicèn's reality. A calming reality distilled in his mind. Against all odds somehow, out of nowhere, the battle for Durge Helm was won.

Brown and red dust hazed off the ground mixed with the lighter wisps of smoke from the freed souls above. He slowly turned his back on the beast that had saved his life and looked up at Draul. Their eyes met and the hatred set in with a new found intensity. One question rose above all that rained in his mind as Durge Helm recovered in the aftermath of the battle. A brutal question that he asked himself, turning back around to stare into the intense eyes of the Dragadelf once more... His heart began to beat quickly again, before he breathlessly whispered.

"Who am I?"

RAVENSP.

CASPARIA

ARI'

ELCARIA

ÐRETHAI ÞÁ'

Betrayals Unfold

Alex, Pirocès and Dancès trudged through the streets of Casparia. Their hands bound while the pale onlookers of Elcarians looked at the trio with disgust and shame.

How could this have happened, Alex thought? He looked over towards Pirocès who didn't look back. They all were kept out of earshot from each other on their descent into the city depths. Pirocès was looking very much worse for wear, his dishevelled face matched his clothing which looked desolate and rugged. Dancès looked very much disorientated from the blast. He must have taken most of the hit when they bombarded through the door. Another turn of events that Alex could have done without. Not to mention the fact that Dalarose was there. But why, he kept thinking? Was he Elcarian after all? Or was he just there to his utter annoyance? Like a fly that refused to be swatted. To betray Alex now must mean that in some capacity he had betrayed Rombard Hill and informed Casparia of all Landonhome's significant movements. Maybe he was the reason for tensions rising so high between the two realms.

But more importantly to Alex was his burning desire to find out how in Rolgan Brody could have done what he did? His best friend, who he accepted into his family as uncle Brody to his son, had betrayed him. Alex's muscles in his jaw ached from the clenching, his teeth grinding on every tooth. His nostril hairs were whistling as his furious breaths fired out. The sweat from his armpits and hands soaked his garments as they found themselves at the bottom level of the city. His haunted thoughts made him angry and vengeful.

It made sense to him, the more he thought about it. Brody must have known someone very powerful. Powerful enough to know of Alex's true identity, which he was believing more and more. They must have known that Felder hid the stone and that the only way they could extract it was through Alex himself, the true-born son of the King. They must have known that Jàqueson shared the same blood as Alex and therefore took him for their own. Blessèd only knows what they would do to him. Every possible thought pinched his heart. Pirocès was right. Along with many other things he said, his son didn't come to have Malerma by chance. Brody deliberately infected him, he concluded. The thought made him curdle inside again as that defeated feeling was back and more potent than ever.

The thought that Mirabella was the one who took Alex and rode him out of the event of The Dragasphere filled Alex with such a contrast of emotions. He was grateful to her for managing to get him to safety and live a life he loved, but at the same time, she put him at significant risk by telling him about the stone in the first place. None of it would have happened had she not told him. How could she have been so careless? His only guess was that Mirabella was not even remotely aware that the discovery of The Time Stone was part of a trap and that she told him in the knowledge that it would be safe.

The familiar rainbow of thoughts rained inside his head but he had no idea how they got caught. Pirocès said it should definitely have worked, whatever it was that he did. All in all, he was not in the slightest hopeful for what was going to happen next.

The very bottom level was much quieter than the levels above. No more prestigious than the upper levels in decor, but the personnel certainly looked more important. A vast tunnel lay before them leading so far down, Alex could not make out what was at the other end. Torches lit the way down impressively well as they trudged towards the end. The Elcarian guards kept their eyes on the trio the whole way, waiting for them to talk so that they could quieten them down. The further they got down the tunnel, the more aesthetically pleasing it got. Finally, some art and craftsmanship within what Alex thought was a very unimpressive venture. Statues of Elcarian ancestors, Màgjeurs casting spells, the reading and studying of books. Symbols of individuality, the ethos and identity of the Elcarians. They were halfway down the tunnel before Alex could finally make out what was at the end.

Piroces and Dances of course knew, but Alex noticed two vacant thrones side by side, one bigger than the other. The colours of black, purple and gold entwined in the fabric of the cave-like aesthetic.

Inside the throne room to the right was a large clearing that looked out onto the lands of Elcaria below. As it was nightfall by that point, they were lucky the moon was still present which shone its blue and silver light into the room. In addition, crystals captured the lights of the moon and torches nearby. Beside the two thrones on either side, laid two curved tables which could potentially seat at least ten people each side. All seats were empty as they entered.

"You are in the summons of our King," one of the guards spoke, placing them in the middle of the room. "You must not speak unless spoken to from this point. Any communication between yourselves unless permitted could result in instant death. You will wait here for the trial for your crimes."

"Dalarose certainly loves a court drama," Alex thought.

The three were left isolated from each other in the middle of the throne room, waiting for something to happen. Alex was cautious not to speak or make eye contact with the other two, as desperate as he wanted to find out exactly what happened.

"I am so very sorry!" Piroces said.

Alex felt the red in his face burning at his communication. To add to this, he noticed out of the corner of his eye Piroces, even looking at them both directly.

"I was sure it would work."

"Are you out of your mind?" Dances harshly whispered. "Shut up, you fool!"

"Well. Well. Well. Isn't that a pity?" the slimy voice of Dalarose came into fruition. "And yet I would have hoped for a fair trial at least. You'll burn for this you old fool."

"Better to die than live as a traitor to your people, Dalarose!" Piroces sneered.

"What? You seem to be mistaken. I didn't say you'd be dying while burning..."

Another sadistic smile squeezed out onto his taut cheeks. He made his way past the trio to take up a seat on the very edge of the table. Not that Alex could see, but he could feel Pirocès desperately trying to conceal his horror at what was going to happen to him.

The sliding bolt of a door was heard and the tall doors behind the thrones opened slowly. Out came the Elcarians who didn't look too much different in terms of their attire and complexion. The only main difference being that the colours of purple and gold shone slightly brighter. All the chairs began to fill as they filtered into the room, all remaining standing until appearing from behind the thrones were undoubtedly the King and Queen of Elcaria.

King Caspercartès was a lot younger than Alex envisioned and far more muscular and lean than the rest. His shadowed eyes were striking and his pursed lips gave him an intensity which justified his crown.

The Queen however, was much smaller and very beautiful. Cute and almost innocent in her gaze. Alex noticed that the sight of her agitated Pirocès. Once both the King and Queen were in position, they sat and the rest of the room followed.

After a bit of adjustments from the room, a female Elcarian addressed the court.

"In the presence of the King, he requests that you explain a number of crimes committed against the realm. The charges relating to both Elcarians are simple. The attempted destruction of studies and work of the realm which binds and protects us, and all that collaborate in their activities. The charges relating to the nobleman however, are still unclear. We assume he is here in collaboration with the assailants, but we need clarification."

"Indeed," Caspercartès' angelic voice calmly said. "A foreigner that comes into our walls and is complicit in crimes will be punished accordingly, no matter what the filth of man thinks in Rombard Hill." Every Elcarian listened to his words with complete admiration. "But to say I am disappointed would be an understatement. You shame us all Pirocès."

"Is that so?" he replied, attempting to remain regal in his stance. "The greatest shame is the madness that has taken over this once great city."

The King smirked at his remark. "Madness, you say? I am told you came here to sabotage the lovely work that we put together," he said with a hint of irony. "What shames us is your presence here. Did you really think that it would work you fool?"

"Honestly? No," Pirocès confidently said.

"Then why shame our ancestors by giving up your life so cheaply? Not that it had much value anyway."

"I think you know why," Caspercartès' face turned a little sourer, before laughing to himself.

"Pity! Such a pity. You really were lost when I came to you. I did not realise you were so far away that you could not see yourself - "

" - I came to lay my eyes one last time on the one I loved more than anything in this world... And now I have. Fleurcès - "

" - You insipid swine!" Caspercartès angrily spat, interrupting Pirocès and standing abruptly in the process. "You dare not say her name! You dare not talk as if you once knew her! You dare not even look at her! The fact that you pollute our air with your filth disgusts me. You shame us all to be called Elcarian."

Pirocès' front was very much strong and stable, but the blows were landing behind his eyes. Alex gathered that it was Fleurcès who he had fallen in love with. From the tattoos and writing on his body, it was clear he had deep affections for the Queen and that they had past relations that Pirocès could not let die.

"I have returned to the one I love. You do not need to follow him any longer Fleurcès. Be free of him. I have come to save you!"

The Queen looked a little uncomfortable on her throne at his words.

"Loved you?" Caspercartès scoffed. "Oh, dear, oh, dear. You are lost. She never loved you, Pirocès. She only ever loved me."

The Queen's expression remained the same, almost a little frightened to dare say anything to upset the King. She kept her gaze away from a pleading Pirocès.

"That's a lie, and you know it is," Pirocès carefully said. He felt like he was walking on a tight rope. "Fleurcès, please! Come back to me!"

"Did you not hear me!? I said, she only ever loved - "

" - I heard you very clearly, but I do not believe it. She loves me still. I can feel it."

Caspercartès shook his head with mock sympathy.

"This is breaking my heart, Pirocès. Let's ask her, shall we? Come here, my Queen."

Fleurcès nervously arose from her throne, maintaining her coy appearance all the way. Pirocès had expected her to comfort him in some way with a reassuring look or gesture, in recognition of the love they had once shared. Instead, his heart squelched as it truly broke.

The sight of Fleurcès placing both her hands on the King's cheeks and the embrace of their lips crushed him. It was the way she touched

Caspercartès that was proof to him, it was no act. It was a real and deliberate kiss, proving they were utterly faithful to one another. The same love they once shared a lifetime ago, although this time it was not his to bear. They dragged out the uncomfortable moment as they held their kiss for a moment longer.

"Such sweet justice," The King whispered, lustfully staring into her eyes. "Such passion. Do you see it now? Or would you like another reminder?"

Pirocès' stance did not change, but Alex could see the light had completely gone from his eyes. They weren't bloodshot or even tearful. Instead, they were filled with defeat, a resignation.

"How did it feel my Queen?" Pirocès' droned voice hummed. "How did it feel to pretend to love me before stealing every piece of my work?"

Alex realised there was much more going on that Pirocès ever knew. It was her, she stole his work.

"Pirocès," Fleurcès' voice drifted into the courtroom. Her voice was in the same angelic tone as the King's. "No Elcarian does not recognise your work and contribution to our cause."

"Except myself," Pirocès stubbornly said.

"But what you must understand is that I did what I had to do for our people. Only our new King could have given us the means to thrive. Dianarcès was too old and too foolish to give us hope. We needed a new identity, new ideas... We needed you." Her words filled him with an emptiness inside. "But then when you turned your back on our people, I did what I had to do."

"I trusted you with everything I had. And you went and turned your back on me. All of you! It was not my work that I turned my back on, it was the manipulative nature of your King I turned away from!" he spat.

"*Your* King now is it?" Caspercartès' eyebrows rose. "Your time with the noblemen has made your mind weak and soft. We are now a people to be feared. We are now strong in the land of Terrasendia. Before everyone just laughed at us. The Questacèrean elves, the dwarves of Handenmar, the Màgjeurs on Mages Wreath, they all saw our attempts to learn new ways and become a voice as feeble, but no longer. I have given Elcaria that voice. A voice to be feared."

"How?"

"... You will see. Very soon, or perhaps not. Your time has come to an end Pirocès. There will be no statue for you. No memorial. Just a memory. Which we will find a way to erase for good."

Pirocès' gaze was fixed on the King who returned it in the same fashion. Neither one of them flinched in the standoff.

"Perhaps there is another way my King?" Fleurcès suggested. "Maybe the ultimate punishment is to remind him of our love?"

Pirocès began to weaken at the knees at the thought and what was coming his way. Her voice started to escalate with vindictive evil.

"Perhaps death is too easy a punishment for someone whose crime was so terrible. He should live out the rest of his days with a broken heart. He should be reminded that treason is punished by his soul being taken away and replaced with an image of us, my King? To live the rest of his life in true pain. A pain worse than that of The Understunde. Wouldn't that prove more fearful to the rest of the world?"

Her newly found strength was never in doubt in Alex's mind. It turned out she was more evil than the King.

Caspercartès laughed in admiration of Fleurcès.

"See how fierce our Queen is? I agree, we shall rip your worthless soul from you, and all that will be left is your broken heart, to remind you of your treason."

"I shall do it myself," Fleurcès said. Caspercartès' laugh grew louder.

"How appropriate. Show him the meaning of a true Elcarian. Have fun," Caspercartès encouraged. Pirocès felt nervous.

"Fleurcès-" Pirocès pleaded.

Before he could plead for her to reconsider, she walked towards him and quickly swished her hand horizontally through the air which sent him flying back into the wall. The impact broke his body like a branch snapping at the weaker points. Alex and Dancès were bound by the guards, unable to tear their bonds and help. With nothing they could do, they looked on helplessly. The Queen then raised her hand and dragged the frail body of Pirocès kneeling before her.

"Have you ever witnessed Soul Mancing before nobleman?" Alex's eyes lit up. Soul Mancing was what Pirocès told him about, being the most evil form of magic to ever exist. The practice by a monarch he assumed would mean an instant declaration of war were it ever brought to common knowledge.

Pirocès' front shattered to pieces. He pleaded with the Queen which was immensely heart-breaking to witness. The King and all the Elcarians smiled and laughed at his pathetic attempts to save his own life.

"No? Let me educate the nobleman!"

With one hand pointed at Pirocès' chest, the other was by her side. She was using a protecy of some sort which Alex could not recognise. The colours of purple and black in front of both hands as they channelled through her body. Pirocès could not move, he was bound by this magic. As the dark energy intensified, Pirocès started to scream violently. The piercing wail was so intense and hideous that the smiles of the Elcarians drifted away. He struggled and wormed as best as he could, but his body was stiff like a poisonous swelling. Alex was utterly mortified at what was happening. He of course, imagined in the darkest part of his imagination what it was like, but seeing it with his own eyes was truly horrific.

All of a sudden pieces of flesh started to rip from Pirocès' chest, as if an invisible knife was carving into his body slashing out blood and tissue, creating a hole in Pirocès' chest. Shortly into the carving, small white orbs started to leave his body. Twinned and mixing with his blood, they formed a much bigger white orb with streams of red inside. Gradually increasing in size, the orb floated from the middle of Pirocès chest and toward Fleurcès' hand. His soul was forming. His living soul was being ripped from his body. The eyes of Pirocès were dying the more his soul was being extracted, until the intensity diminished and the blood and soul formed a perfectly delicate white orb which floated into the hand of the Queen. She slowly closed her palm around the magical light which disappeared into her grasp, before softly taking a breath to digest what had just happened… Pirocès' soul was hers. Forever. To control, to manipulate and more importantly, to punish.

His body froze in his kneeling, pleading position. His eyes were dead. No life and no movement in his dead body. To prove this, the King swayed towards the lifeless kneeling body of Pirocès. His stealthy footsteps making no sound in the room filled with deafening silence. He placed his palms elegantly onto Pirocès' cheeks.

"Such a waste of Elcarian blood," and just like that, with a quick and robust motion, he snapped Pirocès' head towards his brother who was directly behind him. The sound of his neck snapping sent shivers down Alex's spine as it echoed out onto the province below. Dancès looked on and tried his best not to react. Instead, trying to stay emotionless and not show weakness. Pirocès' corpse crumpled to the floor.

"How do you feel, my Queen?" Caspercartès said as he looked at the mangled body of Pirocès.

"... Invincible," she said as the room stayed silent. You could hear a pin drop it was that tense. The King softly smiled.

"Indeed, a pure demonstration of how far we have come."

"I can hear him! I can hear him, my King," she said with a smile, closing her eyes to focus on Pirocès' voice in her head. She was enjoying the power she held over his soul.

"What is he saying?" the King said with genuine intrigue.

She let out a wicked laugh which seemed to echo into the valleys below and beyond.

"He's pleading for his life back. Why? I'm telling him, why? He's with the woman he loves for the rest of his life. Why would he want that to change? We can give him that at least."

This made the order laugh once more. Alex felt genuinely sorry for Pirocès and what had happened to him, but a more considerable concern to him was the growing fear that they did not yet realise Alex's true identity. He could only hope that it would remain unknown to them and he would not be dragged into the same fate.

"I think it would be prudent to move on," Caspercartès said. "Let Pirocès serve as a reminder to us all of our strength. What do you make of your brother now, Dancès?" His enthralling power gave him the arrogance to play God. Dancès did not respond, instead he remained totally still. "Very well," the King said impatiently. "We shall show you the same regard shall we?"

"If I may, my King," Dalarose interjected, making his way into the court. "I believe I have some knowledge that cannot wait further regarding these two. But firstly I have not had the chance to thank you for entrusting me so far hence."

Caspercartès pointed a smug and satisfied look towards Dalarose.

"My trust in you appears to be justified. Your information has been vital to our cause."

Alex knew it. He knew Dalarose was a snake. He hated the Màgjeur so much, he would gladly put a sword through his back.

"What is it you wish to share?"

"You will not believe what I have discovered. I implore you to reach out to *him*."

"To our lord?" The King asked.

"Yes, to *him*." Alex was very confused. He thought that Caspercartès was considered their lord. Was there someone that the King of Elcaria answered to? For the first time, Alex noticed Caspercartès appearing slightly on edge.

"What have you found, Dalarose?" Caspercartès carefully asked.

"Dancès here has committed a crime so dark and so terrible to us, he should not simply be allowed to die. Instead, he too should suffer the same fate as his traitor brother, in a condition that mirrors that of The Understunde." The whole room shuffled as the commotion was clearly of shock. "The crime that Dancès has committed, is the withholding of knowledge that could benefit the realm."

"And what concealment is this?" Fleurcès asked.

"The concealment of this nobleman's true identity, my Queen."

Alex's heart once again thudded out of his ribcage. He felt like his soul had skydived to The Understunde already.

"Elcarians of this court, this man is the son of the High King on Terrasendia."

Everyone in the court sat frozen with their mouths agape. The atmosphere in the room absorbed any essence of life. Even Caspercartès struck a stunned look.

"We are standing in the presence of Ramerick, son of Felder."

Alex stared directly at the floor, avoiding eye contact with everyone as he knew this was not a welcomed truth.

"You say this man is the lost Blood Monarch?" The King said, truly taken aback. "Ramerick you say?"

"As is compulsory among monarchs, the name of the prince or princess shall have relation to the man or woman that brought them onto this world. Ramavell was the Queen's midwife. They both share the term 'Ram' as a symbol of tradition."

"How came you by this, Dalarose?" Fluercès asked. The room in between speaking was so dense and silent, you could hear the faintest of sounds. Lip smacking, the shuffling of clothes, the drawing of breath. Alex even thought that they could hear the echo of his heart pounding inside him.

"Pirocès here performed the blood ritual, which we all are aware uses the art of clairvoyance to detect if somebody is alive. Unfortunately for him, he did not destroy his ritual when he left his chambers in Rombard Hill." Alex felt more than gutted. Once again, another let-down. "I broke into his chambers myself and constructed what they had done, to which I too heard the term *Ramerick*, said by none other than King Felder himself. I could not believe it, my King. Upon my discovery, I left Rombard Hill immediately to inform you of what I had seen and where these two had gone. On my arrival, my suspicions were correct. Dancès holds the art of clairvoyance as we all know. He used that to help locate his son, which the nobleman could not find without his help. As I had suspected, the two were indeed clairvoyanting their way as Pirocès sought to destroy our work. I detected what they were seeing and confirmed what I heard. This man is *one* of the true borns of Felder."

"One of!?" Caspercartès said.

"Indeed. It was also revealed that the Queen did not give birth to one child, but to three. In which they all escaped in time during the construction of The Dragasphere."

Caspercartès lightly gasped. "Terrasendia was not aware of this. Was this something Dianarcès would have been made aware of?"

"Oh, for sure my King. Another reason to justify your rebellion. Which is why I urge you to reach out to *him*. Tell him what we now know. He will want to hear this for himself."

"Our lord?" Dancès finally droned into the conversation. "You talk as if you speak for all of us Dalarose, but you have never mentioned you can reach *him*. That is something you kept for yourselves. All of you. But why hide such a crime I wonder?"

"Careful Elcarian," Dalarose cautioned. "You are on thin ice!"

"How carefully should I tread? Imagine if The Blessèd knew of your crimes? What you have just done to my brother? My crimes are not worse than yours, I assure you. Nor yours, Caspercartès. Do you honestly think I do not know of whom you speak?" The face of Caspercartès turned more angry and intense. "My only question is why? Why turn to the worst of us all?"

"When you are a leader of your people, you would do what needs to be done to ensure their survival."

"And you turn to the inventor of Soul Mancing for hope?"

Again the whole room was transfixed on Dancès' accusation.

"You dare not speak his name!" Caspercartès hissed.

"... Melcelore."

The room gasped in horror of hearing his name spoken aloud before them. Dancès shook his head at the King, almost sympathetically as if he felt sorry for him.

"You turn to Melcelore."

Suddenly Caspercartès cast a purple and black wave of energy at Dancès which did not throw him back but instead inflicted a tremendous amount of pain onto Dancès who trembled to the ground.

He managed to scramble to his feet before the King sent another dark purple bolt right into his chest which that time thrust him towards the edge of the clearing, again inflicting searing pain. Dancès' head hung off the edge of the throne room. He took a moment to gaze sadly at the beauty of the land lit up by the blue and white of the moon beneath him, before looking down to the terrifying drop to which he struggled to see the bottom of.

"You're just like your brother, traitor's blood!" Caspercartès spat.

"Blessèd help me if ever I were to call you my King again," Dancès struggled for breath. "You shame Elcaria and everything it stands for."

The King seized him upright with his protecy and made him kneel before him, looking out onto the open plain as he approached. He barely resisted as he braced for the inevitable death coming for him, standing strong in his beliefs. The drop and slope of the rocky mountain would create vertigo amongst the strongest of stomachs, but Dancès was not afraid of his impending doom.

"Such a waste. Such a waste of Elcarian blood."

Dancès turned his head to look to the King.

"I have also seen something else which I daresay you too have already seen. The prophecy of your downfall, and my retribution." Caspercàrtes' face turned even more intense. "May my soul haunt yours for all eternity."

"And how would you know?" his breathing clearly affected by the curse-like words being fired at him. "You do not possess the art of *true* clairvoyance and therefore the ability to foresee the future."

Dancès smiled at the King. "... Do I not?"

"Perhaps we should listen to what he has to say," said the slippery voice of Dalarose. "We may need him to confirm to truth-"

Before the King could make a decision, Dancès used the distraction to his advantage, breaking free from his bonds from the King's protecy with his own and, with what little strength he had left, he ran straight off the edge of the throne room and let gravity take him. Dancès was no more.

The Order was shocked at his swift suicide, but none more so than the King who stood in absolute disbelief.

"Silence!" the King demanded, visibly shaken. Elcarians were a superstitious people and the curse of a dead man was said to be very taken very seriously. "I do not know of that he spoke. I do not possess his skill, I cannot tell!"

"My King," came the seductive voice of Fleurcès. She offered her hand out in attempt to calm him as he paced frantically at the curse.

"He cursed me, Fleurcès! He cursed me!!" Caspercartès shuddered.

"His words mean nothing. You are a King. You are stronger than this. Curses and whispers don't affect great Kings like yourself, only the the ones who believe them to be true."

"What did he see? I need to know!"

"Nothing," Dalarose placated him. "He saw nothing I assure you. Our Queen is right this is nothing but a ruse. You were going to execute the man for his crimes. He knew he was going to die and said what he had to say to exact any sort of revenge. There is no prophecy, my King." Caspercartès felt calmer after their soothing counsel but still appeared tense and uneasy. "How could our Lord fail? The greatest Màgjeur ever to walk this world? He has already defeated his greatest adversary in the high King and his plan is fully in motion. You are very much a part of that plan. He needs you!" his words seemed to snake their way into the King's unsettled mind and land successfully, with the King slowly nodding in acknowledgment.

"You're right. Only false Kings could be affected by such empty words and promises," he said, encouraging himself.

"Besides, he did not possess the art of *true* clairvoyance. So… It was all a broken curse," he confirmed smiling once more. "We have already lost two Elcarians tonight. One whom we did not want to see take his life taken so unnecessarily, but what of the lost monarch here?" he indicated to Alex, who felt powerless as he looked on.

The whole event had opened Alex's eyes. There was so much more going on than he had ever imagined. Everything he had learned was all so poignant, yet so pointless as he came here to find his son, but ended up being caught up in a political debacle.

"Would you see him come to a more violent fate than that of the treacherous brothers?" Dalarose continued. The Elcarian Order looked on silently as the King debated the decision inside his head.

"I would," Caspercartès concluded.

Alex could think of nothing but his son at that moment, and how he had utterly failed him, his fruitless attempt to save his life.

"… But not by us, but by *him*. By our Lord!" Caspercartès ordered. "Call our bands. We shall bring our Lord a mighty gift."

"At once, my King," said one of the members of the Order as he left through the double doors.

"May our Lord become the true ruler on Terrasendia, and may the work of Elcaria, The Banamie and all those who support him, relish in his success. Let's prove to him as true followers that we once again are a force to be feared. May he harvest in the blood of Felder, and absorb the right to rule, once and for all!"

Suddenly the sound of a massive explosion erupted from the hallway. The dust and smoke quickly plumed from the hallway and into the throne room. The thick smoke clouded the room while several guards began running down the hall to see what had caused the explosion. The Elcarian Order were stunned as they all leapt from their chairs.

"What is the meaning of this?" Caspercartès demanded.

Alex had only one explanation. Pirocès' rune which he must have managed to successfully execute after all. His plan had worked. In the chaos of the explosion, the Elcarian guard loosened his grip on Alex and he used the opportunity to fling his head backwards into the nose of the guard. The crunch of his nose breaking and blood spattering was heard as he wriggled out of his bonds, cutting them on a shard of glass from a goblet which fell onto the floor from the table, using the smoke as cover. Knowing he would never make it out alive without leverage, he made a run for the only one he could bargain with. He grabbed the broken glass and found the one he was looking for.

Amid the clearing dust and cloud, the visibility started to clear relatively quickly. Caspercartès looked around to see where Alex had gone. He turned to members of The Order and to Dalarose before he figured out who Alex had taken hostage. He slowly turned around, with a horror-strewn face.

"Allow me safe passage out of this city... And I promise you, on the word of a nobleman, I will not cut her throat," Alex warned with the broken glass wedged into Fleurcès' neck.

He managed to grab her and drag her to what seemed like the edge of the world. The picture of the moon beaming down onto them and the crisp night sky in the background gave the King a sense of foreboding and fear as to what could potentially happen. Caspercartès knew he could possibly save her with the magic he possessed but the razor edge of the glass pressing into the main artery on her neck was far more immediate. He would not be able to react quickly enough to stop an intended flick of Alex's wrist.

"Safe passage, you say?" Caspercartès tried to calm and compose himself. "Put down the glass."

This made Alex deliberately and very slowly breathe at the threat.

"I think not. If I am who everyone says I am, I will not last long."

"If that is true, then let her go. Why waste blood you never intended to spill? Come, nobleman. It's not in you to do this."

Alex found Caspercartès' weakness. He was genuinely showing his vulnerability at the value of the Queen's life.

"Will you allow me to go?"

"... I will."

"Don't do it!" Fleurcès snapped. "He won't do it. You know he won't!"

"Quiet!" Alex ordered.

The Queen started to laugh with her mouth closed.

"He can't kill me. If he kills me, who will save his son?" she slowly and softly said.

And with that, Alex knew his last card was played. He knew that Fleurcès had figured out his Achilles heel in return. He knew that she was aware that the value of his son's life meant infinitely more to him than that of his own life, which gave her leverage.

"His poor son. Helpless. Weak. Going to die. You've played your little trick nobleman, or should we call you, Ramerick!"

"I swear to The Blessèd I will - "

" - You can swear all you like, but you will not kill me, I know this for a fact."

"Is that so? If I kill you and jump off this edge, I like my chances. I won't survive of course, but at least if I die, you can't have my soul. I'm guessing it'll make its way to The Gracelands pretty quickly after the fall. So it appears we are stuck."

"Hmm. It would appear so," said the King. "We may not be able to use your soul... But we could always use your sons."

Alex once again, felt outwitted and outplayed, out of his depth with people that played the game too well. The King continued sinisterly.

"Imagine your son seeing the same fate of poor Pirocès... His little chest carving open. His childish scream begging for mummy and daddy to make it stop. His heart breaking. The life leaving his eyes and let's not forget... He will feel... Absolutely... Everything. Unless... You are alive. His last hope."

The King's cruelty drew a tear from Alex's brave face, trickling down underneath his chin. He knew deep down it was all over if he killed the Queen.

"You know where he is?"

"Of course, do you not think we know who took your son? Our Lord has more allies than you think. Terrasendia has been blinded for too long. He is heading in the same place as you. To *him*. To our Lord... Now release my Queen," he said more forcefully. "Or I will make you watch your son's soul being torn and ripped right from his chest."

Alex had had enough and buckled under the intense pressure of the situation. He made up his mind and was going to cut her throat, all he needed was enough strength to do it... But that strength did not come. It did not present itself because deep down, he had hope that he could still save his son. Hope that against the odds, if he was alive, he had a chance. A chance to see him again.

The sound of glass chinking on the floor confirmed Alex's decision. The Queen was released from his grasp, a small slit on her neck drew a faint line of blood but was by no means fatal.

"Ramerick, son of Felder," a relieved Caspercartès said. "You may prove to be your father's son yet. Bind him!"

* * *

Alex felt like death with the weight of everything that had just happened. He knew he was alive but felt his mind floating elsewhere, like a horrible dream he was lucidly a part of. Alex's hands were bound once again as he was trundled off to the higher levels of the city and loaded into a cart, where they set off to the doom and presence of Melcelore. As they passed the remains of the room that was destroyed, he overheard the Elcarian's anguish and turmoil at the work that had been lost in the explosion.

"It's all gone!" he heard. "Every bit of it! Destroyed!"

Pirocès planned it all along, he knew it would work and the last piece of his puzzle was to look upon the Queen. He was there, somewhere in Fleurcès' existence. Not that in the grand scheme of things it was his priority, but knowing that Pirocès had accomplished what he set out to do and knowing what Elcaria was really up to, made him feel that the world was a safer place for doing what he did.

Alex was lucky enough to have a tiny window in the rattling cart as the Casparian band journeyed along the bridge leading out of the city. The horses they had rode in on were slaughtered as they ventured out. Alex once again felt the sting of helplessness.

He constantly thought about everything that had happened and how one's life could be so tragically overrun. The secret unknown to him, that he was in fact, one of the sons of King Felder and his true identity uncovered. He occasionally wondered where his two lost brothers had ended up. Where they alive, he thought. Why was it him that had to endure such turmoil? Wherever they were, it did not concern him more than where he was headed.

Alex did wonder how Melcelore was operating while allegedly buried inside the darkest and most impenetrable tomb, but seeing him in Dancès' dimension made him realise he must have found a way to escape. Perhaps the most alarming concern was that if he really was in Felders Crest, The Dragasphere must have some form of a breach or a way in and out. Otherwise, they would not be taking him to Melcelore, but where could that possibly be, Alex pondered. And to put another level of horror on top of that, should he be taken inside The Dragasphere, he would essentially be in the presence of the legendary Dragadelf which he could not fathom. Standing so close to one of those creatures in a false dimension was scary enough. He had hoped that it would never come to that.

The sense of time was no longer in Alex's reality. So much information to process and so much weight laid onto his shoulders, he felt like a failure. His mind turned to Brody and how it all started with him. How could a man be so evil and cruel that could start such a tragedy? The image of his face churned Alex's guts. It was the most intense feeling Alex could feel at such a time. He hated the man, he wanted to turn to the deepest darkest corner of his mind and hurt him in such a way that gave him any sort of justice. Even then it would not have been enough to justify the pain he had felt as a result of his betrayal.

Thinking about the Time Stone that he stole made him even angrier as he could have used it to cure his son once he found him. The fact that such an essential part of history and relevance was now in the wrong hands scared him beyond words and it was now a bigger problem than first feared. Brody the snake. Branmir on the other hand was the polar opposite. He had saved his life twice. He spared a thought for him too in his lowest hour. How he wished he was still with him then. And Garrison, and Joric, he could do with hearing all their voices right now.

Was there any hope, he thought again? He promised the dead mother of his child he would see her again. A promise that encouraged him to continue this nightmare in the hope his fortune would turn around. How deep would he need to go to get his son back? He kept thinking that his blood must be worth something. He only wished he had the chance to use it.

The final thought that ran through Alex's head as his body swayed and rocked gently from side to side in the cart, was how similar a position he was in, to that of his son. Imagining that he was in the same position, in a cart, heading towards the same fate. The only comfort Alex could think of was that in the horror of where they both were heading, they would see each other once more.

At that point, he couldn't care where he saw his son, anywhere would do. Just his presence, his embrace or even just their eyes meeting would give him what he has needed since his life, his home and his family were snatched away from him. He reminded himself of the promise he made to Amba and extended on that vow.

"I am a nobleman. I am true to my word. I will see you both again."

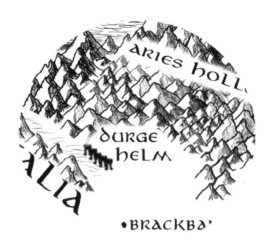

ARIES HOLL

ÐURGE hELM

ILIA

◆**BRACKBÐ'**

Swift Justice

Beneath the mountain of Aries Hollow laid a chasm no bigger than Meigar's cave. Attached by the wrists, Draul's imprisoned body was chained by more than just iron shackles that stretched his arms out wide, connecting between the two walls either side. Among his binds was a bracelet of magic implanted by Meigar himself which illuminated a white and blue colour at the wrists. The chains did not cause any immediate pain but were so tight, he was unable to kneel without feeling the strain in his armpits.

Standing before him in the dark cave-like aesthetic, lit only by torches and the setting dusk glaring in from the large entrance, were Alicèn, Meigar, Hiyaro and Luanmanu.

"End of the road," Alicèn declared to a defeated and resigned looking Draul. His head heavy and his eyes closed shut. "Your philosophy, your ideology, your existence means nothing. Your people are finished."

"Then have me killed," Draul mumbled. The chains tightened slightly as Draul began to fatigue and tire.

"Killing a defenceless prisoner? We're not like you. We don't murder the helpless."

"Ironic. You think we are the murderous ones?"

342

"There is no *we* any longer." A gentle shiver rippled through Draul's clothing. His bowed face hid his unravelling emotions. "My biggest regret is that so many people fell into your trap. Good people. Honest people. People who deserved a better life than the one you offered... But you can still help them. Tell us what you know," Alicèn pressed.

The shivering stopped as Draul froze. "What I know?" Draul whispered. The crispness in his weakened voice still seemed to echo around the walls.

"The men here want you dead. Help me, and I assure you of your safety."

"And I assume these bracelets are for *my safety?*"

Draul knew the nature of the survival chains, with the idea to preserve the life of the host. Designed mainly for stopping the use of The Protecy, but also to torture, which he found hugely ironic.

"Intimidation, is it?"

"It's up to you how this goes," Alicèn gently warned.

"You would never do it. You're a man of the realm, Alicèndil. True to your word. You want me to come quietly?" his rhetorical answer caused him to raise his head and pierce his interrogator with a venomous glare before a sickening smile grew on his face. "You've not been paying attention."

Out of the shadows, slowly emerged the colossal head of Alicèn's Dragadelf, appearing behind his master to return the unforgiving stare. Draul could not truly establish his intensity, clearly frightened at the prospect of what he was facing. The atmosphere in the room grew sharp as a knife edge, as if something could happen at any moment. The watching three grew nervous in the Dragadelf's presence, clearly not fully trusting that Alicèn had it under control. They feared above all that Alicèn would call Draul's bluff. If that were the case, their faith in their Durgeon and his mental state would provide very challenging.

Its deathly growl gently simmered as it slowly circled its enormous carriage around the prisoner, ducking its bouldered spine elegantly underneath Draul's chains, half in the shadows of the chasm, facing him at all times, as if it was sizing up his next meal. The gloopy saliva drooped from its jaws filled with sharp teeth. Alicèn's eyes remained cool. Deadpan. A relentlessness ran through him, a power he was not used to. Even though he could not understand where it came from or why the Dragadelf was under his command, he marvelled in the feeling of immense power he now possessed.

"As I said, it's up to you how this goes," Alicèn quietly said, the only one who remained calm in the dragon''s presence, as it continued to circle its prey.

"You think I will break?" Draul grew more defiant. "I have seen more than you know. I have seen the one who will truly avenge this world!"

"You speak of Melcelore?"

Draul began to laugh his booming deep laugh once more, but this time a hint of mania could be heard in his tone.

"Oh my dear boy! You have done your research, haven't you? But I fear you really have no idea what is upon you! For all on Rèo."

"How did Melcelore escape from his tomb?" Alicèn's obsession with his long-standing theories accelerated his press. A sense of urgency and lack of patience seemed to intensify his eagerness for answers.

"I gave him the means to escape before he went inside. It was his plan all along. He was the only one who saw what was coming. Only he foresaw The Dragastone. Not even his greatest adversary could see, and he promised me greatness when he arose."

"So you betrayed Felder."

Suddenly the Dragadelf let out a horrifying roar upon hearing the name *Felder* which Alicèn felt in his own mind. A connection to that name which felt like it hurt them both to be associated with. Nonetheless, that connection grew surprisingly strong. The beast's movement became a little more vigorous as its sides brushed the walls, crumbling debris onto the ground. Luan placed his hand on the hilt of his sword, ready to spring into action should he need to. Meigar quickly stopped him from drawing, even though he shared the same growing concerns. Draul tried to hide his increasing panic.

"He was wrong. Wrong to do what he did. He created the demon Melcelore became. He ordered the genocide of the hundreds of thousands who died in The Dragasphere and he was somehow a hero!?" he shook his head in disbelief. "He committed a crime so dark, Sarthanzar would have welcomed him as a brother."

"What is Melcelore's plan?"

"… A fate. A purgatory. His signature punishment for all that oppose him," Draul's tone became more mysterious.

"You're speaking of Soul Mancing?"

"You cannot stop him."

"Tell me how he got The Boldemere and a Dragadelf passed the spell. What is down there, in The Draughts?"

"See for yourself! Search the darkest corners of your mind, your heart and your soul, and then you might catch a glimpse of your fate."

Alicèn grew angrier. He had no idea why. Ever since the connection had been established with the Dragadelf he felt a vulnerability. Not in a way that weakened him, but in a fearless, reckless way that freed him to act on his own impulses and emotions. He felt that invincible feeling once more, leading him down the path of impulsiveness. It gave him license to feel the bubbling anger easier to act upon.

"So you will not help us then," Alicèn's voice had a more sinister undertone to it which alarmed the other three. They had never heard their Durgeon speak with such a villainous tone.

"Surely he wouldn't do it?" Luanmanu thought.

They could all see in Draul's eyes that he was truly trapped. No matter how much fright was truly in his eyes, they also knew there was no chance he would bend... Through Alicèns eyes however, they saw something more immediate. An inevitability.

"I sure hope these chains last..." Alicèn blankly announced, almost completely unrecognisable in his newly found position of power.

He could practically hear the thuds of Draul's heart pounding against his steel breastplate as the Dragadelf sinisterly came about face to face with his prey, its glaring eyes fully accepting his next victim.

"DRAUL!" Luan interjected. "BREAK!" A final plea in his voice suggested Alicèn was fully prepared to call his bluff.

Draul worryingly darted his eyes back and forth at everyone in the cave, hoping that one of them would stop his burning fate. They did not. Almost looking as worried as him, they looked at him with great shame before staring one final time at Alicèn.

"May your soul, forever belong to Sarthanzar!" Draul's voice shook as he made his final declaration. Luan, Hiyaro and Meigar could not bear to look any longer.

And with that, Alicèn did not hesitate, nor move a muscle. He continued his possessed gaze onto his helpless victim. He opened up the connection with the Dragadelf in the same way he did with his protecy. Feeling its power, its strength, and its burn, and issued his command with merciless intent.

Not an ounce of sadness appeared as the Dragadelf's belly erupted its molten fires onto Draul. His deep, masculine screams were prolonged with Meigar's survival chains holding Draul's existence together. The severity and intensity of heat made the bracelet struggle to maintain its purpose. Alicèn stood alone, reflecting in his eyes with the colours of orange, yellow and spatters of burnt blood as the chains could not prevent parts of Draul's flesh melting apart from his bones.

The unnatural power of invincibility burned through Alicèn's body once more. It felt right to him in that moment. Totally right... But knowing that some part of him felt it was entirely wrong. A war of righteousness raged in his mind, blocking out the desperate wails of his victim.

When the screams finally stopped, he stared into Draul's eyes which were bright white, rolling into the back of his head briefly. Something was happening to him which brought his mind away from the torture. His beady eyes quickly appeared back into his head and he stared at Alicèn through the continuing furnace.

"Good Gracelands!!" Draul's frail voice declared under tremendous amounts of pain he could no longer feel, having just seen what he had seen. "*Ramacès!!??*"

A sudden surge of anger came from absolutely nowhere inside the darkest part of Alicèn's soul. Why had the name *Ramacès* filled him with so much hatred that it filled him with instant revenge? Almost as if hearing that term felt like a secret he was entrusted to protect. That natural impulse he experienced soared to the surface again, erupting with a violent hatred that he could never have imagined any man alive to have.

Coincidentally, the survival bracelet could no longer hold Draul's life in place. The reinforced iron chains still held their binds, while Meigar's smashed as the magic floating away. At that point, Alicèn commanded the flames to cease before using his pressurised surge of anger to thrust an almighty punch right into the gut of Draul, squelching his flesh on impact. The feeling of hot steel easily seared through Draul's midriff as Alicèn left the hilt of his Meigarthian sword against his victim's belly. Draul's eyes were truer than Alicèn had ever seen in a man. With his connection to the Dragadelf broken, Alicèn quickly realised what he had done, truly petrified at how different a person he had just become. With heavy regret and instant remorse, the sympathy flooded back into Alicèn's soul. He tried to salvage through his utter panic whatever information he could.

"Who am I? Who is Ramacès?" Alicèn demanded through gritted teeth, juxtaposed to his weakened eyes which had never been so desperate for an answer. "And Melcelore, what's his next move?"

The life in Draul's eyes was fading as his ghost slowly left him.

"I was wrong... It's not him... It's him..."

His blank stare suggested that all Draul could see was this image in his mind of what he had just seen in his mind as the flames radiated through his body.

"It's him…"

He struggled for breath one last time before the fight for oxygen became too great. Draul's eyes became wide, still and motionless. He was dead.

What on Rèo had just happened? No one beneath Aries Hollow dared move, save the gentle swaying of the Dragadelf which lurked, half in the shadows. Draul's outstretched burnt carcass hung by the wrists, haunting the chasm. What was it that he saw amongst the flames? Such distaste never sickened Alicèn so much.

"What have I done…?" he was still in complete disbelief at his abhorrent and heinous actions. He dared not speak to his comrades, petrified that if he spoke, it would make what just happened all real. He tried to deny it, wondering at what point he would wake up.

"Alicèn…?" Meigar gently approached behind him.

He dared not get too close. Even a Màgjeur of his power remained cautious, unable to determine confidently whether the same treatment would not be laid onto him.

"Can you hear me?"

Alicèn slowly turned, his breath heavy and remorseful. His wide teary eyes, unable to blink and release its stream down his face. The terror-stricken Durgeon almost pleaded to his friend.

"What am I?"

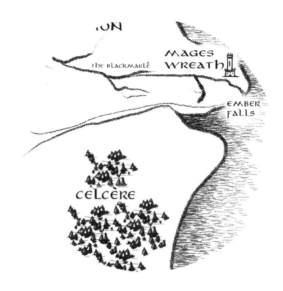

A Just Fate

The city of Mages Wreath had restored order. The people crept out of their homes and refuges as the ghost of the Charzeryx lingered. Its haunting created an air of stillness amongst the eerie streets.

Ramalon was once again bound and brought swiftly to the court of prosecutions to decide his fate. In the absence of the recovering Davinor, Lestas Magraw resided as head judge, followed by a panel of several other members of The Magikai in Anelene, Dorovir and several others he did not recognise.

Nothing mattered to him anymore. All hope of peace had completely disappeared. He passively listened as Magraw addressed the room, listing the crimes he was accused of which included: murder, attempted murder, the creation of a threat to state security, the obstruction of state defence, conspiracy to protect illegal dwellings, improper code of teaching, theft of the Charzeryx and above all else which wasn't illegal in itself was his blatant lack of remorse, which he guessed was justification for digging up every single piece of dirt they could.

Ramalon found it ironic that through all of that, there was no mention of the actions of Davinor, which significantly contributed to every one of those crimes. He didn't for one second wonder why Davinor did not have The Magikai engage as soon as he saw Arinane. He knew that he wanted to see how much power Ramalon could muster at the peak of his wrath and madness. The attraction, the allure of the enormous amount of power he wanted to witness only for him to dream of having the power himself.

He could hear the low, gravelly tune of Magraw's voice but struggled to process much of his speech. He was forbidden to speak as it was deemed that his actions consequently deemed him unworthy of the right to a defence, but it perhaps was to Ramalon's preference as he accepted his fate. Magraw had officially entitled him as a Rògar of the State, who as a result of their unforgivable deeds, were stripped of any civil rights on Terrasendia. Not many Màgjeurs had ever delved into crimes so serious to warrant the title but strangely enough, the term Rògar sat right with Ramalon. *Rògar Ramalon*, an exile, truly alone. It suited him, despite his impending doom as it empowered him.

"And quite frankly the most dangerous Màgjeur to have ever set foot on Mages Wreath," Magraw finally concluded.

With the additional sentence to live out the rest of his life in the solitary bards of the capital of Questacère itself, Lathapràcère. Ramalon did not flinch, nor react as his death warrant was signed. In normal circumstances, it was also procedure for the convicted to give up their protecy stone for it to be destroyed. Ironically, he wondered why he was never asked to do so. He thought he had a pretty good idea as to why as he left the hearing emotionless and with zero remorse.

Accompanied by a band of roughly thirty members of The Magikai, he was escorted on foot to the capital. Several Windermares were also travelling with them, carrying supplies and rotating Màgjeurs ahead of the three-day voyage. Not even their beauty and wonder made him remember the awe they inspired in him during The Fall. A significant sign to him that he really had gone past the point of no return.

As the band journeyed their way through the streets of Mages Wreath, he was expecting an uproar of the civilians to attend and show their disgust at the monster they thought he was... But not one soul was seen. Ramalon took satisfaction in knowing the only reason that was possible was that they had honestly never seen someone so frightening. Another reason to take a small victory in his stride.

The band had cleared the main gates of the white city. Ahead of them lay rocky green hills and open plains as they skirmished down. Ramalon turned his body to look upon rays of sunshine bursting through the clouds onto the city, before willing the shadows to seize up and stop the light, for which it did to his satisfaction. As he indulged in one final look to the place he had lived all of his life, he hoped that it was a sign of things to come.

He continued to stare absently at the horizon as they marched south. Not many thoughts ran through his mind, however he did briefly spare a thought for Haldane and wondered what had happened to him before his mind turned passive once more and he could no longer muster the power to think straight.

His eyes were utterly vacant as the life seemed to have left them. All he felt now was a means to an end. Just flesh, blood, bones and a bit of skin hold it all together. His light had gone. His mind had gone. He had been defeated in every way possible. The nuggets of empowerment he had found through everything were the only thing keeping his muscles moving.

As dusk approached, they had already been on the trail for many hours having set off just after dawn. They did not rest until they stopped to deliver the most despised man on Questacère. The scenery did not change at all. Still the same old grey stones, green and brown hills which they journeyed across. As Ramalon wobbled across the foundations, his mind finally came to a blank. He wasn't frightened at the notion of spending his entire life locked away. Every step he took was a sign of acceptance that his life was effectively over.

The shingles of the grass gently came to Ramalon's attention. He furrowed his eyebrows because he noticed that they were blowing eastwards in the direction towards the sea. He thought that was unusual as the winds from the coast without exception always blew inland. Ramalon didn't make too much of it, but he felt a particular strangeness in his passive state. Almost a mini battle was taking place between his mind and his soul, one telling him he was done, the other telling him to get ready.

"Do you smell that?" Ramalon asked the closest of Màgjeurs.

"Quiet!" the Màgjeur barked.

He did indeed smell something genuinely terrible, not dissimilar to that of the burning of flesh he experienced while furnacing his students. It grew so strong to the point where it seemed to him that he was the only one to smell it. Why was no one else even clocking the pungent fumes that suddenly appeared? It was hard to describe, but it reminded him of one thing... Death.

Suddenly a huge gust of wind hurtled toward them along with a ball of fire crashing over the top of the hill. The enormous gale of wind sent the whole band of Màgjeurs including Ramalon flying backwards, hurtling collectively to the ground. Smoke and dust appeared from the blast and hazed above them before they saw the shadow of spread wings, a bulky carriage and a long thick trailing tail flying directly above them.

"It cannot be," Ramalon whispered aloud.

The first thought was that it was Arinane flying to his rescue, somehow resurrected once more, but that was impossible. His body had undoubtedly been destroyed for good. The only possible thing it could have been scared even Ramalon to his core, which was confirmed by the Màgjeurs bellowing.

"DRAGADELF!!!"

"RUN!!!!!! RUN!!!!!" Màgjeurs yelled in terrible panic.

Upon the wailing desperation to escape the wrath of the Dragadelf, it let out a mighty roar as it turned about, heading straight for the band once more. The deafening roars were much louder than Arinane's, and Ramalon's survival instinct suddenly kicked in. He had no idea why, but his mind performed the most significant U-turn he could have imagined. He listened to his soul impulsively and ran straight for the nearest boulder, hiding behind it while his hands were still bound in chains. He was not stopped by any of The Magikai. Considering the circumstances, they had much bigger problems on their hands. The rumours they had heard from Septalia were true, a legendary Dragadelf had managed to escape.

It breathed a whirling tornado of fire onto the Màgjeurs, carving open any defence they had mustered to try and defend the incoming attack, but to no avail. Their wards were not strong enough and were completely obliterated by the flames as they turned to ash before it. The Dragadelf continued its fires onto some of the fleeing Windermares too. Their desperate neighs mid-flight were short-lived as their death was swift. Their ashes floating down behind their falling bodies as they crumbled on impact down to the ground.

Ramalon's chains suddenly broke off of his wrists. The owner responsible for chaining him had clearly turned into ash. That similar smell of death perfumed the aroma in the air. He watched on as the Dragadelf turned about once more with a sense of frightful happiness as he couldn't believe it. His enemies were utterly overwhelmed and a sense of justification in him was brewing stronger and stronger.

Having resigned to the magnificent power of the beast, The Magikai fled their separate ways in desperation. This perfect tyrannosaurial lizard breathed this time a hurricane of fire, consuming everything within the gorge they fled from. Several more Màgjeurs were caught up this time until there were less than half of the original band left.

Ramalon's happiness turned into madness once more as he intensely watched on, willing for more destruction. He had no idea why, but he felt a sense of responsibility for the creature. It was as if he was the one taking the credit for the destruction and it was him doing this to them.

The firestorm had set alight the nearby shrubberies, turning what was once green and full of life into charcoaled waste. He peered around the corner of the stone before trying to get a closer look at the scene. In one short attack, the land looked as it had been at war for days as the dragon-breath simmered and burned away. Ramalon scanned for signs of the Dragadelf before its heavy landing rumbled the ground behind him.

Ramalon slowly turned around to confront the legendary creature. The beast turned his attention to him and reared its huge body as it roared ferociously in front of Ramalon. The stench of its breath rippled into his hair and clothes, his blind confidence somehow knew that no fires would be laid onto him.

What on this land was happening, he thought? It just lingered idly in front of him, quietly judging with its narrow eyed snare. He had nothing but frightening respect for something so powerful and majestic. He stared into its relentless eyes which looked back down at Ramalon. Compared to Arinane, it was the perfect creature, fully grown and perfectly developed in every way. Everything was in proportion, its silver-grey scales were in perfect formation while the vertebrae on its spine were like marbled rocks, holding the phenomenon together. This particular Dragadelf was tinted white amid the colour of its carriage and sails. A remarkable coincidence as it was Ramalon's favourite colour.

He briefly wondered why he wasn't being roasted alive at that point. Why he had attacked his enemies but not him, it owed Ramalon no allegiance and no favours. The Dragadelf answered to no one. They were the most powerful beings ever to exist on the world of Rèo, but by nature the only thing they were captivated and possessed by was power itself. Did the Dragadelf recognise a power greater than itself in Ramalon? Nothing he could say or think of gave him privilege enough to witness such beauty and terror... But it did not last long.

The feeling of awe and mesmerisation soon started to fade as another immediate feeling took its place. That power he felt through his protecy stone was becoming more and more potent and felt the connection grow stronger by the second. He had no idea why, but the most bizarre and crazy notion came to Ramalon. He felt somehow that the Dragadelf belonged to him, which both confused and delighted him because it was almost the same feeling he had with Arinane, but he definitely was not sharing his soul with a Dragadelf.

The power of his own stone combined with the sheer terror of the beast permitted him to feel undeniably invincible. Tripled with his madness he indulged in the ideas of what he potentially now held in his hands. He wanted to do one thing and one thing only and nothing was going to stop him from indulging in this request.

Was the Dragadelf somehow involved in the behaviour of his protecy stone, he thought? Was he somehow connected by some sort of magic or blood that he was not aware of? With no time for answers, he noticed some of the escaping Màgjeurs fleeing nearly out of sight on one of the far hills. With a growing confidence in this new found establishment of ownership and possession with the beast that was becoming more and more believable, he indulged in his insane impulse, fully expecting it not to be fulfilled.

To his gleeful surprise, the deep sound of burning crackles was heard coming from inside its strong neck as the Dragadelf's head wriggled slightly in preparation. Ramalon's eyes narrowed, looking at the fleeing Màgjeurs before trying his luck with what he turned into a command…

"Kill!" Ramalon whispered.

With a mighty roar, the Dragadelf did not hesitate in obeying his command and thrashed away, ripping up hills and trees, smashing boulders as he hurriedly hunted its prey.

Ramalon watched on in delighted horror as the fires rained down on his enemies, listening to every one of their soul ripping cries as their flesh was torched alive. Each heavy breath he drew filled him with more and more satisfaction. He felt the rare feeling of happiness as justice was being dealt at his own hands. He did not know how or why it was happening, all he did was marvel in the glorious opportunity that was presented to him. And to the opportunities that laid ahead.

The corners of his lips sharpened and slowly widened apart. Ramalon's vendetta had begun.

Book One

Dragadelf - Protecy Unbound

(2019)

Book Two

Dragadelf - Shoulder to Shoulder

(2020)

Book Three

Dragadelf - The Band of Brothers

(2021)

A Word on Pronunciation

The re-spelling of names, portrays the correct pronunciation and not the purity and fluidity of speech

"Alexandao" … Alex-an-dow

"Ramalon" … Ramalon

"Alicèndil" … Ala-senn-dil or Ala-senn for short

"Rèo" … Ray-o

"Questacère" … Questa-sair

"Lathapràcére" … Latha-pray-sair

"Màgjeur" … May-jur or Major for casual speech

"The Blessèd" … The Ble-sid

"The Durge/Durgeon" … The Durge / Dur-jun

"The Magikai" …The Maj-i-kai

"Jàqueson" … Jake-son

"Joric" … Yoric

"Branmir" … Bran-mir

"Brodian" … Bro-dian

"Gracène" … Gray-seen

"Pirocès" … Piro-seas

"Dancès" … Dan-seas

"Caspercartès" … Casper-sar-teas

"Fleurcès" … Fleur-seas

"The Skyurch" …The Sky-urch

"Ildreàn" … Ill-dre-anne

"Xjaques" … Xjax

"Arinane" … Arra-nane

"Draul" … Draul not Drool

"The Reinhault" … The Rine-halt

"Hiyaro" … He-yaro

"The Boldemere" … The Bol-demere

"Charzeryx" … Char-zer-ix

"Dralen" … Dra-lun

"Drogadera" … Drog-a-deera

"Felder" … Felder

"Aristuto" … Aristuto

"Max Meigar" … Max Mi-ga

"Ethelba" … Ethelba

"Wemberle" … Wem-berley

"Thorian Mijkal" … Thorian Mi-kal

"Zathos" … Zathos

"Eveleve" … Ev-a-leev

"Mavokai" … Mavok-i

"Davinor" … Davinor

"Lestas Magraw" … Lestas Magraw

"Thakendrax" … Thake-un-drax

"The Ancient Drethai" … The Ancient Dreth-i

"Melcelore" … Mell-se-lore

"Soul Mancing" … Soul Man-sing

"The Understunde" … The Under-stund

"Sarthanzar" … Sarthan-zar

"Ramacès" … Rama-seas

"Ramerick" … Rama-rick

Printed in Poland
by Amazon Fulfillment
Poland Sp. z o.o., Wrocław

60298904R00211